Praise for BEST EATEN COL[

'Chilling and thoroughly gripping thrille:

'I had so much to do this weekend and have spent most of it devouring your book. Just finished it. Sheer genius.'

'Loved, loved, loved it! Send me another!'

'I admire any author who can hold my attention so thrillingly from beginning to end.'

'Much superior to Girl on a Train.'

'REALLY enjoying it!! The part where the email disappeared made my heart thump! I love it when you read a book and can picture yourself as a character in it and it took me back to those early days after I had the kids and would be feeding them in the dark in the middle of the night'

'I was consumed by the story - and it stands tall as an outstanding read amongst anything I've read.'

'Fast-paced, terrifyingly believable, chilling at times ... the kind of book that's hard to put down.

The part where ... was BRILLIANT! I was feeling totally relaxed that ... and then Boom!

About the author

Tony writes pacy contemporary thrillers. Exploring different themes, but all sharing Tony's thought-provoking plots and richly-painted characters.

Highlights of his early career include (in no particular order) three years as an oilfield engineer in the Egyptian desert, twelve years managing record companies for EMI Music in Greece, India and across Eastern Europe, running a caravan site in the South of France and being chauffeur to the French Consul in Sydney.

Having survived the Dotcom boom, he went on to be a founder of the world's largest website for expatriates, a major music publisher and a successful hotel technology business.

In amongst this, Tony found the time to backpack around the world twice (once in his twenties and once in his fifties), learn six languages (including Norwegian and Greek) and to find a beautiful Norwegian wife.

He now lives in Oxfordshire and writes full-time. He is fifty-eight and married with three children and four grandchildren.

Also by Tony Salter

Tony's second novel, The Old Orchard – a tense domestic thriller – was released in November 2017 to widespread acclaim.

Tony will publish his third novel, Sixty Minutes, in early 2018.

He is currently working on the sequel to Best Eaten Cold.

You can find out more about Tony at www.tonysalter.com

BEST EATEN COLD

Tony Salter

www.tonysalter.com

ETS Limited

Dawber House, Long Wittenham, OX14 4QQ

First published in Great Britain in 2017 by ETS Limited

ISBN: 978-0-9957977-0-3

CONTENTS

For Gro

Prologue

Had he moved? Was she imagining it?

The girl in the blue jeans stood up, cramp searing through her right thigh. How long had she been sitting there, still as a rock? Three hours? Four?

A pathetic grey dawn crept into the kitchen as she walked over to the body. He wasn't dead; she could see the gentle rise and fall of his chest and the mist of his breath ebbing and flowing on the tiles. Amazing how he could still be stubbornly holding onto life.

The hammer lay next to him in a pool of black blood. It would be covered with her fingerprints, but the whole house was covered with them, so it probably made no difference. His hands twitched rhythmically every four or five seconds as though from a regular, repetitive electric shock.

Brain damage or recovering consciousness? An important difference.

There was no time for weakness and indecision. She'd been working towards this moment for weeks and everything was prepared. If he woke up, there would never be another chance.

Finding the money was the first lucky break she could remember in years. Twenty-three thousand, four hundred and ten pounds in small notes — she'd counted it over and over. The stupid man didn't even trust the banks.

All that money, stuffed into carrier bags and hidden under a loose floorboard. It was enough for her to make a clean escape, to build a new life and to start again.

Looking at him now though, her strength and resolve began to fade away and the old fear returned; familiar icy fingers knew just where to squeeze to lock her in place. She could never forget the consequences of previous defiances. Even as a small child, she'd learned the value of obedience. Each time she'd tested the limits of that obedience, she'd learned — or rather she'd been taught — that the boundaries were absolute and unchanging. His way was the only way.

1

There had been times – especially after her mother had died – when she'd lost control; her rage and frustration seeking release through small acts of resistance. The punishments which followed weren't only painful. They were also degrading and humiliating in ways which intensified her feelings of worthlessness. How could someone like her dare to hope for a bright future?

She looked down on him once more and her decision was suddenly clear.

Enough. Whatever happened to her afterwards, enough was enough.

He must never be allowed to abuse and degrade her again. Not her nor anyone else. She would stop him. She would finish it here and now and then she would build a life for herself where no-one was in a position to control her.

She would call the shots and others would follow.

Something physical had snapped inside her. He had abandoned his basic responsibilities and betrayed the most important primal trust. Trust could no longer be part of her life. That was how it must be. She was on her own. From now and forever, the only person she would rely on was herself.

She took a knife from the kitchen drawer. The long, thin boning knife which was normally used to prepare the rabbits he sometimes shot – when he was sober enough to hit one. As she crouched down beside him, she finally understood her nightmare was coming to an end.

She wasn't ready to push the blade into his heart and stop his life, but she would do what was necessary to make sure he could never hurt anyone else as he'd hurt her.

It didn't matter if he lived or died after that.

Coming Home

Staying safe online demands time and discipline. Protecting personal data can become an obsession and will affect your quality of life. If you don't think you need to worry, you may prefer to ignore the risks. However, the decision should never be taken lightly – for the unlucky few, clawing back a stolen life can prove protracted, painful and, in some cases, impossible.
"How much is your Life Worth? Protecting your Identity in a Digital World."
JJ Martin, Insight Business Press 2015

Before Sam was born, there were a couple of weeks when I didn't believe I'd ever stop being so fat and pregnant.

After stopping work, time slowed as though someone had thrown it into a vat of treacle. I was excited and overwhelmed but that only made it worse. Excitement, frustration and impatience don't respond well to treacle time and Rupert didn't know what had hit him. He would come in from work and find himself swamped by an onslaught of meaningless, pent-up, semi-hysterical babble. Still, good training for the coming years, I supposed.

I'd read somewhere that there are two distinct ways in which women remember their first pregnancy. Some have strong memories of the process and the journey from conception to birth: the pregnancy itself; the change in body shape; the scans; the 'shall we find out if it's a boy or a girl?' discussions; the 'will our baby be healthy and normal?' worries; the discomfort; the pain of the contractions; the white agony of the birth and all of the mess involved before, during and afterwards.

For others, the slate is magically wiped clean when they hold that tiny, mewling thing for the first time; nervous, unsure fingers quickly learn and grow in confidence as the moment of truth when it moves from being an *it* to a *he* or a *she* kicks off a second wave of euphoria. Memories of the journey itself slip back into the past.

I was definitely in the second camp. It's not as though I couldn't remember what had happened over the last nine months; it was simply that my mind chose to wrap it up in rose-tinted cotton wool when confronted by the strength of my joy as I looked at our little boy, now cradled in Rupert's arms.

Rupert looked at me with a smile. 'It's Sam, then?'

'Sam, it is. And he's perfect.' As the words left my lips, I started crying and laughing all at once.

The John Radcliffe didn't allow partners to stay overnight and Rupert left me and little Sam at around nine o'clock.

I was exhausted, but still as excited as a Christmas Eve five-year-old and the night passed in fits and starts. I did get some sleep in between, but spent long hours propped on one elbow looking at the tiny little bundle lying next to my bed. I knew I should let him rest and had to fight my desire to pick him up and hold him close at every opportunity.

I woke from the edge of a dream to feel a hand gently shaking my shoulder.

'Time to wake up dear,' said the nurse. 'I've brought you a bit of breakfast and a nice cup of tea.'

'Thank you,' I said, looking over to Sam's cot to check he was real and not just part of my dream. 'That's very kind.'

She helped me to sit up and set the tray in front of me. I was starving and feeling slightly queasy. Hopefully a little fruit and toast would help to to settle my stomach.

'Have you seen your lovely flowers,' said the nurse. 'They're beautiful.'

'Oh, how gorgeous,' I said, noticing them for the first time despite the fact that the bottom of my bed looked like a florists shop.

'I've left them wrapped,' she said. 'You'll be going home later, so it's easier. Would you like to see the cards?'

'Yes please.'

She took the messages from the bouquets and put them on the tray before turning and walking away.

I guessed Rupert's parents might have sent flowers, but the others were a mystery.

My guess was right:

> *Congratulations Rupert and Fabiola. Another generation of Blackwells begins. Well done. Love Virginia and John*

The first surprise was Rupert. He never bought me flowers:

> *It had to be yellow roses. Thank you for being with me. Looking forward to being parents together. All my love. Roop xxx*

What a softie!

The third card was a bolt from the blue and made my heart leap:

> *'Well done Fabs. You're the first of us. Many congrats. Charlie, Amanda, Jen & Debs xxxxx*

I hadn't heard from the girls in years and had thought they'd given up on me. I couldn't believe that they'd sent flowers.

My eyes were blurred with happy tears as I saw Rupert pushing open the double doors and striding towards me.

'Hey babe,' I said, holding his hand as he looked down at his new son.' Thank you for the beautiful flowers. A first, I believe?'

'Well, you've got to start somewhere,' he said. 'I tried to get some at the hospital shop yesterday, but they didn't have any yellow roses.'

'Well, these are beautiful and I also have a lovely bouquet from your parents ...'

'... who should be here in a few minutes ...'

'... and, totally unexpected, from the girls I used to share a flat with at uni.'

'Really?' Rupert said. 'I thought you guys had fallen out.'

'So did I,' I said. 'But maybe not as much as I thought.'

'That's great,' said Rupert, now only half-engaged in the conversation. He pointed down at Sam who had opened his eyes and was pushing his tiny, pudgy legs up and down into the blanket. 'Can I?'

'Of course,' I said.

The maternity ward was pleasant enough as hospital wards go –

friendly staff and a decent group of fellow newbies – but I was happy to go home. It was the start of the real thing. Rupert and I needed to do things by ourselves without a safety net. We were terrified, of course, but kept reminding ourselves that we were reasonably sensible people and we weren't the first parents to go through this.

My only slight worry was Rupert's mother who lived only a few miles away. I was convinced she didn't think much of me at the best of times and it was easy to imagine her 'just popping by' once or twice a day and sticking her oar in. I didn't want that to happen. This was something we needed to manage by ourselves. We would make mistakes, but they would be our mistakes.

Rupert had promised he would speak to her and make sure that she respected our privacy, but I wasn't holding my breath. Virginia was a Home Counties, middle-class wolf mother; her slim, blonde and chic exterior neatly concealed a force of nature with the skin of a rhinoceros and a lifetime of training in getting her own way.

Home was a charming, but tiny, terraced house in Jericho, which was probably the best place to live in Oxford. Central, but with a strong village feel to it and a mix of students, young families and a shrinking core of people who'd lived there for ever. Not as edgy as my old place in Camden but, then again, neither was I.

All of the houses on our street were painted in different pastel colours and we arrived home on a sunny Saturday morning to see our neighbours from the blue side standing in the street, chatting and waiting for us to arrive.

John and Julie were a few years older than us – early thirties maybe – and we got on well. They were keen to see the new baby and their three-year-old son, Jake, was the most excited of anyone. He was zipping in and out of view, running up and down the path waving his arms and shouting at the top of his voice.

I guess Rupert must have given them the nod about when to expect us because they'd blocked off a parking space right outside the house and had even tied a couple of balloons on either side of the wooden gate.

'Glad to be home?' Rupert said, turning to me as he switched off the engine.

'God, yes,' I said. 'I can't stand hospitals ... Feels strange bringing him back though.' I looked at Sam calmly sleeping in his baby seat. 'It's going to be completely different now, isn't it?'

'Yeah. It will be. I haven't got my mind around it properly yet, but we'll be fine. One step at a time.'

I reached forward, took his hand and squeezed it, loving his attempts at confident reassurance, but doubting he believed a single word of it.

Sam was still tiny, and I'd only been in hospital for two days but, what with clothes, baby paraphenalia and all my beautiful flowers, there was a huge amount of stuff which needed to be carried into the house, and it took us a while to get inside.

Rupert had the fridge well stocked with champagne and started filling glasses while John and Julie gathered around me and little Sam. Jake was hopping up and down shouting 'wanna see baby' and demanding to be picked up.

The conversation was predictable and would prove to be the identical dialogue which would fill my life for the following six months. That was, of course, when it wasn't just me and Sam on our own. Our private conversations would be even more mindless, and totally one-sided if you don't count screaming for food or attention as a meaningful contribution.

'He's gorgeous,' said Julie. 'Such a little squidgeable bundle. Can I...?' She reached out towards us.

'Of course,' I replied, knowing I would have to get used to this. 'Here you go.' The transfer was less than elegant as I was finding it difficult to hand him over or put him down while still supporting his neck and making sure no bits of clothing or wraps were caught up in the process.

John and Julie spent the next few minutes with huge grins on their faces – the same faces that were seriously invading Sam's personal space – muttering a string of inanities. 'Who's a lovely boy then? Is that Daddy's nose? He's such a cutie ...' Meanwhile, Jake dangled from John's arm, and stretched his hand towards Sam like the hand of God on the roof of the Sistine Chapel.

Staying with the Michelangelo imagery, I did my best to keep a serene Madonna and Child expression in place as I silently screamed. 'Careful, don't drop him, watch his bloody neck, don't let Jake stick his fingers in his eyes for crying out loud. Did any of you wash your hands?'

Meanwhile, Rupert passed round the champagne, I took Sam back with no visible panic or desperation, and we all raised our glasses. Rupert looked at me and said, 'To the two most beautiful people in my life. Sam and Fabiola. Cheers!'

Although the baby-showing-off routine was amazingly repetitive, in many ways I never got tired of it. You saw the best side of people at times like these. They looked at the small, helpless child in your arms and wished him well, wished him a long and happy future. It was a basic human response which was pre-programmed into us.

It was a time to forget all of the complexities of life – to forget your jealousies, your frustrations and your fears. A time to put them all aside for a brief moment to celebrate this new life and give him your blessing.

After they'd gone, it was only the three of us at last. The real beginning of the next stage of our lives.

'D'you fancy giving him a bath?' I said.

'You sure?' said Rupert. 'Wouldn't it be better if you did it this time? I've got no idea what to do.'

'And I do?' I said. 'You'll be fine. I'll help, but you need to start at some point.'

Lots of people had told us how important it was to avoid making baby care an exclusive mother-child thing and it made complete sense. Apart from protecting Rupert's feelings, I couldn't imagine being stuck with doing absolutely everything.

Rupert filled the small plastic bathtub while I undressed Sam.

'Is that the right temperature?' he asked.

I checked with my elbow as I'd been shown. 'Perfect.'

'Not too much water?'

I laughed. We really did make a pathetic pair of first-timers. 'No. I'm sure it's fine. You're not planning on dropping him in are you?'

'Just trying to get it right. Give me a break.'

Rupert was a big guy, very physical, but he was gentle and controlled with little Sam who, at a fraction under three kilos, wasn't much bigger than Rupert's hand.

I suppose it was predictable that Sam would start to scream as soon as Rupert took him and put him into the water, but I wasn't sure which of them looked more upset. Sam was quickly red-faced and struggling for breath but the look of despondent failure on Rupert's face was almost comical.

'What did I do wrong?' he said, lifting him up.

'Nothing, you idiot,' I replied. 'It's normal. Wipe his bottom and his willy with the flannel and then give him a cuddle. He'll be fine.'

Rupert wrapped him neatly in a soft, yellow towel and paced up and down hugging him gently into his chest. Sam calmed down quickly enough and Rupert's expression changed to one of contentment and pride. 'You dress him,' he said, passing him to me. 'I'm worried I'll hurt him getting his arms into the suit thingy.'

What he was probably worried about was making sure his little son became my problem again before he started crying, but I resisted saying anything.

I eased Sam into his sleepsuit and, after a quick feed, put him in his cradle. We both stood and watched as he scrunched his face, wriggled his arms and legs a few times and then slowly melted into sleep.

I was exhausted but I could have sat and looked at him for ever. Such a perfect little thing. Impossible to believe the two of us had created that life.

I was awake long enough to register Rupert putting a pillow under my head and kissing me on the cheek. I don't know if he heard me mumble 'Grazie caro mio. I love you ...' before I drifted off.

I was determined to begin writing a diary. I'd lost the habit when I was at university and had been banging on about starting again for years. Sam's birth was the perfect trigger as I didn't want to forget a single thought or feeling.

Rupert had offered to set me up on a web-based diary site but, like everything else in life was moving online, I insisted on doing it the old-fashioned way. There was something about the tactile presence of a physical sheet of paper – the restrained pace and rhythm of the pen following words onto the page. I also loved the action of opening and closing the diary before and after each entry. It gave a sense of permanence and, for me, brought back memories of childish excitement – secret thoughts safely locked away by a pink ribbon.

We compromised as we usually did. Rupert set up a page on a website called LifeCake – social media for your baby – where we could post photos and thoughts about Sam as he grew and which we could share with friends and family, but he also bought me a beautiful brown leather diary with soft, creamy, unlined pages and a black ribbon. I was, after all, a twenty-eight-year-old married mother and my days of pink ribbons were definitely over.

I made my first entry when I got up to check on Sam in the middle of the night. I was exhausted but wanted to set down a few words to remind me of the feelings of pure, naked euphoria which were threatening to overwhelm me.

I failed miserably. How do you put those kinds of emotions into words? But it was good to have tried and I never missed a day after that, through good times and bad.

By writing down my feelings of joy and gratitude, I hoped to avoid jinxing things again. After so many stupid mistakes in the past. I knew I didn't deserve this fairytale happiness; all I could do was cross my fingers and hope things would turn out differently this time.

I hadn't held on to much of my former life; there was only enough to half fill the olive-green shoebox where I kept my personal papers.

I rested the new diary carefully on top of the mess of documents: old passports; birth certificate; marriage certificate; the paper part of my driving license; my parents' death certificate; the boring, recycled record of my existence.

I was just closing the lid when a flash of pink shouted out from the drabness. My teenage diary was half-hiding at the bottom of the box, hiding badly in its garish, vinyl shell. Little wonder that I'd wanted to move on to something classier.

My mum and dad had given it to me for my thirteenth birthday and, although I'd almost grown out of the pink diary stage of life by then, I'd ended up being quite a diligent diarist for a few years. The small volume was packed with my teenage hopes, dreams and reality: boys, smoking, drinking, a career as a famous model/singer/actress/poet, the usual.

The writing was excruciatingly childish and embarrassing and, as I leafed through my adolescence, I scrawled a mental Post-It to burn the diary sooner rather than later.

There was one exception. I knew what I was looking for and turned to the final entry, made three years after its closest neighbour. It had been written by a different person. An adult.

12th June 2007

I never thought I'd write here again, but I had to talk to somebody.

I've had the most incredible week of my life. Probably the most amazing experience I'll ever have.

The trip to Germany and the G8 protests were massive 'firsts' anyway. I've never done anything like that before. I've never even been out of England.

There were thousands of us, continuous noise and tension everywhere, and the toilets were unbelievably disgusting. I've led such a sheltered life. It's pathetic.

But that wasn't it. I need to write about Jax.

I'd been put in her tent, but she didn't have much time for me to begin with. Jax had been going to demos for three or four years and spent most of her time with the hardcore protesters. Most of the time, I wasn't sure she even knew I was there.

But I noticed her. Even though she was ignoring me, I could already feel it – the fire which always burns inside her like a tiny sun.

She's not that beautiful. Slim and pretty enough with fragile, porcelain features framed by a short, spiky frizz of dark hair. She moves with a dancer's grace and, while she looks fragile, she's not at all - every muscle,

11

every sinew is iron hard and sometimes I imagine I can actually see her skin glowing.

Most of the time, her body and her features are at rest, a sullen slouch which has a little 'don't mess with me' about it, but just a little. It's only when something lights the fire inside that you see the true Jax, or rather one of the true Jaxes.

If something makes her angry or she feels threatened, she becomes a cornered vixen oozing defensive aggression. That was the only side of her I saw during those first days and even then, just once or twice. Her anger isn't something I would ever want directed at me.

It wasn't until I saw the other side that I understood how special Jax really is.

She wanted to borrow a towel from Kurt, who was one of the hard-arsed communist bureaucrats-in-waiting at the reception tent. Kurt was dismissive to begin with, spouting tired, comradely explanations of why he couldn't help, why making an exception would destroy the people's project.

Jax let him finish and then she simply looked at him and smiled. I saw the light of that single smile reflected in his eyes and watched as his resistance evaporated. He reached for the towel and handed it to her without another word.

It was then that I first realised how much I wanted her to shine that light on me. I wanted it more than anything I'd ever wanted before.

I only had to wait two more days for my wish to come true, but they were such long days. I spent my time with Daz who was sweet and kind, but all I could do was to think about her. I struggled to eat more than a few mouthfuls at a time and, with Jax breathing softly only an arms length away, I hardly slept.

And then it happened.

I wasn't expecting it. The big protest was planned for the following morning, everyone was tense, and the camp was dark and strangely quiet as I walked over to the wash area to clean my teeth. A couple of bare, yellow bulbs were creating golden puddles in the corner of the tent and I saw that Jax was already there, standing by one of the metal basins.

She asked to borrow my toothpaste and, as I handed it to her, our fingertips touched. She smiled.

It was like being bathed in liquid honey. We stood silently, a single statue joined through those few square millimetres of skin contact. I felt her strength and passion flow through me, an electric river which thrilled every cell of my body.

It was a moment from Greek mythology. Jax is a Goddess — fascinating and frightening, intense and in control. I couldn't believe she cared about me.

But then she leant forward slowly, rested her warm fingers against my cheek, and kissed me.

That was it. We've been together every moment since. It's like a fabulous dream - every sound, every touch, every colour is brighter and richer than before. I'm floating above my old life which now seems drab and uninteresting in comparison.

All I want is to be with her and, for some wonderful, inexplicable reason, she seems to want to be with me.

Is this what love is?

Family Life

If you use a standard online email provider, even inexperienced hackers can easily capture your primary password as long as they have access to your email address and mobile number. (Detailed procedure: Ch 7, Section 5). In most cases, this then gives them full access to all of your emails, contacts, calendar, photos and personal documents without your knowledge.
"How much is your Life Worth? Protecting your Identity in a Digital World."
JJ Martin, Insight Business Press 2015

The first five or six weeks after Sam was born were a blur of new experiences and showing off. I'd heard some horror stories about sleeping problems, eating problems, colic, jaundice or parents too afraid to touch the baby in case they break it. You name it, every one of these disasters was lying in wait for me and Rupert. As it turned out, we were either incredibly lucky or amazingly talented new parents and most things went smoothly. Apart from the sleeping, of course.

I had a great midwife and a health visitor who made me feel confident and vaguely in control. She was called Joyce and was one of those slightly annoying people who seem to be happy all of the time. Her smile looked 'genuinely' genuine, not forced at all, and she radiated peace and satisfaction.

After her first visit I'd been left feeling strangely envious and sad, which didn't make much sense when I looked at how lucky I actually was.

She'd finished weighing Sam and he was lying happily on his blanket looking up at his new mobile and watching the sun glint off the shiny silver angel's wings which dangled protectively above him.

I handed Joyce a cup of tea.

'Everything seems fine,' she said, closing her notebook. 'His weight is right in the middle of the range and that rash has gone away completely. He's a lovely little boy.' She took a big slurp of her tea and looked at me. 'What about you, Fabiola? How are you coping?'

'I'm fine,' I said. 'Tired, of course. He's up for a feed two or three times in the night. Rupert would help if he could, but he's got a lot of work on at the moment. Pretty normal stuff I suppose.'

'Hmmm. Maybe? Is there such a thing as normal? You sure you're all right?'

'I'm sure, There's no need for you to worry.'

'You do look tired and a bit gaunt. Have you lost weight?'

'A little. I sometimes forget to eat, what with everything else.'

'I understand,' she said, taking my hand in hers. 'It's a difficult time for all young mothers. But you must look after yourself. It's important you keep up your strength.'

'I know and I will make a point of it. Thank you.'

'What about little Sam? Are you enjoying being with him?'

'Oh yes,' I replied. 'He's the most perfect baby. Every time I look at him, my heart skips a beat. We're fine, really. Everything's OK.'

Joyce hadn't finished with me. 'What about friends?' she asked. 'You've not lived here long, have you?'

'No, it's less than a year since we moved out of London and I've taken a while to settle in.' I didn't particularly want to go into the details of my non-existent social life. 'Rupert grew up in Oxford and still knows a lot of people. And he's got his work, of course.'

'And family?' said Joyce, the bit clearly between her teeth. 'Are any of your family nearby?'

'My parents are both dead, but Rupert's parents are still in the same house he grew up in. It's only up the road, so we see quite a lot of them. Especially his mum.' I rolled my eyes. 'She's here most days.'

Joyce smiled. 'How's that working out for you? I think I'd have killed my mother-in-law if I'd seen her every day. Especially straight after my first was born.'

I couldn't hold back my snort of laughter. Joyce had a great deadpan way of saying things. 'Surprisingly well,' I said. 'I was dreading it before but, somewhat ironically, Virginia's visits have turned out to be the high point of my day.'

'Why somewhat ironically?'

'Have you met Rupert's mum?' I said, still giggling.

Joyce shook her head.

'Well, she's quite proper. Very posh. And I don't think she's ever approved of me.'

'But you're getting on OK?'

'Yeah. She's great with Sam and mostly manages to keep her mouth shut when she thinks I'm doing something wrong. And, let's face it, if it wasn't for her I probably wouldn't see anyone all day.'

'Sounds a bit lonely,' said Joyce, standing and picking up her bag. 'It'd be good if you could get out a bit more. Join some baby groups. There's a lot going on round here for young mothers.' She walked out to the hall. 'I've left a couple of leaflets on the table.'

'Thanks Joyce,' I said, as I opened the door for her. 'I'll do that.'

She set off down the path and, as I watched her cheery, bouncing stride, I was shocked by how pathetic and lonely my answers had sounded. That wasn't me. I would need to get my act together.

I heard the key in the front door about two hours after Joyce had left and just as Sam was waking from his nap.

'Yoo-hoo. Only me.'

'I'm in Sam's room,' I shouted. 'Getting him up. Why don't you put the kettle on? I'll be through in a minute.'

By the time we got out to the kitchen, the tea was made and the table laid neatly with proper cups and a plate of fresh home-made blueberry muffins centre stage.

Virginia gave me a polite hug and a kiss and reached out for Sam.

'Come here, you lovely little boy,' she said. 'Did you have a nice sleep?'

'I don't know how you do it,' I said, handing him over. 'Those muffins look amazing.'

'Oh those.' She waved one hand dismissively. 'I knocked those up this morning. They're easy to make and I thought you needed fattening up.'

That was rich coming from her. Thin as a rake, I doubted if she'd manage a single mouthful of muffin herself.

'You're the second person to say that to me today,' I said. 'Maybe I should listen?'

'Important to keep up your strength for this little one.' Sam was lying happily in her arms, looking up at her with eyes wide open, his tiny, pudgy fists squeezing each of her little fingers as hard as he could.

'Message received,' I said, grabbing a muffin. 'I'll start with one of these.'

Virginia smiled. She was making me feel like a broodmare, but right then I was happy enough to accept the role. As long as it came with freshly-baked muffins.

While I was feeding Sam, we chatted about this and that for twenty minutes or so. There was definitely something important on her mind though; the small talk was her clumsy version of a polite introduction to the real subject.

'I've been thinking about Sam's christening,' she said eventually. 'Have you had any thoughts?'

'No. Sorry. None at all. I struggle to think about anything these days.'

'Of course. That's completely understandable. Is he still up in the night?'

'At least twice, sometimes more. I'm in a total daze most of the time. It's getting better though.'

'Good.' Virginia smiled as I put Sam down onto his play mat. 'In the meantime, I'd be happy to take on boring tasks like the christening if you'd like.' She waited until I was sitting down again. 'I assume you actually want a christening?'

We'd had the audacity to get married, just the two of us on a beach in Thailand, without telling anyone in Rupert's family; there was still plenty of smouldering resentment about that, and I had no intention of making things worse by refusing a christening.

The fact she was offering to organise it was no surprise. Virginia loved that sort of social event and, more than anything, she loved to be in control.

'Of course we do and it would be great if you could help. Thank you, Virginia.'

'You're welcome. That's what family's for,' she said, visibly relaxing. 'There are a couple of tricky issues though ...'

'Really? What?'

'Well, obviously, we'd love to have it in our village. At St Peter's. It's a beautiful church, we know the vicar well, and we could have the reception in our garden right next door.'

'It sounds lovely,' I said. 'What's the problem?'

'Well, you're a Catholic aren't you?'

'Oh, I get it,' I said, relieved that she'd finally got to the point. 'Don't worry about that. I am a Catholic, but I'm not exactly practising. As you say, St Peter's is a lovely location and your garden is fabulous.'

I was obviously saying all of the right things and Virginia smiled. 'That's a relief,' she said. 'I must admit I've been worrying about it for a while. These things can be so difficult.'

I couldn't help thinking the world was full of slightly more difficult things, but it wasn't the time or place.

'It's really no big deal. As far as I'm concerned, Sam can make his own choices about religion when he's grown up.'

'What about your friends and family? How many do you expect to come?'

'I'm not sure there'll be any family,' I said, looking for a stone to crawl under. 'Since my parents died, I've lost touch with most of them.'

'That would be a shame,' she said. 'But it's completely up to you, of course. I'll just need to know numbers at some point.'

'Of course. I might get in touch with some old university friends, but need to think about it. Would it be easiest if you co-ordinated the guest list with Rupert?'

I suspected the christening guest list was one of those family minefields, like 'who goes where at Christmas?', which was best avoided.

Thinking back to where things began to go wrong, it probably all started there.

On Thu, Sep 25 2015, at 9:33 AM, Rupert Blackwell
<rupert.blackwell@savilles.com> wrote:

*Darling, Hope you're having a good day. Mum's just
sent me suggestions for who to invite to the
christening. I've attached the list. It's only family and
their friends so far. Who do we want to add? She
suggests a maximum of ten more which seems about
right. Give Sam a kiss from me. See you at about six.
Roop XXXX*

On Thu, Sep 25, 2015 at 10:39 AM, Fabiola Blackwell
<fabiola.blackwell@gmail.com> wrote:

*Thnx Roop, I'll have a look later. Sam's OK but quite
needy this morning. Fabi XXX*

Sent from my iPad

On Fri, Sep 26, 2015 at 11:03 AM, Rupert Blackwell
<rupert.blackwell@savilles.com> wrote:

*Fabi, I forgot to chase this last night. Too much on.
Can you look at it? Roop XXXXX P.S. Don't forget I'm
staying at Mum and Dad's tonight. I'll have a few
glasses of wine with Dad and don't want to drive. You
sure you'll be OK?*

On Fri, Sep 26, 2015 at 15:03 PM, Fabiola Blackwell
<fabiola.blackwell@gmail.com> wrote:

I've had a look and it seems fine. Are we thinking of

*inviting some of my London gang to the christening?
I've not heard from Jax at all. Probably still seriously
pissed off with me. We'll be fine just me and Sam
tonight. It'll give me a chance for some peace and
quiet :-) XX*

Sent from my iPad

_____

On Fri, Sep 26, 2015 at 18:03 PM, Rupert Blackwell
<rupert.blackwell@savilles.com> wrote:

*Fabi, Seriously? Jax!! Not sure that would be such a
great idea. What about those old uni friends you
mentioned? I can't believe I've hardly met any of them.
Let's chat tomorrow. If you need anything ring me on
the home number - mobile reception's still crap at Mum
and Dad's. I'll miss you both. Roop XXXX*

_____

On Sat, Sep 27, 2015 at 2:07 AM, Fabiola Blackwell
<fabiola.blackwell@gmail.com> wrote:

*Roop. Sam's not having a great night. Up twice
already. Hope you had a nice evening. Don't be too
late in the morning. You're probably right about Jax but
it does feel like I'm just cutting ties and that's not really
fair. It's not as though there's any real justification. Fabi
X*

Sent from my iPad

_____

On Sat, Sep 27, 2015 at 5:27 AM, Rupert Blackwell
<rupert.blackwell@savilles.com> wrote:

Fabi, Depends how you define 'no justification' I guess.

That letter was full of some pretty explicit threats. I can't sleep either. Love Roop

---

On Sat, Sep 27, 2015 at 5:30 AM, Fabiola Blackwell
<fabiola.blackwell@gmail.com> wrote:

Jax didn't mean all of that. It was a huge shock when I decided to sell the flat. The letter was only a knee-jerk reaction. XXX

Sent from my iPad

On Sat, Sep 27, 2015 at 5:32 AM, Rupert Blackwell
<rupert.blackwell@savilles.com> wrote:

Maybe, but that wasn't how I read it. Let's not stress about this on email at five in the morning. I'll be back by ten-thirty. Try and get some sleep. Roop XXXXX

On Sat, Sep 27, 2015 at 5:34 AM, Fabiola Blackwell
<fabiola.blackwell@gmail.com> wrote:

I'll try. See you in a bit. It wasn't actually so great being on my own btw. XXXXXX

Sent from my iPad

I found it surprisingly difficult to be on my own overnight. It's not as though Rupert was able to help much when Sam woke up anyway. He usually wanted feeding and I was the only one who was physically qualified. But it did make a difference to have my man lying there beside me to provide a bit of moral support, even when he was flat out and snoring. I wouldn't have fancied being a single mum and going through that phase alone, that was for sure.

The whole christening saga didn't help. It was never a good idea to have important conversations by email and especially not in the middle of the night. One reason why people kept telling me not to have my phone in the bedroom, and to give myself some time away from screens and the intrusive tentacles of digital connectivity.

Easy to say, but I was finding myself more and more reliant on emails and social media to help me to break out of my isolation bubble and I couldn't imagine being disciplined enough to cut back. I loved every moment of being with Sam but that didn't stop me feeling bored and lonely for much of the time, even when he was awake.

The great thing about social media was that it never slept, and it didn't care whether it was three in the morning or three in the afternoon. A good reflection of my life at the time.

I'd been pleasantly surprised by how many old friends had sent me congratulation messages after Sam was born. After university, I'd gradually come to accept that none of them wanted anything to do with me any more. I hadn't been imagining things; for years, any comments I tried to make on their Facebook posts were ignored and would usually kill the thread.

But now, even a few of the guys from London had been in touch and seemed to be genuinely pleased for me.

But nothing from Jax. Not a single word.

Whether Rupert and I had discussed the christening guest list by email or face-to-face, the results would have been the same. My friends from London weren't 'suitable' and it was too early to be sure I would be able to patch up relationships with my university friends.

The main reason why we'd avoided a proper wedding in the first place was that the church would probably have tipped over; the right-hand side would have overflowed with Rupert's family and friends and my side would have yawned empty as the grave.

What would Jax be up to while Sam's soul was being handed over to God?

Saturday morning, soon after midday. Probably sitting, legs crossed, on the floor of some dodgy bedsit with a few of the others, maybe Joe, Daz, Linda and Sal, smoking the first spliff of the day and preparing to save the world yet again.

I missed that crowd. We'd been so close, so tight, for over five years and I couldn't believe we'd drifted apart so easily. It must be two years now. How had I become so good at burning bridges?

I wasn't the only one to blame – it takes two to tango – but I knew Jax would have pinned the responsibility on me anyway. Getting together with Rupert, that was the ultimate betrayal. I'd gone over to the other side and become a part of *them*.

It had all come to a head when I sold my flat. I'd bought it with money inherited from my parents and then lived there with Jax. When I moved to Oxford to be with Rupert, I let Jax stay on; I felt bad enough about our break up and couldn't face making it worse. True to form, Jax had turned out to be a lousy tenant.

When Rupert and I were ready to buy a house together and I needed to sell the Camden flat, I knew there would be trouble. That was when Jax sent me the letter.

Rupert was right and I was kidding myself. It was a horrible letter. Malicious, threatening, vengeful and not something to be brushed aside and forgotten. We had our new life and Sam to think about now, and it was best to leave those days behind me.

Ghosts of Puglia

Growing concerns about long-term privacy and the potential of personal profile damage were the main drivers behind the success of Snapchat and the various copycats which have arisen since Snapchat launched in 2011. Hackers and identity thieves have been using bespoke 'snapmail' software for many years. True snapmail (where all trace of a received email is removed at a fixed time after receipt or reading) can only be implemented on infiltrated email accounts.

"How much is your Life Worth? Protecting your Identity in a Digital World."
JJ Martin, Insight Business Press 2015

I woke up in soft steps. I'd been dreaming, but my dreams stayed behind and forgotten as the real world seeped in. I could feel a gentle almost-tickling touch on my face and opened my eyes. There was Rupert, sitting on the edge of the bed, smiling down at me and stroking my cheek with the backs of his fingers.

The morning sunlight filled the room and I felt as though I'd slept forever.

'Buon giorno, cara,' he said, holding out a glass. 'I've made you some fresh orange juice.'

My scrambled thoughts started to congeal. 'What time is it?' I croaked.

'A little after ten,' he said. 'You slept for almost eight hours.'

'Bloody hell! We've got to be there at twelve. You should've woken me earlier.'

'Calm down,' he said, with a smug smile. 'You needed your sleep. I've got everything under control. Sam's just gone down for his nap and I'll get him ready when he wakes up. You only need to worry about yourself.' He was puffed up with pride – like a little boy.

'You sure?' I said, taking the glass from him. 'I feel like I've died and gone to heaven.'

'Nothing so exotic. You can sit on your cloud for a bit longer, but then you need to get your arse into gear. Bacon and scrambled eggs. On the table in five minutes.'

He'd even laid the table and bought some flowers. No prizes for arranging them, but that wasn't why I married him.

'Are you sure we've got enough time,' I said, still feeling we should be in full panic mode.

'All under control. I'm not totally useless. I've even got Sam's outfit laid out and ready to go.' He filled a mug with freshly-brewed black coffee and handed it to me. 'As long as we're out of here by eleven-thirty, we'll be fine. It's our show after all.'

'You're such a sweetie,' I said. 'And no-one ever said you were useless. I don't think I've felt this well rested since Sam was born.'

'Well, you'll need to be. It'll be the first time you'll have met half my family and I'm sure they'll want to give you a proper grilling.'

'Oh joy!' I said. 'I'll do my best, but promise you'll come and save me if I need it.'

'You'll be fine. They'll love you. What's not to love?'

I got up and went over to give him a hug. 'I don't know what's got into you this morning, but I like it. Now, let me grab a shower and get dressed or your clever plan will go properly pear-shaped.'

Rupert's parents, John and Virginia, lived in a small village just north of Oxford. It was more of a hamlet than a proper village but, somewhat greedily, the village had its own beautiful Norman church and a huge vicarage.

It was an impressive house, almost an imposition, with grey limestone blocks and sharply angled eaves brooding from three stories up. Seven bedrooms, swimming pool, tennis court and two acres of gardens.

Naturally, John was Church Warden and, as he was quite the charmer, the old ladies who did the flowers had made a special effort for Sam's christening. The church looked beautiful and the ceremony went off without a hitch. There were about forty guests;

all, as expected, were from Rupert's side of the family with the exception of our neighbours, John and Julie, and a couple of Rupert's Oxford friends.

I did have one trick up my sleeve, however, and I smiled every time I remembered that the Carlantino family wasn't totally absent from proceedings. I'd been pretending that my family's absence wasn't a big deal, but it obviously mattered more than I was willing to accept.

After my parents died, I put my inherited share of their belongings into storage, thinking there would be time enough to sort through them later. That never happened, but I would go to the storage unit once or twice a year and look through things. I had broken with everyone from home by then, but wasn't prepared to completely give up on my memories. I never told Jax, who would have made some snide remark about 'bourgeois sentimentalism' or 'needing to throw off the shackles of tribe and family'.

One of the more special items which I'd inherited was a lace christening dress, delicately hand-stitched and coffee-cream with age. My grandfather, Nonno, once told me it had been in our family for six generations and, a few weeks before Sam's christening, I drove up to Bedford and dug it out of the storage unit.

We may have been poorly represented physically but Sam played his part in keeping the family line unbroken. As I looked out behind the congregation, I saw row after row of Puglians stretching into the distance, cheerfully bright in their Sunday best, beaming smiles lighting every face and rough-fingered blessings tracing the sign of the cross into the dusty air.

Not there in body, but welcoming him into the family nonetheless.

'What a beautiful Christening dress, Fabiola,' said Henrietta. 'I've never seen anything quite like it. Virginia told me it was a family heirloom.' She leant close to my ear and whispered. 'She also said you fought tooth and nail to make sure that Sam wore your family's dress rather than the Blackwell monstrosity. Well done! It takes a strong woman to stand up to my daughter and win the day. I

26

certainly gave up years ago.'

Henrietta was my favourite Blackwell, still fit and feisty at seventy-eight and nobody's fool.

'I'm sure it was much more civilised than that,' I replied, laughing. 'Virginia understood how important it was for me and, as I didn't have any family coming, she was happy to give in.'

'I doubt that, my dear, but you're very gracious.' Henrietta sipped her champagne through a smile. 'Now tell me about your family, if you don't mind.'

'Not so interesting, I'm afraid.' Thinking about my family made me feel sad and empty. 'I've lost touch with them all now. They originally come from Peschici, down in the South-East of Italy. It's a small fishing village. Apparently more touristy these days, but I've not been there since I was twelve.'

'And your parents emigrated to Bedford. Why was that?'

'No. It wasn't my parents who emigrated, or at least not by choice. My grandfather moved over to work in the brick factories after the war and he brought his wife and children over about five years later.'

'How interesting,' said Henrietta. 'Did a lot of Italians come over at that time?'

'Yes, loads of them. And they brought a lot of the southern Italian culture over as well. Everything was still very traditional back then. Do you remember the part of The Godfather where Al Pacino goes back to Sicily and falls in love with the local village beauty?'

'Of course.'

'Well, you'll remember they go walking together – strolling arm-in-arm along a dusty track – but, when the camera pans backwards, you see about twenty chaperones following a few paces behind. I doubt it was actually that bad for my Mum and Dad but, from the stories I've heard, it wasn't far off.'

Henrietta laughed. 'I can just picture it. It's one of my favourite films and there's something about Al Pacino ...'

'Yes, he's got a certain brooding smoulder, hasn't he?' I said, amused to be sharing a moment of lustful idolatry with Rupert's grandmother. 'My father looked a bit like him when he was younger. Anyway, it was all different by the time we kids came along and my parents' generation struggled to cope with the changes.'

'Fascinating.' Henrietta appeared genuinely interested although, as she was from a background where making conversation was simply good manners, I doubt I'd have been able to tell if she wasn't. 'But a shame you've lost touch with your family. You should do something about that. Sooner rather than later. Family endures when all else fails.'

'You're right, and it makes sense that you're saying that today. I've mostly managed to avoid thinking about them over the past few years but, since Sam was born, and especially today with everyone gathered together to celebrate his arrival, I've felt there was something missing.'

Henrietta arched an eyebrow. 'How do you mean?'

'Well, I want to connect him to my side of the family but, apart from the dress, I can't. I really wish my brothers and sister were here but I couldn't face inviting them and having them refuse to come.'

These thoughts, seeds of regret, had been germinating quietly in the back of my mind for months, ever since I held Sam in my arms for the first time. He was the start of a new generation and needed to be placed into the jigsaw puzzle of family history; he needed to fit both into his past, and his future.

My own decisions had been mine to make – although I was questioning many of them now – but I had no right to leave Sam hanging one-handed from a single family tree, even if it was from the sturdy branches of an English oak.

Most Sunday lunches after mass, Nonno Roberto would tell us stories of home and how, as boys, he and his friends would hunt and forage in the woods and mountains which surrounded his village.

Storms were brewing in northern Europe, but there had been a few golden years before the sun became stained with bitterness and blood, and they roamed free as young wolves through the last remaining fragments of the ancient forests. They had their own kind of oak trees – I couldn't remember what they were called – and Nonno would often say that the English oak was the connection which had made him happy to adopt England as his home.

The British weather was terrible and he worried that the people had lost their standards and morality but, as he would often tell us while sitting indoors in his nice warm cafe, 'take a woodland walk here, on a crisp sunny day in late autumn and you could be in Puglia'.

Although it wasn't strictly legal, he'd made my father promise to scatter his ashes under a huge oak in Odell Great Wood, just outside Bedford. He loved the tree and wanted to be connected through unseen root networks to the oak forests of his youth.

Nonno had lived long enough to bury his son and, when he'd died himself a year later, it had fallen to me to keep my father's promise. I went to the tree alone and sat in solitary silence under the massive canopy until long after dark. I've never been back.

I looked up from my champagne glass to see Henrietta watching me carefully before reaching over and touching my hand; just a stroke of a feather but enough to send an electric shiver up and down my arm.

'You have a sad soul, Fabiola,' she said. 'It's not too late to go back and mend those bridges, you know? To do what your heart is telling you to do.'

'Thank you,' I said. There was nothing else to say.

'Now, I've monopolised you long enough.' Henrietta snapped seamlessly back into her 'conversation at cocktail parties' mode. 'You should go and save your son from his grandmother. He looks like he's had quite enough.'

As I walked over to rescue Sam from Virginia, I thought back to my comforting vision of generations of Carlantinos crowding the church and stretching out into the churchyard and beyond. There was something which jarred uncomfortably with my memories but refused to take shape, it was sand sifting in a sieve, slipping soft and silent through the mesh.

The strangest thing happened later that night. I picked up an email at about six in the morning when I was up with Sam. The message was unusual and upset me but, later on, when I went to read it again, it wasn't there; it wasn't in my trash, nor in any of the other email folders. It had vanished completely.

Rupert was in the kitchen, making coffee, when I came out of the shower.

'Morning sweetie, did you get any sleep at all?' he said, handing me a cup.

'Not so much, he was restless most of the night and then there was an email which really got under my skin.'

'That's the last thing you need, I keep telling you to stop checking your phone during the night. You're online way too much these days. Who was it from?'

'Well, that's the weirdest thing. It wasn't from anybody. It just had a row of asterisks where the sender's address normally is.'

Rupert was much better than me with computers and anything technical and I recognised the familiar look which implied I had probably pressed something by mistake, or selected the wrong option somewhere. Nothing was more guaranteed to wind me up.

'OK, that is strange. Let's have a look then. Maybe I can find out something from the header info.'

'That's what's even crazier,' I said. 'It's gone.'

'What do you mean, gone?' By then, he had the phone and was fiddling away, but the frustration in his voice and his energetic tapping and scrolling told me that the 'stupid thing I must have done because I was a woman' wasn't as easy to find as he'd expected.

'Gone, as in I can't find it. It's not in any of my folders, not in my trash, not in my sent items, not in my spam, nowhere. I checked on the iPad too. Nothing.'

'That doesn't make any sense, Fabi. Emails don't just disappear. You must have done something. What did you do after you read it?'

Well, that question was predictable, and so was my furious reaction. 'I didn't bloody do anything. Why does it always have to be something I did? I read the mail – several times actually – then went to check on Sam and to make a cup of tea. When I went to look for it again, it wasn't there.'

Rupert was smart enough to realise his mistake. 'OK, OK, I'm sorry, I was only trying to help. I wasn't accusing you of anything.' He was still looking at the phone but there was no eureka moment.

'It doesn't make any sense. You've still got messages in your trash so it hasn't been emptied. It must be somewhere. Any chance you were dreaming?'

'No, for fuck's sake. Of course I wasn't dreaming. Do you think I've gone pazzo just because I gave birth? That's such a typical bloody bloke thing to say.' I took a few seconds to calm down and sip my coffee. 'The mail wasn't about anything as such and there was only one sentence. 'You should have listened!' That was it.'

'Beats me. I can't find any trace of it,' Rupert said, handing me back the phone with a sheepish smile. 'The only thing which might have happened is that it was some sort of spam which slipped through and then the mail software identified it and removed it afterwards. I wouldn't worry about it.'

I finished my coffee and sat at the small kitchen table while Rupert went to get Sam ready to go out. We'd added an extension at the back of the house which made the kitchen much bigger and we'd put a hexagonal skylight in the roof at the same time. A narrow beam of cold morning sunshine spotlit the dust which spiralled upwards as I plumped down onto the cushion. We needed a cleaner, and soon. Would it be too decadent and bourgeois to get an au pair?

God, how my attitudes had changed in just a couple of years. What would Daz or Linda have thought about that? Thinking about them was enough to make me give myself a good ticking off, a mental slap on the back of the hand because of the conversation I should probably have with Rupert about the political side of my life in the years before we met. The conversation I kept putting off.

It had been bad enough when he'd learned about my relationship with Jax. I'd avoided telling the whole truth for over six months. I hadn't exactly lied to him at any time, but I'd always known that he'd assumed Jax was a man and I'd never said anything to disabuse him of the notion.

The fact I had a long-term relationship with another woman wasn't a big deal for me. I've always preferred men and it had no impact on my relationship with Rupert. I didn't think of myself as gay in any way. The thing with Jax was simply something which

31

happened; there was something about her ... something unique and exciting.

I hadn't been sure how well Rupert would take it though. He was such a straight-laced public school boy, full of thoughtless pseudo-homophobic jibes about people being 'bloody benders', 'nancy-boys' or puerile innuendos about 'back passages' and 'bending down to pick up the soap in the showers'.

His ridiculous old-school approach to sexuality was the main reason why I'd been wary of telling him that Jax was a girl in the first place and, once I'd missed the opportunity to say it upfront, it became easier and easier to avoid as time went by. I'd never had any intention of letting the two of them meet after all.

Rupert and I met fairly randomly when I was out for drinks after work. A group of us were standing on the pavement outside the Lamb and Flag in Covent Garden and Rupert came up to me with an outrageously cheesy chat-up line. It was ridiculous, but he had a gorgeous smile and, although he had no idea, brilliant timing. Things with Jax were becoming difficult and I was probably looking for an excuse to make my escape.

We went out for drinks a few times and then one night I ended up staying over at his place. I was never a one-night-stand sort of girl but with Rupert it was right. I'd not felt that way about anyone for a long time, if ever.

We'd been lying in bed afterwards, chatting and got into one of those idiotic conversations which seem to spring up in the confused first-time moments when a whole tombola full of emotions is spinning and rattling around – satisfaction, pride, embarrassment, guilt, hope, fear – all mixed up together. We ended up on the subject of 'favourite sexual fantasy' which, as it turned out, was not the best idea.

Rupert's favourite was a classic, or at least a classic for a middle-class English male in his mid twenties. He imagined surprising a lesbian couple, in action as it were, and being asked to join them. It didn't take much imagination to see what would happen next as, of course, they found him so attractive that they stopped being interested in each other and devoted themselves to giving him pleasure. Way, way too close to home and there was no way I was going to bring up the topic of Jax's gender immediately after that.

I didn't mind so much, he didn't mean anything by it. He was at ease with the few gay couples in our London social group and would blithely use the same language in front of them. I suspected, however, that he would see me having been in a same-sex relationship for five years in a somewhat different light, which was why I avoided the issue for so long.

I'd told him eventually although there were still other things which I'd never mentioned and needed to. It would have to wait as that morning wasn't a good time to talk about anything serious. I hadn't slept well and was tired after the christening.

The email was also still niggling away at the back of my mind, but it must have been some weird webmail thing as Rupert had said; it wasn't worth worrying about on such a lovely day. We'd been looking forward to strolling down to the town centre and simply wandering about, looking at some of the colleges, grabbing a coffee and enjoying a peaceful Sunday.

'We're ready,' came the shout from the hall. 'See you outside.'

'OK, just coming.' As I got up and reached for my coat, I remembered the other thing which had been worrying away at the edge of my mind like a puppy with an old blanket. The vicar had been about to do the water-splashing thing with Sam and I'd been looking at everyone gathered in the church and the rows of imaginary Carlantinos. Right at that moment, a dark figure had stood up and slipped out through the open doors. I hadn't seen who it was but, for some reason, it gave me the shivers.

Timing is Everything

Once password access to email accounts has been acquired, it is possible to upload a Calendar Jogger. This will adjust the displayed time of a calendar appointment and is often used in the case of full identity theft to allow the hacker, or an accomplice, to attend a meeting in place of the victim. Calendar Joggers can automatically reset themselves leaving no trace of the 'jog'. The original appointment remains unaffected.

"How much is your Life Worth? Protecting your Identity in a Digital World."
JJ Martin, Insight Business Press 2015

I couldn't believe the weather. It had been gloriously sunny for two weeks, but then it started tanking it down, blustery gusts conspiring with overflowing gutters to spread bucket-sized sheets of extra wetness as a random bonus.

It was a couple of weeks after the christening and I had an appointment to take Sam for the third, and last, of his baby injections.

Our doctor's surgery was on Beaumont Street which was only fifteen minutes walk away and, as it was almost impossible to find a parking space anywhere nearby, driving wasn't an option.

Not only did I need to time my excursion to fit in with sleeps, feeds and nappy changes, I also needed to allow for the time spent configuring the rain cover for the ridiculously-expensive, high-tech pram, finding the waterproof bags for all of the stuff I needed to take with me, and finally dressing myself for wet weather.

Normally it would have been a pleasant stroll, but the weather made it a nightmare. The appointment was at ten o'clock and, despite allowing twenty minutes extra to organise myself, we were still ten minutes late by the time we arrived and I was sweaty, stressed and soaked to the skin.

'Good morning. Sam Blackwell for his five-month injection. I'm sorry I'm late,' I panted out. 'I thought I'd allowed enough time for all of the wet weather hassle, but clearly not.' I peeled off my raincoat, managed to open the pram cover and released Sam.

'Good morning, Mrs Blackwell. Let's have a look.' The receptionist turned to her computer and then looked down at her watch, shaking her head slightly. 'You're a bit early, I'm afraid. I have you down for twelve o'clock, not ten.'

'Are you sure?' I said, taking out my phone. 'I only checked this morning. Look I have it here.' I opened the calendar and passed her the phone.

'That's right. Twelve o'clock,' she replied, handing back the phone. 'The same as I have in the system.'

'But that doesn't make any sense ...' I took back my phone and looked at the evidence in full retina-screen technicolor. 'I only checked an hour and a half ago and I'm certain it said ten o'clock. I must have a much worse case of baby brain than I thought. I'm so sorry. Any chance of an earlier appointment?'

'I'm sorry, Mrs Blackwell, we're very busy. It'll have to be at twelve. Sorry about that.'

It shouldn't have mattered as there were lots of lovely coffee shops only a short walk from the surgery but, when you take into account the hassle of managing a baby, and the fact that we were completely soaked, the whole morning was turning into a complete disaster.

I'd fed him right before we left and he wouldn't need a sleep for a couple of hours. Now everything was out of synch and, to make it worse, I was furious with myself for being such an idiot.

I called Rupert; I needed to talk to somebody and to vent a few of my frustrations.

'Roop, you won't believe it. I've messed up Sam's appointment at the doctor's and arrived an hour and half early. I'm unbelievably pissed off. You're not around for a coffee, are you?'

'Oh, what a pain,' he said. 'That's not like you and you must've got soaked. I can't get away, I'm afraid. I'm in Summertown now, and meeting a client in twenty minutes.'

My surging irritation and disappointment at his inability to drop everything and come running immediately were, of course, wholly unreasonable and I managed to maintain an approximation of a cheery voice. 'OK caro mio, not a problem. It's just a bit of a pain what with feeding and sleeping times. His routine is going to be royally messed up, and I feel like such an idiot for getting the time wrong.'

'Don't beat yourself up about it,' he said. 'You're still up two or three times in the night. It's no surprise you're tired. Look, I have to run. I won't be late tonight. Love you.'

'Love you too.' I put the phone in my bag and started preparing to go out in the rain again. For some reason, my irritation slipped seamlessly into sadness and I felt tears threatening the edge of my eyes without warning or permission. I turned away from the other people in the reception and busied myself settling Sam back into his pram while I told myself to get a grip. It was only a messed up appointment and I wasn't even late. Really not something to get upset about.

As it turned out, Sam and I ended up having a pleasant enough time at the Ashmolean coffee shop; he was well behaved, and afterwards he didn't even complain about the injection. The rain had stopped by the time we set off for home, the wind had blown itself out and, walking up Walton Street, I remembered how much I liked living in Oxford.

I grew up in Bedford which was one of the most boring towns in England; there was absolutely no point in comparing it with Oxford, or anywhere else I've lived for that matter.

My granddad, Roberto – we always called him Nonno – was in the last wave of Italians who came over in the late fifties to work at the Marston Valley Brick Company. There was a huge shortage of labour after the war, I guess a huge shortage of able-bodied men was more the case, and a lot of building going on. Marston and a couple of other firms brought over workers from southern Italy, where there was no work or money.

Nonno was a hard worker and soon got a real job as a shift supervisor. He managed to make a deposit on a small terraced house a year later and sent for his family, which included my dad, also called Roberto, who was seven at the time. Nonno made sure his children, the boys at least, had a good education and, by the time I went to secondary school, the two Robertos, father and son, owned a chain of three coffee shops.

It was a strange life growing up in the Embankment, Bedford's Little Italy. We were, in many ways, normal English kids, but our home culture was still Italian. We spoke Italian in the house, ate Italian food, never missed mass on Sundays and there was absolutely no question about who to support when international football was on.

The more I thought back to those years growing up, the more I realised that they had been wonderful times. I wasn't planning on conceding that Bedford was anything other than boring, but, leaving that aside, we lived in a great community and my family had been kind, loving and usually very entertaining. I was never a religious fanatic but I was a good Catholic and I had my faith.

Every Sunday, when I was a child, we would have a big lunch at the largest coffee shop. It was closed on Sundays and we would be anywhere from ten to twenty people, all lined up on pushed-together tables, just like the traditional family lunch under a vine terrace which is an obligatory part of every Italian film I've ever seen.

My favourite was the *polpette di melanzane*, fried aubergine balls, which were always deliciously crunchy and we would always have ice cream afterwards, big balls of hazelnut and pistachio, covered with flaked nuts and smothered with shiny chocolate sauce.

The women would clear up while the men moved over to a corner table to smoke cigarettes and drink their coffee and grappa. They would pretend to be discussing important matters but everyone knew the conversation was about football and, even if politics did come up, it was much more likely to involve a ranking of politicians' wives than anything serious.

Having a child, or even thinking about having a child, had changed me in so many ways. Growing up, I'd never seen or appreciated that Nonno, and my parents to a lesser extent, had made huge sacrifices to make sure their children would have the basic opportunities in life which hadn't been possible for them.

What an ungrateful little bitch I must have been, pompously regurgitating my Marxist dogma; my adolescent passion and deep, deep certainty blithely brushing over the fact that I'd never had a moment's real hardship in my life. Too blind to imagine what they must have needed to overcome simply to survive, not to mention the inner strength and faith it must have taken for them to not become bitter and resentful. To keep on smiling and laughing despite everything.

I looked around me as I walked through the comfortable, middle class streets towards my lovely house – owned, not rented – with my expensively-dressed baby in his seven hundred and fifty quid pram, and realised how much I'd changed over the past year. I no longer thought about making the world a fairer place. I thought, somewhat subconsciously, about how I could help my children succeed.

I was no different from my parents, grandparents, and almost all other parents, and had no intention of trying to be. When it came to any of the important decisions relating to my children – schooling, friendships, travel, sports, whatever – I would do whatever I could to give them an unfair advantage.

The world wasn't fair but I no longer had time to change anything. My instincts screamed at me to focus on making sure my kids were part of the winning team and I would follow those instincts. Family had to come first.

By the time we reached home, Sam was happily asleep in his pushchair and I decided to walk around for a while to enjoy another ten minutes of peace in the sunshine. I was struggling to remember what had compelled me to be such a nasty, selfish piece of work back then and I wanted to understand what exactly had triggered my change of heart now.

Having my first child was obviously part of it but the process had begun earlier, possibly even before I met Rupert. I wondered if it might have been something as simple as the fact that I'd grown up, but I couldn't help worrying that I might have allowed Jax to drive a wedge between me and my family. By freeing myself from the relationship with her, I had also freed myself to question a lot of other things.

Every time I'd gone home, I'd needed to deal with a belly full of sniping from Jax which, in retrospect was plain nasty. She resented anything I thought, felt or did which wasn't about the two of us and our relationship. Why could I see it so clearly now, but hadn't been able to back then?

People can be so blind when they're wrapped up in a relationship. They will endure lifetimes of misery and abuse and fail to see what's right in front of them. Their myopia may be driven by unquestioning love and adoration, warped obsession, a sense of obligation, guilt or the pressure of society, but the consistent part is the fear which rushes in if the blindfold is removed. That moment of truth as you stand, blinking mole-like in the bright sunlight, naked and exposed.

I didn't want to believe I'd been that blind and wondered if I was still giving Jax too much benefit of the doubt to protect my ego from the full extent of my stupidity? If half of the half-memories were half-true, she really was a monumental bitch. How could I have loved her so much? What did that say about me?

Writing these thoughts in my new diary would help me remember. Putting them down on paper, reading them a few times, giving myself time to think, that would make things clearer.

It was too late to do anything about my parents and grandparents except for visiting their graves and praying for them, but I did want to go back out to Puglia and show Rupert and Sam my roots.

While I was putting a reminder in my calendar to have a look at flights to Puglia and to discuss the idea of a short holiday with Rupert, I couldn't resist flicking back to my morning appointment. It was there at 12:00, clear as day. I didn't see how I could have got it wrong. There was nothing wrong with my eyes and it made no sense. No sense at all.

Maybe there was something wrong with the phone? Next time I was in town I would have to go into the shop where I bought it and ask someone. In any case, I would double check on the iPad in the future just in case.

I needed to get my act together. I had a job interview in a couple of weeks as an assistant editor for Oxford University Press and I couldn't be late for that. My old boss in London had made the introduction, but it was a one-off favour. My networking has always been pathetic so I couldn't hope for other lucky breaks if I messed this one up.

The job was part time, three days a week and didn't start for three months which suited me perfectly. Sam would be almost nine months old by then and I'd paid a deposit for a provisional place at a great little nursery down the road. I loved being with Sam, but couldn't help feeling that being isolated from adult company was starting to mess with my head.

The Best Laid Plans

Most anti-hacker protection assumes the hacker has a traceable ambition such as theft, blackmail or concealing criminal activity. The most dangerous kind of identity thief is much more patient and has less obvious goals. They may go for extended periods with no activity. Reading emails, observing appointments made and waiting for the right opportunity. In such cases, it is extremely unlikely that the victim will ever become aware that their identity has been compromised.
"How much is your Life Worth? Protecting your Identity in a Digital World."
JJ Martin, Insight Business Press 2015

Rupert was bathing Sam and singing him to sleep and, while he was happily engaged, I set to work transforming our small living room into an Italian trattoria. I quickly laid the table, switched all of the lights off, scattered lit candles on every flat surface I could find and opened up the wood burner.

I'd been preparing all day, or at least whenever Sam had allowed me to, and the food was almost ready by the time Rupert got home from work. It had been a long time since I'd felt so energised and efficient and it felt good.

'Wow, how did this happen?' Rupert's reaction when he came back in was exactly what I'd hoped for.

I smiled and pulled out his chair. 'I thought it was about time we had an Italian evening. What's the point in marrying a sultry Italian goddess if life is only shepherd's pie and curry?'

'Something smells good,' said Rupert, picking up the bottle of wine from the table and peering at the label in that faux-sommelier way which all men develop eventually. 'This looks nice. More expensive than our usual plonk. You're up to something aren't you?

I'm not objecting, but I know what you're like.'

'Am I really so transparent?'

'Sorry, Fabs but, honestly, yes you are. I bend the truth for a living and am pretty good at smelling a rat, but you'd lose a lying competition with a four-year-old. It's fine though. Pretend I didn't say anything. I like the game and I don't want to wait too long to taste whatever it is that smells so good.'

'OK,' I said. 'We'll forget about your unjustified devious suspicions and put them down to the paranoid delusions of a professional slimeball. The wine is a Primitivo from the old country by the way. I managed to find one that comes from a vineyard just outside my family's old town.'

'Perfect,' said Rupert, taking a big slurp. 'I don't think I've had Primitivo before. It's delicious. My kind of wine.'

Rupert's dad had a big wine cellar full of expensive, special bottles which he'd been collecting for years, and Rupert knew a lot more about wine than most people his age. Fortunately he was self-aware enough to avoid slipping into the 'notes of cherry, infused with undertones of chocolate and blackberry' wine snob bullshit which was, in my view, the best way to ruin a good bottle of wine.

On this occasion, I'd done my research and prepared my spiel. 'Actually, you probably have drunk Primitivo before. It's the same as Zinfandel in the States, but with a different name for some reason. Primitivo is the original name though, and it's the main red wine grape in Puglia which is where it was originally grown. This is the real thing, not some American rip-off.'

'Well, la-di-da, who's the wine snob now then?' he said. 'I'm impressed.' He leant back and breathed deeply as I put a steaming plate of food down in front of him. 'Now that's what I'm talking about. It looks stunning.'

It wasn't fine dining, only spaghetti and meatballs, but, apart from the spaghetti, I'd made it all by hand, slowly cooking the tomato sauce over hours, using only fresh herbs and even getting the butcher to mince the beef on the spot for me that morning rather than using ready-minced. It smelt of home and glistened in bright colours on the plate, begging to be eaten. I think my mother would have approved.

I'd cheated with dessert; the ice cream wasn't home made, but the chocolate sauce was, and I certainly wasn't hearing any complaints from the other side of the table. Rupert finished scraping the glaze from the bottom of his bowl and looked up, a cheeky grin lighting his eyes.

'That was amazing. Now I remember why I married you. Consider me one hundred per cent primed and ready to hear whatever grand scheme you've been cooking up.'

I laughed, also reminded of why I'd married him. 'OK, guilty as charged,' I said. 'I'll start at the beginning. You remember I was upset that none of my family were there for the christening?'

'Of course, I do. But you've never explained why you fell out with them so badly, so I'm swinging in the dark.'

'I know darling, and I will explain one day, I promise, but not right now. It's difficult for me and, the thing is, I'm realising that the main reason why it's so difficult is because I've started to see that it was all my fault.'

'Oh come on ...'

'... let me finish. I've managed to convince myself for years that everything I said and did was justified but, the more I think back, the more I realise it's total bullshit. I was a selfish spoilt brat and my judgement where friends were concerned turns out to have been total crap.'

'Whooah, tell me what you really think,' said Rupert. 'Seriously though, give yourself a break. We all did stupid, thoughtless things when we were kids.'

'Maybe, but there are degrees. In any case, the point is that I want to try to get back some sort of connection to my past. I don't expect I'll ever speak to my brothers and sister again, but I'd like to find out more about my parents' family back in Italy and I want you and Sam to know more about that part of me.'

'Is that it?' said Rupert with a big grin. 'You want us to visit your family in Italy? Sounds great. When can we go?'

I felt the softness of tears coming as my shoulders sank and my head dipped down with release, before I took both his hands in mine and looked up at his sweet, cheery face. 'You are a lovely man, Mr Blackwell, you do know that, don't you. I love you so much.'

We sat in silence for a long while, holding hands in the candlelight while, with impeccable timing, Dean Martin crooned 'That's Amore' in the background. Thank heavens for Spotify and its playlists. Eventually Rupert stood up.

'I'll start to clear up,' he said. 'You go and check on Sam.'

When I came back in, he was bent over the sink, scrubbing the griddle pan.

'Well, as you might have guessed,' I said. 'I do have a bit of a plan. Firstly, I think we can afford it and secondly, I think we should go in the first week of December – in three weeks.'

'OK, so not hanging around then?'

'No. I've got my interview next week and the job starts at the end of February, so it makes loads of sense. You've got that week of paternity leave saved up, so why not?'

'I can't think of any good reason right now, but ...'

'Plus, the weather will hopefully be lovely, it'll definitely be rubbish here, and Sam's still small enough to drag around without too much trouble. I've been emailing back and forth with one of my relations in Puglia. It's my cousin, Alberto, and he speaks perfect English. If we go, he says we can stay with them and it would be easy for him to take a few days off work to show us around. I remember him from my Nonno's funeral, he was the only one who was able to get over here. You'd like him. I know you're busy at work but I think this would be great for us and some fresh Italian air and sea breeze would make me feel better.'

'All right, take a breath,' said Rupert. 'The idea sounds great but can I have a few days to think about it? You're obviously all over it and very keen. I just need a little time to get up to speed and to check with work. Have you looked at flights?'

'Of course, you know me. Once I get going, I cover all of the bases. There are lots of flights to Bari and Brindisi, RyanAir are the cheapest but we both hate them, so I thought we'd probably end up with Easyjet as the slightly less unpleasant option. I've applied for a passport for Sam and had email confirmation that we'll get it in time. I think we can do the whole trip for not much more than a thousand quid which we can afford in any case, and definitely if your Q3 bonus comes in.'

'Bloody hell,' said Rupert. 'I'd forgotten how frightening you can be when you're in organiser mode. I'll know about the bonus tomorrow, so why don't we decide then.'

I hadn't managed to wean myself from the habit of checking emails and social media in the middle of the night. I'd stopped breastfeeding, but Sam still woke up needing a bottle and I usually took the graveyard shift. Rupert was working so hard.

It was a lonely time, sitting in the shadows watching Sam enjoying his milk and waiting for him to drift off again – not alone, but still lonely. I found it all too easy to let my mind drift down dark avenues and my phone gave me a lifeline to reality.

It was almost five in the morning. The clocks had gone back and the night sky was softening a bit around the edges – not that it was ever properly dark in the centre of town. Sam was done with his pre-breakfast, eyelids heavy with milk. I checked my email once more and there it was, just like before.

No sender, only a row of asterisks where the name should be, and a single line of text, 'I hope your interview goes well tomorrow. Don't be late.'

I hadn't imagined it. Something was going on. I had no idea what, but here was the proof. I put Sam back into his cot, a bit roughly maybe, and ran next door to show Rupert. Now he would believe me.

It took some vigorous shaking to wake him before he sat up in bed looking confused and worried. I expect I painted a pretty picture, standing over him, waving my phone at him like a mad person.

'What's going on?' he said. 'Why's Sam crying? Is he OK?'

'Yes, he's fine,' I snapped. 'I didn't wait with him because I wanted to show you this. I've had another mail. Just now. I wasn't imagining it. Look.' I handed him the phone.

'OK, OK, calm down. Let me see.' He took the phone and looked blankly at it for a few seconds, before handing it back. 'You'll have to show me Fabi. The last mail I can see was a few hours ago and it's some spam from Hidden Escapes.'

'No, let me show you. It tells me not to be late for my interview. It's right here.'

But it wasn't. It wasn't anywhere and I felt the darkness closing in on me. I couldn't have imagined it, but it was gone. Was I losing my mind?

Sam was screaming now, but I sat on the edge of the bed transfixed, staring at the phone and gulping for air like a dropped fairground goldfish while Rupert ran next door to calm him down. The poor baby was very upset, struggling in his own way to breathe through the red-faced outrage of his rough treatment and neglect, and it took ages for him to settle.

By the time Rupert had the chance to pay any attention to me. I'd moved from my petrified catatonia to an equally dysfunctional state of girly sobbing.

'I don't understand what's going on,' he said, stroking my cheek with the back of his fingers. 'You really frightened me just now. Something's obviously not right, but I don't have a clue about stuff like this.' He lifted my face gently and looked down at me. 'Don't worry, we'll figure it out somehow. We'll work it out together.'

'Am I going mad?' I said. 'Is that what you think? I don't feel like I'm going mad, it's just ... it's just ...'

'Come on darling, you lie down and try and rest. You've been up half the night. I can call in late for work today and Sam won't need feeding for a few hours. Try and get some sleep and we'll talk later.'

He walked out and closed the door gently, leaving me to lie back on the bed, frightened eyes fixed on the elephant-shaped water stain which should have been painted over months ago after we had the roof fixed. Sleep came eventually, but it was full of demons.

Just the Job

Another version of the Calendar Jog is used to modify location. The address can be changed in a confirmation email, or in the co-ordinates which are sent to the device's mapping software. The result is that the victim arrives on time for their meeting but in the wrong place.
"How much is your Life Worth? Protecting your Identity in a Digital World."
JJ Martin, Insight Business Press 2015

It was after ten by the time that Rupert came in to wake me, carrying Sam on one arm. 'I wanted to leave you longer,' he said, 'but I need to be at work in half an hour or so.'

He was trying hard to appear normal and chirpy which was his standard response to most problems. So British and I loved him for it.

'I'll come out,' I said. 'You put the kettle on and I'll deal with muggins here.'

We sat in our small living room for a while, sipping our tea and focusing on little Sam. Anything to avoid the conversation which we both knew was coming.

Rupert broke first. 'Did you manage to get any sleep?' he asked.

'A little,' I replied. 'But it took a while.'

The silence slipped uncomfortably back between us and lingered.

'Look ...' we both blurted out at the same time before stopping dead with awkward laughs.

'You go ...' said Rupert, waving his hand in what I supposed to be an attempt at gallantry.

'OK. I'll try.' I shifted round on the sofa so we were facing each other. 'I'm not imagining any of this. I saw the emails, I checked my calendar. I get that there's no evidence, but I'm not that tired and

I'm not going mad.'

'Nobody's saying you're going mad,' said Rupert. 'If it turns out you're confused and forgetting things, it doesn't mean you're losing your mind.'

'Doesn't it?'

'Of course not. There might be some perfectly normal explanations for it. Lots of women have issues after their first child.'

'But that's my point. If I accept that possibility, then I've got to accept the possibility that I might have been imagining these things, and that's a slippery slope.'

'Perhaps,' he said. 'But it doesn't need to be such a black or white thing. I really think you should consider that it could be simply because you're overtired.'

Acid bile burned in the back of my throat. Rupert had already decided everything was in my head. That hadn't taken long.

'Maybe we could get an au pair or a nanny?' he continued. 'So you can get a bit more sleep. I can't see how it can have anything to do with your phone. I've checked your emails and calendar on mine, and on the PC.'

My head snapped up. 'What? You've checked my mails and calendar? Have you been spying on me?'

'Oh, for fuck's sake! You know I know all your passwords. Don't be so bloody paranoid. I was only trying to help.'

'Right,' I spat out. 'Of course you were.' I picked Sam up and stomped out to put him down for his nap.

What was wrong with me? Rupert was trying to be supportive and all I could do was jump down his throat.

When I walked back into the living room, Rupert was standing with his back to me. He was stirring his tea with a rhythmic chinking of the spoon as though it might calm him.

I wrapped my arms around him. 'Sorry ... Sorry ... I didn't mean that. I'm not myself. Please just ignore me.'

He turned me gently around and kissed me on the forehead before looking into my eyes, his brow crinkled with worry. 'You sure you're up for the job interview?' he said. 'We could always push it back a few days. I'm sure they wouldn't mind.'

'You're a sweetie,' I said with a smile. 'But, don't worry, I'll be fine. I've checked the email confirmation and I even called yesterday to confirm the time.' I held up a pink Post It note. 'Look, I've written it down, just in case.'

'Sounds like you've got it covered,' he said. 'Try and get some more rest when Sam goes down.'

'I will. I promise.'

He finished his tea with a gulp and got ready to leave, but the sleeve of his jacket had twisted up on itself. He had several abortive tries to ram his arm in, before tearing the jacket off to unravel it, muttering curses under his breath. I'd never seen Rupert like this. He was usually so relaxed about everything.

I put my hand on his arm, took the jacket and untangled the sleeve.

'I'm fine, darling. Really,' I said.

'I hope so,' he said. 'But ...'

'What?'

'I think you should go and see your GP. Will you do that? For me?'

'I'll think about it. Give me a few days though. Is that OK?'

'Of course,' said Rupert. He held my face in both hands and kissed me. 'Good luck with the interview. I'll see you later.'

I was feeling much better by the time Virginia arrived. Excited, energised and, though I said it myself, looking pretty sharp. I wasn't going to let a couple of stupid overreactions get in the way of my interview. As Rupert said, I was probably just overtired.

The Oxford University Press offices were on Great Clarendon Street which was only fifteen minutes walk, so I had time for a cup of tea with Sam and Virginia before I left.

'Rupert says you've been finding everything a bit stressful recently,' said Virginia. 'Do let me know if there's anything I can do.'

God, that woman had a way about her. Even an ostensibly kind offer of help could come across as a snide and superior put-down.

'Oh, did he say that?' I replied with a smile. 'Well, you know what a worrier he is. I'm a little tired maybe, but that's not so surprising.'

'But are you sure you're ready to go back to work?' Virginia always had an agenda. 'He's still so little. And it's not as though you need the money.'

'Well, actually we do need the money, Virginia. We've got a big mortgage and things are tight on only one salary.'

'Come Fabiola, you know John and I have offered to help out financially while you've got young children. It would be our pleasure.'

'Yes, I know you have, and it's extremely generous of you both, but Rupert and I want to stand on our own two feet. I'm sure you understand.'

'I do, of course. But it seems a shame to create this additional pressure. Especially if you're still feeling fragile after the birth.'

'I'm fine.'

'I hope so. You need to take care of yourself and, in any case, you appear to have enough money to go gallivanting off to Italy at the drop of a hat.'

I had no intention of dignifying that little, barbed comment with a response. She was getting worse rather than better as we got to know each other. What had Rupert been saying to her? He was such a mummy's boy and she could twist him around her little finger.

In any case, I needed to get out of there. Virginia was doing nothing to enhance my positive interview attitude.

'I'm sure we'll be OK Virginia. The job doesn't start for three months, and it's only part-time.' I picked up my bag and coat and opened the door. 'Thanks for looking after Sam. I'll be back about six-thirty, but Rupert should be back well before then anyway.'

As I left the house, I found myself thinking about my years with Jax. It all seemed so long ago and so far away. I was annoyed with Rupert and his mum and amused myself by imagining what Virginia would say if she found out about my relationship with Jax.

Rupert had promised not to say anything and had kept his word as far as I knew. I couldn't stop myself smiling as I thought about dropping it into conversation at Christmas dinner or some other family gathering, 'Oh Virginia, did I mention that my previous partner was a woman?'. She would blow a fuse.

When I'd eventually got around to telling Rupert, I'd been quickly reminded of why I'd been avoiding the conversation for so long.

I hadn't give him any warning and it hadn't gone down well.

'Jax always hated The Clash,' I said, late one evening. It was a few weeks after Rupert and I moved in together, but before we got engaged. 'She said they sold out.'

'Sounds pretty typical of Jax as you've described him,' said Rupert. 'Contrary for the sake of it ... Hang on a sec. What do you mean *she* said they sold out?'

'I mean that she said they sold out.'

'Are you telling me Jax is a woman? You never told me Jax is a woman.'

'Well, to be fair, you never asked.'

By now, Rupert had his hands and fingers out in front of him as though he was trying to milk a cow and was clenching and unclenching his fists repeatedly. He'd also pitched his voice a couple of octaves higher. 'But I thought the two of you were in a relationship?'

'We were. The fact she was a woman was one of the things which never came up when we talked about her.'

'How could something like that not come up, for Christ's sake?'

'We didn't talk about her much anyway and I guess I didn't want to do anything to screw up things up between us.' I attempted a sheepish grin. 'Sorry.'

'So you're telling me you're gay? Or bi-, or something?' The sheepish grin hadn't worked and Rupert looked very distressed.

'No, caro mio. I'm not gay. It's just ... Well, Jax was different. It was a craziness that turned into a thing, that turned into a longer thing, and after a while I couldn't figure out how to go back.'

I thought about those first moments at Rostock and the years which followed. Looking back from the outside, I could now see the cracks and the brooding darkness, but from the inside, it had been amazing – a wonderful, perfect dream.

'Actually, I said, 'for the first few years, I didn't want to go back anyway. We were soul mates. I was besotted with her.'

'Bloody hell,' said Rupert. 'I never wanted to know too much about Jax because I knew you were in with a fairly edgy crowd. But Jax being a girl, and you being a lesbian. I didn't see that coming.'

'I wasn't a lesbian. I'm still not. I don't know how I can get it through to you.'

'Easy to say.' Rupert had been almost shouting by this stage. 'But I still don't see how that works. Five years in a same-sex relationship sounds pretty close to a slam dunk to me.'

'What I mean is that I've always fancied men, before, after and during my time with Jax and she's the only exception in my life.' I could see I wasn't getting close to convincing Rupert and began to worry that I'd made a huge mistake by telling him. 'I can't explain why it happened with her, but I think that, if you'd met her, you might understand.'

'Really? And why's that?'

'There was something about her, a kind of strength, which attracted me. I suppose it also frightened and excited me; she wasn't only strong, she was reckless and a bit crazy as well.'

'... And that's supposed to be attractive?'

'Yes, but I don't understand why any more. I suppose I was going through a phase where that was what I thought I needed.'

'Shit, I have no idea what to say. Let's park this for now, I need to think about it and more talk won't help.' Rupert had managed a half laugh. 'I suppose I should find it hot, but I don't.'

Things had been awkward for over a month, but after many long conversations and explanations, it had all settled down. I actually realised he'd probably become proud of it in a warped male fashion. He'd managed to convert me. I was happy enough to humour him – some fights aren't worth having.

I was early and wandered around the shops on Great Clarendon Street before strolling down to the OUP head office. I was looking forward to the interview. Spending some time out of the house would make all of the difference.

Rupert was in the living room with his mother when I walked in. He leapt up and ran over, wrapping his arms around me and hugging me tight. 'Christ, Fabiola, are you OK? We've been so worried. It's almost ten o'clock.'

I held him closely, burying my face into his warm neck, sobbing quietly. Words didn't want to come.

I didn't hear Virginia approach until she spoke, pulling Rupert's arms gently away from me. 'Go and make yourself useful,' she told him. 'Make us all a nice cup of tea.'

'And you,' she continued once he was in the kitchen. 'You come and sit yourself down. You're not hurt, are you?'

I shook my head.

'Good,' she said. 'Then there's no rush is there? Let's have a cup of tea and maybe you'll feel like telling us what happened in a bit.'

I nodded and sat down on the sofa next to Virginia. Her nearness reminded me of what the empty black hole in my stomach was telling me. I wanted my mother. I felt as alone and helpless as I had after my first day of secondary school. Mum always knew what to do and what to say. That's what mothers do. They understand. But, although she was being kind, Virginia wasn't that sort of mother.

Half a cup of tea later, I felt calm enough to start to tell them what had happened.

'I got there bang on time. After walking up and down Great Clarendon Street for ten minutes, I rang the bell at twenty-five past. I was totally thrown when a fireman answered the office door and told me the offices were closed for a fire inspection.'

I looked at Virginia. 'I suppose Rupert's told you what's been happening with me recently?'

'Yes.' she said. 'He's worried you're overtired and I suspect he's right.'

So the Blackwell diagnosis was agreed. That was all sorted then. I would have time to worry about that later. First I had to finish my story, which wasn't going to do much for my defence.

'Well, I started to panic straight away. It was too much to take in and I was struggling to breathe.'

Both Virginia and Rupert were perched on the edges of their chairs by this time.

'The fireman was very kind,' I went on. 'I guess they're trained to deal with panicking people, and he calmed me down quite quickly. I then tried calling the number I had from the email but got no reply. After trying it again and again, I found the number on the web and got through to Mr Byatt's assistant, who told me I was supposed to be at their other offices, behind the book shop on the High.'

'And they didn't bloody tell you?' said Rupert.

'I'll get to that,' I said. 'It was already five o'clock but she said that, if I went straight there, Mr Byatt would still be around for another hour or so and would see me.'

'So did you go?' Virginia asked in a soft voice.

'Yes, I ran all the way. I must have looked a complete mess by the time I arrived. I probably spent more time catching my breath, apologising and trying to explain, than I did actually talking about the job.'

'And you found out what happened? How the mix up occurred?' said Rupert. I could see from the looks on both of their faces that they had a good idea of what might be coming next.

'Yes. I spoke to Mr Byatt's assistant afterwards. She told me she'd emailed me to confirm that the job interview wouldn't be at their normal offices because of the fire inspection. She was quite defensive as though she thought I was accusing her of something. She said she'd even sent a second email to be sure.'

'Well, did she?' said Rupert.

'What do you think?' I said, a black curtain falling as I watched Rupert draw his own conclusions.

'I was sure she hadn't of course,' I continued. 'I wouldn't have missed something like that and I'd even cut and pasted the email into my calendar. By this time I was talking nine to the dozen like Carrie from Homeland when she's off her medication.'

'So, what happened?' said Virginia.

'What, apart from me terrifying a poor twenty-year-old secretary?'

'Yes. Had she sent the emails?'

'It was exactly the same as the other times. I'm certain I'm right, but when I go back and check, it's just as they say and I look like a crazy, disorganised idiot. I even went to check the note in my calendar and there it was, clear as day.'

I picked up my phone and showed them.

Please note that the interview will not take place at our main offices on Great Clarendon Street as they are closed for a fire inspection. The interview will take place at our retail shop at 118 High Street and we look forward to seeing you there at 16:30. Please ask any member of staff to direct you to Jason Byatt's office.

'There's no way I'm getting the job now,' I said. 'Why would anyone want to employ someone who can't even get to their interview?'

'How dreadful!' I had the impression Virginia was in full agreement about my suitability for employment. 'But that must have been hours ago. Where have you been?'

'I walked. I must admit that I went to Brown's for a large glass of Pinot Grigio first, but afterwards, I just walked. I couldn't face coming home.' I looked at Rupert, trying to choke back my emotions. 'I couldn't face looking at you and telling you what had happened. I couldn't bear to see that look in your eyes.'

Virginia didn't look at all happy and it was clear Rupert had no idea what to say. There is a special look which people have when they're in the presence of someone who has a mental illness. I worked in a nursing home for a couple of years in my teens and could spot it a mile off. Seeing it in the eyes of someone you love is bad enough but then you realise they're about to bring out the special 'slow, calming voice' as well. It was unbearable.

This couldn't be happening. And I hadn't even asked about Sam since I'd come in. What was wrong with me?

Giving in

One of the easiest ways to track and monitor an individual is via their mobile phone. Bugging and tracking software such as mSpy is widely available and allows remote operation of all of the phone's functions including location, sound/video recording and call monitoring. Often used by parents, partners or employers, it can be installed in minutes.
"How much is your Life Worth? Protecting your Identity in a Digital World."
JJ Martin, Insight Business Press 2015

It took me a few days to calm down after the disastrous job interview. I didn't get the job, but there were no surprises there and it seemed to be the least of my problems. I couldn't get over the fact that I'd only been thinking about myself and hadn't worried about Sam at all. Not the behaviour of a good mother by any stretch of the imagination.

Did I love him properly? I thought I did, it certainly felt like it, but then how could I be so self-absorbed and neglectful?

Rupert continued to be a perfect husband on the surface but he must have been terrified and I was sure he was checking up on me all the time. When we'd talked about getting an au pair, he'd suggested we might get a nanny-cam to keep an eye on her. Had he already installed one to keep an eye on me?

Then again, when I tried to imagine how I would react if the tables were turned, I couldn't see myself behaving as well as he was. He was strong, calm, loving and positive, reassuring me continuously that this was only a short blip and everything would be fine.

I suppose his attitude helped him to keep his own fear and worry under control as well; he was like a colonial army officer standing in the middle of a riot, a battle, a thunderstorm or a plague of locusts.

Standing firm, speaking clearly and calmly and spreading confidence to everyone around. All will be well.

I wondered sometimes whether there might be too much of the oak tree in his approach rather than the blade of grass. If the winds continued to blow stronger and stronger, was there room to bend and flex, or would he reach a point and suddenly snap? I hoped I'd never need to find out.

Rupert had clearly learnt his practical positivity at the feet of a master and I don't know how we'd have managed without Virginia's help. She came over for three or four hours every day and took charge. Although she was often sharp and bossy and I didn't feel comfortable in the role of patient or invalid, her presence gave me the chance to have more sleep. The doctor had also given me some mild sedatives.

I had promised Rupert I would talk to someone and we had gone to the surgery together, the day after the abortive interview. I got on well with my GP who had two young children of her own and, although she took the situation seriously, she suggested that my issues might simply be driven by exhaustion, and that we start by trying to get me properly rested and take it from there. Hence the sedatives and Virginia.

It didn't take long for me to start to feel much better, helped by the rest and the fact I'd agreed not to leave the house at all or to use my phone or any other electronic device. This meant I was unnaturally cocooned and wrapped in cotton wool. While it was wonderful to feel my mind becoming my own again, I couldn't imagine enduring this level of house arrest for long.

Combine that with the over-cautious, over-caring behaviour of Rupert and Virginia and it wasn't so different from what I imagined life in a mental hospital would be like. Everyone speaking slowly and softly, nothing to make the patient excited. Gentle classical music, nice cups of tea and calming drugs. One Flew Over the Cuckoo's Nest comes to North Oxford!

Fortunately Sam wasn't signed up to the Nurse Ratchett 'patronise the patient' programme and he carried on as normal, happy and smiling some of the time but blasting the cotton wool to all corners of the room when he wasn't getting what he wanted. A welcome breath of normality in what was, in many ways, more like a waking dream than real life.

After five long days, I declared I was feeling much better, was well rested and needed to engage with the world outside our small house. I started by checking my emails and social media; there were no unexplained, unattributable emails, only the normal mix of spam and trivia and a Facebook message from an old friend from university, Charlie Taylor, saying she was in Oxford for a few days and would love to meet up.

I wasn't surprised there weren't any strange emails as I was certain Rupert was now checking my accounts regularly and he would have said something. A bit creepy to be spied on like that, but I had nothing to hide; my secret thoughts and worries were confined to my handwritten diary in any case.

I called Charlie and we agreed to meet for a coffee at Quod which was next to her hotel. Virginia was there to look after Sam so I would have at least three hours to enjoy my freedom. A bit melodramatic perhaps but that was how I felt as I stepped out of the front door and set off down Walton Street. I had already almost forgotten the reasons behind my confinement, and escape was wonderful.

I had a bit of time before I had to be at Quod and popped into Waterstone's to see what was new. The Booker prize had just been awarded and there were two tables featuring the short-listed books and a big display for the winner, a book about the Japanese work camps in the war. Even though it looked dark and depressing, I've always made a point of reading the Booker winner and picked up a copy.

I was excited about seeing Charlie. She'd been on my Politics and French course at Bristol and was my best mate for the first two years of uni. We ended up in the same halls in Stoke Bishop and, in our second year, we shared a flat in Clifton with four other girls.

Charlie spent her year abroad in Toulouse while I was in Paris and, when we came back for the fourth year, we somehow drifted apart. I hadn't seen her since and I wasn't sure why not. There'd been something about a French boyfriend, which might have been it.

I was early but Charlie was already there, very smart in a black skirt and white blouse. I had no idea what her job was – her Facebook page was minimalist to say the least – but she looked important and successful.

We hugged and kissed and made all of the noises good friends do when they've not seen each other for a while, before sitting at a table and getting down to proper catching up.

'You look great,' I said. 'Very chic and professional. You were always the high-flyer though. What are you up to?'

'Oh, fairly boring stuff actually,' said Charlie. 'I work for an MP, but I'll tell you more about me in a minute. What about you? Married, and a mother too? I didn't see that coming. You've not brought your baby with you?'

'Well, someone's got to do the marriage thing and both of my boys are gorgeous,' I said, feeling a surge of pride. 'Sorry I didn't bring Sam with me. I left him at home with the mother-in-law because I wanted to have a chance to properly catch up.'

I took out my iPad. 'Look. Here he is,' I said. '... And here he is with Rupert.'

Charlie reached for the iPad and started scrolling through the photos. 'He's very cute,' she said. 'And Sam's quite sweet as well.'

I snorted cappucino foam across the table. 'Well you haven't changed. Remind me never to introduce you to my husband.'

She giggled. 'Don't worry, you're safe. I'm spoken for. He's called Anthony and we're getting married next year.' She flashed a massive diamond in front of my eyes.

'Whoa! It's huge,' I said. 'You must be over the moon. But, bloody hell, we're all getting so old. How did that happen?'

'No idea,' Charlie said. 'You turn your back for ten minutes and ...'

'I know. Look at me. I ended up with a baby.'

'I think we know how that happened though. Don't we?' She'd always been famous for her dirty laugh. Rich, throaty and full of innuendo.

'Totally busted,' I said. 'I can vaguely remember something ...'

I finished my half-hearted attempts to wipe the foam off the table and my bag. It was lucky I'd missed Charlie's smart white blouse.

'It's been so long,' I said. 'I don't understand why we've not seen each other all this time. It's crazy. Thanks again for the flowers. They were a brilliant surprise.'

'No worries,' she said. 'It wasn't just me. It was all of us. We thought that, now Jax is out of the picture, we might get to see you again from time to time.'

'What's Jax got to do with it?'

'You must know,' she said. 'The last time I tried to call, Jax answered your phone and made it very clear you weren't interested in seeing anyone from the old crowd. It wasn't the only time that happened.'

'Jax said that? How weird? I've no idea where she got that from.' I looked at Charlie. It wasn't the sort of thing she would make up. 'It does explain a lot though. Do you see everyone else from the flat?'

'Yeah. And a few others. We all get together at least once a year and I see Amanda most weeks. We're catching up just before Christmas down at my parents' house. You should definitely come.'

'I'd love to. That would be brilliant. I miss you guys.'

'Perfect. Done deal. I'll mail you the details. No excuses this time.'

'I promise,' I said, smiling as a trail of happy, giggling memories popped behind my eyes like bursting soap bubbles on a sunny day. 'I'll bring Sam, but don't tell them I'm coming.'

'Good plan,' she said. 'I can see their faces already.'

'Great. That's sorted. You wouldn't believe how excited I am. Now, tell me about your MP. Who is it and what do you do for him or her?'

'OK. Well I've just started a new job. I went through the usual grind of unpaid internships and general dogsbody jobs before getting anything decent, but I've now been promoted to Senior Parliamentary Assistant to Simon Armitage.'

'What, the young, tasty one who got a cabinet job a couple of months ago?' I said, genuinely impressed. 'I wouldn't throw him out of bed, whatever his politics.' He was a Tory, of course. Charlie had a typical public school background like so many Bristol Uni students. Grew up in Surrey or Hampshire or some such Home Counties ghetto.

'It's strictly professional unfortunately and I don't think he's the type to play away from home.' It was great to see Charlie again and I felt like we'd jumped straight back to the old days. I'd missed our pointless, puerile banter. 'But I've got Anthony now, so ...'

'And you're Senior Parliamentary Assistant to a cabinet member before you're thirty, that must be some sort of record?'

'I doubt it, but I'm way younger than most of the others, which is tricky as they're a bitchy bunch. Nothing I can't handle, though.' Charlie smiled and looked at me. 'But, much more importantly, how did Fabiola 'I'm going to change the world' Carlantino end up a posh, young married mother in Oxford?'

I shrugged my shoulders. 'You tell me. Shit happens, I guess.'

'Start at the beginning. What happened to you, Jax and that guy Darren? An interesting ménage à trois if ever I saw one.'

'Not so much to tell, really. Daz was a sweet guy, but I never fancied him. I know he had a big thing for me, but I didn't have eyes for anyone but Jax at the time.'

'What about the lovely Jax? I never figured out why she hated us so much?'

'What complete bollocks!' I said. 'Jax didn't hate you. Why would she?'

'Beats me,' said Charlie. 'But she did.'

'Anyway.' I didn't feel like digging deeper into that strangeness. 'Me and Jax were together for five years – until a couple of years ago. You know how it is? As time goes by, people change and sometimes they change together and in a good way, and sometimes they don't. Jax was getting closer to the violent factions and even our anarchist friends were starting to distance themselves from her.'

'Well, that doesn't surprise me one little bit,' said Charlie. 'She was always scary mad.'

'That might be a bit harsh,' I said. 'But anyway, it was as though I woke up from a trance one day and realised we didn't actually have much in common, even though we'd been together for five years. It was a hell of a shock.'

'So, it was you who broke it up? I can't imagine Jax taking that well?'

'She didn't. I made myself scarce after we split, but from what I've heard, she wasn't a happy bunny.'

'Ta da,' said Charlie. 'Why am I not surprised? It's funny you talk about being in a trance though; that was what we all said at the time – that you were under some sort of spell, that you were bewitched.'

She took a sip of her coffee and continued. 'Once you and Jax got together, your other friends were cut out of your life, just like that. We'd been best mates and then I was suddenly a fascist representative of the system. It was like you'd joined one of those religious cults.'

'God, I'm sorry. I had no idea.'

'Really? Are you serious? You must have known.'

'Yeah, totally serious. I think I was caught up in this crazy whirlwind of new ideas and experiences, including the fact that she was a girl. I probably thought you were all jealous.' Picking at the scabs of my past with Jax was both painful and surprisingly compelling. 'I'll tell you one thing for sure. I'm glad to be free of it.'

'Yeah. I can imagine,' she said. 'Anyway, who gives a fuck! It's all in the past. Let's forget about it.' She looked up at the clock. 'Shit. I have to go. Simon's speaking at the Union in twenty minutes and, seeing as I wrote the speech, I should probably be there.'

'No problem,' I said. 'I'll get the coffees.'

'Thanks,' said Charlie standing up. 'Let's catch up properly very soon, definitely before the Christmas thing. With Rupert and Anthony maybe? And I definitely want to meet little Sam. I'll give you my mobile number and you can text me.'

'That would be great. You'll like Rupert. He's one of your lot.'

I went to get my phone from my bag but couldn't find it anywhere. I emptied the bag on the table and felt the first fingers of panic knotting and twisting in my gut as I realised it wasn't there.

I needed to stay calm. I had probably dropped it somewhere when I was getting my wallet out. I wasn't imagining anything. I'd simply misplaced my phone.

The thing was that it was brand new – I'd persuaded Rupert to get me a new phone in case my problems were somehow linked to my old one. I'd also set up a new password on my email account, to make sure – just because you're paranoid doesn't mean the whole world isn't out to get you, after all.

Losing the new phone on my first day out again would be a disaster. I must have dropped it somewhere. There was no point in panicking until I'd checked.

I took a deep breath and turned back to Charlie. 'I think I've left my phone somewhere. Can I borrow yours to call my number?'

'Sure,' she said, handing me her phone. 'But be quick.'

Six long rings later, someone answered. 'Hello?'

'Hello,' I said. 'I'm dialling my own phone which I appear to have mislaid. Who am I speaking to?'

'Oh, I'm glad you called,' the voice answered. 'This is Jennie from Waterstones. I work on the front till and someone handed in your phone about an hour ago. She found it on the floor.'

'Thank God for that,' I said. 'Thank you. You're a lifesaver. I'll be along in about twenty minutes to collect it.'

'That's a bloody relief,' I said to Charlie, handing her back her phone. 'I could really do without losing my phone right now.'

Charlie was obviously anxious to leave. She handed me a scrap of paper with her number on it and gave me a hug and a kiss. 'It was wonderful to see you. Call me soon,' she said, and rushed off.

Although I knew it would be there waiting for me, I found it difficult to breathe until I finally got my phone back from Jennie at Waterstone's. I quickly checked to make sure no-one had used it to call Australia or India or somewhere outrageous, but all was fine. God knows how I'd managed to lose it from my handbag in the first place but, in the list of idiotic things I'd been doing over the previous few weeks, it wasn't even appearing in the top ten. Everything is relative.

I still had an hour to spare and no great desire to sit and chew the fat with Virginia, so I took the opportunity to go and pick up the euros which I'd pre-ordered for our Italy trip. It was now only only a week away. I already had the parking and flight confirmations printed out and in a folder together with our passports and as many contact details for Italian relations as I could find. I then only had two outstanding tasks on my to-do list: cash ,which I was about to sort out, and Sam's shiny new passport which was due to arrive on the following Monday.

There was a little place called Senli Cash & Go on Broad Street which gave much better exchange rates than all of the traditional places – there were some advantages of being stuck at home with an iPad and a broadband connection – and I had my Euros in minutes.

With one of my two remaining tasks completed and my phone safely zipped into my bag, I felt buoyant and carefree for the first time in ages. I would show everyone I hadn't lost the plot and could still be trusted. It was time to snap out of this negative spiral and to get on with life. I would put everything behind me and get back onto an even keel.

The low, winter sun glowed in an opalescent sky as I cut down Great Clarendon Street on my way home. I might have been fired up and feeling positive, but I found my feet superstitiously crossing to the other side of the street as I went past the Oxford University Press building.

'Hi Virginia. Sorry I'm a bit late.'

'Oh. Don't worry,' she said, whispering. 'It was only fifteen minutes and I'm not in a hurry.' She nodded her head behind her. 'He's asleep. Been down about half an hour. We had a lovely afternoon. What about you?'

I could tell Virginia had been worrying about me being late, which was ridiculous. I suppose I wouldn't have minded if I'd believed she genuinely cared about me and my well being, but it didn't feel like that.

It was as though she was more concerned with building ammunition to bolster up some kind of warped, smug, I-told-you-so, schadenfreude. I was pretty sure I knew exactly what was going on in her head. I might be going crazy, but it didn't make me a complete imbecile.

I could just imagine her. 'I did try to tell you, Roopie. She's a pretty girl, but not the right sort. No real backbone and too many secrets. There's no smoke without fire, you know. You should have listened to me.'

We both kept our thoughts to ourselves, of course.

'I had a great time, thanks. I was so happy to catch up with Charlie after all of these years. It was as though I'd seen her yesterday.'

'I'm pleased,' she said. 'It's important for you to have friends around you.'

There it was. The obligatory smear of innuendo. Only missing the end of the sentence '... when you're in such an emotionally fragile state.'

'What does Charlie do?' she continued. 'Is she married?'

'Not yet. She's just got engaged. I don't know if she'll have much time for marriage though – she's a bit of a high flyer, career-wise.'

'Really?'

'Yes. She's Senior Parliamentary Assistant to Simon Armitage.'

'What? The Simon Armitage?'

'Yes.'

'And she's the same age as you?'

'More or less.'

'Well, that is impressive. A good friend to have.'

I suppose I should have been happy I was earning some extra Brownie points by association, but it wasn't going to make any difference. Virginia had made up her mind about me and nothing was going to change that.

The Old Country

Email remains key to our Internet life. Most transactions – banking, income tax, company tax, car tax, grant applications, online purchases, flight reservations, hotel bookings etc – can be managed online. Confirmation is almost always by email. We have learnt to be afraid of email spam but, when a confirmation email is expected, most of us trust the content without question.

"How much is your Life Worth? Protecting your Identity in a Digital World."
JJ Martin, Insight Business Press 2015

It was Tuesday afternoon and I was beginning to panic. Sam's passport should have arrived the previous week and we were flying on the Friday. Everything else was ready, I had the tickets and the car parking receipt, Alberto was going to meet us at Brindisi airport, I'd checked everything a hundred times. All I needed was Sam's bloody passport.

I didn't want to get Rupert involved; he was working long hours to finish everything before we left and this was supposed to be my trip, where I would organise every detail and prove in some childish way that I was still capable of behaving like a competent adult.

Telling Rupert about the passport would have exactly the opposite effect, but I had no choice. If it didn't arrive in time, we would have wasted all the money and wouldn't be able to go.

He didn't come home until well after seven, by which time Sam was asleep and I was already the wrong side of two large chardonnays and a whole bowl of cashews.

'I'm worried about Sam's passport,' I blurted out, before he'd even taken his coat off. 'It hasn't been delivered yet.'

'That's not good,' he turned to look at me. 'You said it was due last week. Just let me get in the door though. Is the Samster asleep?'

'Sorry, I've been stressing about it all day. Yes, Sam's out for the count. Do you want a glass of wine?'

'I could murder a beer actually. I've been talking non-stop for the past three hours. Bloody demanding clients.' He waved both hands at me, fingers crossed. 'It's looking very good for a big deal in the next few weeks though. That'll pay for Christmas if it comes through.'

'That's amazing,' I said, trying to control my trembling fingers as I handed him a bottle of Becks. 'You're turning out to be quite the star.'

'Well, I wouldn't go that far but I think we're in good shape for now. So, tell me about Sam's passport. Have you been in touch with the passport office?'

'I've tried, but it's impossible. I can't get through on phone or email and I can't make the bloody status-tracking link work. It keeps rejecting me and won't let me change or update my password.'

I hated the idea of being the useless female technophobe and I wasn't totally incompetent, but technology really did seem to be conspiring against me. It was like trying to pick up a freshly-landed fish as it gasped and flapped on the riverbank; each time I thought I had a good grip, it would slip away and leave me holding out my empty, slimy hands and looking like a fool.

'It's a government site,' said Rupert. 'What do you expect?'

'To tell you the truth, I expect it to bloody work,' I said. 'And I expect to be able to manage it without needing help. I really didn't want to get you involved with this after everything else, but I'm terrified I might have missed something obvious. I'm trying so hard, but I don't trust myself any more.'

'Don't worry, darling,' he said. 'We need to work as a team and you don't need to prove anything to me. I'm sure there's a simple solution. Let me have a look.'

He picked up the iPad and started searching through my emails.

'Here we go,' he said. 'They confirmed your online application on the tenth of November and asked you to send your signed declaration form, photos and supporting documentation. Ridiculous bureaucratic bullshit. What's the point of building an online application system if you still need to send in the paper forms? Did you send them off?'

'Yes,' I replied. 'I even did it registered post and got a receipt but, in any case, they sent me a confirmation mail a couple of days later, saying they'd received everything they needed and I should expect the passport by the week commencing November twenty-fourth. Last week.'

'I can't see that email,' Rupert was giving me that look again. 'The only other one you have from the passport office is dated on the fourteenth of November, confirming receipt of the application, but saying the photo of Sam isn't valid because your hand is visible.'

'What!' I thought he must be teasing me for a brief moment. 'That wasn't what the email said. It said everything was fine and gave me an estimated delivery date. I wouldn't have invented that. Why would I make something like that up, for Christ's sake?'

'I don't know Fabi, all I can do is read what's in front of me. Emails don't just change.'

'Well, I don't bloody know either. You must remember it. You've been reading all of my emails anyway, haven't you? I know you have.'

'Yes, I've been checking your mails, but I haven't been reading everything. I wouldn't have bothered to open an email like this. I haven't been trying to spy on you. Only to help.'

'Well it would've been helpful if you'd actually read this particular email at the time wouldn't it? Then you'd know I'm not making it up and that something is going on.'

'Fabi, I've got no idea what's going on and I get you're frustrated and scared, but before we start looking for people to blame, let's focus for a moment on the practical issue of getting Sam's passport in time. So you definitely didn't send them a new photograph?'

'No, why would I?' I said, close to tears. 'I just told you I got an email telling me everything was in order. Why would I bloody do anything except wait for the passport?'

'OK, OK. Give me a break here, it's not as though it's my fault. Why don't you grab me another beer and I'll have a look at out options.'

He sat on the sofa, head down and focusing on the iPad. I had no idea what was going though his head, and it may have been me imagining things, but his voice had been cold and flat, and I was afraid he was properly angry this time; his tense, almost business-like posture a sign of how much effort it was taking for him to avoid shouting at me and telling me what a bloody idiot I was. Again.

'All right,' said Rupert, looking up. 'We might be able to do a fast track premium application. They don't normally do them for first passports but it's worth trying. It costs more and we'd need to go to London on Thursday to pick it up, but it's all we've got. The phone lines are open until eight. Let me give them a try.'

'Thanks Rupert. I'm so sorry about all of this. I only wanted to make everything work smoothly. To show you I haven't become totally useless and crazy.' I managed a half-smile. 'Not panning out so well, is it?'

Rupert laughed. 'Well at least you haven't totally lost your sense of humour. Don't worry, if this doesn't work out, my dad's best friend from school is something big in the civil service. He might be able to pull some strings. We'll sort it out. There's no need to get upset.' He went off into the garden to pick up a better phone signal, leaving me standing there, powerless again.

The last thing I wanted was for Rupert's parents to get involved. Virginia had definitely decided that I wasn't a positive addition to the Blackwell family and I suspected that, were we in Victorian times, she'd already be furnishing an attic in the vicarage to hide me away.

We don't always get what we wish for as I realised when Rupert came in from the garden.

'There's good news and bad news,' he said. 'I got through to someone at the passport office and they confirmed that you can't do the premium service with a first passport, even for a baby. The only option is a Fast Track but it takes a week.'

'So, is that the good news or the bad news, or both?'

'That's the bad news. The good news is that I spoke to my dad and he's sure his mate will be able to help, especially as you made the original application a while ago. He's calling him now and we'll hear more in the morning.'

'Thank you darling.' I held him tightly, pressing my face into his chest in search of strength and comfort. 'I feel so bloody useless and I'm scared of what's happening.'

'I know,' he said. stroking my hair. 'But I'm here for you. You mustn't worry.'

'I know you are, but I don't think you understand.' The panic was there the whole time now, just below the surface. 'It's as though there's someone, or something, alien hiding inside me. It's never there when I'm looking for it, but as soon as I get comfortable, as soon as I let my guard down, it does something to trick me.' I could feel my pulse throbbing into my temples like a jungle drum. 'And I think it's growing. I don't think it's going away or getting weaker, I think it's waiting, waiting for a time when I'm weak, when it can hurt me again.'

'Try not to worry,' he said, strong arms almost squeezing the breath out of me. 'It sounds awful, darling, it really does. I think you probably still need to get some professional help. I'm completely out of my depth with all of this, and I don't know what I'm supposed to say or do.'

'I understand,' I said. 'Neither do I.'

'Anyway.' He let me go and looked at me. 'We'll get this passport mess sorted and enjoy a nice week's holiday. We can then have a think about how to find you the right help when we get back. Maybe after Christmas?'

Of course, John's friend was able to sort things out, that was inevitable – but it wasn't hassle free. Rupert needed to take an extra day off work to come into London with us, and I couldn't begin to imagine what John and Virginia would be saying about me behind the scenes.

Organising the trip had been a glowing beacon in the darkness of the previous few weeks; it was going to be the way in which I proved to myself, and to Rupert, that I was OK. That I was going to be OK.

But I'd failed miserably and it was as though my legs had been swept from under me. I couldn't do anything right and no-one had any reason to believe in me any more.

Fortunately, the rest of my planning seemed to have worked out well and, as I couldn't do anything to undo the passport fiasco, I decided to try to make the best of it and to focus on enjoying our first holiday with Sam.

There's nothing quite like an airport at five in the morning. The lights were unnaturally bright and the thousands of stoned zombies milling around Gatwick South's Terminal shuffled noiselessly across the polished floor.

I stopped breathing as the guy at passport control took Sam's shiny new passport. He spent ages looking back and forth between the passport, his computer screen and little Sam, who was wriggling happily in his baby carrier. If he'd taken any longer, I think I'd have passed out.

Then we were through, and on our way. It would help for us to get away for a few days. We needed a break. I spent every day walking on a thin sheet of ice which could crack at any time, but if I could only make it to the other side of the lake, I would be safe.

'I'm just going to the loo,' said Rupert. 'Will you wait around here?'

'Sure. I'll take Sam,' I said, reaching over to undo the clips on the carrier.

'That's fine. I'll only be a minute. He's settled now.'

'Don't be silly. You're going to the loo. Let me have him.'

Rupert lifted Sam carefully up and handed him to me. 'Happy now?' he said. 'I'll see you here in a couple of minutes. Don't wander off.'

He looked over his shoulder twice as he walked off and I began to understand. By the time he came back I was certain.

'Are you worried about leaving me alone with Sam?' I snapped at him as he walked towards us.

'What are you talking about? Of course not.' I could see the guilty look in his eyes.

'I don't believe you. You're lying. You don't trust me to look after my own son. Have you got any idea how that makes me feel?'

'Fabi, it's not like that,' he said, open hands and puppy dog eyes pleading at me. 'I just didn't think it was worth disturbing him.'

'Bollocks.' I passed Sam back to him roughly. 'Absolute fucking bollocks. I'm going to get a coffee. I'll see you on the plane.'

The plane had started boarding by the time I got to the gate and I could see Rupert pacing up and down next to the huge windows. Sam seemed to have had enough of the day's disruptions and was red-faced and screaming.

I tapped Rupert on the shoulder.

'Hi there,' I said. 'Let me take him.'

Rupert stared at me before lifting Sam into my arms. 'Here you go. He's been like this for twenty minutes and they've started boarding.'

'I know. I can see the sign. He'll calm down in a minute. Look, can we just forget about earlier. I don't know what came over me.'

Sam was toning down his screaming notch-by-notch and was gradually moving on to a sequence of racking, hard-done-by sobs.

'OK,' said Rupert. 'I get that things are tough for you, and I want to be patient, but I don't see why you need to accuse me of stuff like that. It doesn't seem fair.'

'If there's anything I've learned over the past few weeks,' I replied. 'It's that nothing makes sense and nothing is fair. The unreasonable rules apply.'

Alberto was waiting for us at Bari airport holding a cardboard sign and a big bunch of flowers. I'd been half mad with grief when I'd last seen him, but would have recognised him anywhere – he looked exactly like my father had in his thirties, the same beaming smile, the same rosy, shiny cheeks, he even had a combover which wasn't fooling anybody. Just like my dad.

Sam had slept on the flight and was back on fine form, even happy to have his cheeks pinched by Alberto. I'd never figured out why Italians always did that – as a general rule, babies, and kids of all ages, hated it almost as much as someone trying to put suncream on their face, or wiping their mouths. 'Get your massive hands out of my face, you big person! Careful of my eyes. Why are you pinching me? Can't you see it hurts?'

Rupert and I had agreed on the plane that we wouldn't discuss any of the troubles I was having and we would try to treat the trip almost like a second honeymoon – to the extent it was possible considering the demanding and intrusive presence of a six-month-old baby.

It was easy to say, but there wasn't much I could do to hold back the dark thoughts and doubts which swirled on the edge of my consciousness. As we were coming in to land, I looked at Rupert and Sam both dozing beside me and made myself a promise to find a solution to my problems so I could look after them both.

Alberto was charming and, as expected, spoke perfect English; I could almost hear Rupert sighing with relief.

'So, Rupert,' he said as we walked to the car park. 'Is this your first time in Italy?'

'No. I've been once before. To Rome,' said Rupert. 'But it was on a rugby tour so we didn't do anything cultural and, as you can imagine, my memories are a bit, shall we say, "foggy".'

'And how's your Italian?' said Alberto.

'Non-existent,' said Rupert. 'I've been totally useless. I keep meaning to but I'm not good with languages – typical Englishman, I suppose – and I keep putting it off. I've promised Fabi I'll do better when we get back. She always speaks Italian to Sam.'

'Don't worry,' said Alberto. 'I'm sure you'll pick it up. It's much easier to learn than English and it is much more beautiful. The scholars all claim Sanskrit is the language of the Gods, but every Italian knows better.' He turned to me and Sam. 'So Fabiola, you're teaching Sam to speak Italian already? I like that. We need to keep some family traditions, even so far away.'

'I'm doing do my best,' I said. 'It's not so easy in Oxford, though. There are lots of people studying Italian at the university, but not many real Italians and the ones I've met come mostly from the North.'

'Ah,' said Alberto, 'that is a problem. Rupert, you must understand that the northerners always look down on us. They say we're lazy idiots and everyone here is either a farmer or a mafioso.' It was difficult to tell if he was joking or half-serious. 'I think they're jealous because we have more sunshine, better food and much more beautiful women. It's best not to talk to people from the North.'

I could remember hearing similar comments growing up. Twenty per cent of the population of Bedford were of Italian origin, but not just any old Italians. Almost everybody was from the South and proudly partisan. The conversations meandered from amusing, good-natured rivalry, through bitter recriminations, to declarations of war and independence and back again. I suspected that the amount of grappa consumed was the key determining factor.

'Rupert,' I said, trying to sound as serious as possible, 'this is worth remembering. When the conversation turns to politics here, the best thing for you to do is to be quiet and non-committal. Nod and pretend to agree. If you've had too much to drink and can't avoid it, tell them you're married to a southern Italian from Peschici and hope for the best. The same goes for football. And women.'

Alberto burst out laughing. 'Don't be so cruel. We're not that bad. Sometimes we might get a little carried away and excited, but it's all just good fun. OK, if you tell someone you support AC Milan ...'

It was only half an hour's drive to Alberto's house, which was a small, but pretty, modern villa in the Valle Castellano, about a mile outside Peschici. We were welcomed by his wife, Maria, their ten-year old son, Luigi, and two enormous, fluffy Alsatians who appeared friendly enough, but were definitely too big and boisterous for Sam.

Alberto and Maria seemed to have put their entire life on hold in honour of our visit and we had a full programme laid out – visiting old aunts and uncles, exploring the region and gorging ourselves on the most amazing fresh food. I don't think I've ever eaten as well, both in people's houses and in a series of seaside restaurants, set out on the rocks or nestled into small harbours.

Rupert even started to pick up some Italian as he sat with the boys after one dinner or another, drinking his coffee and grappa. Sitting in my place with the other women, I had the impression that feminism might take a while to reach this part of the world, but everything appeared harmless enough. Maybe my guard was down because the environment was so familiar.

It was not exactly beach weather and the nights were already quite cold but, for the whole of our trip, there was not even a wisp of cloud to smudge the perfect blue sky and I felt a million miles away from the cold, grey Oxfordshire December.

Maybe things would be better when we got home.

There was one thing in particular I'd been keen to do on the trip. The week before my disastrous job interview, the three of us had taken a trip to Odell Wood to visit Nonno's oak tree. On the way there, I'd told Rupert and Sam all about Nonno, as much as I could remember, as much as I'd ever been told. We'd nestled together under the tree, drinking coffee from a thermos and indulging my memories. I didn't cry but remember being unable to continue after a while and we sat there quietly as the sun went down, wrapped up in the warm blanket of my memories.

Before we went home, I took a small handful of the leafy, black humus from the base of Nonno's oak and put it in a small ziplock bag to take to Italy. Fortunately it hadn't aroused the suspicions of either airport security or Italian customs.

I'd asked Alberto if he could try to track down any of Nonno's old friends from after the war, the ones he used to hunt and forage with as a teenager. As with everything else, he'd come up trumps. Giuseppe was eighty-five, but still wiry and fit from a Mediterranean diet and a lifetime of hard, physical work. He was happy to take us to some of their old hunting grounds, but there was a sadness in the shadows of his parchment eyes when he told me how few of them were left.

Rupert had decided to stay behind with Sam as it was a long walk and the conversation was going to be exclusively in colloquial Puglian Italian. This allowed us to set off early and to take our time over the route, stopping as often as we wanted, pretending to look at something beautiful or interesting, but mostly making sure we neither pushed old Giuseppe too hard, nor offended his male pride. In reality, he could probably have outlasted both me and city-softened Alberto but, as the point of the trip was for us to be there in the forest, the frequent stops felt right.

We did have a target for the walk. Giuseppe believed he could guide us to the exact spot where Nonno had shot his last boar, on their final hunt together before Nonno had left for England. After two hours of walking through rolling hillsides of beech trees, mingled with lush ivy, ferns and the occasional giant yew, the forest gradually transformed and the beech faded away to be replaced by Turkey oak – I had finally found out what Nonno's oak trees were called – and maple trees. This was now the forest which Nonno had always talked about when he told us stories of home.

It was midday when we arrived in a small clearing. Giuseppe stopped and turned slowly, smelling the air and nodding his head gently as he looked around. He pointed to a huge, old tree at the edge of the clearing.

'*Laggiù*,' he said, '*è qui che il cinghiale è morto.*' 'Over there, that is where the boar died.'

I walked over to the tree; sharp December sunlight paved the forest's soft, mossy floor with a random mosaic of black and gold and the silence of the dense woodland was absolute. I stood for an age under the ancient oak, both palms pressed into the bark until I could feel the gnarly texture imprinting itself deeply into my skin.

I tried to imagine Nonno as a young twenty-eight-year-old standing there proudly over his kill – elation at his victory not quite covering the hidden ball of fear which lay cold and secret in his stomach. What would England be like? Was he making the right decision? He'd heard stories from people who'd been and come back before their contracts were over, but not so many from those who'd stayed.

If he could be so brave for his family, why couldn't I?

The image of the young man was hard to hold onto and my memories took me back to the face I knew, the paterfamilias ruling benevolently over his small family kingdom. Eyes which held years of experiences – including the boar hunt which ended here – good and bad, joyful and tragic. Eyes which still managed to twinkle with mischief despite what they'd seen until, near the end, the death of my parents snuffed out the glow from one moment to the next.

I took the small bag from my pocket and gently, but with no great ceremony, sprinkled the dirt around the base of the old oak, completing the circle of Nonno's life as I whispered soft words.

'Bentornato, Nonno. Mi dispiace che sia voluto così tanto tempo.' 'Welcome home, Nonno. I'm sorry it took so long.'

Breaking Point

Hacking isn't confined to the internet. If you need to press your wireless key fob twice to unlock your car, a nearby hacker may be spoofing the sequential encryption by using a radio blocker to intercept and record your key signal. When they walk up to your vehicle a few minutes, hours, or days later, it will only take them one button press to get inside.
"How much is your Life Worth? Protecting your Identity in a Digital World".
JJ Martin, Insight Business Press 2015

I started seeing a counsellor just before Christmas.

A counsellor. Me. Those are words I thought I'd never say.

But I had to do something. I'd thought I was getting better for a while after we got back from Italy, but my lapses were still happening. Not many and with no pattern, but I'd begun to avoid making any arrangements and preferred not to go out on my own. It wasn't only messed up appointments and emails, and it was generally little things, but each one built on the others and appeared huge to me. The evidence was building steadily. The evidence which said, 'This is happening in your mind. You have a mental illness.'.

I was still fighting it though. I wasn't prepared to accept that I was losing control. Not quite. I made a note of each occurrence in my diary and read and re-read it, over and over, hiding myself away and desperately trying to find some other explanation for what was going on. But, however hard I tried, I couldn't find any patterns which made sense, and even I could see that I was starting to behave like a secretive, obsessive paranoiac.

The most recent incident had happened a week earlier when I'd gone up to Marks and Spencer's food hall in Summertown. I couldn't ask Rupert to do everything. It wasn't fair as he was working so hard and then had to deal with my emotional baggage when he came home. I suppose the car park meltdown was the thing which finally pushed me over the edge and made me realise I couldn't go on without help.

I was in a good mood. Sam was beginning to show signs that he might consider using the night as a time for sleeping, rather than an opportunity to torment me. He was also becoming very funny, especially as he learnt to eat solid food.

Virginia and John had given us one of those Scandinavian Tripp Trapp high chairs; it had a big plastic tray with raised edges, which was proving to be extremely useful as Sam experimented with the myriad different approaches to solid food consumption.

These were, in no particular order: spitting out, swallowing, gargling, biting the spoon and a skilful combination of simultaneous swallowing, spitting out and wiping everywhere. I was sure he would progress to the smiling cheekily and dropping on the floor stage soon enough but, for now, that was beyond him.

He was still small, so didn't interfere with the shopping expedition as he dangled, face-forward in his baby carrier, happily distracted by the bright lights, the people everywhere, and the shiny shapes of tins, jars, bottles, boxes and bulging bags. It was more fun than the Early Learning Centre and Sam was vocal in his appreciation as each new delight went into the trolley. He had developed a particular stuck-pig squeal which he would mix up with his other new talent, that of blowing raspberries.

The adventure was wearing thin after about half an hour and the checkout queue was definitely not as enjoyable. By the time we'd paid, I think he'd decided shopping might not actually be everything it was cracked up to be.

It had been sunny when we arrived but, as we came out, a light drizzle was falling and it was already getting dark. No wonder people got sad, or rather S.A.D., over the winter months. Spring was a long way off and it was definitely going to get worse before it got better. I thought idly about moving to Italy.

I dragged the trolley up over the conveniently placed curb, manhandled a grizzling Sam into his car seat and put the bags in the car. It was only after I'd got in and sat down that I saw the plastic envelope tucked under my wipers.

I'd bought a parking ticket for two hours and had stuck it on the inside of the windscreen. I remembered fumbling about in the glove compartment for coins. I'd been there for less than an hour, so it couldn't have been a parking fine. But it was. Of course it was.

Failure to display a valid ticket. It should have been easy enough to dispute as it patently wasn't true, but the ticket was nowhere. Not fallen on the floor, not on the dashboard. It was as though it had never existed. I couldn't believe this was happening. I knew that I'd bought a ticket.

It wasn't as though I'd bought the bloody thing a week earlier, it was less than an hour and I could clearly remember looking for the coins, going to the machine, putting the money in, listening to the stupid beep-beep-beep noise that the machine made as though it was impersonating a reversing truck, taking the ticket and sticking it onto the windscreen. I didn't *think* I'd bought a ticket. I *knew* I had.

Sam was screaming his head off by this point and my brain was about to explode. Every breath was tugging my head back and up with short, rapid gasps and pulling my stomach into my throat. This couldn't be happening to me. It couldn't. It simply couldn't.

It was only when I heard tapping at the window that I realised I was making more noise than Sam, banging my hands on the steering wheel again and again, screaming and shouting obscenities at the top of my voice. I turned to see a small grey-haired woman leaning towards me and peering down through heavy glasses, obviously assuming I was a madwoman who'd stolen a car and a baby.

I grabbed hold of the steering wheel with both hands, squeezing as tightly as I could while I tried to bring my breathing back under control. Her patient, concerned face must have been hanging there for a long while, framed by the misty glass, before I felt it was safe to wind the window down.

'Is everything all right dear?' she said.

'Yes, thank you, I'm fine.' I managed to force a smile, or at least a grimace. 'It's just the third parking fine this week and my husband will kill me.'

'Well, if you're sure you're all right ...' she said, and turned away, probably muttering to herself about the absence of decorum and self-control in the youth of today.

I've never been emotionally fragile. Not even slightly. There were times when I'd wallowed in self-pity for a while after breaking up with someone or losing a job, and I was usually a major pain in the arse when I had PMS – but who wasn't? Until recently, though, my glass of water had always been half full.

There had been one big exception; when my parents died, there was suddenly nothing left in the broken and empty glass. Not a single drop. Their death came out of the blue and shocked me to the core. One minute they were there and then suddenly they were gone.

But my reaction didn't mean I was emotionally weak. Losing them had been totally unexpected and they were much too young.

Which was probably why Deborah's first serious question rocked me back on my heels.

Deborah was my counsellor. Deborah Horsley, mid thirties, gentle West Country accent slipping through from time to time, she appeared to be a kind person and exactly what I expected from a shrink.

We'd done the form filling, introduction thing and spent about fifteen minutes talking over the story of my life so far. It was all very superficial and probably designed to put me at my ease. I also assumed she needed a bit of context if she was going to be able to help me, but I was impatient and I wanted to talk about what was happening to me there and then.

'So, Fabiola, tell me about your relationship with your father,' she suddenly said, out of the blue.

Talk about a sucker punch. Where had that come from?

'Isn't that a bit of a cliche?' I said, crossing my arms and sitting back in my chair. 'Surely there's more to this than, "They fuck you up, your Mum and Dad"?'

Deborah smiled. 'Yes, there's a bit more than that, but it works best if you go with the flow. I'll do my best to help you but it'll be much easier if you trust me. Tell me about your father. Were you close?'

'Until a year before my parents died, we were very close,' I replied, picturing my dad's shiny-cheeked, smiling face as he welcomed someone new into the coffee shop. Everyone was his favourite customer and his easy, happy charm was universally captivating. 'I loved my mother as much, but Papa and I had a special bond. We were on the same wavelength.'

Deborah leant towards me, holding my gaze. 'So what happened a year before they died? What happened to break your bond?'

I looked away and down to my shoes. Over the past few months, I'd had a lot of time for introspection and the realisation that my parents would never meet Sam inevitably rose up in my thoughts – a dark leviathan writhing, sinuous and yellowed-eyed, just below the surface.

Whenever I thought about them, my natural grief was muddied by guilt over the way I'd behaved in the year before they died; instead of embracing remorse, my perverse response was often to become angry instead. That was the peculiar thing about those times when you felt guilty and you actually deserved it. It was easy to become bitter and resentful of the people you'd wronged. After all, it was their fault that you felt bad in the first place.

When they couldn't answer you back, the cycle of twisted self-justification fed on itself for a while but, unless you really were a total shit, it wasn't a healthy long-term approach. I'd been thinking a lot about that conflict but wasn't ready to share my fledgling conclusions with a stranger. 'Look Deborah, could we focus on what's been going on recently, please? After all, that is why I'm here.'

'OK. If that's what you prefer. We can come back to your family later. I don't think we can ignore them though. These things are so often interrelated.' She looked at her notes. 'I understand you've been experiencing some confusion and memory lapses, is that right?'

'Yes. It started soon after Sam, my son, was born – just under nine months ago. I've found myself mixing up appointments – arriving too early, too late or going to the wrong place. I've also imagined receiving emails and have forgotten about other emails which I've received or sent. Nothing like this has ever happened to me before and I'm beginning to think I'm losing my mind. I'm being so careful to check and double-check everything, but I keep slipping up. It's as though a hidden part of me is deliberately trying to sabotage my life.'

'Yes. I see. I can understand how you might feel that way and it must be extremely distressing,' she said. 'Is it affecting your sleep? Other areas of your life? Social? Work?'

'All of them,' I said. 'Sleeping was a mess anyway, but it's got worse. I was hoping to have started a part-time job by now, but that was one of the things I screwed up by going to the wrong place for an interview. I don't have any close friends around here and I was relying on getting back a little normal adult contact through work.'

'I'm surprised to hear you don't have close friends. You come across as someone who'd have a good social life.'

'I used to. I always used to. But I moved in a different circle for a while and lost touch with my school and university crowd. Since we've been here, it's been difficult. I've met a lot of Rupert's friends but it's going to take me a while to fit in.'

'And you can't get back in touch with some of your old friends? We tend to have the most uncomplicated, trusting relationships with the people we bonded with during our formative years.'

'I'd love to and I've tried, but it's actually a perfect example of how I'm behaving and how pathetically insecure I've become. I was invited to catch up with a lot of old university friends before Christmas and was really looking forward to seeing them, but then it didn't work out.'

'What did you mean by, 'it didn't work out'?'

'I couldn't face going. It was straight after a couple of memory lapses or whatever you want to call them. I was too afraid to go.'

'That's a great shame,' said Deborah. 'It's important to have people who you trust around you. And you're absolutely certain your problems aren't issues with technology or simple mistakes?'

'I don't see how they can be,' I replied, biting back my irritation. 'There have been too many incidents plus we've checked my phone and iPad again and again and there's nothing wrong. My husband, Rupert, is good with techie stuff and he's double checked with other devices as well. I even persuaded him that I should have a new phone a few weeks ago and I've changed all my passwords. I want to believe it is something external, but I haven't found a single thing to back that up.'

'What about your husband? Is all of this having an impact on your relationship?'

'Absolutely. Rupert is being incredibly patient, but it's clear that he doesn't believe he can trust me any more. He's beginning to check up on me and to treat me like a child. I hate it obviously, but I do see his point. Some of my lapses have cost us real money.'

'So, are you saying that the basis of your relationship with Rupert has changed?'

'Yes. We're no longer equals. We've moved into some sort of warped parent-child relationship which isn't what either of us signed up for. Going back to your first question, I loved my father, but I never wanted to sleep with him.'

'That doesn't sound good.' Deborah was writing a lot of notes. 'It's something we'll need to address in due course.'

'I understand, but I'm sure Rupert and I will find a way to figure it out. We're both adults and we still love each other. The real elephant in the room is the danger that something I do could put Sam at risk. What if I forgot to pick him up from somewhere or left him behind? I would never forgive myself.'

'I would be surprised if anything like that happened,' she said. 'The maternal instinct is deeply ingrained in our psychological make-up.'

I wasn't convinced. Since the incident in the car park, I'd become certain Rupert and Virginia were spying on me and checking up on everything I did. They didn't trust me to be alone with Sam, I could tell.

I lifted my head and looked up at her. 'Please help me to figure it out, Deborah. I can't go on like this. I really can't. I'm afraid of what might happen.'

Deborah reached over and took my hand in hers. 'Don't worry,' she said in her calm, sensible voice. 'We'll find our way through to the other side. As I said at the start, we'll have a minimum of six sessions and more if we need them. I would like to go into more detail about these incidents but, before we do that, were you aware that confusion and memory lapses are well-documented consequences of the grieving process? It may not be a factor but, over the past few years, we've moved on a long way from the simple "five stages of grief" theories and we shouldn't exclude the possibility that you're undergoing a delayed response to the loss of your parents.'

'I didn't know that, but I don't believe my parents' death has anything to do with what is going on. This is something that's changed recently, and is happening to me right now. They died six years ago. I was sad. I'm still sad. I do feel guilty and I will try and explain why at some point, but that isn't what's behind this.

'This is as though some malevolent spirit in my subconscious is toying with me, tormenting me, punishing me for some reason. I'm still not sure whether I should be seeing a counsellor or an exorcist.'

Deborah lived about twenty minutes walk from home but, as Virginia was looking after Sam until after lunch, I had the rare opportunity to take a solitary walk and clear my mind on the way home. I looped through Port Meadow to breathe a bit of green (ish) air, but my real destination was Brew – a special little coffee shop on the Banbury road which I loved.

I liked Deborah and hadn't found the process as embarrassing or painful as I'd feared, but it was still difficult to imagine sharing my innermost thoughts and fears with a stranger. I suspected it would become easier and easier as we progressed, but would I ever share every sordid detail of my family history with Deborah? I wasn't sure.

I was probably no worse than the average obnoxious teenage girl until Joe. It all started there, and the three months we spent together changed everything back in Bedford in ways which couldn't be undone. I probably always knew it would work out like that, but I went ahead anyway. It wasn't as though I was underage, I was seventeen, or almost seventeen, and he was only thirty-six. But that wasn't the point; I wanted to grow up, to become an adult woman so that I could make my escape and Joe was my exit visa, as well as being charming, intelligent, good looking and wanting me. He courted and seduced me and I was besotted.

I should point out that, not only was he thirty-six, but he was married and with a second kid on the way. That added a bit of spice to the situation. Oh, and he was my politics teacher. Yes, I knew it was wrong, and I knew it would have consequences, but I didn't care. I wanted to break free from the chains which were holding me down, the chains of my conservative Italian family, the chains of the class system, the chains of the patriarchy, the chains of bloody Bedford. I don't think I wanted to shatter them quite as catastrophically as I did, but teenagers have never been renowned for measured judgement.

It went much more wrong than I'd expected, although I hadn't thought much about the consequences anyway. The affair was too exciting and illicit and dangerous to worry about such petty details. He said he loved me and that he was going to leave his wife for me. I suspect I was mostly flattered and having fun but, when you're suddenly picked up and plonked down into the middle of a Hollywood movie, there's nothing to do but play your part until somebody shouts 'cut!'. And so I did.

Looking back, it was easy to see that I was much more of a child than I thought I was at the time and, when the shit hit the fan, my world changed forever. He lost his job, his wife kicked him out, and there was some talk about whether he should be prosecuted.

The sad thing was that he professed his love for me throughout the scandal. The more he'd write to me, the more I felt creeped out and began to see him as a pathetic old git – perving over young girls – who'd tricked me. It made me feel dirty and stupid.

My family, of course, went apeshit and all sorts of things were said in the heat of the moment. My grandmother wasted few words, at least not to my face. 'Puta' was quite enough for her. My parents tried to understand, but struggled enormously.

After Joe, nothing was ever the same again. I'd certainly shown everyone how far I was prepared to go in order to distance myself from my small, insignificant life in Bedford and, within what was still a southern Italian peasant community, most people were happy enough to see me go.

I must have been unbearable at the time and so sure of everything – opinionated, arrogant and happy to exploit and abuse the fact that I was a bit smarter than those around me. A complete and utter pain in the arse.

Our family survived the final six months – until I finished my A-levels – by avoiding each other. My brothers and sister were a few years older than me and, somewhat perversely, they had ended up even more like traditional Italians than my parents were. We weren't very close, but I had expected them to take my side, at least partly. I was wrong, and the disapproval in our house coated every available surface like mildew.

When I moved to London after university, I stopped even going back home to visit. I had hardened myself to the tears, cries of 'why are you treating us like this Fabia?' from my mother, stern, sad words from my father and grandfather, 'can't you see what you're doing to your mother?' and hurt, but pretending not to care, bickering with my friends and siblings, 'well fuck you Fabs, if you think you're so much better than us, stay in fucking London then'. And now? Now, looking back, it all appeared to be so pointless and petty and mean.

Why had I made such a big effort to finish the job I'd started with my affair, to estrange myself completely from my home and my family? Surely it couldn't have only been because of my politics? That wasn't reason enough. However hard I thought back, I couldn't come up with any single specific reason, although the continuous anti-bourgeoisie sniping from Jax probably hadn't helped.

It was as though I'd been overtaken by a temporary madness and had simply dug my heels in, driven by a dogmatic certainty that trying to live my life as an urban radical and pop home for a nice Sunday lunch was the ultimate hypocrisy.

Then, without warning, my parents died and all of the bad blood was washed away by shock and grief. I stayed for over a month with my older brother Roberto and his family. They took care of me while I tried to find a way to move forward. In fact, we all took care of each other.

I was the baby of the family but my brother Paulo, who was six years older than me, took our parents' death the hardest. He just gave up, and he never got going again. In the six months that followed, he lost his job, his wife left him and he became a virtual recluse, sitting at home watching endless reruns and mindless reality TV. As far as I was aware, he never found his way out of that hole.

They'd been out Christmas shopping at the Harpur Centre. It was Sunday after Mass, the only time they had free to be together and to catch up on a bit of normal life. The car came full pelt out of a side street without looking and broadsided them across the road, sending their old Fiesta spinning into the path of a small truck. My mother had died instantly, and my father never recovered consciousness, although he hung on for a few more hours, long enough for the family to get to the hospital and to be there at the end.

Except for me. I'd been too late to hold his warm hand one last time, but I'd been too late for a long time. The hospital had put them side-by-side in a small chapel where I sat alone with them and said everything I wanted to say and should have said earlier, words which had formed soundlessly as I sat on the train, my blank eyes barely registering the dismal brown fields sliding by. Words of regret, of gratitude, of respect, of love and of loss.

The young guy driving the car which hit them had apparently been uninjured and, according to the witnesses, he'd simply reversed and driven off. It was a white Audi TT, either stolen or belonging to some spoilt rich kid, with a numberplate beginning with BK or BH. My two brothers Roberto and Paulo had spent hours every day for weeks afterwards, cruising around Bedford looking for a white Audi with a smashed front end, adrenaline-fuelled and ready to jump out and chase down our parents' murderer. No-one was surprised when they found nothing but then again, neither did the police.

I often wondered if the driver had read about what happened in the papers. Did he care? Did he carry guilt with him for the rest of his days, or was he one of those soulless shaven-headed zombies whose ability to feel guilt or remorse had been excised at an early age by a fight-or-die world of anger and violence. I hoped that, even if he was in the latter group, there would be a moment, like the elusive green flash of a tropical sunset, just in the space between waking and sleep, when he would see everything with open eyes, understand truly what he'd done and feel the pain of guilt scour him from head to toe. If not, it would have to wait, but I had no doubt about what would happen when he met my parents' God. He was not the forgiving type.

I saw much more of my family in the year that followed and had been especially pleased to have re-forged my bond with my grandfather, Nonno, who had always been my hero. He was the same hard, gnarly Puglian oak he'd always been, holding the family together throughout the nightmare. Still solid and unbending on the outside, I could see he'd been hollowed out by the loss of his only son and was struggling to find answers to the biggest questions of all. For him, life had stopped having a point. He was going through the motions, not least because, as a good Catholic, he didn't have an alternative. I think he enjoyed our time together, and was happy I had come back into the fold, but it wasn't enough.

As it had turned out, the family reconciliation had been short-lived. Nonno died less than a year after my parents, and I was foolish enough to take Jax to the funeral. It was unclear quite how things had kicked off, but words were said which couldn't be unsaid and I hadn't spoken to any of my family since. Looking back, I didn't understand how it could have happened. Why had it been necessary to pick sides like that?

Blast from the Past

Most phone bugging software sits quietly hidden in the operating system, recording activity data as specified by the hacker. It functions whether the phone is turned on or not and is extremely difficult to disable. The only way to protect yourself is to employ a security expert to check your device or to never let your phone out of your sight.
"How much is your Life Worth? Protecting your Identity in a Digital World".
JJ Martin, Insight Business Press 2015

By the time I got to Brew, the sun was out and I allowed myself a moment of optimism. During the half-hour walk from Deborah's, I realised that, even though it had only been the first session, I did feel better.

I'd been fighting this every inch of the way, heels dug in deep and dragging furrows in the dirt like a tug-of-war anchor on the losing side. Everything is straining as the white tape inches closer and closer to the centre mark. Veins bulge and pop, muscles burn and fade but you keep trying to hold your ground, just a little more, just a few seconds longer.

Until, all of a sudden, you stop trying. The decision to give in and stop fighting comes in a rush, almost as a surprise, and you tumble forward over the line with disappointment and relief flooding over you in equal measures.

Accepting that I might have a problem was a relief. It gave me back some element of control in contrast to the feelings of spiralling panic which had been threatening to overwhelm me. It would take time, but Deborah had assured me that my issues were not unusual and, whatever was behind them, we would be able to find a way to manage them. My intransigent, pig-headed certainty that I couldn't be imagining any of this was, in fact, blocking my path of recovery. It did make sense but that didn't make it easy.

Brew was unashamedly hipster; filled with beards, cool specs, vinyl records and a whole slew of authentic retro touches; I settled down at one of the four two-seater tables with a cup of Sumatran Gegarang – one of the three specials brewing that day – and checked my phone for messages.

After a few minutes, a burly guy in a black donkey jacket eased himself into the chair opposite me; he was heavily bearded and wearing a thick woolly hat, but I would have known him anywhere.

'Daz?' I said, eyes wide with surprise. 'What the fuck are you doing here?'

'Take it easy, Fab, stay cool,' he said, looking up briefly and smiling before shifting his gaze back to his coffee. 'Don't make a scene. Just chill.'

Darren, better known as Daz, was one of the original members of our London group, the only one apart from Jax who'd been there at the Rostock G8 demos in 2007. Although it was difficult to imagine looking at him, he was a senior mental health nurse and apparently very good at his job. I hadn't seen him, or any of them, for over two years.

He was being very shifty but he'd always had more than his fair share of paranoia, and I knew it would be easiest to play along.

'The question stands,' I said, quietly and not making any sort of scene. 'It's great to see you, but what the fuck are you doing here?'

'I followed you from your house. I needed to see you. Look, have you seen Jax?' he mumbled, his interest in the cup of coffee undiluted.

'No. You must know that,' I replied. 'She didn't exactly react well to me leaving, and then when I sold the flat ... Well, I assumed she must've turned all of you against me.'

'Yeah, she did hang you out to dry at the start but there was no surprise there. We all knew what she was like,' he said. 'And she disappeared not long after. No-one's seen her since.'

'What? Not at all?'

'Nope. Thin air. But she's always been a few sandwiches short of a picnic.'

'I'm starting to understand that,' I said. 'Can you believe I never saw it at the time? I must have been so blind.'

'Yeah. Actually, I can believe it,' he said. 'That was her trick, wasn't it? Making people see and feel what she wanted them to.'

'But we were together for five years. I should have seen something.'

'You were different Fabi. I think you were the only person she ever cared about. The only one she trusted.' He dragged his eyes up from the table and looked at me. 'You should have seen her after you left. She completely lost it for a while. I've never seen anything like it.'

'Sounds terrifying.'

'It was, and it might have been part of the reason why we didn't keep in touch. We figured you were better off out of it.'

'Fair enough. I did want out anyway and I knew where you were. So, anyway, why are you looking for Jax now and what's with all the cloak and dagger bullshit?'

'I've not been looking for Jax. I've been looking for you. I wanted to give you a heads up. The cops have been asking around, looking for Jax. Something to do with March 2011, the TUC anti-cuts rally.'

'That turned out to be a heavy day.' I said. 'My last protest.'

I wasn't going to say anything to Daz, but I knew something had gone down with Jax that day. I'd lost sight of her early on. She'd been sly and secretive all morning and, as we were walking through Trafalgar Square, I remember turning to say something to her but she'd vanished.

I hadn't seen her again until she'd slunk back to the flat at about five in the morning, covered in dirt and what looked like food waste, with a big cut on her forehead.

She wouldn't tell me what had happened and made me swear not to say anything and to tell everyone we'd been together the whole time. I'd agreed and, by that stage in our relationship, had no desire to know what she'd been up to anyway. I think I'd been ignoring her more volatile sides all along; it was only around then that the blinkers were coming off and I was beginning to see what she was actually like.

'Yeah. The bloody black bloc ruined everything.'

Daz had been deeply upset by the way the media had focused exclusively on the violence and destruction carried out by a tiny percentage of protestors. He wanted to make the world a fairer place but cared about more than just breaking the system and destroying the rich. He hated the violent fringe with a passion.

'That was probably why it was my last march,' I said. I finished my coffee and looked at him. He looked like a tramp but he was genuinely a good person, a good friend. Maybe my judgement wasn't totally screwed up? 'It's good to see you, but you didn't come up to Oxford to reminisce. The police are looking for Jax? What's that got to do with me?'

'I don't know. My guess is they've picked her up from the security videos and it must be something bad if they're still on her case after three years.'

'I guess.'

'Well. It's only a matter of time before they connect her, the flat and you. I'd expect a visit one day soon and I thought you'd want to give your bloke a bit of context before the plod comes knocking.'

'Thanks Daz.' I wasn't quite sure how I was going to give Rupert any sort of context. 'It's really appreciated. I always knew there was an angel under that scruffy beard.'

'No problem. Solidarity and all that,' he said. 'Have you got any idea what she might've got caught up in? Did she tell you anything?'

'Not a clue. We were separated before we got to Trafalgar Square. The whole thing was a bit of a zoo.' I stood up and put my hand on his shoulder. 'Listen, I've got to get back to rescue the baby from my mother-in-law. Thanks for this. Will you say hi to everyone from me? Are you still with Linda?'

Daz looked at me closely, his eyes locked on mine as if he could tell I knew more than I was letting on. 'Course I will Fab. Yeah, Linda and me are still an item. Apart from you and Jax leaving, nothing's changed and it probably never will.' He put his hand on top of mine for a moment, still holding that penetrating gaze.

As I got up and walked out of the cafe, I heard him say, almost to himself. 'You take good care of yourself, Fabi.'

'Roop, I need to tell you a bit more about Jax,' I said.

We were sitting at our small dining table scraping up the last smatterings of a delicious apple crumble which Virginia had magicked up when she was here earlier. That woman really was like the home economics professor from Hogwarts. It was frightening.

The wood burner was oozing warm comfort in the corner, Sam was happily asleep, and a dozen candles were scattered around to complete the romantic winter evening scene. I suspected I was about to ruin all of that by shoving a king-size spanner into the works, but didn't see an alternative after what Daz had told me.

I could see Rupert had been about to lick his bowl but, hearing the tone of my voice, thought better of it, and sat back in his chair like a naughty boy. 'Ouch,' he said. 'You sound serious. You sure you don't want to do this another time?'

'Better now,' I said. 'I think you should know everything about me, but you might not like it so much.'

'Try me,' said Rupert. 'I might surprise you.'

'OK. Well, I popped into that new coffee place, Brew, on my way back from seeing the counsellor. You remember the one I told you about?'

'Yup. I think so. What's that got to do with Jax?'

'I'm getting there. Anyway, I was sitting having my coffee when this bloke sat down at my table. He was being all secretive and weird and it took me a couple of seconds to realise it was Daz. D'you remember him?'

'Of course,' said Rupert. 'We met him a couple of times at the Kings Arms. He was strange but seemed nice enough. Clearly totally in love with you though. Like a puppy.'

I laughed. 'So you're not totally brainless and lacking emotional intelligence then? Surprising for a man.'

'Come on Fabs, give me a break. We need to know how to protect our females from rogue males.'

'Well, anyway, that wasn't why he was there. He wanted to tell me something about Jax. Something important.'

'Hang on a sec,' said Rupert. 'How did Daz know you were going to be there?'

'He told me he followed me from home.' As I said it out loud, I realised how bad that sounded.

Rupert was well ahead of me. 'What! So, firstly, how the hell did he know where you live? And secondly, you're saying he waited outside our house, then followed you secretly and waited for another hour outside the counsellor's house before following you to the cafe?' He was standing up by that point and his voice had become squeaky with outrage. 'And none of this strikes you as worrying? How long was he waiting outside the house? Is he out there now?'

'Fucking hell,' I said. 'Of course you're right. It just didn't click because I was listening to what he had to say about Jax. It's very creepy.'

'Creepy is a bloody understatement.'

'But I'm sure Daz is harmless enough. He always looked out for me.'

'Well, you say that, but I've got no idea what these people you used to know are actually like. Are you sure he's not dangerous? We've got Sam to worry about now.'

'You're right, of course. I'll speak to him. Maybe you should come?'

'Too bloody right I'm coming,' said Rupert. 'Anyway, tell me what he told you about Jax and we'll get back to him sneaking around later.'

'Well, it starts at the christening and what Daz said triggered the memory,' I said. 'D'you remember that I told you I saw someone sitting at the back of the church during the christening? Someone who crept out before the end of the ceremony?'

'Yes. A woman. But you didn't recognise her, did you?'

'No,' I said. 'But I think I do now. I'm sure it was Jax. She looked completely different, but I've got this gut feeling it was her.'

'How sure?' said Rupert.

'Pretty sure. But then she was gone so quickly and it was right at the critical moment. I wouldn't put it past her to have shown up unannounced though. It's just the sort of thing she'd do.'

'That's also very creepy,' said Rupert. 'What is it with these people?'

'What can I say? They were an unusual bunch. I know it sounds crazy, but when I first started to have my problems, a part of me was afraid that Jax was somehow behind them.'

Rupert frowned. 'That's probably not a healthy way of thinking. You said the counsellor was helpful, didn't you?'

'Yes, I was surprised at how much better she made me feel.' I put my hand on Rupert's arm feeling his muscles tense against the cotton of his shirt. 'Don't worry. I don't actually believe anyone else was involved. I was only telling you what I thought at the time.'

'Good.' I suspected Rupert had decided to file away my 'Jax vision' in the same drawer as all my other visions. 'But that wasn't the main revelation was it? What else do I need to know?'

I gave him a potted summary of my meeting with Daz and what he'd told me about the police. I also told him what had really happened that night.

'The thing is,' I said. 'If the police do come around, what do I tell them?'

Rupert stared at me wide-eyed. 'You tell them the bloody truth, for Christ's sake. I can't believe you're even asking that question.'

'But I promised her that I'd say she was with me. I gave her my word.'

'And so what? Haven't you seen and heard enough now to realise she's a crazy vindictive bitch? She might have done something terrible that night for all you know.' He held both hands out in front of him, palms upwards as though in supplication. 'Why would you consider, even for a nanosecond, making yourself an accessory? You need to stop and think about this. Think of me, think of Sam.'

I reached over the table and took his hands in mine. 'You're completely right, darling. I just needed to hear someone say that. If they come, I'll tell them the truth. Of course I will.'

Love and Protests

I love Fabiola. I always have. I know it's pathetic and I don't have a chance, but I don't mind. I call her Fabiolous, because that's what she is, and all I care about is that she's all right.

When Fabiola was going to Paris for her third year at university, the idea almost did me in. I couldn't imagine going a whole year without seeing her, but I'd just started work after college and it wasn't as though I could zap over to Paris every week. I did manage to get there three times but the distance between us tore me apart.

I think she always liked me too – not in *that* way – but I reckon we're friends. I never wanted to push things too far, so I got in the habit of hanging around out of sight even when we weren't supposed to be doing something together. That way, she could see lots of other people and not feel I was in her face the whole time.

She got what she wanted and I got what I needed – which was to be close to her all of the time, to watch her smile, walk, read a book or whatever.

It sounds creepy and I probably come across as a bit of a sad stalker, but it's not like that. I've needed to sneak about a lot to keep an eye on her, but I would never cross the line. Even though our relationship is never going anywhere, I've always been happy enough to simply be near her and to see her as often as I could.

I would do anything for her. Literally, anything. I know it sounds sad, but I don't care. We're all made differently and Fabiola is my thing. She's my dream girl.

The days we spent together at the G8 in Germany were probably the best of my life, even with that bitch Jax ruining everything. It was the first time I'd ever done anything like that. The summer of 2007, I'd just turned twenty-one and I'd never been abroad before.

I'd started going to meetings of the BAF, the Bristol Anarchist Federation, a few months before the summit and knew I'd found my place.

I was in the last year of my mental health nursing degree at UWE, which used to be Bristol Poly, and I was spending a lot of time working shifts at the hospital.

Getting involved and seeing the true situation from inside made me more and more angry every day; funding had been slashed, the system was systematically failing the weak and the vulnerable and, as for 'care in the community', it was clearly a load of bollocks dreamt up by the accountants. I knew, even then, that things were going to get worse, rather than better. So much for progress.

It's not like I grew up in a political household, my dad might have talked politics, but not at home. He was either at work or down the club every night and we never saw him. My mum was a floating shadow, a church mouse with the volume cranked right down, and this amazing ability to silently materialise next to you, or behind you, wherever you were and whatever you were doing. Maybe she had her own thoughts and opinions but she'd never dare express them.

As I got my hands dirtier at work, literally and metaphorically, I realised I needed, and still need, to stand up, to take part and to do something to try to make a difference, rather than simply lounge around and watch society go down the tube. The BAF gave me a way to do that. The members weren't exactly normal, but there were plenty of people like me who only wanted a place where they could try to make their voices heard, to speak up for all of those people who couldn't speak up for themselves.

We were a mixed bunch, and at the other end of the spectrum were the hard-core anarchists who, to be honest, could probably have been soldiers or mercenaries if the wind had been blowing in a different direction when they were making their life choices. They had plenty of self-righteous passion but you could see in their eyes that it was violence and destruction they craved. The politics was an excuse, a circular, cast-iron justification for any extreme behaviour.

Some of them were very scary and would have fitted in well at some of the more secure hospitals I was starting to work in.

When I heard that the BAF was organising a protest trip to the G8 summit in Heiligendamm, I was one of the first to sign up. The idea of the leaders of these eight – or seven, depending on whether Russia was behaving itself – countries sitting together in a posh hotel and deciding what should happen to the whole world was plain wrong. I mean, it was like we were still in the Dark Ages. Going to the G8 summit to remind them that not everyone saw things the same way was exactly what I needed.

I signed up for the trip to Germany before Fabiola joined the BAF, but Jax had already been a member for a year or so. I knew I didn't like her from the start – she was always such a smart-arse alpha bitch and seemed to enjoy putting people down – but there were about fifty of us going, in two battered coaches and I didn't expect to see too much of her.

Fabiola appeared on a rainy Wednesday evening in early May, less than a month before we were due to leave. A couple of mates from her course at uni were already members and had persuaded her to come along. We were mostly a dull, drab bunch and then Fabiola walked in and lit up the room.

It was like the girl in the red coat in that Spielberg Holocaust film, everything else is shades of grey and black, and there is this one bright figure moving through the scene, standing out in sharp contrast. Although, come to think of it, it's a rubbish comparison because that girl was there as a symbol of horror and tragedy and there was nothing of that in the way Fabiola shone as she came in.

It's always the same for me when I talk to her, talk about her or even think about her. I wish I was a poet or writer, someone who could dip a hand into their mind, take out a handful of golden corn and, flicking their wrist like an old farmer, spread it evenly onto the page. I manage to get tongue-tied and stammer even in my own head and am guaranteed to say the wrong, clumsy thing when I'm speaking out loud.

Another thing I love about Fabiola is that, in spite of my

consistent, fumbling oafishness when we're together, she's always been nice to me. She sat next to me at that first meeting and, out of everyone there, she decided to speak to me first.

'Hi, I'm Fabiola. Sorry about the name. It's Italian.'

'Hi, I'm Darren. Most people call me Daz though. Like the soap powder.'

She laughed, a rich, deep laugh. 'Cleans whiter than white then? Nice to meet you Daz. Have you been coming here for a while?'

'Not so long,' I said. 'Only for a couple of months. It's a great group.'

We stepped quickly through the repetitive dance of where we came from, who studied what and where and how come we'd ended up where we were. By luck, my mouth was on autopilot as the rest of me was being consumed from inside out by Odin's lightning strike, or had I been cracked on the skull by Thor's hammer. Whichever one, it certainly wasn't a little arrow prick from some poncy Greek cherub. I suspect that, when I wasn't speaking, my mouth was hanging open like a village idiot. Luckily the first speaker rescued me.

I expect the guest presenters were talking passionately about important and interesting topics but I only heard white noise as I stared fixedly ahead, every part of my body tingling with the sense of her presence, scant inches away. God, I had it bad. What an idiot.

When the talk was over, the club president reminded everyone about the trip to Germany and I felt the electric touch of Fabiola's fingers on my shoulder.

'Are you going, Daz?' she said. 'What do you think about it?'

I turned to her, fighting to keep my voice under control. 'Yeah, I'm going. I signed up straight away. I think it'll be brilliant and everyone says there'll be loads of us there from all over the world. You've got to do something, haven't you?'

'I guess so, but it's all quite new to me, even though I am studying politics. Have you been on lots of protests then?'

'No,' I replied. 'This will be my first. It's all pretty new to me too and I can't really afford it, but I knew straight away that I needed to go.'

'I'm very tempted,' she said. 'Maybe we could meet for a coffee in town tomorrow, or on Friday, and you can tell me a bit more. Would that be OK?'

Of course it would be fucking OK. I mean, how OK does OK need to be for fuck's sake?

'Yeah, sure,' I replied as calmly as possible. 'Tell me when and where.'

We agreed to meet at the Boston Tea Party on Park Street at eleven the next day and she stood up and put on her coat. Not even slightly red as it turned out.

'I have to run,' she said. 'Thanks for your company, Daz. It's been so nice to meet you. See you tomorrow.'

'You too, Fabiola. See you at eleven.'

And then she turned and walked through the door. I could swear that the room dimmed as she left.

After that first meeting and our coffee date, Fabiola decided to come to Germany and she signed up at the next BAF meeting. I introduced her to a few of the other more-sensible comrades who were going and she seemed to get on well enough with them. I can remember spending those weeks wandering around with such a fixed grin on my face that my cheeks actually started to ache.

We left from outside the university union in two knackered, old, white buses which had clearly had a former life doing school runs until they were considered too worn and manky even for that. I guess there is a natural evolutionary cycle in the life of a bus but it goes in reverse, starting with the higher strata of civilised coach tours and conference transfers, descending through club coach trips to daily school runs and eventually finding its way back to the primordial ooze of student trips like ours.

As it turned out, the thirty-six hour bus journey was a lot more comfortable than the five days we spent in the protest camp at Rostock where eighty thousand others were waiting for us. We arrived late in the afternoon, having walked the last four miles with our tents, packs and food and the atmosphere was incredible.

The camp was surprisingly well organised, considering this was all put together by a bunch of volunteer enthusiasts. There was a reception tent and even street names; the main street was Via Carlo Giuliani, after the young antiglobalist killed in Genoa by carabinieri in 2001 and Rosa Luxemburg Avenue was where the Marxists were hanging out. We were in Durruti Boulevard, together with all of the other anarchists.

All incredibly well organised, considering ... The consequences of tens of thousands of protesters, mostly young and broke, living in the same space for several days were totally predictable: mud, rubbish, food waste, disgusting portaloos, even more disgusting makeshift latrines. It was a miracle we didn't all get dysentery.

It didn't seem to matter though as we were all fired up with the righteousness of what we were there for and a bit of discomfort was a small price to pay. It's amazing what a bit of quasi-religious fervour can achieve.

For the first couple of days of the protests Fabiola stuck to me like a limpet. I didn't mind the crowds or the growing stink and squalor – not so different from Reading festival and I'd been there every year since I was fourteen – but it was different for her.

It wasn't because she was posh, at least not by Bristol University standards, but she was classy and I got the impression that she'd led a pretty sheltered life until then. Whatever it was, she was definitely finding life in the camp hard, especially the way a large group of people can take on a life of its own, like it's a separate creature and we are just individual cells.

Mobs always have something exciting about them, you can see it at a footie match or a big stadium gig, but a major protest has something different, especially when there is a violent side and a lot of police. A network of invisible electric wires links everyone in the crowd and guides them to move backwards or forwards, left or right like a shapeless, but still intelligent, jellyfish, or one of those amazing black clouds of twilight starlings that you see on the wildlife programmes.

Once you're a part of the mob, you're hardwired into the larger being and you hand over the freedom to act on your own. You're forced to ebb and flow with the crowd.

Definitely exciting, but a bit terrifying, as people have become more and more independently minded and expect to have control over their lives. I was a bit different; I loved the feeling because I wasn't so desperately happy with myself as an individual and got a kick out of being part of something bigger, something which accepted me as me, with no criticism or snide put-downs. Anyone who's always been the last one picked for a team – any, and every, team – would understand how I felt.

Fabiola was different. She would always have been popular and loved. It showed in that easy smile and her gentle graceful movements. You could see how she would have grown up as a little, golden princess surrounded by admiring courtiers. Not so easy to give that over to the mob, to let that huge, gelatinous thing take control and lead you where it chose. Good news for me though, as I fell happily into the role of knight protector and spent more time with her than I could ever have hoped for. I like to think that was when we became real friends.

Rostock was definitely violent though, and I've never agreed with that. Some people said there were over four thousand in the 'black bloc', the mask-wearing, black-clad chaotics who seemed to enjoy violence as an end in itself and came armed with stones, Molotov cocktails and worse.

This time there was a much bigger problem to deal with than the few hundred who'd caused so much damage at previous summits in Prague and Seattle, and the police struggled from the start, despite all their armoured vehicles, tear gas and water cannons.

Those first two days passed in dream-like euphoria. I was doing something positive to help the world and this amazing, beautiful girl had picked me as her defender and companion against all of the odds. I suppose, if I'm honest, I did begin to allow myself to imagine our relationship could become something more, something bigger than just friends. What a moron!

Us Bristolians had a small area to ourselves in the camp with a bunch of girls' tents on one side and the boys on the other. Lady Luck had it in for me big time; she'd arranged it so that Fabiola was sharing a small two-man tent with Jax. I'd already decided Jax was not a nice person and the only saving grace was that she and Fabiola didn't seem to be hitting it off so well. They shared a tent but, apart from that, Jax was hanging out with her crowd and Fabiola with hers. And that was me.

It was on the morning of the third day when it all changed and it didn't take long for me to realise what an idiot I obviously was. Fabiola strolled up, gorgeous as ever, but now Jax was walking beside her, laughing and joking.

'Hi Daz,' said Fabiola. 'You know Jax don't you?'

'Morning. Yeah, I know Jax. Hi, how's it going?'

'I'm great thanks, Daz,' said Jax, smiling at me. 'Mind if I tag along with you guys today? My crew are up to something heavy and I don't think they want a newbie around.' It must have been the first time she'd ever looked at me, let alone smiled. Manipulative bitch!

'Sure, no problem,' I said. 'The more the merrier.'

And that was that. Our twosome became a threesome and, day-by-day, it became clearer that I was the spare – and redundant – prick at the wedding. Fabiola was blind to all of Jax's little tricks: the way she'd manage to find a way to stand between us, slick little twists in conversations to move me out of my comfort zone, a little touch here, a whisper there. It was nothing I could compete with.

I could see that Fabiola was hero-worshipping Jax from the start. I have no idea how Jax did it but was smart enough to know that trying to mess with people's heroes always ends badly, so I did what I've always done – kept quiet and made the best of it.

Looking back and thinking about that time, there was always something frightening about Jax. She had a magical power over people. Even though I'd never liked her, and was cursing her every minute of every day for coming between me and Fabiola, she could always turn that around with a look or a smile.

If she wanted to, she could make anybody feel like they were the most important person in the world, and get them to follow along with whatever she wanted. It wasn't a good experience. Jax could charm you against your will with her devil's charisma but, when she switched it off, she left you confused and blinking in a world of greyness.

Of course, I was only in that spotlight a few times, when I was needed for something. Once Jax had Fabiola in her sights, she kept her there all of the time and I could almost smell the smoke rising from the intensity of her charm offensive. Fabiola didn't stand a chance and there was nothing I could do.

On the day of the actual summit, we were with a group of five or ten thousand, mostly peaceful, demonstrators, part of a co-ordinated action to block the eastern gates of the summit hotel. This mob had an intelligent mind and knew what it was doing; a sea of rainbow flags gave the media the spectacle it was hoping for and we came prepared with waterproof tarpaulins to protect against the water cannons and sacks of straw to defend against police batons and to build barricades.

The demonstrators outnumbered the police maybe three to one and slowly moved forwards in a five-fingered formation, a gloved hand, towards the gates. The police could see the weakness of their positions, and were thrashing about with their batons, but we stayed strong and kept moving forwards, just like the salt protestors in the film Gandhi, shaming the police with our refusal to either back off, or to repay violence with violence.

The noise was incredible and the chaos seemed to go on for hours, but it was probably no longer than fifteen minutes before the police realised they had no chance and ran. We had won, the gates were blockaded and no-one was going to get in or out that way.

I can still remember the feeling of adrenaline-fueled elation rushing through me as I looked around and saw that we'd done it.

I remember even more clearly the way the feeling drained away when I realised Fabiola was nowhere to be seen. She and Jax must have split off into a different finger as we formed up. I wanted to share the moment of victory with her, but Jax had made sure that didn't happen.

She wanted Fabiola all to herself, whatever it took. Why couldn't Fabiola see that? Why couldn't she see what Jax was like?

After Fabiola moved to Oxford, I knew she wouldn't want people like me hanging around and ruining her new life, but I've still kept an eye on her. Not only to have a chance to see her but to make sure she's OK as well. I never let her see me though and I can only get enough time off work to be there every couple of weeks. Still it's better than nothing.

He seems all right, that Rupert bloke, but I don't like the look of his mother. Not sure why, but I don't trust her. Snooty, hard-faced bitch if you ask me. It looks like he's kind to Fabiola – which is what I care about most – but something's wrong and I can't put my finger on what it is.

On the face of it, everything is going well – new baby, husband, nice house – but she doesn't look happy at all. She looks scared.

I've seen that look a lot. Whenever we get a new patient on the ward, they've got the same look of disbelief. 'This isn't me. I'm not supposed to be here. There's nothing wrong with me. You've made some sort of mistake.'

It's the same look every time, but why would Fabiola have it? It doesn't make any sense.

A Clean Bill of Health

Mobile phone spy software allows the controller to bug conversations at will. Even with the phone switched off, it is possible to activate the microphone and record nearby speech. Times can be manually controlled or pre-set. Recordings are then forwarded to the hacker when the phone is next connected to WiFi and automatically deleted afterwards leaving no trace of the activity.
"How much is your Life Worth? Protecting your Identity in a Digital World."
JJ Martin, Insight Business Press 2015

This was my sixth, and hopefully final, visit to Deborah. I'd been coming once a week for an hour each time – with a break for Christmas and New Year – and, as I got to the door of her office, I realised a part of me was going to miss the sessions.

I had been so much better since I started. No more incidents and I was completely myself again, although I could still taste the fear and panic which had been eating away at me only a few weeks earlier. Even thinking about it made me tense up and start looking for an escape route, somewhere to run to, somewhere safe.

That was possibly the most debilitating part of the whole situation. My instincts screamed at me to flee, but you can't run from yourself and I had needed to find some way to push those feelings back down inside me, however strongly they were screaming at me to do something, and to do it fast.

It had been difficult to accept it was a part of me, that I had the potential to lose my grip on reality in that way. It put me somehow into a different category of human being. I wasn't an axe-wielding psychopath, but I had been suffering from a type of mental illness and, although it was objectively fairly mild, it hadn't felt mild to me.

There was such a lot of stigma attached to problems of the mind and I was the sort of person who would always have subconsciously seen mental fragility as a flaw, a weakness and something to pity. Definitely not something which could apply to me.

As with every previous session, Deborah didn't waste any time with social chit chat. She wasn't interested in me telling her how I was getting on, her approach was to follow along with various threads and themes across the sessions and to allow me to reveal my progress to her, and to myself, in the context of those evolving themes and unravelling threads. The most interesting revelation for me was the way in which I would so often be surprised by what I said and thought.

'How are things with Rupert?' she asked as I sat down. 'Are you having good sex again yet?'

This was a topic which we'd dipped in and out of several times already. Over the past few months, Rupert had taken on the role of carer and I'd found it difficult to see him as I had before. Our life hadn't been entirely celibate since Christmas, but I'd lost most of my passion and desire. I didn't really get turned on and ended up faking it more often than not, which made me feel awkward and uncomfortable. It wasn't only me and my mental state though, some of it was definitely coming from his struggle to deal with the way our relationship had changed.

'I think we're getting there,' I said, smiling at Deborah's now-familiar bluntness. 'We're both beginning to see the funny side of our hang-ups and the last two times we've made love it's been much more like it used to be.'

'Good. And the business with Jax and the police?'

'Rupert's still worried about that. He feels betrayed by me keeping those things secret and possibly a bit thick for not figuring them out for himself. He knew we were involved in political activism but chose to ignore it. Now he's been forced to face up to it, he doesn't understand what we were doing and why. It upsets him. To tell you the truth, looking back, it upsets me too. I can't quite see the person I was then as "me" if you know what I mean.'

'Of course I do, Fabiola. It's understandable and not so unusual. Lots of people have periods of their lives when they become fixated on a goal or a mission which appears to come from nowhere and can disappear just as quickly. These passions are often associated with a strong personal relationship with someone powerful and manipulative, often possessing an evangelical charisma of sorts. I think that was how you once described Jax to me?'

'Yes. That's exactly it.'

'It might be politics, it might be marathon running, but religion is probably the most common. It's also not at all unusual for people to feel disorientated, confused and disappointed when they look back on the relationship after it's over. Did the police ever contact you about Jax by the way?'

'No, but it's funny you should bring that up,' I said. 'I had a text from Rupert ten minutes before I got here and two police officers are coming around this evening to see me. I doubt it's a big deal though.'

'No, I'm sure it won't be. It might even represent some sort of closure for that time in your life.'

'Maybe?' I smiled. 'But that does sound like a bit like a bunch of psychobabble, doesn't it, Deborah?'

Deborah laughed, a deep throaty laugh. 'Fair enough, guilty as charged. It appears my work here is done. As far as I can tell, we've made some great progress and, everything else being equal, you stand a good chance of putting this behind you as a one-off experience. I'm recommending to your doctor that you carry on taking the fluoxetine for the next six months and we can have another session then to check everything's on track. Don't forget that one of the side effects can be reduced libido, so that may have an impact and, of course, if you have any more episodes like before, or panic attacks of any kind, you should go and see your GP straight away.'

I stood up and went over to give her a hug. 'Thank you Deborah. I do feel much better and I'm sure I'll be fine. I'm so grateful for your help.'

'You're very welcome Fabiola, it's been a pleasure.'

It was more like seven o'clock when we heard the knock at the door.

The police must go to special door-knocking school where they learn their technique for delivering a clear, sharp, not-to-be-ignored knock with the command and authority which is missing from an ordinary civilian knock. There was, of course, no point in mentioning the fact that we had a perfectly good doorbell.

There were two of them standing there. 'Good evening Mrs Blackwell, my name is DI Johnstone and this is my colleague, DI Simpson. We're sorry to disturb you so late. Is this a convenient time?'

'It's fine,' I said, standing back to let them pass. 'Please come in and sit down. My husband told me you'd be coming this evening.'

Another thing they must teach at police school is the perching-on-the-edge-of-the-sofa pose. Make sure you don't get too comfortable, you're on official business, after all. It didn't take long to get them suitably perched, each warming their fingers around a mug of hot tea.

They made quite a pair, DI Johnstone was early-forties, tall and composed of skinny, sharp angles, from his pointy elbows and knees to his perfect roman setsquare nose. In contrast, DI Simpson was a few years younger, curvy, petite and blonde and probably not much over five foot tall. She would never have got into the police in the bad old days before it was decided that height restrictions were discriminatory.

'So, what can I do for you?' I said.

DI Johnstone cut straight to the chase. He took a photo out of his bag and handed it to me. It was blurred and grainy, probably taken from a CCTV camera, but there was no doubt about who it was.

'Do you recognise this woman?' he asked.

'Yes, of course I do,' I replied. 'It's Jax Daniels. As I expect you already know, we lived together for almost five years until a couple of years ago.'

'Yes, we are aware of that. We're interested to know if you've got any idea of Ms Daniels' whereabouts, or any thoughts on how we might locate her?'

'No, sorry, I'm afraid I've not heard from her for almost two years. We didn't exactly part on good terms and, as far as I understand from mutual friends, she's disappeared.'

'Thank you,' he said, handing me another photograph. 'And what about this?' It was a photo of a dark-grey backpack next to a white, numbered card.

'Well, it looks like a daypack which I used to have, but I can't be sure from the photo and it was a pretty common brand. Loewe or something like that. I lost it years ago.'

'... And when was the last time you remember seeing it?'

'As far as I can remember, the last time was when Jax borrowed it on the day of the London TUC demonstration in 2011. She was wearing it when we were separated and didn't have it with her when she came back.'

'Did she say what had happened to it?'

'No. But she made a bit of a habit of borrowing and losing my stuff, so it wasn't a big deal.'

'OK,' he said. 'I'd like to come back to that in a minute if I may. Just one more.' A third photo was handed over and I could feel DI Simpson's gaze burning into the side of my face as I looked at it.

It was a picture of the same backpack with two old-fashioned light bulbs and a nasty looking folding knife resting on top. I looked up at DI Johnstone, still acutely aware of DI Simpson's intense scrutiny.

'It's two light bulbs and a knife. I'm sorry, what is it that you want to know?'

DI Simpson replied this time, and I turned to face her. 'This is what we found in the backpack. The light bulbs are filled with ammonia. We would like to know if you've ever seen them, or the knife, before.'

'No, of course not,' I replied. 'I think you'd better explain what's going on here.'

DI Johnstone took back the lead, 'We'll explain as much as we can,' he said. 'But, before we do, I'd like to go through what happened that day, to understand a bit more about your movements and those of Ms Daniels.'

Rupert was sitting next to me on the sofa and jumped into the conversation.

'Look, this is sounding a bit like an interrogation. Is my wife under suspicion of some sort? Should we be asking for a lawyer?' He turned to me. 'Are you OK with this darling?'

I gave his hand a squeeze. 'Yeah I'm fine, thanks.' I turned back to DI Johnstone. 'I'll tell you what I know but I hope you understand it was three years ago and I don't remember every detail.'

I went through the timeline of that day as accurately as I could, finishing with Jax coming in at five in the morning in a mess, but didn't mention the part where she asked me to promise to say we'd been together.

'That's about it, I'm afraid,' I said, once I'd finished. 'That's all I can remember. Now are you going to give me some idea of what this is all about?'

DI Johnstone shifted forward on the sofa. 'I'll share as much as I'm able to,' he said. 'But you have to understand, this is an ongoing investigation and there's a limit to how much I can say.'

Rupert and I both nodded, and he continued, almost reciting from a script like he was giving evidence in court, part pompous and part droning and dull.

'During the protest, I expect you know that a violent minority, a so-called 'black bloc', of about five hundred people were unusually active. There was property damage, random violence and they fought running battles with the police. We'd been under a lot of public pressure following the kettling containment strategy we'd used in previous demonstrations and were taking a deliberately low touch approach. In retrospect, it was a big mistake and we were unable to control the violence as the perpetrators were too spread out and fast moving. We were being led on a merry dance, as the saying goes.'

DI Simpson stood up and walked over to the window where she stood silently gazing out into the night.

'But it wasn't so merry,' said DI Johnstone, looking over at his partner. 'Thirty-one police officers were injured on the day, some seriously, and one officer in particular was hit in the face with an ammonia-filled light bulb. The injuries eventually resulted in him losing the sight of both eyes. All of this was widely reported at the time but what is not well known is that, twelve months later, that officer took his own life.'

'Oh my God,' I said, bringing my hand up to cover my mouth. 'How terrible. But you're not suggesting Jax was involved in that, are you?'

'I'm afraid that is exactly what we believe,' he said. 'Although the violent protesters were all masked, we have video evidence indicating that Ms Daniels was directly responsible for the attack, which appears to have been deliberate, planned and unprovoked. We found the backpack in some bins at the back of a Chinese restaurant in SoHo. As you could see in the photo, the backpack contained two more ammonia-filled light bulbs and a knife and had clearly been abandoned in a hurry. Unfortunately, we were unable to identify Ms Daniels until recently and, in fact, believe she was living under an assumed identity in any case.'

'What do you mean by 'assumed identity'?' I asked.

'It appears that her name and legal persona were built around the documentation of a child, Jacqueline Daniels, who died six weeks after birth in nineteen eighty-six. Among other things, we have evidence that a copy of the birth certificate of the deceased child was used to register for a social security number a little over ten years ago. The Jax Daniels who you knew never existed.'

I sat speechless and open-mouthed, desperately trying to think of examples or evidence which would show that they were mistaken. Facts, history, anything that would allow me to explain to them that it wasn't true. We had been together for such a long time, known each other inside out, shared everything, or so I had thought.

There must have been something but, hard as I tried, I couldn't find a single concrete fact. She'd claimed to have grown up in Uxbridge I thought, or was it Acton? How could I not know? I'd never met anyone from her family, not a single schoolfriend, I didn't even have an idea of where she went to school. I sat there like a lemon, not knowing what to say or think.

The sound of Sam crying had never been so welcome. I needed a couple of minutes of normality to get my thoughts in order. I changed his nappy and, when he was ready, paraded him around the room to say goodnight. When I put him back in his cot, he went back to sleep without a murmur. God, it must be so much simpler to be a one-year-old.

DI Simpson seemed to understand how stunned I was. She turned from her position by the window and walked over to me as I came back. Almost too close. 'Don't worry Mrs Blackwell, I am sure this all comes as a bit of a shock. I want to assure you that we have no reason to suspect you of being involved in this situation at all. Our video evidence backs up what you told us, so you shouldn't worry on that account.'

I could see she was upset. For whatever reason, this was personal.

'One thing I can assure you of however,' she said, each word filled with cold anger. Her blue-grey eyes were fixed on mine, hard and unblinking. 'This will not be dropped. We will find her and we will bring her to justice however long it takes.' Bubbly blonde and pocket-sized maybe, but the package came with a sharp edge. 'If you think of anything, however small it may appear, or hear from her, or about her, in any way, please call us on this number. In the meantime, be cautious. She is an extremely dangerous woman.'

And that was that. Half of my adult life, turned into a lie.

The End of the Beginning

A lot of hackers get their kicks from breaking down huge security walls. Leaving some anarchist propaganda on the Pentagon's website or pulling a bunch of correspondence from the GCHQ mainframe and publishing it online. That doesn't rattle my cage, and it's not what I'm best at either. I'm not a good enough programmer to deal with the heavy-duty corporate system security although, back in the day, I'd have been happy enough to break in and smash up the mainframe with a sledgehammer.

I'm much more about personal data security – that's what I do. I'm a personal online security consultant. I help my clients to protect their identities and, almost by definition, they tend to be wealthy, high profile and paranoid. I charge a lot for my time. When I'm not working, I like to ferret around and find holes in the system and tricks to exploit them. It's always been a hobby of mine and it keeps me on my toes.

After Fabiola left, I lost the plot for a while. It all seemed pointless without her and, in any case, I was bored with being an anarchist and I'd made a few mistakes which might be coming back to bite me.

It was time for Jax Daniels to disappear for good.

With a fresh identity in place, I started putting a lot more effort into my consulting work and I'm now making good money – over a hundred and fifty grand a year.

Meanwhile I still have my private project ...

... And phase one has come to a perfect end.

Fabiola – along with everyone around her – is convinced that all of her problems over the last six months were in her mind, the result of some sort of post-partum brain fart. That idiot counsellor has added a white coat seal of approval to everything; she's been professional, kind and supportive and has convinced Fabiola she did have mental issues but has responded well to treatment. It's such a load of bullshit.

Thank God I got the phone software loaded in time, those counselling sessions are hysterical and I've been playing them over and over. No-one suspects for a moment that anything sinister is going on. They've all decided that Fabiola has been imagining everything, the poor dear.

My favourite was the parking ticket. Such a small thing, but such a big impact.

I needed to be nearby to remove the ticket but it was easy to track her using the GPS on her new, compromised phone. I should probably have left straight away, but couldn't resist staying to watch what happened.

I'm so happy I did. For a moment or two, I thought she was actually going to break the steering wheel, she was hitting it so hard. And the little old lady coming to help was just priceless. You really couldn't make up stuff like this.

I didn't mind not being invited to the christening. Not especially. It was the last in a long series of rejections which, deep down, I did understand. Honestly I did.

Fabiola had a new life – new friends, new family – a much shinier, cleaner version of life. I understood why she wanted to distance herself from me, from the past. Our relationship wouldn't sit well in her new squeaky-clean world.

I get it. I'm not a fool. I can understand the whys and the wherefores, but – and I need to be absolutely clear here – understanding and forgiveness are two very different things in my world.

Until the child came along, I think I'd assumed that Fabiola would see the error of her ways and come back to me. I wouldn't have been too proud. I'd have taken her back. I'd have made her grovel first though, made her suffer for all the times she made me suffer.

But then I saw the smug grin she had on Facebook after it was born and, when I read those emails about the christening invitation list ...

Well, if she thought I was just going to sit here, hurting all of the time, watching them have a perfect time with their child, she obviously never knew me at all.

I went to the christening anyway, sat at the back of the church and made my own vow. I didn't have anything against the child, and I wasn't planning to hurt it, but I would break up their happy little family if it was the last thing I did.

It was quite ironic, I suppose. A bit like Sleeping Beauty. A christening curse from an evil fairy. I guess that would be me, then.

I didn't enjoy listening in to her conversation with the police so much. Traitorous bitch. So much for promises.

I'm not worried. They'll never catch me. I'm a bloody identity thief – if I can't hide, who can? I've got my new identity and I've broken contact with anyone who knew me as Jax.

The new 'me' died with both of her parents in a car crash, twenty-four years ago. She's five years younger than Jax and Jax was one year older than I actually am but I've always had that ageless 'gamine' look anyway. Let's face it, given the option, what girl wouldn't want to shave four years off her age overnight?

I'm no longer the sort of person who gets involved with protests and I look completely different. It only took a few – very expensive – cosmetic tweaks, but even my mother wouldn't recognise me now.

Jax Daniels was a great name though and I'll miss it. No more 'on the rocks' jokes for me.

Anyway, back to Fabiola who has been miraculously 'cured'. It's time to take a break and let everyone believe it's true.

If she has no more episodes for a year or so, she will relax and any nagging suspicions will fade. The human mind is so good at pushing dark episodes like this into its hidden recesses.

The dance isn't over though. Jax may no longer exist, but I will always remember.

I'm in this for the long game and when Fabiola has a relapse – as she will when I decide the time is right – everything will come flooding back.

It won't be so easy to control next time.

It Ain't Over 'til it's Over

Once an identity thief has control over the victim's email, phone communication and calendar, the opportunities for exploitation expand exponentially. If the right care is taken to delete traces, it is extremely difficult for the victim to see that their privacy has been compromised. The reasons why hackers are caught are, as with most other criminals, motive, greed and impatience. Where the motive is obscure and the criminal is in no hurry, they are unlikely to be identified.
"How much is your Life Worth? Protecting your Identity in a Digital World."
JJ Martin, Insight Business Press 2015

'He loves it. Thank you, Virginia. It's just perfect.'

Sam was concentrating hard on his pasta, making sure it didn't stick to the pan.

'Don't forget, Sam. *Tu sei Italiano*. The pasta must be perfectly al dente.'

'Va bene, mummy.' He looked up at me, still stirring furiously. 'It andenty. Look.'

I picked up two plastic bowls and held them out, 'Is it ready? Can I have some? What about some for Granny too?'

'OK,' he said with a big grin. 'It ready now.'

Sam's lips were scrunched up with intense concentration as he carefully filled two bowls with the spaghetti before spooning on the sauce. 'All gone,' he said eventually.

I handed Virginia her bowl and we both dutifully pretended to eat, making slurping noises and loudly praising the food and the perfect cooking of the spaghetti. Sam, however, had moved on to whatever he had in the oven and was no longer interested; we left him to it and joined Rupert and John on the patio where they were hoarding the champagne and smoked salmon blinis. The late spring sunshine was just high enough to climb over our neighbour's wall and warm up our garden, blossoms were everywhere, and it felt as though summer was right around the corner.

John was one of those men who didn't have much time for babies. I don't think he saw the point of them, but he'd begun to become much more engaged as Sam started to become a little person. When Virginia and I walked over, he was completely absorbed in watching Sam cooking away happily in his new kitchen and a big, proud granddad smile lit up his face.

'So, he likes it then?' he said. 'It looks as though he's well on his way to winning MasterChef already.'

'Yes, he's a little star,' I replied, picking up my glass. 'It's a brilliant present, thank you both. He's going to have so much fun with it.'

Winning Masterchef! I didn't understand why everything had to be so bloody competitive all of the time. Virginia was the same and Rupert not much better. I wasn't anti-competition as such, not someone who wanted to avoid sports days and ban ability streaming in schools, but there should be limits and I wasn't convinced it was necessary for every single activity in life to be part of a Darwinian challenge.

Luckily for Sam, I was his mum and, if I had anything to do with it, he'd learn to keep all of these things in perspective. That being said, I did have every intention of making sure Sam learnt to make the best Italian food in Oxford before I was done with him. I'd always felt that a small dose of hypocrisy never hurt anyone.

'I'd like to propose a toast,' said Rupert, with a little cough. 'Well, actually, two toasts. The first one is obvious. Happy second birthday, Sam. It's been a great year and here's hoping the next one will be even better.'

'Happy birthday, Sam. Cheers.' We all lifted our glasses in his direction, but he was totally oblivious to the wave of well-wishing, and much more concerned with how he was going to fit his fire engine into the oven.

Rupert continued, turning to his parents. 'The second toast is equally important and I wanted to say how lovely it is to have you so close by and to thank you for all of your help and support over the past two years. To family!'

He was clearly relieved that his parents had got the birthday present right as relationships, especially with Virginia, were still strained. Something had changed during the dark period which I'd been through after Sam was born. I'd been back to normal for over a year but there was still a carefulness between us which persisted like a stubborn stain.

I couldn't put my finger on what was driving it, but I had this gut feeling I couldn't trust her, and I suspected she felt the same way about me. It made for an undercurrent of tension which was always tugging away beneath the oh-so-civilised surface.

Rupert's dad was OK, but he lived in such a different world that I never found spending time with him particularly relaxing either. We seemed to drift inexorably towards topics of conversation which were totally alien to me. Not only when he was ranting on about some amazing pheasant shoot he'd been on, or a clever acquisition which had made them squillions in fees. Even when we were on my home turf, politics, I soon realised there was no point in trying to open up a debate.

I suppose I was no more likely to agree with John's point of view than he was with mine, but at least I was always ready to revisit things and hear the pros and cons one more time. In any case, I was moderating some of my more extreme views now I was looking at the world from a mother's perspective.

It's easy enough, in theory at least, to fight for something which goes against your own interests if you believe you're fighting for a greater good. When you have children, however, it seems that you instantly lose the right or ability to do anything which is in conflict with their interests. We think we're so sophisticated, civilised and intelligent but we're not so different from most animals when push comes to shove.

John was politically informed in his own way but stunningly intransigent. The only slight chink in his armour had been during the 2014 election when a few of his shooting friends had started supporting Nigel Farage and UKIP. That was a step too far for John and, in the process of distancing himself from them, he was forced to challenge some of his own dogmatic beliefs – especially on immigration.

It was only a momentary chink in his armour, however, and it didn't take long to close that up. A tweak here, a tweak there, tighten a few straps of self-justification and everything was back as it should be.

Still, he wasn't a bad man and we're all made from different cloth. I probably needed to be a bit more tolerant and accepting. Something to work on going forward.

'So, Fabiola. You've got yourself a job, I hear?' he said. 'Back to publishing?'

'Yes,' I replied. 'I'm going to be an assistant editor at Oxford University Press. It's the same job I applied for a year and a half ago, back when ... well, you remember?'

'Yes, of course I do, but it's water under the bridge isn't it? No point in dwelling on the past. My mother always used to say you should never waste your time on things you can't control, and let's face it you can't control the past, can you?'

'Your mother was a wise lady by the sounds of it, although choosing what to worry about is often easier said than done,' I said with a smile.

'When do you start?'

'I start in two weeks. I'll be working three days a week to begin with – for the first six months or so – and then we'll see.'

'That sounds wonderful,' said John. 'And Sam's off to school?'

'Well, I'd hardly call it school. We've managed to get him a place at this wonderful little Montessori nursery in Summertown. We were very lucky as they'd had a cancellation on the day we went in to visit, and the whole set-up is perfect for him. I think it's a great opportunity for him to have a chance to play more with kids of his own age.'

Virginia had been talking quietly to Rupert in the corner, but I wasn't slightly surprised her bat-ears had picked up on our conversation.

'Of course, it's totally unnecessary, darling,' she said, stepping towards us. 'I've told Fabiola and Rupert a hundred times I'd be happy to look after Sam rather than sending him off to be with strangers all day. The poor little thing's only two years old, after all ... and it's so expensive.'

This was a familiar subject and, as on previous occasions, I resisted pointing out that a few hours a day of healthy play and socialising at a Montessori nursery was somewhat less traumatic than being sent away to boarding school for months at a time.

Rupert had been packed off to board full-time at some place in Hampshire a few weeks before his seventh birthday and, even when he came back to Oxford to go to St Edwards, he'd still been a full-time boarder, including weekends. This was despite the fact that his family home was less than ten miles away from the school. Another conversation which wasn't worth having, but Sam would be going to boarding school over my dead body.

'Come on, Mummy,' said Rupert. 'We've been over this a million times. We both really appreciate how kind you are to offer to help even more than you already do, but we think it'll be a good experience for him.'

'But he's only a baby, darling,' said Virginia.

'He's two years old. There'll probably be a few tears to begin with, but he'll get over those and then he'll have a great time. You've been to see the school. Tell Dad what a lovely place it is.'

'Well,' said Virginia. 'I must admit that it did seem to be clean and well run but ...'

'No need for 'buts',' said Rupert. 'He starts next week and I'm sure he'll be fine.'

Rupert's parents stayed on for another hour or so until Sam went down for his nap, but I continued to be annoyed with Virginia until well after they'd gone.

'Can she never, ever drop anything?' I said to Rupert. 'Thanks for stepping in, but it's unbelievable how she can go on and on about things. Has she always been like this?'

'Sorry, 'fraid so,' he said. 'I did warn you.'

'I know you did, but she's way worse than you said she was. I seriously think she's hoping Sam doesn't get on at nursery, so she can charge in on a bloody white horse and save the day ... And then tell us we should've listened to her in the first place.'

'That's probably taking it a tad far, don't you think?' said Rupert, cheeks flushing vermillion. 'I mean she's doing her best. She's actually been very helpful and anyway there's a limit to how much you get to lay into my mother without pissing me off.'

'Fair enough, sweetie pie,' I slumped down on the sofa. 'I didn't mean to go on about it. I'm tired, and I guess I'm a little stressed about sending him off myself, not to mention starting work the week after.'

The Lighting of a Fire

Most modern smartphone spyware can set filters and automatic flags to respond to pre-programmed actions of interest. These may be notifications when the victim is near a particular location, automatic diversion of specified incoming phone calls or setting recordings to be activated in certain places. This focus avoids excessive battery consumption, which is the only real risk the software might be detected.
"How much is your Life Worth? Protecting your Identity in a Digital World."
JJ Martin, Insight Business Press 2015

Sam was on excellent form as we walked down to the nursery. As his speech developed and he began to build up a real vocabulary, he'd developed the habit of standing still before any serious pronouncement and putting on his most serious face.

He would then lift one hand up, index finger pointing skyward like a Roman senator in the forum, before sharing his few words of wisdom with us. Invariably, we'd only manage to hold serious faces for a few seconds before bursting into laughter. Like almost all two-year-old games, it could be repeated ad infinitum and, to be fair, was funny every time.

The slight issue was that the frequent oratorical stops meant slow progress down the street and eventually, we had to find an acceptable distraction. So, after about fifty 'one, two, three, wheeee' swings, we'd arrived at the gates. It was lucky Rupert had taken the morning off, as one-parent swinging just doesn't stack up.

We weren't too worried about him fitting in at nursery. He'd been to a few playgroups over the past year and, when it wasn't raining, we went to a nearby playground where he had a few little friends of the same age. I suspect we were more worried about how we'd feel as we walked away for the first time. He was still so small.

The cloakroom inside the main door was a scene of complete chaos; twenty or so tiny children were running about randomly or sitting on the floor, some crying, some laughing, most shouting at the tops of their voices. In the midst of this were almost twice the number of giant parents, trying to help or to get out of the way, all of this without treading on one of the small bodies which were spread out everywhere.

It didn't take us long to change Sam's shoes and put his bag into a locker. We managed to escape without treading on anybody's children and went inside to his new classroom. His age group were red squirrels and there was a huge, bright-red squirrel painted onto the classroom door. Five or six children were already inside with the teacher and I knelt down in front of him.

'Sam. Mummy and Daddy have to go to see the headmistress, Mrs Stanton, and sign some papers ... Will you be OK? ... We'll be back in five minutes.'

'OK Mummy,' he said, before striding into the room. He stopped after three or four paces, half turned and lifted his hand in a half wave. 'Bye Mummy. Bye Daddy,' he said, before turning again and running to join the others.

Rupert looked at me with a big grin. 'I think he'll be OK,' he said.

Mrs Stanton stood as she saw us and quickly ushered us into the office. 'Mr and Mrs Blackwell, I'm surprised to see you both here today. Can I help in some way?'

Rupert and I looked at each other and I could tell he was as confused as I was. 'Good morning, Mrs Stanton,' he said. 'Isn't it usual for the children's fathers to come along on their first day? It is a big deal for us both after all.'

'No, no, it's not that, Mr Blackwell. It's just ... just ... well, I wasn't expecting to see either of you here today.'

'Why on earth not?' my voice was trembling. 'It is the first day of term, isn't it?' Surely I couldn't have got the date wrong.

'Yes, it is. Of course it is. But, as you cancelled your son's place last week ...'

'You did what?' said Rupert, turning to me.

'I did nothing of the sort,' I said to Mrs Stanton. 'I have no idea what you're talking about.'

'But I had an email from you last Wednesday,' she replied. 'Apologising for the late notice, and explaining why Sam wouldn't be able to join us this year.'

'I'm sorry. There must be some mistake,' I said. 'I didn't send any email.'

'I can assure you that we did receive an email, Mrs Blackwell and we replied straight away. We have copies in your file but, in any case, as you know, we spoke on the phone.'

'What? No we didn't.' I had no idea what was going on. 'We've not spoken since the time I visited with Sam's grandmother, about three weeks ago.'

'But I called you, Mrs Blackwell,' she said, her firm, schoolmistress authority brooking no interruption. 'I spoke to you on Friday afternoon. You told me that you didn't think your son was ready and asked us to defer the place until next year. You must remember. It was only three days ago?'

'No. No. We didn't speak,' I said.

'We most certainly did,' she continued. 'I explained why I couldn't give you a guarantee, but that I would be able to put you at the top of the waiting list for the three to four year-old entry.'

Before I could reply, Rupert jumped in. 'I'm sorry, but I'm totally confused. We had a confirmed place for Sam and we've already paid for the first term, haven't we?'

'Yes. And normally the payment would not be refundable as you cancelled at such short notice. I discussed this with your wife, however, and we agreed that, as we had several people on the waiting list, we would exceptionally make a full refund in your case.'

The nightmare was starting again, my heart was pounding, two iron hands slowly tightening around my throat as I struggled to get my words out. 'But I didn't send any email and we didn't speak on the phone.' I was flicking my gaze between the two of them and felt myself stepping up and back, out of my body, so I could look down on them both together.

They were staring at me with frightened eyes like two rabbits transfixed in car headlights. Why were they frightened? I was the one who couldn't breathe. This was happening to me. This was my nightmare.

'Are you all right, Mrs Blackwell?'

'Fabi, what's wrong? Come and sit down. Let me help you.' Rupert's strong arms around me were warm and comforting, but I still couldn't breathe and was certain I was having a heart attack.

'Water,' I croaked out. 'Please, water.'

I stayed in my disembodied state for almost an hour afterwards, watching everything from above but still aware of the stabbing pain in my chest and my struggles to breathe. I managed to tell Rupert about the chest pains and he rushed me out to the car, leaving Mrs Stanton promising to make sure Sam was looked after until we got back.

By the time we got to A&E at the John Radcliffe, the pain had receded but, as I was presenting with acute chest symptoms, they rushed me straight through and I sat in a dismal, white curtained cubby hole for forty minutes while a string of doctors and nurses came in and out, alternating between asking questions and poking, prodding and palpitating.

Eventually a nurse took me back out to the waiting room where I could see Rupert perched on the edge of his seat, slumping forward with his hands clasped behind his head. He looked alone and miserable. I walked up to him and tapped him on the shoulder.

'Fabi,' he cried out, leaping to his feet and wrapping his arms around me. 'Are you all right? Was it a heart attack?'

'I'm fine, darling. Apparently it was only a panic attack. I'm sorry, I feel like such an idiot. I seriously thought it was my heart this time. It was much, much worse than last year.'

'It doesn't matter, cara mia. As long as you're OK, nothing matters.'

'You are the sweetest man,' I said, kissing him. 'I really don't deserve you.'

The doctor had prescribed me some strong sedatives, but only for a couple of days and had told me I needed to see my GP straight away. After collecting these, we drove straight home.

On the way back, Rupert explained that he had arranged for his mother to collect Sam from the nursery and to have him for a sleepover, so there was no stress and I would have time to recover.

I had almost forgotten about the nursery debacle what with the fear, fuss and kerfuffle of being whisked off to hospital, but it didn't take long for the whole nightmare to come flooding back and for me to realise that my problems were by no means over.

In fact, they were just beginning.

When we got home, Rupert refused to talk about any of it and insisted I went straight to bed. I didn't think there was any way I would sleep with all of the half-formed, flashing images which were tumbling around in my mind but, whether it was the exhaustion from the panic attack, the sedatives or simply the safe feeling of being tucked up in my own bed by Rupert, I was out for the count in minutes and slept for fourteen hours straight.

By the time I surfaced the following morning, breakfast was ready laid on the table – a big fruit salad, fresh orange juice and a pot of green tea. Rupert had taken another day off work and had been busy. I wondered again what I had done to deserve someone like him but had a moment of doubt when I thought about how much I depended on him; as household provider, father to Sam, lover, confidant and the only real friend I had left. Was that healthy?

Breakfast was only the beginning. Like all men who've been clever, good boys, he was eager to share all of his achievements.

'OK, Fabi, I've been busy and things aren't so bad. Shall I tell you?'

I sat down, poured myself a cup of tea and managed half a smile. 'Go ahead. It seems I'm in invalid mode again, so I might as well stick with the programme.'

'Yes, that's a good plan. It won't last, so enjoy it while you can.' Rupert sat down opposite me and plonked an A4 pad onto the table. 'Right, well, first of all, you've got an appointment to see Dr Mayhew at eleven-thirty.'

'Wow. Not easy to get on two hours notice.'

'True, but I was persuasive.'

'I'm impressed. So what else have you done that's so amazingly clever?'

'I spoke to Mrs Stanton and she's agreed to put Sam top of the list for next term. It's ninety-nine per cent certain he'll have a place at the beginning of September.'

'Oh my God. That is incredible. After yesterday's performance, I'm surprised she wants anything to do with us, or rather with me. I suppose you've checked the emails?'

Rupert lifted his head from his papers. 'Yes. And the call history on your phone. I'm afraid it all matches with what Mrs Stanton said, but I don't want you to worry about that right now. Let's just focus on getting you well. I was so scared yesterday. I thought I was going to lose you.'

'Well, the way I'm going, you'd all be better off without me anyway,' I said, looking deep into the brown whirlpool of my tea. I could feel my voice cracking as the memories rushed in. 'I can't believe this is happening again. I was so sure it was all over.'

Rupert pulled his chair next to mine and took hold of my hands. 'Don't be an idiot,' he said. 'We wouldn't know what to do without you. You know that. Anyway, the last bit of the puzzle is that my mother's agreed to look after Sam until September while you're at work and I'll be back in time to help in the evenings. That way you'll be able to relax and concentrate on finding your way in the new job.'

I couldn't hold back the tears any longer and buried my face into his shoulder, squeezing him close with all my strength.

'Thank you, darling,' I sobbed. 'Thank you.'

I wasn't tempted to say what was lurking at the back of my mind, which was that Virginia had got what she wanted after all. No surprises there.

Rupert hadn't quite finished. 'One more thing. I know you're keen to start the new job and we could certainly use the money, but you have to promise me that your health will come first. If the GP says you should wait, you have to listen. OK?'

'OK, va bene, caro. Prometto che.'

The Slippery Slope

The power of knowing where someone is, and where they're going to be in the future, cannot be underestimated. It allows the hacker to know when it is safe to break into a home or office or alternatively to plan ahead, to lie in wait for the victim, and to spy on them directly.
"How much is your Life Worth? Protecting your Identity in a Digital World."
JJ Martin, Insight Business Press 2015

I'd always thought that "absence makes the heart grow fonder" was a ridiculous cliché but, for any young parent experiencing their first days back at work, it hits the nail clean on the head. Having completed three days at my new job, I found myself loving every moment of my first full day back at home with Sam.

My attention and focus had shifted – turned about somehow – so that I was able to concentrate on enjoying all of the little amusements and pleasures being with a young child can provide, rather than merely surviving the onslaught of demands and counting the hours until bedtime and wine o'clock. The contrast probably wouldn't continue to be as bright as this, but it was great while it lasted.

Being back in an office had been a shock to the system, but I would get over that soon enough and, after what had happened a year earlier, and again the previous week, I was amazed and grateful to have finally made it back to the real world. I'd become more and more certain that everything was conspiring against me to ensure I would never get there.

Following my terrifying panic attack and the whole nursery business, I'd assumed starting work was out of the question. If something like that could happen to me out of the blue, how could I expect to hold down a responsible job?

This time, it had been more than a simple mistake or trick of my imagination – there was some other secret, hidden person inside of me, writing emails and making phone calls on my behalf.

Unless it wasn't a person inside of me, but was actually someone else? A real person who was trying to drive me insane, like in that old black-and-white film. I couldn't imagine who would do that, or for that matter, why and how? Virginia was the only possible candidate. She definitely had it in for me. But it was a ridiculous idea; thinking crazy, paranoid thoughts wasn't going to help me in any way.

I'd been expecting my GP to prescribe a strict regime of rest and isolation, to warn against taking on any potentially stressful responsibilities and certainly to advise against starting a new job after almost three years out of the market.

I suppose I needed to accept that my judgement was always going to be wrong. Dr Mayhew had been kind and sympathetic but didn't seem particularly worried. She'd said it was not unusual to have a relapse of the kind of symptoms which I'd experienced before, but there was no reason to assume that it was anything other than an isolated incident for the time being.

With everything so fresh and raw in my mind, I hadn't been so convinced it was a one-off but, when the person in authority was telling you what you want to hear, there seemed to be little point in arguing the toss. Dr Mayhew booked me a follow-up appointment for two weeks later, upped my dose of Fluoxetine and that was that.

Rupert was being incredible as always, his strong arms holding everything together, but Virginia seemed even colder and more distant. I could see the almost-physical effort she needed to avoid saying 'I told you so' and her smug martyr act – as she took up her burden of helping us out by looking after Sam – was so rammed full of hypocrisy, it almost made me scream.

It did get us out of a bind though. A bind which was entirely of my creation, so I understood I needed to button up and use my lips for polite, grateful smiles instead of screams, regardless of what I thought or felt inside. Saying anything to Rupert was out of the question; he was even more defensive of his mother than usual, and completely blind to the way she manipulated everybody to get her own way.

Luckily I had a friend in my diary. It didn't answer back, judge me or make me feel guilty when I let rip with my honest feelings and frustrations. Even there, I was a bit conflicted and needed to put my feelings in context. Virginia often made me uncontrollably angry, and I knew she really was a self-centred cow, but I was grateful for the help. I'd needed to get back a small slice of normal life, and I wouldn't have been able to do it without her.

Why did everything need to be so bloody complicated?

Dr Mayhew had been much too relaxed about my situation and I could only see two possible explanations. Either she was simply out of her depth or she was underplaying everything to keep me calm. Was she talking to Rupert behind my back? I would need to keep my eyes and ears open.

She had mentioned one thing which was new and different; she'd suggested I join some sort of self-help group, either online or actually face-to-face. There were a number of links to official monitored groups on the health service website as well as a load of private groups on Facebook.

Her advice was that they all had their own strengths and weaknesses and I should try a few before deciding which one was right.

I opened a thread in one of the first groups I stumbled upon and realised that it wasn't going to be easy:

Sara: 24-04-2016 : 23:17 (new therapist)

Change is hard. My T is retiring around the end of this month. 7 years w/him. the Transition has been a main topic during T for a couple of months.

I didn't think it was going to be a big deal. But I had my first real spike of fear this weekend, listening to inside talking, while doing the dishes. I suddenly remembered T is going and BAM.

I think he'll be relieved actually. My T, I mean. He's been worried that I don't seem to be expressing attachment.

Apart from the fact that I didn't have any idea what she was talking about, there was something deeply disturbing in the cold, disinterested tone of her posting. I trusted Dr Mayhew's advice, but I wasn't one of these people.

They weren't all as bad as that one, but most of the forums were still very strange places to be; alien worlds with disembodied voices talking in their own language and code: acronyms and labels; lists of drugs; things that worked; things that didn't work (more often); sad, hopeless life stories of abuse and neglect and, inevitably, soppy, dippy images of calm, tranquil places tagged with upbeat, greeting-card messages of hope and happiness.

This wasn't me. These people were really ill and many of their stories were heartbreaking. It wasn't me but, like lowbrow reality TV, I felt a voyeuristic compulsion to know more about many of these characters.

I spent hour after hour trawling through discussion after discussion and, with a bit of focus and translation, I slowly came to realise that, behind the strangeness, many of the posters were actually ordinary people with real medical issues. Not aliens or raving psychopaths after all.

I told Rupert what I was doing but everything about the subject made him mumble excuses and look at the floor so I didn't get a chance to go into details. I suppose the normal 'me' would have been even more uncomfortable and cynical than he was, but by then I was desperate and prepared to try anything.

Signing up as a member of a group was a big step – for starters, was the group really as confidential as promised? – but the private forums were apparently much more interesting and I wanted to get involved and see where it took me.

Fabi: 17-05-2016 : 11:30 (memory lapses)

Hi everybody. First time, so please bear with me.

I've been suffering with memory 'glitches' for over a year. I see things which aren't there or do things without remembering I've done them – nothing huge (yet!) but always self-destructive in some way.

I went to a counsellor a year ago and it seemed to have got better, but now it's back with a vengeance and I just had a pretty horrible panic attack.

My GP doesn't seem too bothered and no-one in my family is able to help, but I have a little boy of two and am worried about him.
What should I do?

John: 18-05-2016 : 06:47 (memory lapses)
Sounds a bit like Dissociative Identity Disorder (DID) to me. Do you ever feel like there's someone else inside you? Most people with DID have lots of different 'parts' but not all. I've only got one other and she only appears from time to time. When she does, I always need to clear up some sort of mess after her.
I am always looking over my shoulder and haven't been able to trust anyone for years. It makes life almost impossible for me sometimes.
Have you spoken to a therapist?

Fabi: 18-05-2016 : 11:34 (memory lapses)
Thanks John. That sounds a bit more extreme than what I'm going through, but I'll do a bit more digging.
I do sometimes feel there's an evil spirit inside me doing these things, but I think it's just me trying to explain what's going on.
Your situation sounds terrible. Good luck.

'Come on Sam,' I said. 'Let's get you in the car and we can go and look at the ducks.'

I'd been back at work for a two and a half weeks and was beginning to settle in to what was not a particularly challenging job. It was one rung down from my previous role as Senior Assistant Editor in London, and the pace of life at Oxford University Press was a bit more 'measured' than it had been at my old publisher. Perfect for now, and there would be time enough to move into roles with more responsibility in the future.

Chatting on the forums seemed to help as well; maybe Dr Mayhew was more on the case than I'd given her credit for. It was a great release to be able to talk anonymously about my fears.

I texted Rupert to let him know where we were going. He'd asked me to promise to tell him my plans whenever I was going out with

Sam. I wasn't comfortable with the idea, but agreed on the proviso that it was only for a few weeks.

Rupert wanted us to give his mother a present to thank her for all of the help she'd been giving us, and I'd agreed to go up to the Aga shop in Woodstock to buy her a stupidly expensive cast-iron frying pan.

I felt good as we left the house. Sam was smiling and happy and I allowed myself to imagine things might be coming good after all. Dangerous thoughts and very premature. Speaking too soon could easily jinx things and I reflexively crossed my fingers and made the sign of the horns to ward off the evil eye.

Growing up, my mother had been a firm believer in *il malocchio* and always wore a gold horn around her neck to ward off the bad luck. Perhaps I should have taken those superstitions more seriously?

It was only a short drive to Woodstock – I would get the frying pan and then Sam and I were going for a long walk in the grounds of Blenheim Palace. Blenheim is one of those glorious stately homes with beautiful, landscaped parkland sloping gently down to a huge lake. Sam loved ducks, or kak-kaks as he called them.

Parking in Woodstock was always tight, but I was lucky and found a place straight away. Once Sam was tucked up nice and warm in his pushchair, I bought a parking ticket, put it in the car and took a photo of it on the dashboard for good measure.

We were only a few yards away from the car when the alarm started, the over-loud, incessant scream tearing apart the tranquillity of the town and setting my teeth on edge. I fumbled the key out of my handbag, unlocked the car, locked it again, and waited a few seconds. It seemed to be OK.

But, after only a couple more paces, the bloody thing went off again. I couldn't believe it. There always seemed to be something going wrong. Maybe I'd left one of the windows open. I checked carefully, opened and closed the boot and locked it again. Hopefully that would solve it.

I turned back to Sam, ready to get on with the day, but the pavement was empty.

The pushchair wasn't there.

'No, no, noooo ...' I wailed as I ran towards the spot where he'd been – not more than ten feet away – and looked frantically up and down the street. Nothing.

There was nobody in sight and I didn't know which way to go. He had to be somewhere nearby.

I ran into Barclays bank, pushed aside the customer at the counter and put my face to the teller's window.

'Have you seen a black pushchair with a little boy? Just a few moments ago,' I said, begging and praying with all of my heart.

'I'm afraid not,' said the woman behind the glass. 'Is there a problem, do you want me to call the ...'

I was already out of the door and running back down the street.

The Post Office was only a few yards away and I barged in just as I had at Barclays, pushing in front of an elderly lady who was being served by a young, serious-looking man behind the counter.

I looked at the man, panting and probably looking like a crazy woman. 'Excuse me. Have you seen a black pushchair with a two-year-old?'

'Yes, I have. He's in the back,' he said. 'I'm so pleased to see you.'

My heart leapt like a young salmon and the breath left my lungs in a whoosh. 'Really! Oh my God, I'm so relieved. How did he get here?'

'Someone brought him in a few minutes ago. They said they'd found him abandoned on the street. I've just called the police.'

'Can you get him please.'

'Of course,' said the man.

Sam was still strapped into the pushchair, confused and sobbing. Luckily, he hadn't had time to get into a proper state. He saw me, lifted his arms and shouted 'Mama'. I picked him up and squeezed him as tightly as I could. 'Oh, Sammy. I was so frightened. I didn't know where you were.'

The man coughed theatrically. 'Excuse me. How do I actually know you're the baby's mother? This is all a little unusual.'

'Of course I'm his bloody mother,' I said. 'Isn't it obvious?'

'Well, you do look like you might be, but maybe it would be better if we wait for the police to come anyway? Just in case.'

I didn't have time for this jobs-worth idiocy. I only wanted to hold my little boy. 'Whatever,' I said, holding Sam out in front of me and smothering him with wet kisses as he wriggled and giggled. 'Do whatever you need to do.'

By the time the police arrived, Sam was calmly tucking into a packet of banana biscotti, but I had worked myself up into quite a state. This was too much. I knew I hadn't imagined it. Someone had grabbed Sam while my back was turned and wheeled him into the post office. I couldn't think why, but something was going on, and this time I'd be able to prove it.

The policewoman couldn't have been much more than twenty-one – policegirl would have been more like it – but she seemed competent enough.

Having established the basic facts, she turned to the clerk. 'So, what exactly is the problem?' she said, clearly still confused.

'I didn't want to hand over the baby to this lady without some sort of proof that she was his real mother,' he said.

'Don't be so bloody ridiculous,' I said.

She turned to me. 'Please calm down and watch your language, madam. Are you the boy's mother?'

I took a deep breath. 'Yes, of course I am. Look there must be a way I can prove it. I have my driving license.'

She took it from me and wrote down my name and address carefully with precise, pianist's fingers. 'Thank you, but you see, that doesn't actually prove that ...'

The elderly lady was still there. She stepped between us and looked at me. 'Do you have any photographs, dear? Ones with you both together?' she said.

'Of course. I've got hundreds on my phone. Look ...'

The policewoman took the phone and scrolled though the photos, smiling at the cutest ones. 'That all seems in order,' she said. 'That's proof enough for me.' She turned to leave.

'Hang on,' I said. 'Someone grabbed my baby from the street

while my back was turned. And that's it? That's all you're going to do?'

I must have been shouting as all three of them took a step backwards.

The policewoman turned back to me with a weary expression on her face. She'd clearly met people like me before. 'I see,' she said. 'You're saying that someone grabbed your baby, wheeled him ten yards into the post office and left him? Why would anyone do that?'

'I don't know why,' I said. 'But it wasn't me. Surely there must be CCTV that can show who brought him in?'

The policewoman turned to the clerk with a questioning eyebrow raised.

'Of course there is,' he said. 'But we don't need it.'

'Why not?' I snapped, fed up with being pushed around and not taken seriously.

'Because I can tell you who brought the pushchair in,' said the clerk. 'It was Trevor Eames, the landlord at the Lamb and Flag. He said he found it just outside the door.'

Cry for help

A research study was carried out by Manchester University in 2013 on the subject of online security and password use. The results were startling. According to the study, 45% of people use only one password (unchanged for over a year) and a staggering 95% of people use three passwords or less (unchanged for over two years). By breaking the security of the weakest sites used by the victim, a hacker will normally gain full access to the most secure.
"How much is your Life Worth? Protecting your Identity in a Digital World."
JJ Martin, Insight Business Press 2015

'What the fuck is this?' Rupert was waving his phone at me like a crazy man as he stomped into the house.

'Daddy, Daddy, Daddy.' Sam had heard the door open and was piling down the hallway like a train, arms stretched up and forward. He crashed into Rupert who scooped him up and threw him into the air. 'Daddy, come see what I make. Come see.'

'OK Sammy, I'm coming.' He put Sam down and allowed himself to be dragged through into the living room. 'Let's go and see what you've made.' As he passed me, he handed me his phone with a scowl. 'I really don't know what you're trying to do, Fabi. One of my mother's friends saw this first and shared it with her. What's wrong with you?'

I had no idea what he was talking about and stood there, shocked, for a few seconds before looking at the phone. It was open to my Facebook page and a posting which I'd apparently made earlier that afternoon.

> *'Anyone interested in joining a local support group in the Oxford area for anxiety and depression?*
> *I need a place where I can talk to like-minded people who know what*

I'm going through – to share our thoughts and feelings and help each other to cope.

I've set up a members-only group at https://www.facebook.com/ ADSG-Oxford. If it's not for you, please share with anyone you think might want to join.'

It was on my page but I'd not been on Facebook for a couple of days. I'd thought about setting up a local group, but I hadn't done anything about it.

My finger hovered over the link. Whatever was behind it must be terrible.

There was only one post:

Admin 17-05-2016 14:47

Welcome to the Oxford Anxiety and Depression Support Group. I am hoping this will be a place where people with similar issues can share their thoughts and feelings openly and confidentially.

From a personal perspective, I need to talk to someone. I've been ill for almost two years now. I thought I was better, but I was wrong.

My husband tries his hardest, but he doesn't understand what I'm going through, and my mother-in-law is an interfering bitch who hates me. She's almost convinced my husband he shouldn't be leaving me alone with our son. How awful is that?

And I don't know whether I actually can be trusted with my son any more. I thought I'd lost him today. He was missing for fifteen minutes and I don't understand how it happened.

I don't only want to talk to doctors - I want to talk to people who actually UNDERSTAND!

I was still standing there minutes later when Rupert came back carrying Sam. 'It's way past your bedtime young man. Say goodnight to Mummy and give her a kiss.'

'Nigh-nigh Mummy,' said Sam, stretching forward to plant a wet slobber on my cheek. He thrust the book he was carrying at me. 'Toot-toot.'

'Nighty-night, little one,' I said. 'Is Daddy going to read Thomas for you?'

'Yeah, toot-toot,' he replied, and disappeared into his room.

Rupert must have been reading to Sam for at least twenty minutes but it was all a blank to me. When he came back, I still hadn't moved, hadn't thought; for all I knew, I hadn't taken a single breath while he was away.

He was good at compartmentalising. I guess it came with working in sales. He'd been calm and gentle as he dealt with Sam but was instantly just as furious as he'd been half an hour earlier. Maybe more so.

'Are you telling me you didn't do this?' His red, angry face pushing into my personal space snapped me out of my trance quickly enough. I'd never seen him like this.

'Of course I didn't fucking do it. I'm not fucking crazy.'

'Well, you've had your moments ...'

'You bastard, what's that supposed to mean?'

'I mean you've got a lot of history, this is *your* Facebook page and the group is registered to *your* account.'

'But I didn't ...'

'... And you can't stand my mother and, let's face it, this is exactly the sort of thing you would write if you thought no-one would see it ... And what's this about almost losing Sam?'

'I was going to tell you about that tonight. I just haven't had a chance because you've been shouting at me since you came through the door.'

'So it's true then,' he said, shoulders slumped and arms hanging lifeless by his sides. 'And I have to find out on Facebook?'

'If you give me a chance I can explain. It turned out not to be a problem. Everything's fine. You know I'd never let anything happen to him.'

'I don't know what the hell I know and don't know any more,' he said, looking like he was about to burst into tears. 'And I certainly don't know why I should trust you about anything.'

'You can trust me. This wasn't me. Someone is out to get me.'

'Don't start with that ridiculous, paranoid crap,' said Rupert. 'I thought this was all in the past but now it's much worse than before. You know what my mother's like. She'll see it as a direct personal attack and she's already worried about Sam.'

'What the fuck has he got to do with her,' I screamed. 'He's our son, for Christ's sake ... But, anyway, it wasn't me.' I was crying now, proper Oscar-winner tears running down my cheeks. 'If you don't believe me, then I haven't got anybody who will.'

'I want to believe you, but I'm struggling and I've already got two missed calls from Mummy.'

'Mummy? For Christ's sake, Rupert, you're not six years old. Can't you call her Mum like a normal person? She's still got her claws in up to the quick hasn't she?'

'You're upset, and I'm not rising to that. And keep your bloody voice down or you'll wake Sam. Look, it's easy enough to find out.'

He reached over, picked up my phone and held it in front of me so I could see what he was doing. He then started selecting options, giving me a running commentary in a slow voice as if he was talking to Sam. 'If you go to Facebook and pick Settings from the main menu, then Security Settings, you can select Active Sessions. This tells you which devices have logged on to your account, when and where. When was the post made?'

I still had Rupert's phone in my hand, open at the offending post. 'It was at 15:15 today.'

'OK, let's see,' said Rupert. 'Facebook for iPhone on iPhone5 ... that matches your phone ... last posting at 15:15 at ... give me a sec, I just need to put this into Maps ... here we go. It says that the session was active somewhere on the Banbury Road, right here ...'

He showed me the phone with the map location and he must have seen how my shoulders sagged. He definitely noticed when his phone slipped through my numb fingers and clattered onto the hard tiles.

'Jeezus. That's a bloody new phone. What's wrong with you?' he shouted, bending to pick it up. 'So, you were there?'

'Well, it looks like the cafe I go to, and yes, I was there this afternoon. But I didn't ... You've got to believe me. It must have been someone else.'

'So, someone else went there at the same time and made the posts pretending to be you, did they?' He slammed his phone down on the counter, walked to the French windows and stood facing out into the garden. I could see his shoulders rising and falling and his angry exhalations misting the glass. He turned around slowly, staring at me with red, swollen eyes. 'Do you have any idea how crazy you're sounding? Apart from anything else, how would anyone know you were going to be there?'

'I don't know and I don't bloody care Rupert. I didn't sit in the cafe, enjoying my machiatto and quietly creating a stupid Facebook group which will most probably ruin my life.'

It was only then that I noticed Sam, standing by the door, bottom lip quivering 'Mummy,' he said. 'I scared.'

The rest of the evening passed in the kind of fuzzy blur which anyone who has had an exceptionally high fever, or dabbled in the wrong sort of drugs, would probably understand. Although aware of everything going on around me, I had become disengaged, distant and doll-like in my passive compliance.

Rupert put Sam back to bed and then started to work on deleting the post – which was continuing to attract comments, shares and likes – and closing the group, which already had over a hundred member requests.

I almost didn't recognise my husband as I watched him tap away, his frowning face twitching with frustration and anger while he struggled with impenetrable menus and options. Meanwhile I sat in a bubble of defensive disbelief, having lost the will and energy to defend myself or argue my case. I was increasingly feeling like a bit-part player in my own life.

Apparently, closing a group in Facebook is not easy and even removing a post can be tricky. The history always stays and, if you're not careful, the original post resurfaces after a while.

Rupert did the best he could as a first step and then poured himself a large whisky before calling his mother. I only heard one end of the call, but it wasn't difficult to fill in the gaps.

'Mummy, it's me ...'

'...'

'Yes, I know you've called five times. I needed to speak to Fabiola, put Sam to bed and get that awful post deleted from Facebook first.

I'm sorry ...'

'...'

'No, Fabiola says it wasn't her. She didn't do it ...'

'...'

'Yes, I know it was on her Facebook account, but she says someone must have hacked it. And it's not true that she doesn't like you ...'

'...'

'Yes, apparently there was some incident with Sam today. I'm trying to find out what actually happened ...'

It went on for half an hour and got worse and worse. I was hoping Rupert would continue to defend me and take my side but, in the face of what was bound to have been a biblical onslaught, his resistance crumbled and I heard my future unfold in half-heard, half-imagined snippets.

History was being written for me and, even protected by my bubble, my heart sank down and down as I realised no-one else was ever going to believe me and, even worse, they might all have a point.

'...'

'Yes, I'm sure it wasn't intentional. I don't know exactly what happened but of course she's grateful for everything you've done to help. We both are ...'

'...'

'Yes, I promise. I'll make sure she gets an appointment straight away. No, no. Sam's fine. Look, don't worry Mummy, I'm dealing with it.'

'So, everything sorted then?' I said, after long, silent seconds had stretched into minutes. 'Are you going to tell me what I'm supposed to do next? Or maybe you'll send me an email?'

'There's no need to be so bloody sarky, Fabiola.' I'd never seen Rupert stay angry for so long. 'I'm trying to sort your mess out – again – and I'm getting pretty fed up with it.'

'Well, how do you expect me to feel? I'm sitting here listening to you and bloody Mummy decide everything between you. It's my fucking life you're discussing and it's like I'm not even here.'

'That's absolute bollocks and you know it. I'm doing the best I can and you're not the only person involved in this mess, you know?'

'So you didn't just promise your mother I'd go back to the shrink then?'

'Well, yes I did.' At least Rupert looked slightly sheepish. 'But you're not going to disagree are you?'

'Probably not. I have to do something, but it's got fuck all to do with your mother what I do. It wouldn't surprise me if she's behind everything anyway.'

'Don't be ridiculous,' said Rupert.

'Is it so ridiculous? She always wanted to spend more time looking after Sam, and now she's got what she wanted. And she never liked me. Not from the start. I'm not good enough for her little Roopie.'

'Are you serious?' Rupert screeched. 'Are you saying my mother is some sort of witch who's making you do things you don't want to? Or maybe poisoning your tea to make you crazy?'

'I don't know,' I said, my voice now flat and emotionless. 'Are you going to deny she's getting what she wanted?'

'Of course I am. I hate this paranoia. It terrifies me. It makes me afraid you took too much of the wrong sort of wacky baccy or whatever when you were in London.'

'Wacky baccy?' I said with a sneer. 'You really are a straight-arsed plonker sometimes, aren't you?' I'd had enough of being pushed around. 'I mean, seriously, no-one's used the phrase wacky baccy since Bill Clinton didn't inhale in 1968.'

Rupert hated to be reminded of what a conventional, sheltered upbringing he'd had and, when we first started going out, he always used to rabbit on about how boring I must find him. Like most couples we knew each other's weaknesses well, and I was set on going for the jugular.

He was still struggling apoplectically to splutter out some sort of retort, so I ploughed on. 'Have you ever actually *done* anything, Roopie dear? Taken any sort of risk? Lived even a little bit?'

There was a long silence as we stared at each other, neither willing to break the gaze.

'Well, it seems I took a pretty big risk on you, doesn't it?' Rupert didn't sound angry any more and I knew he was close to tears. 'How would you say that's working out for me?'

And at that, he turned and walked out.

Mother-in-law's Tongue

Phone bugging software isn't always used by malicious hackers. The majority of purchases are legitimate and over 65% are made by concerned family members. Not only worried parents and suspicious spouses, but also the children of aged parents and dementia sufferers. Research indicates that 85% of subjects are unaware of the software's installation.
"How much is your Life Worth? Protecting your Identity in a Digital World".
JJ Martin, Insight Business Press 2015

I wasn't childish and pig-headed enough to refuse to go to a counsellor simply because Virginia had insisted that I did, but it did cross my mind more than once. I was finding it more and more difficult to resist channeling my fear and frustration into anger; it felt better and Virginia was such a good target.

The reality was that I had no choice about going back to a counsellor. I'd known in my gut that the mess with the nursery shouldn't have been brushed under the carpet so easily. Mistakes and misunderstandings are one thing, but the situation had moved beyond that.

The cold and terrifying reality was that I was capable of doing or saying things without any awareness, or knowledge, of my actions. The fact that these random acts of semi-conscious, sleepwalking, zombie behaviour were, step-by-step, sabotaging everything which I loved or cared about made it doubly terrifying.

Rupert's dramatic storming out after our fight a few days earlier had been short-lived; he came back after five minutes but then didn't speak to me or attempt any kind of reconciliation. He just took a pillow and a duvet and settled onto the sofa for the night. It was only later that I figured out why.

In different circumstances, he probably would have gone out for a few drinks and crashed at a mate's house to make sure I fully understood how upset he was. The only reason why he had come back was because he didn't trust me to look after Sam.

Could I blame him? Did I still trust myself? The possibility that I might not was too awful to contemplate. Sam was my constant. He needed me without question, judgement or qualification, and that need was the anchor which was holding me in place while everything around me was being swept away. Having him gave me the strength to weather the storms which were threatening to rip me away into dark waters where wild eddies and tugging undertows were waiting. Without him, I would have nothing.

I called Deborah the morning after the Facebook fiasco and we talked for ten minutes on the phone. She was disappointed that my problems had recurred and told me she was surprised by what had happened. She also made it clear that she no longer believed she was the right person to help me; she would speak to a couple of friends and colleagues, but suspected I should probably be seeing a psychiatrist rather than a counsellor.

I was disappointed and the idea of starting from scratch again filled me with dread. On the other hand, she was giving me advice which went against her own financial interests so I had to assume she was being objective and professional.

And it appeared that I needed all of the help I could get.

'Good morning, Mrs Blackwell,' said Dr Mayhew. 'Please, take a seat.'

It had taken three days to get an appointment with my GP; meanwhile there had been no sign of the ice in Rupert's heart melting. I was lonely and desperate and struggling to contain the rage which boiled inside me from morning to night.

'Good morning, Dr Mayhew,' I said.

'I listened to your phone message,' she said. 'I understand there have been more problems since your panic attack at the nursery?'

'Yes. That's right. Much worse and it's now caused a huge divide in our family. Rupert is barely speaking to me and, as for my mother-in-law ...'

'That's such a shame. I was hoping it would be an isolated relapse.'

'No such luck. I actually lost Sam for a few minutes in Woodstock. I have no idea how it happened and I know I'm not a bad mother, but that's shaken me more than anything else.'

'Have you spoken to your counsellor?'

'I spoke to her a couple of days ago, but she said she couldn't help me and that I probably need to see a psychiatrist. I don't care what it is. I need some way of resolving this. I'm not sure how much longer I can cope.'

'Are you still at work?'

'No. I lasted three weeks – which was great – and then everything fell apart again. I've been on sick leave since Monday.'

'Well, for starters, I think you need to take some more time off. I'll write you a note. In retrospect, it seems likely that it was a mistake for you to go back to work. Trying to juggle too many balls at the same time inevitably creates additional stress.'

'But it didn't feel like a mistake and I felt less stressed at work rather than more. I'll be leaving them completely in the lurch. They'll have to fire me.'

'You mustn't worry about that,' she said. 'You need to focus on yourself for now. And, in any case, they can't fire you. It's illegal.'

'OK. I'll try, but it's easier said than done. What about me? What can I do to make this stop?'

'I agree with Deborah. There seem to be some serious underlying issues here which need to be addressed. I know a psychiatrist at the John Radcliffe who's very good. He's a bit stuffy, but he's worked wonders with a couple of my patients. I'll write you a referral.'

'Thank you. Do you have any idea how long it'll take to get an appointment.'

'I can't say until I've spoken to him, but I'll stress the fact that it's urgent, and you should hopefully get something in the next couple of weeks.'

'Two weeks! That's a long time. What am I going to do until then?'

'If we can get you in that quickly, it will be a great result. He's a busy man, I'm afraid. Like all of us these days.'

'Yes. I do understand. I'm sorry. I just need to do something to make this stop.'

'Of course you do. I'll do my best but, in the meantime, you should get as much rest as possible and try to avoid stress.'

Dr Alastair Pettigrew had an office at the John Radcliffe hospital and that set the scene for a sea change in the way I thought of my illness. No-one likes hospitals; there's something about the way they involve a handing over of control which triggers a deep fear in all of us. Walking down those antiseptic, blue corridors did nothing to put me at ease.

As small children, we are happy to be thrown high into the air, never questioning our simple faith in our parents. They will be there to catch us. That's how the world works.

As we grow and mature, we develop a more complex and nuanced understanding of the world around us and many of us become wary of simple faith and blind trust. Hospitals and churches both expect that faith and trust and I found it difficult to force my feet over the threshold of either.

Dr Pettigrew seemed to be a pleasant enough man, and reminded me of a slightly remote father figure from the 1950s. I could imagine him sitting in his armchair – reserved for Father of course – horn-rimmed glasses on the mahogany side table next to a pipe, or maybe a small cigar, a serious, self-satisfied smile playing at the corners of his lips as he listened to Radio 3 or the Goon Show.

His initial goal seemed to be to let me talk – without comment or guidance – and I was ready. Following my collapse at the nursery, my thoughts had been corkscrewing inwards in spirals of despair and my mind was brim full.

I would have found it easier if the normal me had been able to see some evidence of my crazy self, but I couldn't remember anything. Even some sort of trace memory would have helped. Glistening tracks of snail slime clinging to the cracks in my memories – clues to the paths of my secret activities.

But I had nothing. Plenty of hard, incontrovertible evidence of my sins, but I still wanted to shout out that it wasn't me, that I would have known. A big part of my conscious mind continued to believe there was nothing wrong with me. Now, that was crazy.

Psychiatrists probably have to work hard to get most patients to open up. Not me. I talked almost non-stop for two hours. I talked until my throat was sore. Repeating myself of course, but each repetition dug a little deeper and stretched my mind around the patterns and themes which had now become my life.

The first and strongest was, perhaps unsurprisingly, my growing sense of loneliness and isolation. One subject but so many different elements: I had no contact with my family, my parents were dead and my brothers and sister wouldn't return my mails; the limited family which I did have through Rupert had never liked me and certainly didn't now; all of my friends had slipped through my fingers like so many grains of sand; the one true friend who remained, Rupert, appeared to have given up on me and who could blame him?

The common thread was obvious. I had been responsible for the breakdown and destruction of each of these relationships, but I had no idea why. Since I was a child, I'd always been lucky, healthy and surrounded by wonderful, kind and warm people. As I talked and talked, cycling through the litany of my broken relationships, I couldn't see any logic, no reason why I should have consistently been compelled to undo everything which made my life good.

Each individual element could easily be rationalised and explained away, but when they were all brought together, they formed a coherent narrative which was difficult to ignore and even harder to explain.

Dr Pettigrew sat and listened, his sole contribution the occasional scratch of pencil on paper and the clearing of his throat every few minutes. I remember thinking that the scene was only missing the lonely shlick-shlock swinging of a pendulum clock ticking away time, second by second.

It was only a few baby steps from talking about my loneliness to launching into a rambling exposition about the steady erosion of my sense of identity and self worth. I didn't know who I was any more and I didn't trust this stranger in my skin.

This, of course, led to the biggest fears of all, which floated underneath everything like a hidden armada of paralysing jellyfish. If I was capable of doing things without control or awareness, how long would it be before something I did, or said, actually harmed Sam. Leaving aside the damage my condition was doing to my relationship with Rupert, was my son at risk?

I could sense a change in dynamic when I started trying to explain my feelings about Sam. Dr Pettigrew sat forward on his chair and the pencil stopped its scratching. Maybe he'd only been doodling before.

'What makes you feel you might be a bad mother?' he asked, breaking his silence for the first time in half an hour.

'I don't think I am,' I said. 'But I don't think any of these things are actually happening to me either. Whatever I think though, they are happening. When I lost him the other day, it was only for a few minutes, but I don't have any memory of how it happened. That's what I was trying to say before. If I don't have any control of my own actions, how can I be sure about anything?'

'Well, we have to work on the assumption that we'll find a way to give you back full control of your actions. That's what we're here for. The problem is that it may take some time, and I'm worried about the stress these concerns are creating. Is it possible for you to arrange your daily schedule so there is always someone else around when you're with Sam?'

'So you think I should be worried? You're saying you agree that I might be a risk to my own son?'

'No, Fabiola,' he said. 'That's not what I'm saying. If you're going to get better, it's important that we try to limit your stress, and this is clearly causing you a lot of anxiety. If you can take away that element, it should allow you to relax more and to focus on becoming well.'

'I suppose that makes sense,' I said. 'I can probably arrange something in the short term, but how long do you think it'll take me to get past this?'

'I'm afraid I can't possibly say at this stage,' he told me. 'We've only just started and, as you've rightly identified, the fact that you have no memories at all of these episodes does potentially make things more complicated. You need to take a long-term view and to recognise that there's a possibility there may not be a cure as such. Lots of people lead perfectly normal, happy lives despite experiencing regular lapses of this nature. It's not as difficult as you might think to build a coping structure into your daily routine and, as long as the episodes remain infrequent, they don't have to make such a difference to your regular life.'

'You mean I might always be like this? For ever?'

'I'm saying it's a possibility which we need to consider, but it's not the end result which we hope to achieve. For now, you need to be patient, I'm afraid. We'll know much more after a few more appointments.'

Fortunately, we were coming to the end of the session as I didn't feel up to talking more about this Domesday scenario. He'd glossed over the real conclusions but they were clear enough to me; it would be better if I wasn't alone with Sam, and there was a possibility I would never totally recover.

Rupert would remain a carer and, as Sam grew up, he would start to become one as well. What sort of life would that be? For any of us?

On my way home, I wondered why I hadn't shared my more morbid thoughts with the good doctor.

A long-term, active member of one of my self-help forums had recently committed suicide – the site was full of condolence messages – and I couldn't help wondering if Jude was in a better place now. A majority of the messages seemed tinged with envy and someone had started a specific thread on the subject.

> ... *Anyone else jealous of Jude? It must be amazing to be free. She had the courage.*
>
> *Yeah. Easy to talk about. Not easy to do.*
>
> *If I ever get there, I pray I have her strength.*
>
> *If you're gonna do it, you've got to do it properly. Have a look at this*

website to see why.

OMG. I never knew that. Terrifying.

Yeah. I don't think I'll ever have the guts, but if I do, I'm not going to do half a job. I know how I'll do it and I've got everything ready ...

I'd followed the link and quickly fallen into an amazing world of websites dedicated to people whose lives were in crisis.

Even though Rupert and Sam would probably have been better off without me, I wasn't seriously considering anything drastic. That didn't stop me spending hours trawling through the reams of content; the websites were detailed, diverse and strangely compelling. They ranged from esoteric Plath-analysing sanctuaries for teenage girls' angst to the unbelievably practical.

My initial reaction was that it should be illegal to discuss suicide in public like that. Surely offering advice on the various methods and selling kits online was wrong?

Most of the sites had links to support organisations, but not all of them, and the matter-of-fact way some websites acted as impartial DIY manuals for taking your own life shocked me deeply. Who wrote all of this stuff? Why?

There were even suicide websites devoted to Catholics. Of course suicide was a sin against God but apparently the official Church line was more nuanced:

Grave psychological disturbances, anguish or grave fear of hardship, suffering or torture can diminish the responsibility of the one committing suicide ... We should not despair of the eternal salvation of persons who have taken their own lives. By ways known to him alone, God can provide the opportunity for salutary repentance. The Church prays for persons who have taken their own lives.

Well, no-one ever told me there were get-out clauses when I was being taught the rules. They certainly kept that quiet. But the internet exposes everything, however obscure.

In any case, I wasn't serious about any of this. I simply found it strangely comforting to realise there were many people out there who were struggling profoundly with the ultimate question.

If I wasn't serious, why hadn't I mentioned any of this to Dr Pettigrew? I made a mental note to make sure that I did at the start of our next session.

Virginia and Sam had made a chocolate cake while I was out seeing Dr Pettigrew and Sam was very proud of himself. He'd laid the small table for four people – a place for Daddy when he got home from work – and he was being extremely sweet. If I didn't know better, I would have sworn he was being deliberately kind to me, that he understood I was in a fragile state and was trying to help. Surely a two-and-a-bit-year-old couldn't behave like that?

My relationship with Virginia was beyond repair. There hadn't been much warmth between us even before the Facebook posting and now it was gone for ever. In a way, it was easier and more honest to stick to formal social interaction rather than pretending we actually liked each other. Sam would probably notice as he grew up, but it wasn't the end of the world.

I'd found my session with the psychiatrist draining; it was completely different from the counselling which I'd had before. Apart from anything else, the consultation had lasted two hours which was a long time to be in the spotlight. In addition, Dr Pettigrew seemed to have no desire or interest to support me or to be my friend. It may have been partly a difference in personality, but I knew in my heart that the goalposts had moved.

I was no longer seeing a kind professional who would help me through a difficult period. I was now seeing a medical doctor who would cure me of an illness. There was no value in a soft bedside manner; what were important now were symptoms, diagnosis and treatment.

Dr Pettigrew had known how exhausted I would be and had recommended I go to bed before seven o'clock. He'd also given me some strong sleeping pills in case I needed them. I noticed he had only prescribed two pills. I hadn't shared my deepest fears with him, but was he worried about me anyway?

I desperately wanted to wait until Rupert came home before I went to sleep. I'd hardly seen him since our fight and, although I'd apologised for the things I'd said, he was still distant and I was fighting dark, terrible thoughts. Had something become permanently broken in our relationship? Had I lost him as well?

I held on until six-thirty but, after my chin dropped for the third time and I almost knocked over my teacup, I gave in.

'I can't stay awake, Virginia.' I said. 'I'm sorry, but I think I should put myself to bed.'

'Don't worry,' she said. 'We'll be fine until Daddy gets home, won't we Sammy?'

'Yeah Granny,' said Sam, pointing at the TV. 'Pat?'

'Yes, I'm sure we can watch a little Postman Pat,' she said. 'Say night-night to Mummy.'

'Nigh-nigh mummy,' he said, running over to give me a big hug and a kiss.

I woke in the dark. Suddenly. The transition to consciousness wasn't gentle and gradual. One moment I was in a deep, exhausted sleep and an instant later I was fully awake, pumped full of adrenalin, my nerve ends singing.

I was confused for a few panicky moments; I didn't know where I was or how I'd got there. A moment of genuine terror, but it faded quickly and, as reality pieced itself together around me, I heard the gentle rumbling of voices out in the garden. It was Virginia and Rupert and they were arguing about something while trying in vain to keep their voices low.

The luminous numbers on the alarm clock told me I'd only been asleep for three hours. Not nearly enough. I would need to take one of the sleeping pills. Where had I left them?

I didn't want to interrupt Virginia and Rupert and fumbled around blindly on the dressing table trying to find the pills. The voices were becoming clearer and I couldn't help overhearing what they were saying.

'Do you have any idea what you're suggesting?' said Rupert.

'Of course I do,' replied Virginia. 'I'm not a bloody idiot.'

'Can you imagine what that would do to Fabiola?'

'It would be terrible. But you must think of little Sam. What would you do if something happened to him? You'd never forgive yourself.'

'Nothing's going to happen to Sam. Fabiola loves him more than anything.'

'Of course she does, but how can you be so confident? I know you love her, but I worry it's making you blind. Surely the call from social services must have shaken you up.'

I gasped and covered my mouth with my hand. That bloody police woman at the post office.

'You know it did. But taking Sam away from her? It would kill her.'

'You do exaggerate sometimes, Rupert. There are ways to arrange these things so that it doesn't end up being so awful. I've asked your father to talk to a couple of his QC friends about it.'

'You've done what?' said Rupert. 'Mum, you can't just stomp around in our lives like this without consulting us.'

I could see them clearly through the bedroom window and couldn't believe what I was hearing. Were they seriously conspiring to take Sam away from me?

'I'm sorry but I do think she might be dangerous,' Virginia said, with no intention of backing off. 'She's clearly got some sort of mental illness and I'm not sure you can afford to wait until her new shrink comes up with something. You must do what's best for your son. Haven't you noticed what she's reading?' She picked up the copy of *The Bell Jar* which I'd left on the garden table. 'It's bloody Sylvia Plath, for Christ's sake.'

Rupert wouldn't have known who Sylvia Plath was if she'd dropped on his head from a great height, but it didn't take long for Virginia to share her interpretation of my reading choices.

Inevitably I'd been having a lot of dark thoughts since my world started to implode again, but I can't believe anyone would have been surprised by that. After everything that had happened, it was understandable that I would wonder about the point of it all, but it didn't mean I was going to do anything about it. It just helped to read about other people's thoughts and experiences and allowed me to feel a little less alone.

I'd been shocked when I saw the statistics about how likely most suicide methods were to fail and, worse than that, to fail painfully with long-term physical and mental damage. If I were ever going to do anything, I would do it properly. After all, the whole purpose would be to free Rupert and Sam, to give them a chance to live normal, happy lives without my illness dragging them down any further.

Listening to Virginia calmly trying to persuade her son to accept defeat, unpick his life, and take poor little Sam away from me was a revelation. Much as I'd learnt to despise her and everything she stood for, she had a point.

I was kidding myself. I wasn't going to get better and I might become much worse. What sort of life would that be for my two boys? They would never know what was around the corner. Every moment would be spent waiting for the next surprise.

... And the surprises would never be good.

Each realisation slid smoothly into place with an audible 'whoosh' and 'thunk' – well-oiled bolts slamming closed and sealing tight the gate between before and after. There was no going back.

My diary box was easy to find even though I was groping in the dark and, as I crept silently out to the bathroom, the rumbling voices from the garden faded to silence.

Perched on the edge of the bath, my knees a clumsy desk, I made one final entry in my diary. My mind was clear for the first time, and my decisions made, but I wasn't passive or complacent.

I didn't deserve this impossible choice and it filled me with rage. Was it God? Was it Fate? Whatever the reason, it wasn't fair!

My diary was now at an end, but I had one more bittersweet task.

I carefully tore out a single, blank sheet, laid it on top of the soft cover, and began to write. It didn't take me long – these were words which had been living in my mind for a long time.

I folded the paper over itself three times and tucked it safely inside the diary.

I was still thinking clearly as I walked into the living room.

Neither Rupert nor Virginia noticed me as I walked up to the

French doors and it was only as I pulled them closed and turned the key in the lock, that Rupert saw me.

My wraith-like reflection floated beside him in the garden as he took a step towards me, but I stopped him with a raised hand. I knew he understood as we stood there gazing at each other. That was important.

I'd convinced my conscious, rational self that I didn't have any intention of taking my own life but that didn't match with the preparations which I'd been making, almost subconsciously.

A part of me must have understood that I needed to be ready – just in case – and I had everything I needed packed carefully in a bag.

Looking down on Sam as he slept, I memorised every part of him, burning the image into my mind like a signet ring pressing into red, raw wax. It was all I had time for. I needed to go.

Strange Bedfellows

I'm standing in the shadow of a tree opposite Fabiola's house. I've been here on and off for four days now. Something's going on and it doesn't look good. As soon as I read her Facebook post, I knew there was a big problem.

I can't believe Fabi set up that group and wrote something so stupid. She wouldn't do that. I know it. I don't know why or how, but my gut's been screaming at me that Jax is behind this somewhere.

I only saw Jax once or twice in the weeks after Fabiola broke up with her, but I've never seen someone so totally possessed by anger and outrage. She won't have forgiven or forgotten. I'm sure of it.

Whatever the truth of it, I can see that Fabiola is desperate and is getting worse. I can't just stand by and leave her alone as she crumbles. I'd never be able to forgive myself.

A wedge of light stretches down the path as the front door opens. Fabi comes rushing out of the house, half-dressed, hair messed up and carrying an overnight bag. I know something is seriously wrong. It's after midnight and that witch of a mother-in-law is still there, cooking up some sort of evil no doubt.

Fabiola jumps in her car and pulls out into the road with a screech of tyres.

I have to do something, so I step out in front of the car, waving my arms. She sees me – I'm sure of it – but she keeps on going and knocks me flying across the bonnet of one of the parked cars. I'm thrown over onto the pavement and lie still for a few seconds checking to see if anything is broken. How could she do that to me?

She must be shocked by what she's done because she stops the car, looking back with one hand over her mouth, her wide, frightened eyes scanning back and forth. The moment she sees me stand up and start hobbling towards her, she turns and accelerates away.

I'm still in the middle of the street when Fabiola's husband, Rupert, comes running out of the house. He's clearly upset, out of breath and looking around wildly. He comes through the gate, stares at the spot where the car was and then looks up and sees me hunched over, still half-winded.

'Daz? What the fuck are you doing here?' he says. 'What happened? Where's Fabiola?'

'I tried to stop her, but she drove into me,' I say, trying to control my breathing. 'I've got no idea where she's gone. I only wanted to help.'

Rupert looks like he's about to hit me – which wouldn't be a smart choice as mental health nurses probably spend more time dealing with unarmed combat situations than the SAS – but controls himself with obvious effort.

'Why are you here?' he says after taking a few deep breaths. 'What are you doing hanging around outside our house again? You agreed to stop.'

'I know,' I reply. 'And I did stop coming like I promised ... But when I saw that Facebook post ... She couldn't have written that.'

'For fuck's sake,' says Rupert. 'More paranoia. This is all too crazy for me, but it'll have to wait. Which way did she go?'

I point down the street.

'I need to get after her,' says Rupert. 'She's not herself. Have you got a car?'

'No,' I say. 'I don't know how to drive. But what good's a car? You don't know where she's going.'

'I do actually,' he says, guilty eyes avoiding mine. ' I installed some of that nanny tracking software on her phone last week without telling her. I needed to be able to keep an eye on her.'

'Thank God,' I say. 'But now who's creepy? Let me help. Please.'

'All right. I need someone to follow the map anyway. We'll take my mum's car. Wait here and I'll get the keys. Don't go anywhere.'

Arranging things with his mother takes longer than it should and valuable minutes tick away before Rupert comes back out again. He doesn't say anything; he simply hands me an iPad and jumps into a black BMW, two cars along. I don't know a lot about cars, but it looks pricey.

'Fabiola's the blue dot,' he says as I get in. 'She's on the M40. Let me know when she turns off.'

I'm still getting my seat belt on as we reach the end of the street, skid round the corner and up the Woodstock Road. I've always had a problem with carsickness and, with the way Rupert's driving, keeping a fix on the blue dot is straining both my eyes and my stomach. By the time we get onto the M40 ourselves, the blue dot has already turned off and is on its way to Thame.

'I knew it,' Rupert mumbles under his breath when I tell him. 'She's going to bloody Bedford.'

'But she hates Bedford,' I say. 'Why would she go there? What are you not telling me?'

Rupert sits quietly for a while before speaking. The only sound is the Doppler whoosh as we shoot past late night lorries. 'I think she overheard some things she shouldn't have,' he says. 'And she might have taken them somewhat out of context.'

'What sort of things?'

'Just crazy things my mother was saying about Sam and whether Fabiola was in a fit state to look after him. Thoughtless things. She wasn't serious.'

'Oh Christ. And Fabiola heard that?'

'I don't know. We were out in the garden and I don't know how long she'd been listening. I only saw her as she closed the door and locked us outside.' Rupert's body is rigid, his hands are locked to the wheel and his breath is coming in short gasps. 'She stood there in front of the glass door looking at me with such a sad look on her face. I'm afraid she's planning to do something stupid.'

'You don't mean ... ?'

'Yes. I can't believe I'm saying this, but that's exactly what I mean.'

He takes his eyes off the road for a moment and looks at me. 'It was the way she looked at me. Like she was saying goodbye. She lifted one hand and then turned and walked away. I hope to God I'm wrong but we need to catch up with her.'

I Talk to God but the Sky is Empty

Wireless home networks generally use one of a few models of WiFi router which have a significant range. Most people don't have the knowledge or ability to reset the standard IP addresses, usernames and passwords but, even if they do, hacking these basic units is trivial. Cyber criminals frequently exploit innocent third-party's networks to hide their activity much like the use of disposable 'burner' phones by drug dealers.
"How much is your Life Worth? Protecting your Identity in a Digital World."
JJ Martin, Insight Business Press 2015

Daz took me completely by surprise. I needed to get in the car and away before Rupert figured a way to break through the garden door. I thought I was in the clear and then Daz appeared out of nowhere, standing in front of the car and waving his arms.

I didn't slow down. The noise as the car hit him and knocked him aside was dull and empty and I stopped breathing as he was thrown over the bonnet of a parked car like a doll. I couldn't drive off and leave him unconscious and so I stopped.

I was halfway out of the car to help him – who knows what could have happened? – when I saw him stand up and stumble towards me. I mouthed a silent prayer. He wasn't badly hurt and I was free to go.

Five minutes later, I was out of Oxford and away. My resolve sat beside me in the passenger seat and talked quietly and calmly for the whole drive. I hoped Rupert and Sam would understand my sacrifice and how right I was to make it. I wasn't running away or giving up on them. I was freeing them.

Until I heard Virginia talking, I'd never seriously considered going through with this, or at least that was what I'd told myself. For someone who wasn't serious, I had spent an awful lot of time and effort researching the subject.

It wasn't only the detailed comparisons of the different methods of actually going through with it, it was the amazing insight into why people made the choices which they did. And that was the biggest debate which tore through all of those websites like a bush fire. Could suicide ever be a free choice?

I knew where I stood. Of course, I didn't choose to suffer from mental illness but, as a rational person, I couldn't ignore the overwhelming facts which told me my mind was not completely under my control. There was also a cold, analytical part of me which knew with white-hot certainty that I wasn't going to get better and that the consequences of my illness would slowly destroy the people I loved most.

Maybe not a totally free choice, but not an irrational one and not one made while thigh deep in the swamps of black, sucking depression. I knew what I was going to do and I knew why.

I also knew how. After reading everything I could find, I'd decided helium was the best way. A well-sealed plastic bag, a supply of helium to replace the oxygen inside and it would be quick and painless. By using helium, the carbon dioxide ratios in the lungs wouldn't increase and my body's survival reflexes would be fooled.

I arrived in the car park of the Bell in Odell village. The pub had closed hours earlier and there was no-one around. I snatched up my bag and set off through the black-iron kissing gate at the far end of the car park. I think I would have been able to find my way even without the moonlight but it was easier with fate on my side.

As I stepped onto the footpath, I could hear the sound of my phone ringing from the car behind me. I would have given so much to be able to hear Rupert's voice once more but couldn't trust myself. My heart was melting already as I thought about how distraught he must be, but I needed to be strong.

The phone rang and rang again but with each step forward into the wood, the sound faded until, from one moment to the next, it was gone. After that, there was silence apart from the soft crunch of my feet cracking and crushing the twigs and leaves underfoot.

Nonno's Oak sat in the centre of the clearing as it had for almost a thousand years, regal in its squat permanence; the grace and beauty of youth now compressed into the solid, trustworthy girth of a beloved patriarch. Cold, clean moonbeams turned the dewdrops into quicksilver pearls which I crushed regretfully underfoot.

Spider cracks appeared in my resolve, spreading out with each misty breath. There was not much time.

I opened my bag and carefully laid out the contents. The smooth, metallic curves of the gas cylinder seemed alien and wrong as they sank into the soft, ink-black leaf mould. Everything was out of place and out of time. I checked to be certain nothing was missing and sat down.

My back pressed against the hard bark and I looked up through the branches to the black velvet mantle above. Although I wasn't ready to pray, there was still a chance God might spare me a little forgiveness and understanding. God, Rupert and Sam; I wanted their forgiveness but, most of all, I wanted them to look out for each other.

Hopefully, I would have the chance to make my peace with my father, my mother and Nonno face-to-face. Or not. I would know soon enough.

After one final eyes-squeezed-tight attempt to send a mental message though the night to Sam, it was time.

I was ready.

So Little Time

'She's stopped moving,' I say. 'Two minutes now. In the same place. She's in a village called Odell.'

'I know it. How long 'til we're there?' says Rupert.

'About twenty minutes. Take the next left in half a mile.'

'Call her,' he says. 'The number's under Fabi.'

I let it ring and ring until I hear her beautiful voice. 'Pronto, this is Fabiola. I can't get to the phone. Please leave a message.'

'There's no reply,' I say. 'I've tried six times, and I'm only getting voicemail.'

'Try again,' says Rupert, the rising panic in his voice matched by the engine scream as he throws the BMW into a succession of blind corners.

I try her again and again but I know no-one will pick up. 'She must've left the phone in the car,' I say. 'It still hasn't moved and she's not answering.'

'Shit,' says Rupert. 'Shit, shit, shit.'

We pull into the pub car park less than ten minutes later, gravel flying everywhere as though desperate to escape from our burning tyres. There is only one other car and it's empty.

Rupert is out and running towards a big sign and map at the back of the car park. 'Come on,' he says. 'I know where she's going. There's an old oak tree her grandfather used to take her to all the time. That's where she'll be.'

It's two-thirty in the morning; the moon is full and we don't need a torch, but I'm not much of a runner and struggle to keep up.

167

Everything that's happening seems surreal and I have to keep reminding myself that Fabiola might be in trouble. That's enough to keep me going and to push one leg in front of the other.

Rupert is driving us forwards — we've probably not been running for longer than ten minutes, but it seems much longer — and he still manages to shout out Fabiola's name every few seconds.

There is no reply.

I am almost out of reserves when we stumble out into a large clearing with a massive fat-trunked tree brooding at the centre. This must be it, but where's Fabiola?

Rupert is in front of me at the foot of the tree. He's bending over a figure, crying out over and over, 'Fabiola. Wake up. Wake up ... Please wake up.'

As I reach them, I push him roughly aside, shouting 'Out of my way, Rupert. I'm a nurse.' I know that seconds count when someone's unconscious and roughly pull the plastic bag away from her beautiful, already-slack face, drag her to flatter ground and start to give her CPR.

In between breaths, I issue instructions. 'Call an ambulance. Now,' I tell the paralysed Rupert. 'When you've done that, tell me what's in the gas cylinder. And remember to breathe. You're no use to me if you pass out.'

I know in my heart we're too late but I keep going until the ambulance arrives. If I don't stop the cycle of breaths and compressions, I can hold back the crashing waves of anguish which are rearing over me. Hold back the pain for a little longer.

After the paramedics have taken charge, I walk over to Rupert, who is standing rigid as a telegraph pole, blank eyes staring down in frozen catatonia.

'I'm sorry,' I say. 'I tried as hard as I could, but we were too late.'

Too Late

No-one should ever underestimate the consequences of identity theft. Within our complex civilisation, we have become dependent on a huge range of connections and links to the systems and networks which form the backbone of our world. Our status within these networks legitimises our position within society, controls our ability to communicate with others on all levels, and authorises us to transact within the network. If this status is too badly damaged, we cannot function within society and the foundations of our existence and self-belief may collapse.
"How much is your Life Worth? Protecting your Identity in a Digital World."
JJ Martin, Insight Business Press 2015

I hadn't known what to expect. I suppose I'd always had this clichéd preconception that dying would be warm and fluffy. Gently slipping into cotton wool clouds or maybe enveloped in pain-numbing ice water; Leonardo di Caprio sinking blue-faced, but smiling, into the welcoming depths. Until we face it ourselves, we can never know and it is all too human to imagine a gentle and dignified step from existence to ... what?

With my good Catholic upbringing, and considering the self-inflicted nature of my departure, I was hoping God would give me the benefit of the doubt and the transition would be from existence to simple non-existence rather than the fire and brimstone alternative.

We imagine what suits us and what softens the fear of our looming mortality, so the last thing I expected was the pain. Not quite physical, nor long and drawn out, but a universal lifetime of agony condensed into a single moment as everything which had been 'me' was simultaneously wrenched from each cell of my body.

Billions of tiny rips, sundering my existence from the useless, already-cooling flesh which no longer even contained the memory of who I'd once been.

In that moment of exquisite anguish, I understood everything. Only an instant, my final flash of time, but an instant of infinite duration burning through me in perfect magnesium whiteness. It was all clear now. I'd been right all along, I hadn't lost my mind. Everything that had happened to me was deliberate and malicious and I knew who was responsible. So obvious, so stupid, I should have trusted my instincts. I understood everything now. If only ...

Part 2

Desiderio delle tue mani chiare
nella penombra della fiamma:
sapevano di rovere e di rose;
di morte. Antico inverno.

Desire of your hands bright
in the penumbra of fire:
they knew of oak-trees, roses,
death. Ancient winter.

Salvatore Quasimodo

The World Keeps Turning

When the world's banks decided to disable all online banking software in the autumn of 2025, a fundamental pillar of society started to crumble. Advances in crack-hack technology were making all existing forms of identity protection highly vulnerable and concerns about personal online security soared.

Global infrastructures had become almost completely reliant on internet-based interconnectivity. Without the ability to protect identity and to control online transactions, forecasters were predicting that the world's existing networks — in particular banking and online retail — would collapse within less than five years.

The economic and social consequences of this implosion were predicted to cost the global economy over 25 trillion dollars per year for the foreseeable future.

Luckily for us, those forecasters didn't take into account Julie Martin and Pulsar.

"Pulsar. Behind the Firewall" Sam Blackwell, Insight Business Press 2040

I walked out onto the terrace, rubbing the sleep from my eyes and stretching lazily; I could feel each muscle in my body move as I rolled my shoulders backwards, a pleasant awareness rather than an ache. Julie insisted we ran at least 10k together every day and we combined that with strength training and an hour or more of yoga. I was in better shape than I'd ever been.

Picking up a coffee cup, scratching the back of my neck, arching off the springboard into the pool, even taking the few steps out into the morning sunshine, every movement reminded me of my physical place in the world. I felt alive and in control.

It was already ten o'clock and the air was warm and silky. From the terrace, I could see the whole of the Cap in front of me, everything in its place, green and manicured. It must have taken so much effort to create such effortless perfection.

'Sam? Sam? Are you there?' I could hear Julie's voice through the French doors which led to the bathroom. 'Be an angel and come and keep me company while I do my nails.'

'OK. I'll just grab a coffee. D'you want one?'

'No thanks. I'm caffeined out for now.'

Our suite had a different style of antique Nespresso machine in every room, each one balanced by designer racks of coffee capsules and elegant cups. As there were fifteen rooms in the suite – yes I'd counted – someone had enjoyed themselves helping to make a certain handsome actor a little richer. He must have been eighty years old, but could still be found, sipping a coffee, on billboards at every airport. As he had been since before I was born.

Julie knew him well apparently, but I was yet to have the honour. I had a glimmer of a suspicion they had been a little more than friends once upon a time, but Julie never let anything slip unless she meant to, and something like that wasn't going in the book under any circumstances.

I picked a gold capsule as always. Sumatran Kopi Luwak was the most exclusive option and I couldn't resist the idea of paying extortionate sums to drink coffee made from Indonesian wildcat poo. I should have probably taken my jet-set lifestyle a bit more seriously but couldn't do it. Too much of my mother in me perhaps?

Julie was sitting on a chaise longue in the main bathroom. Dressed in a light silk wrap, chin resting on one raised leg, her focus was absolute; as with everything else she did, perfection was the only option. Her vermillion toenails would be flawless.

I stood in the open doorway, consciously reminding my lungs that I needed to start breathing again. Seeing her like this never failed to stun me for a second or two.

I couldn't believe my luck. She was such a class act and I

struggled to imagine what I'd done to deserve her. Most of my girlfriends before had been shallow, boring simperers, glued to their phones half the time, and already worrying about husbands, babies and country houses.

Julie was nothing like that; she knew what she wanted, had no qualms about asking for it and, if she'd ever failed to get it, I'd certainly not seen any evidence. A bit of a challenge to my male ego at times but it was worth it on so many levels. And tonight was going to be the cherry on top of all of the sweet, sticky icing.

She patted the soft cushion and I sat next to her, my back pressed against her raised thigh, looking out over the perfect blue of the Mediterranean. She wrapped her free arm around my waist and absent-mindedly ran her fingertips up and down my stomach while toenail after toenail fell victim to the strokes of her brush.

I found myself getting hard even though we'd made love only half an hour earlier. There was something about this woman that made everything erotic; the simplest of activities could be touched with a sexual undertone and delicately, illicitly covered with a thin, translucent veneer of excitement, danger and risk.

I wasn't a total moron and there had always been a part of me which knew it wouldn't last, but I'd said that when we first got together and that was more than a year ago. We might last another year? Two? I didn't know and I didn't actually care. Perhaps all of the yoga was getting to me; I was quite content to embrace the here-and-now and leave tomorrow to worry about itself.

'Excited?' she said, removing the offending fingers from my stomach to pick up the bottle of nail varnish. God, even the way she slid the bright, glistening brush back into the bottle was erotic. And the way she was slowly screwing on the lid ...

I looked down at my lap and smiled at her.

'Not that kind of excited, idiot,' she laughed. 'Are you excited about tonight?'

'What do you think?' I said. 'I can't believe it's really happening. I hope you're pleased. And a little excited too?'

'Of course I am. You know we wouldn't be here if I wasn't. You've done an amazing job.'

'Team effort,' I said, standing to let her swing her legs round.

'Maybe so, but you'll take all the credit tonight. I insist.' She stood up, wrapped her hands behind her head and stretched. 'I'll have that coffee now. But none of the cat-shit stuff. Something Italian.'

Glistening Prizes

Julie Martin was already an internationally recognised personal security expert when the systems started to break apart. She was well known on the conference circuit and her 2015 book, 'How much is your Life Worth? Protecting your Identity in a Digital World.' had already become a key text. But when, in early 2023, she started to publish articles predicting a global security meltdown within two years, most people thought she had lost her touch.

Her predictions would prove eerily precise and almost all of the world's foremost experts – including the NSA – were left with egg on their face. Demands for her consultancy services soared and she could have charged astronomical fees. But Julie had other plans.

Pulsar Plc was already eighteen months old by then and, when yesterday's dog's dinner hit the fan, both Julie and Pulsar were ready.

"Pulsar. Behind the Firewall" Sam Blackwell, Insight Business Press 2040

The room fell silent as the lights went up on the speaker's lectern. The small, fat man in a dinner jacket waddled out on stage and up to the microphone. I turned to Julie and whispered, a little too loudly. 'Now I understand why it's called a penguin suit.'

'Shhh,' she replied. 'Behave yourself for once. You're playing with the grown-ups tonight. He's a lovely man, and not everyone can be tall, dark and handsome. I still bet he kicks off with the Frankfurt joke though.'

'Meiner damen und herren. Hertzlig willkommen in Frankfurt,' said the penguin, right on cue. The audience responded with polite laughter although the joke had apparently worn thin about ten years earlier. It wasn't even a joke actually – not even worthy of being called an in-joke. Nothing remotely funny about it at all.

It was my first time but, apparently people had been saying 'willkommen in Frankfurt' since 2030 when the book fair moved from Frankfurt. As far as I could tell, that was it. Simply a reference to the fact that the book fair had once been held somewhere else. People were strange to say the least.

'No seriously guys,' the witty penguin continued. 'Welcome to Cannes and welcome to this Insight Business Press special launch event. I am one hundred per cent certain neither Pulsar nor Julie Martin need any introduction here. Or anywhere for that matter.' He laughed and waved his stubby fin in Julie's direction while the audience craned their sheep-like necks and filled the room with a satisfyingly impressed sotto voce murmuring.

'But you probably don't know much about this evening's main man and, before we tuck in to some delicious champagne and canapés, I'm delighted to introduce you to the author of our new bestseller, 'Pulsar: Behind the Firewall'. He's one of the most talented young biographers I've had the pleasure to work with and I'm sure we'll be seeing a lot more of him in the future. Ladies and Gentlemen, Sam Blackwell.'

A nudge from Julie and I was walking out into the lights. I'd always been confident, but I'd never had to do anything like this and was certain I would freeze and clam up – simply stand there with my mouth open, tongue half out and my village idiot eyes wandering aimlessly around the room. My throat was suddenly as dry as if I were on the third course of a dry cracker eating contest. It was going to be a disaster.

I reached the lectern, shook hands with Dieter Holzmann, who looked a lot less like a penguin at close quarters, and turned to the microphone.

'Good evening, everybody. Thank you all for coming.' The relief of being able to speak surged through me and I took a couple of deep breaths to stop myself leaping uncontrollably from 'can't speak' to 'can't stop'. 'I'm not going to say too much, so the champagne won't have to wait for long.' I looked across at Julie who had a big, proud grin on her face and was struck, not for the first time, by the fairy-tale impossibility of my situation. It's such a human frailty, the fact that, if we are unbelievably lucky and things are going too well, we can't stop ourselves from looking for the catch. Too good to be true.

'I've only got two things I want to say,' I continued. 'The first is to thank Dieter and all of the team at Insight for their incredible, professional help over the past twelve months.' Everyone knew everyone at this event and I waited for the ripple of polite applause to end. 'The second is, of course, to thank Julie Martin. Not only did she commission me to write this book – God knows why – but she's also been unbelievably supportive throughout the process. And, let's face it, it was an easy task for me. The story of Julie Martin and Pulsar is one that writes itself.' This time, the applause was much more enthusiastic and it was clear just being in the same room as Julie was a big deal for most of the invitees. She was properly A-list.

'So, thank you again for coming and I hope to get a chance to talk with a few of you over drinks.' That was it. I'd made it. The lights went down and I felt my whole body sag like an abandoned puppet. I looked over to Julie but she was already being mobbed and I knew she'd be tied up for hours. That was OK. A drink was what I needed most of all.

'So, how come you got such a big credit ... ? Banging the boss, are we?' Susie was a freelance PR working on the launch. She was stunning and knew it. I wasn't sure whether her blue silk dress left everything or nothing to the imagination. 'Julie's a lucky woman. A bit old for you, maybe?'

I smiled and leant towards her. 'A gentleman wouldn't dignify that with a reply,' I said. 'Now would he?'

'I was rather hoping you weren't that much of a gentleman.' I could tell Susie was a believer in getting to the point but, even after hours of trying to empty my self-filling glass of Pol Roger, I was still sober enough to remember to keep my distance from the school of beautiful barracudas which had been circling me all evening.

I could see Julie over Susie's shoulder, talking to a group of important-looking executives but, true to form, still keeping half an eye on the whole room and definitely aware of everything I was up to.

I'd learned early on in our relationship that Julie was unusually possessive and I had no intention of stepping out of line. As I was the star turn, however, the launch party was proving more of a challenge than usual. The whole room was a sweet shop filled with an exceptional array of temptations. Where had they all come from?

I'd never been the centre of attention before. Julie had taken me to plenty of premieres and opening events but I'd always been the 'plus one' and usually ended up trailing behind her while she worked the crowd. Watching her in action was a master class; she never switched off – every air kiss, each witty or pithy aside, the choice of when and how to smile, they were all moves in the huge, multi-dimensional chess game which was her life.

Her business life, that is. Business and personal life were very different for Julie, which was probably the reason why she was so keen to have me seen as the creative force behind the book. I had actually written it – every word – but so had all of the other commissioned ghostwriters behind every celebrity memoir or CEO-Lit corporate puff piece on the market. As a general rule, the ghostwriter wasn't mentioned and was usually contractually forbidden from ever talking about their role.

Everyone seemed happy to live with the deluded idea that all of these illiterate C-list celebrities or highly paid, uber-busy CEOs had managed to find the time and the ability to spend a year or two writing a book. The involvement of an unknown professional ghostwriter was frankly boring and did nothing to sell books.

Julie was different. She did everything possible to push the Pulsar brand, but kept her own profile tightly under wraps. She wasn't exactly a recluse but, like many successful business owners, was skilled in avoiding publicity about her personal life. Stories seemed to slide past, or through, her as though she were a ghost. The Ghost and the Ghostwriter - that was us.

On the odd occasion when the media thought they'd got their teeth into something potentially meaty about Julie, they quickly found out what a cornered vixen – with billions in the bank and some very good lawyers – was capable of. In recent years, most journalists had been pre-warned by their editors not to bother. Messing with Julie Martin was too expensive.

The waiter came to top up our glasses and I looked over at Julie. I managed to catch her eye and she smiled at me. Even from five metres, I still felt the physical jolt. She was so gorgeous and exciting, I struggled to stop myself from standing there slack-mouthed and gawking at her.

'Sam? So are you a gentleman, or not?'

I turned back to the delicious Susie, who may have been very beautiful but was a poor shadow of Julie. 'On another night, in a different time, who knows,' I said. 'But I am tonight. Have you read the book?'

'A shame,' she replied, subtly pulling backwards and away from me. 'But not such a surprise. Of course I've read it. It's my job to have read it. Not bad.'

'Not bad? Is that all?'

'Well, it's definitely better than average, and quite an exciting story for a business book,' she said. 'I'd like to have read more about what might have been though. If Pulsar or something similar hadn't come along?'

'Yeah, that would be interesting, and I've thought a lot about it, but it wasn't the book I was commissioned to write. This was the story of what did happen, not what might have happened.'

'I get that,' she said. 'But there's another story there too. Maybe a novel. You should work on developing it and see what happens.' She put her glass on the table and leant forward to give me a chaste kiss on the cheek. 'Anyway, I need to wander around and do my job. Make sure you let me know if you decide to stop being a gentleman at any point.'

I was having a surprisingly entertaining conversation with Dieter, his wife and our American publisher, but was keeping an eye on the big clock in the corner. I knew we wouldn't stay any longer than scheduled. We never did.

Sure enough, a man in a dark suit walked over to me at exactly eight o'clock. He looked ex-military, probably one of the Guards regiments, but I'd not seen him before. It was hard to keep up.

'We're leaving sir,' he whispered in my ear. 'Rear entrance. Two minutes.'

I was used to the routine by now and made efficient excuses to Dieter and his stout teutonic frau, before following the security guard to the exit. I had no idea what our dinner plans were, but doubted I'd be disappointed.

We'd arrived by helicopter, but the black Mercedes didn't take the turn to the airport and the driver brought the limo to a stop after three or four minutes. This was unusual and I started to run through some of the anti-abduction training we'd been given.

'Is everything OK?' I asked Julie. 'Should we be stopping so soon?'

'Don't worry. Relax,' she said. 'You won't be needing those muscles. At least not yet.'

An invisible figure opened the door.

'Come on,' said Julie. 'Let's go.'

I slid over and followed her out of the car. We'd driven the short distance down to the marina and were parked behind an enormous motor yacht. Its jet-black hull was almost invisible against the night sky and the white superstructure seemed to be floating on air.

'Welcome to the Hesperus,' said Julie, walking ahead of me up the gangplank to a huge deck area empty except for a single candlelit table and two chairs. By the time we'd sat down the limo had disappeared and we were already motoring softly out to the harbour entrance.

'I didn't know you had a boat,' I said, overwhelmed by the shimmering beauty of the bay of Cannes as it gradually opened up in front of me.

'I don't,' she replied. 'But I have a friend who does.'

There is a problem which goes beyond a first-world problem and is reserved for those people who can afford absolutely anything. How do you make anything special when everything in your life is the best?

I hadn't been in Julie's world long enough to really understand how this worked, but was beginning to see that it was possible. If you surround yourself every day with perfection, how do you find something better?

We found it that evening.

The meal was a unique piece of theatre; Julie had flown over a young French chef, Pascal Meillasoux, who was starting to make a name for himself in New York. He'd been in Cannes working on our meal for three days.

Pascal had also chosen the wines. With my extensive experience of drinking fine wines – extensive being a combination of short, but intensive – I'd learned that, beyond about fifty euros a bottle, the price was not the most important factor when picking wines.

I didn't really believe food matching was everything it was cracked up to be either, but the simple art of ignoring the bullshit and choosing wines which tasted good was massively underrated. Pascal didn't put a foot wrong.

The air was warm and silky, the boat was majestic, the staff were attentive ghosts and the backdrop of the Esterel mountains was sublime.

All of the luxury and beauty would have been perfect with or without Julie. But she was on scintillating form – witty, charming, flirtatious and unbelievably sexy, and that added the 'je ne sais quoi' which tipped the balance beyond mere perfection.

And, for a few moments, I almost ruined it.

We were finishing the meal with a bottle of Krug Clos D'Ambonnay and, what with all of the champagne I'd drunk earlier, I should have known that I'd had too much.

'Are you ever going to tell me about yourself?' I said, out of the blue.

'We had a deal, didn't we?' Julie's voice was sharp-edged.

I blundered on. 'I know we did, but you can't blame me for being interested. You know everything about me, but I know nothing about you.'

'And that, you lovely boy, is how it's going to stay.' Julie swept her arms out in a grandiose arc which covered the boat, the inky sea and the rocky cliffs. 'Aren't you happy?'

'Of course I am. I've never been so happy in my life. I'm just curious.'

'Well, you know what happened to the cat. You should learn from that.' She poured the last drops of champagne into her glass and dropped the upside down bottle clattering into the ice bucket. The harsh noise was sobering and I realised I might have just made a big mistake.

Julie sat upright and looked at me for a few seconds. I could sense her weighing up her options. A cool breeze slipped across the deck and I shivered. A few seconds more and then she leant back into her chair and smiled.

'Come over here and give me a kiss, you idiot.' Her voice was soft and sensual. 'I've been wanting you ever since I saw you up on stage this evening.'

Going Back Home

By 2025, most major technology companies and banks were committed to fingerprint recognition as a means of secure identification. When a Russian hackers' co-operative launched a kit which allowed even amateurs to lift fingerprints and create latex simulations, there was widespread panic.

A number of researchers had already recognised that the unique shape of our cardio-rhythms might be a more foolproof option. They struggled, however, to find a way to match the rhythms quickly and accurately.

Julie Martin's 'moment of truth' was to recognise that the technology was already in place to solve this issue. She only needed to acquire the necessary copyrights and patents and to build the right commercial structure.

"Pulsar. Behind the Firewall" Sam Blackwell, Insight Business Press 2040

After Gramps died, it was only a matter of time before Dad decided to sell up in Jericho and move back in with Granny. There was no way Granny was going to sell the vicarage, but it was too much for her to manage and she needed help. She'd been a bit forgetful and loopy ever since I could remember and, without someone around, it was easy to imagine her doing something stupid like falling off a ladder or setting the place on fire.

I think Dad had been quite lonely himself since I left home and it would probably be good for him too. I never quite understood why he never found anyone else after Mum, but there was always something in the way blocking it. I got on well with him — we were good mates — so if he hadn't talked about it by then, it seemed unlikely I'd ever know.

It was after midday on Saturday by the time I got home. Julie had been childish and petulant about me 'swanning off and deserting her' but there had to be some limits and, in any case, I'd promised Dad I'd be there. She'd make me pay later in some way or other, no doubt. Her constant mind games had started to get under my skin, making me feel constrained and claustrophobic and I'd recently found myself wanting to say and do perversely contrary things, simply to wind her up. Not smart, but it gave me a small sense of independence and control.

Uncle Daz was already there, helping Dad to box things up.

'Hey Boy,' he said, wrapping me up in a huge man hug. 'I've not seen you for months. How's it going?'

'Can't complain,' I said. 'You know. Champagne, yachts, five-star hotels, celebrities, Michelin stars coming out of my arse. The usual, really.'

'Yeah,' said Daz. 'Same old, same old. What gets me is that we don't come across each other more often. I guess we're just on different yachts.' His lazy, plummy billionaire's accent was spot on. 'Are we ever going to meet this sugar mummy of yours?'

'I wouldn't hold your breath,' I said. 'I don't think you and Dad'll be meeting her any time soon. She's extremely private.'

'... and we're not good enough for her. I know. I get it. I've spent most of my life not being good enough for people. I'm used to it.'

The great thing about Uncle Daz was that he genuinely didn't give a damn what people thought of him and had no interest whatsoever in the trappings of wealth. He didn't particularly object to other people having stuff, he simply didn't want any of it for himself.

He kept trying to meet Julie because he cared about me and wanted to make sure I was OK, but that was it. Dad was a bit different – it would have been impossible to grow up with Granny without picking up a fair amount of cut-glass snobbishness – but years of friendship with Daz had helped smooth off the sharpest edges.

'Well, that's OK then,' I said. 'Where's Dad?'

'He's upstairs. Been there for a while.'

When I walked into the room, Dad was sitting on the edge of his bed, holding an old shoebox in both hands; his thumbs were pressed tightly onto the lid, forcing it to stay shut as though there were something inside struggling to escape. He was looking straight ahead, eyes half-closed by the effort of keeping the box tightly sealed. I could see his shoulders sagging, his whole body crumpling into the bed, driven downwards by the heavy weight in his hands. He looked shrunken and frail and, for the first time, I realised he was getting old.

'Sam,' he exclaimed, as he looked up and saw me. 'I'd begun to think you weren't going to make it.' He put the box down on the bed and stood up to give me a hug. 'You're looking well.' he said, stepping back to appraise me, hands squeezing my shoulders. 'Impressive! You must be in the gym all the time.'

'And running, and yoga. I've never been as fit. How about you? You looked wiped out when I came in.'

'Oh, I'm fine,' he said. 'I was miles away. You know I could still take you apart on the tennis court, don't you? Muscles or no muscles.'

'Maybe, but not because you're faster and you're not even a better player any more. No, you'd probably win because you're a devious bugger and because there's some small, sensitive part of me that cares. I'll probably always let you win because you'd be so sad if I beat you.'

'Bollocks,' he said, smiling. 'And there's only one way to find out.'

'Tomorrow morning then,' I said. 'No prisoners and, if you have a heart attack, it's my game. Has Granny got the net up?'

'I doubt it, but it won't take us more than ten minutes to sort it out. No excuses.'

'Not looking for them,' I said. 'What's in the box by the way? You looked as though you were going to give yourself a hernia the way you were squeezing it.'

'I'll tell you later. Let's go down and give Daz a hand. I've already been up here for ages.'

After an hour of packing the more valuable, and breakable, bits and

187

pieces into boxes, Dad called a lunch break. We sat around the dining table in front of a big plate of sandwiches and it suddenly hit me like a sledgehammer between the eyes; this had been home for my entire life but it would be the last time I would sit here. I had been so caught up with the book and my crazy, ridiculous life with Julie that I hadn't realised what a momentous milestone it was. Not until that moment. As I looked across at Dad, I could see he'd been thinking about it for a while.

'Penny just dropped, has it?' Dad said.

'Yeah. It hadn't crossed my mind until now,' I said. 'How stupid is that? In a couple of hours, that's it, isn't it? The movers don't want us around tomorrow and the new people get the keys on Monday.'

Daz was watching the two of us carefully and looked at me. 'Your whole life 'til now,' he said. 'Funny to imagine, isn't it?'

I didn't know what to say. Everything was moving too quickly. 'It's the only place where I was with Mum,' I said. 'I'm going to miss it.'

'Me too,' said Dad. 'But we need to move on. Let's you and me have a talk about it after lunch, eh?'

'I read your book,' said Daz, changing the subject. 'It's not bad.'

'D'you think so?' I said. 'Sales are going gangbusters and the reviews are good, but I'm not sure how much of it's down to my writing. The Pulsar story is amazing and that's what sells it.'

'Maybe,' said Daz. 'But that doesn't make it readable, does it? I've read a few of these corporate vanity books in the past and most of them make me feel a bit sick. Lot's of self-congratulatory drivel from overpaid duffers who just got lucky. Your book tells the story like it's an exciting adventure.'

'Well it actually was an exciting time,' I said.

'I know. Don't forget I was actually there,' said Daz. 'Your book took me straight back to the good old days when it looked as though civilisation and society were about to go seriously south. You were only a kid at the time, but you've still managed to get hold of the feeling we all had. What d'you reckon Roops? I know we're both biased but ...'

'I agree,' my dad said. 'You know I don't read a lot, but I thought it was great. I actually wanted to know what happened next all the way through, even though I sort of knew already. You've made a real thriller out of it.'

'Thanks guys,' I said. 'Better than any poncey critics' reviews.'

My dad hadn't quite finished. 'My only issue is that it's still quite difficult to pin down quite what this woman you're seeing is really like. She doesn't feature much even though the book's actually all about her. Why doesn't she want to meet me? What's she got to hide? I mean, I don't think I've ever even seen a photo of her. Certainly none with the two of you together.'

The subject of meeting Julie was top of the agenda every time I saw Dad or Uncle Daz and I knew it would be Granny's first question when I saw her later on. I understood why, but going on and on about it wouldn't change anything.

'You know it's not that she refuses to meet you as such,' I said. 'I'm not going to suggest it to her because I know she'll find a reason to say no. As for what she's like, she didn't want much about her in the book and she's got a thing about photos, but Julie's exactly what you'd imagine her to be – unbelievably bright, always gets her own way and incredibly charming when she chooses to be.'

'Sounds a bit too good to be true,' said my dad. 'What's the catch?'

'I don't know yet, but these last two years have been the best anyone could imagine. I'm not kidding myself though. It won't last forever and I'm sure she'll get bored and find a replacement Sam one of these days.'

'Still sounding like a warm, healthy relationship of equals, sure enough,' said Daz, always happy to stick an oar in.

'OK. I know how it looks,' I said. 'But I'm not fifteen years old. I'm twenty-seven and I've got my eyes wide open. What's the worst that can happen? She gets bored with me and dumps me. She might give me a nice Rolex as a leaving present. I can then get a normal life, meet a girl of my own age, sell the watch, find a normal job, etcetera, etcetera.'

'Slum it with the rest of us, you mean?' said Daz.

'Exactly. The way I see it, I've still got plenty of time. I don't know what I did to deserve this lottery win, but I'm not going to throw the ticket away out of spite or principle. That would be a bit thick, wouldn't it?'

'Fair enough,' Dad said, lifting his hands in mock surrender. 'You've made your point. We're probably just jealous of you gallivanting around while we still have to go to work every day.'

Daz stared at the two of us for long seconds as though we were chimps in a zoo. 'I'm not bloody jealous,' he said eventually.

Once we'd used up all the packing boxes we had, Daz left for London, leaving Dad and me to fiddle about with a few last bits and pieces and take some photos. There's something about a house where all of the personal items have been removed. The furniture's still there, the structure and layout haven't changed, but the soul has gone and what's left is ... well it's just a house.

As I wandered around with the camera, I couldn't help wondering if there was a point in time when everything changed. A single moment when it ceased to be a home – one last item packed, a picture or photo wrapped in cream paper, taking the bins out for the last time. Depressing, pointless thoughts.

The good thing, of course, was that it made it easier to say goodbye. By the time we'd boxed up all of the personal stuff, I was ready.

I saw Dad coming down the stairs carrying the shoebox he'd been holding earlier. He had the strangest look on his face. It wasn't only that he was sad – although he was definitely on the edge – there was something else, a guilty shiftiness. His look reminded me of how I'd felt when he caught me and my mates smoking a joint when we were thirteen. I'd known straight away that I'd crossed a line; he'd always been such a cool Dad and I'd stomped all over his trust. He hadn't blown up or screamed at me like the other parents. He hadn't needed to.

Dad felt bad about something now and what he was holding was important.

'Come and sit down,' he said, carrying the box over to the table. 'This is for you, but I need to tell you a few things first.'

I sat down at the table opposite him and waited. I had no idea what was going on, but this was clearly a big deal for him and he was struggling to get started.

'You know how your mother died ... ?'

I nodded, not trusting myself to speak. How could I forget? I hadn't been told the truth until I was fifteen and I could taste the anger even now, sharp and metallic on the roof of my mouth. How could she do it? And how could he lie to me all my life? There were so many questions and most of them didn't have answers. No-one had been safe from my self-pitying rage.

It had dragged on for months and it took a lot of sessions with a counsellor before I could finally understand why my father had taken so long to tell me. I don't think I ever agreed that it was the right decision, but I did eventually accept that it was made for the right reasons.

As for my mother, I mourned her properly for the first time, but I never forgave her for leaving me and still didn't expect I ever would.

'Well, there are some things which I haven't ever talked about. I've wanted to, but I've never been able to figure out how.'

I felt my shoulders tighten and leant forward across the table. 'Dad, if you're going to throw me another curve ball after all of these years, I'll ...'

'... No, it's nothing like that,' he said, still calm but raising his voice. 'Let me finish. It's about that time. The time right before it happened.'

'All right,' I said, leaning back into my chair. 'Go on.'

'The thing is ... the thing is ... well, I think I could have done things differently. I'm afraid she thought I'd given up on her.' His voice cracked and he covered his mouth and nose with his hand for a moment before continuing. '... and perhaps I did for a short while. I should have known. I should have been there for her, and maybe ...'

He slumped forward onto the table, head in his hands, shoulders softly shaking out his pain and guilt.

I got up and knelt next to him, both arms wrapping him up tightly. 'It's OK Dad,' I said gently. 'It's not your fault. You can't blame yourself. Mum took the decision on her own. I'll never understand why, but it wasn't your fault.' We stayed like that for a long time before I felt able to sit down again.

'Thanks, Sam,' he said eventually. 'I don't think I'll ever change the way I think about it, but I'm glad I got it off my chest.' He looked up at me. 'She would've been so proud of you, you know?'

'So what's in the mystery box, then?' I asked, desperate to change the subject.

'Well, that's the other thing I need to tell you. Your Mum kept a diary. She started it on the day we brought you back from hospital and wrote in it every day.'

'Bloody hell,' I said. 'What does it say?'

'I've got no idea. I've never read it. I know it sounds pathetic but I had you to look after and a job to get back to and then I couldn't face opening up old wounds. I guess I'm afraid she wrote about me not being there for her.'

'One way or the other, it wouldn't have been easy reading,' I said. 'Is that what's in the box, then?'

'Yes. I couldn't bring myself to throw it away. A part of me knew I needed to give it to you one day.'

He pushed the box across the table. I still hadn't taken in the enormity of the situation and looked at the dull, green lid for a while, unsure what to do next. Then I lifted the lid carefully and put it down next to the box.

'Oh, my God.' I had no idea what was written inside, but even looking at the two, smooth brown leather volumes, black-ribbon-tied with neat bows, sent shivers down my spine. 'And nobody's opened these since ...'

'... Nope,' he said. 'I found them in the box twenty-five years ago and they've never been touched.'

I reached in and took out a chunky slab of aluminium and glass. 'And what's this?' I asked him.

'That's her phone,' he replied. 'State-of-the art back then. Cost me a fortune.'

I put the phone back in the box and picked up one of the diaries. The leather was soft and warm in my fingers.

'I don't know what to say,' I said eventually. 'Do you think I should read them?'

'It's up to you,' he said. 'They're yours now. You can do what you want with them. For what it's worth, my advice is that you give yourself a couple of weeks to think about it before doing anything.' He managed a smile and a chuckle. 'Maybe talk it over with your wise, old girlfriend?'

'Very funny,' I replied, still reeling from the revelation that I might now be able to understand what my mother really felt about me and why she did what she did. 'But I think you're right. I'll wait before I do anything.'

I didn't need any time at all to think about whether I would discuss it with Julie. There was no way, not in a million years. We didn't have that sort of relationship.

Take the Money or ...

Matching cardio-rhythms quickly using small and noisy samples had always been a stumbling block. Julie Martin's most significant insight in those early days was to recognise that the problem had already been solved.

Almost twenty years earlier a team of academics from MIT had developed a unique waveform-matching technology to power a music-recognition business. When Julie Martin approached them, they were in financial difficulties and she was able to acquire an exclusive global license for matching cardio-rhythms – fully protected by their patents – for a minimal upfront payment and a small on-going license fee.

By the time the dust had settled, they were making much more from this licence than from their entire music business. It was, however, only a tiny fraction of the billions being made by Julie Martin and Pulsar.

"Pulsar. Behind the Firewall" Sam Blackwell, Insight Business Press 2040

I didn't beat my dad at tennis the next day. I knew I wouldn't, even though I was younger, faster and much fitter. I'd also been having top-level coaching at a string of five star hotels while Julie was off at some important meeting or other. My game was strong and I could compete well at club A-team level or above.

Fat lot of use that was against Dad. Even before we got on the court, he was inside my head and my game fell apart, point by point. There was nothing pretty about his technique; he simply had the knack of putting the ball in a place where you didn't want it to be, spinning in a way which didn't suit you. I couldn't stop myself from getting frustrated and soon started blasting balls out of the back of the court, over swinging at everything and becoming tighter and tighter.

'You should relax more,' said Dad, a big, smug grin plastered all over his face.

That, of course, made it much, much worse. 'You just focus on not having a coronary, old man,' was the best I could manage as I walloped another shot into the net.

'Hah! If you can't even manage to get the ball in play, I doubt I'll even break a sweat. Haven't you been having lots of super-expensive coaching, courtesy of you-know-who?'

I'd missed being home and having my Dad take the piss out of me. He'd started when I was tiny. 'Good training for the real world' he would always say, and almost nothing was taboo. I'm not sure I enjoyed it so much for the first few years, but I gradually developed a second skin which was, of course, his plan all along.

It wasn't a hard, rigid shell which locked in as much as it kept out; it was more of a slippery, semi-permeable membrane which allowed friendly, and not-so-friendly, banter – such an integral part of the relationships between rutting young bucks – to slide past with minimal damage. It didn't work so well with girls for some reason. They seemed to be able to poke their way straight through without difficulty.

Not that I was enjoying being thrashed at tennis by an old man with no style, but there were some consolations. As we shook hands and walked off court, I could see how happy it had made him to keep his undefeated record intact. He wasn't ready to concede anything in the hierarchy stakes and I wasn't in any hurry for our roles to change either. The other, and most important, consolation was that no-one who knew me had been watching.

We went into the kitchen, where my grandmother had already poured two cold beers.

'Hi Granny,' I said, giving her a hug. 'Feeling better?'

'Oh, I'm fine dear. This thing with my heart just sometimes makes me feel a bit woozy. Did you win?'

'He's not there yet,' said my Dad, slapping me on the back. 'The record stands.'

'Oh, you're insufferable, Rupert,' said Granny. 'You've always been so ridiculously competitive. Can't you let the poor boy win for once?'

'The poor boy is twenty-seven years old,' I said. 'And he doesn't need a pity win. Anyway, I'm way better than Dad is now. The thing is that he cheats and uses some sort of witchcraft ...'

'Cheers,' said my dad, lifting his glass. 'Good game. I enjoyed that.'

I took a deep swig of my beer, thirsty enough to delight in the cold, hoppy lager tang at the back of my throat. 'Cheers,' I replied. 'Well played, you old git. Next time though...'

I'd agreed to meet Julie back at her flat before dinner, so needed to catch a train to London soon after lunch. Granny had made my favourite, roast pork, and, however ill she might have been feeling, it was spot on. The juices glistened as Dad carved and the golden crunch of the crackling was only matched by the equally golden crunch of the roast potatoes. Rich, steaming gravy with a jolt of lemon and sage, what more could anyone ask? The vegetables were window dressing and, as always, I got them out of the way quickly before concentrating on the main event. It was like a peg in time.

Sunday lunch with Granny and Gramps had been an institution for my whole life. After Mum died, we rarely missed it and, even when life had become complicated by friends and girlfriends, it remained a priority. It was actually more likely I'd drag them along rather than miss out. I rarely heard complaints.

The train was already moving out of the station as I put my bag up on the rack; the knowledge of what was inside the bag was like a hamster running around a wheel in my head, stupid pointy face grinning at me as its little legs pumped up and down and it squeaked out the same questions again and again. 'What did she write? Did she love me? Why did she leave?'

My dad's advice was good and I was determined to wait for at least two weeks before making a decision – but two weeks of this? I'd be a nervous wreck. The only thing I could think of was to drown the little furry bastard in alcohol but I wasn't going to neck a couple of G&Ts on a Sunday afternoon train. That would be sinking too low.

It would have to wait until dinner and, even then, I knew Julie would try and stop me. She hated it when I drunk too much and we always ended up fighting.

That was fine for her but she didn't have a neurotic hamster in her head and I didn't want her knowing anything about the diary. What else was I supposed to do? I tried some of the meditation techniques I'd learned from the yoga teachers but, as I slowed my breathing and gathered in my thoughts, I was still left either with two diaries nestled in a box, a hyperactive wheel-spinning rodent or, worse now, an image of my mother smiling down at me.

For some reason, I didn't want to take the box home with me. It seemed wrong. Was it because I worried my mother would disapprove of my relationship with Julie? That was ridiculous. She'd been dead for twenty-five years. It wasn't that. It was something about Julie. We'd only talked about my mother once and I can't say it brought out Julie's gentle, nurturing side.

I'd let my thoughts spiral into a dark place, which happened from time to time, and I'd started to explain to Julie that it was because of what had happened to my mother. She hadn't given me a hug or said 'there, there'. She'd become angry, told me to grow up, and stormed out. I suspected she was touchy because she had her own parent issues but it left a mark anyway.

I knew nothing about Julie's family; she lived for her work and, for all I knew, her parents were both dead. Let's face it, Julie and my mother would have been almost the same age, which was clearly a bit weird. It was becoming more and more obvious that I wasn't living in reality. I liked Julie a lot, and we had amazing times together, but now that the book was over, it was time to start thinking about the rest of my life.

That stirred up another basket of rattlesnakes though. I couldn't see Julie reacting well to being dumped, and she would be an influential enemy to make. It would be easy for her to make a quiet call to a publisher or a newspaper. 'I hear you're thinking of taking on Sam Blackwell? I wouldn't if I were you. I can't go into details I'm afraid. As you would imagine, I don't normally make calls like this with regards to junior staff, but in this case, I felt I had to ...'

No, it was absolutely clear. The decision had to be Julie's. I would figure out what to do over the next few months to make it happen. Getting pissed at whatever boring dinner we were going to tonight would be a start. At least the wine would be good. It always was.

In the meantime, I needed a temporary solution for the diaries and the best I could manage was left luggage at Paddington. I bought a small wheelie bag and a padlock, packed the box away and checked it in. Hopefully keeping them at a distance would help to calm my overworked mind.

It was almost six-thirty by the time I got back to the flat and, by then, I had a raft of missed calls and messages. To describe where I lived as a flat might have been be a bit of an understatement. I didn't like the way it was decorated – much too showy-offy – and I shuddered to think how much it might be worth, but as Knightsbridge penthouses go, I couldn't complain.

'You said you'd be back by five,' Julie was not a happy bunny. 'You know how important this dinner is. We need to be out of here in ten minutes at the outside.'

'OK. OK. I'm sorry. You know what the trains are like on a Sunday and I couldn't run off and desert my dad straight away. The move was a big deal for him. And for me actually.'

'Fine, whatever. Just get ready.'

'Remind me where we're going. What should I wear?'

'Bloody hell. Grow up, will you. Don't you even look at your diary? It's the Imperial College fundraiser. I'm hosting it, so we can't be late. Wear the blue Brioni. I've put it out. Now get moving for Christ's sake.'

I sloped off to my dressing room thinking how lightly I'd got away with the exchange. I'd expected to get a full roasting and, when I looked in the mirror, my hair wasn't even slightly singed. I now had a good idea of why she'd gone easy on me this time though; Julie was like a jellyfish – invasive, stinging tentacles everywhere but, in the right light, totally transparent and exposing her inner workings to anyone who knew how to look.

For such a sophisticated and manipulative woman, she was surprisingly childish and vulnerable and she was always going to be nervous and out of her comfort zone at the fundraiser.

She'd arranged to be appointed President of the Imperial College business fundraising programme six months earlier but hated the social obligations which went with it. It was one thing being queen bee at business meetings and conferences; she always knew her stuff and, in any case, people would defer to her wealth even if she did say something idiotic. Tenured academics were different and didn't play by the same rules.

Most of them didn't think much of wealth and tended to judge people on their academic background and whether they understood what was being explained to them. Julie was incredibly smart, but there were times when a professor of applied nanotechnology would leave absolutely anybody hanging with their mouth wide open.

It amused me that, with all her money, prestige and experience, Julie still craved approval like a little girl. I dreaded these events for different reasons. I wasn't nervous and didn't give too much of a damn what these professors thought of me. My problem was that they were so unbelievably boring.

At the last one we'd been to they'd served a multi-bird roast with a partridge inside a chicken inside a duck inside a turkey. It was a perfect metaphor for the dinner itself – pomposity inside pointless formality inside undeserved vanity all rammed into a shell of mind-numbingly-dull scientific twaddle, marinated in mediocre wine and cooked for an eternity.

There was one exception to the rule, and my only hope was to be seated near him. Professor David Bukowski was only a few years older than me and was already a world leader, if not *the* world leader, in nano-genetic research. I'd met him a few times – Pulsar was sponsoring his research – and he was unusually normal. He had a massive brain of course, but managed to avoid all of the defensive pomposity which his colleagues cultivated. Maybe it was because his brain was bigger than theirs? Or because he could still run 10k in less than thirty-five minutes?

Pulsar's technology hadn't stopped with the original cardio-identifier – that had first been hacked over ten years earlier and the whole business of identification and authentication was still growing like tropical bamboo. Everyone wanted a piece of the action and it was all about keeping ahead of the curve. Which was where Prof. Dave came into the picture.

On the face of it, everything was hunky dory in Pulsar heaven. It was still market leader, based on its flagship product, the 'Pulsar Trust', which was a pair of tiny, titanium implants injected into the bicep – one in each arm. They measured cardio-rhythms extremely accurately and were virtually tamperproof. They worked as a pair and, if one was removed from the body or damaged, they immediately de-authorised themselves.

Although easy to insert, people tended not to want to mess with them once they'd taken the plunge, and Pulsar's dominant market share was well established. Pulsar Trust was linked to everything – virtual passports, permanent health monitoring and every kind of smart device imaginable: watches, smart glass, smart lenses, wearables, car locks, door locks, fridge locks for dieters, payments and money transfers. Everything.

Very difficult to hack, but nothing is impossible and, although only a few people were aware of it, the first cracks had been appearing for some time. It wasn't easy but, with recent sensor technology, it had become possible to record heart rhythms remotely and simulate them in playback; a small market was building on the dark web for stolen cardio-identities which could then be used to impersonate the victim. Like every innovation before it, the Pulsar Trust's days were numbered.

Julie wasn't the sort of person to retire and let her business slowly decline. I suspected she didn't give a damn about her thirty thousand employees across the world, but she didn't like to lose. She'd been working with David Bukowski for four years and they were currently running final, live trials of a next generation product, Pulsar Trust 360, which combined the traditional cardio-rhythm implants with on-the-fly DNA matching.

The DNA matching was where David came in; he had developed a radical and unique method of attaching nano-genetic carriers to the haemoglobin cells in the blood. It was all extremely hush-hush but, if everything continued to go to plan, there would be a huge launch event within a few months.

I was showered, shaved and dressed in record time and looking like a perfect, happy toyboy when I joined Julie in the living room. I thought a bit of charm was in order and could sense her tension reduce as I grabbed her coat and held it out for her – half gentleman, half matador.

'Shall we, Senorita?' I said, fluttering the black cashmere gently.

She stood and allowed me to slip her into the coat, laughing despite herself. 'You are a total plonker sometimes, Sam.' She turned and kissed me. 'But a cute and amusing one. Vamonos?'

As we stood in the lift going down, I couldn't help thinking how gorgeous and sexy she was. When she focused her attention on me, it was as though I was stepping out from a dark room into tropical sunshine. Mesmerising and deeply, deeply compelling.

The evening should have gone well after that.

But it didn't ...

'You fucking little idiot.'

'Sorry.'

'What were you thinking?'

'It was Dave's idea.'

'Dave? You mean Professor Bukowski?'

'Yeah, Dave. Went and got the grappa from his room.'

'I've never been so humiliated.'

'I said I was sorry. Not my fault, though.'

'Do you know how important this project is to Pulsar.'

'We only had a little drink.'

'You can hardly fucking stand.'

'I'm fine. Stop shouting at me. And swearing.'

'I'll do what the fuck I want. I should've known better. I really should.'

'I need a piss. Back in a minute ...'

Ink and Tears

May 15th 2013

We brought him home today. Our beautiful, perfect little Sam. I can't believe how small he is. He's so tiny and fragile, it seems impossible that they've left us in charge of him, all by ourselves. He's not got anything to worry about though. I'll look after him and I'll keep him safe forever and ever.

So tired now. Everything's catching up with me. I'll write more tomorrow.

When I woke up, the mid-morning sunshine was burning through the windows and sticking knives into my skull. Why did it have to be so bright and shiny? As I staggered to the bathroom, there was one word on the tip of my tongue (and coating the roof of my mouth). A small, a seemingly harmless word – grappa.

It wasn't my first encounter with that devil's brew but I thought I'd learned my lesson the last time. There is nothing to compare with the acrid, rancid revisiting delivered by a post-grappa hangover belch and the memory should be enough to ensure that 'never again' is diligently obeyed.

Realising I was probably going to die, I double-dosed on paracetamol and iboprufen and plodded back to bed. As I hid from the vicious, uncaring sunlight, I tried to remember exactly what had happened and why I'd broken my sacred no-grappa rule. There were glimpses, flashes of clinking glasses, but not much more. I was definitely in trouble – that was a given – but how much trouble was unclear.

I didn't die but, when I woke up again at half past four, I had a sneaking suspicion Julie would be waiting in the kitchen with a big knife to finish me off. More and more memories were surfacing like dead goldfish and I realised I'd excelled myself at the Imperial dinner. It actually had been Dave's fault though.

I'd ended up in one of the spare bedrooms. No surprise there. Not quite sure how I found my way but Julie would have kicked me out if I'd been half as drunk as I must have been. I guess I'd still been compos mentis enough at the time to find my way to a bed.

A shower helped a lot and I couldn't avoid Julie any longer. Apart from anything else, if I didn't eat something soon I would fall back into the clutches of the grappa devil.

I was ready with my defence arguments as I slunk into the kitchen but there was no wrathful, knife-wielding harridan lying in wait. The flat was empty apart from me and the note on the table:

I'm in New York until Thursday. Back late. We need to talk. Don't bother to call.

Of course. She had a big strategy meeting to plan the launch of Pulsar Trust 360. I was saved for now, but it wasn't over. What if she broke up with me? I wasn't sure I was ready to give all of this up quite yet. Maybe I should have thought things through more carefully?

Worrying about all of that could wait; I had five clear days in front of me and it was time to give the bloody hamster some time off. I grabbed a banana, threw on my jacket and shoes and set off for Paddington. I could get the diaries and a Burger King at the same time.

The box sat on the table in front of me, gaping open, and it was time.

Touching the soft leather was electric; I couldn't stop myself from lifting the diary to my face and breathing in the smell – musty vanilla and chocolate mixed with something else. A familiar scent, but elusive.

As I read the first words, I immediately understood how painful this journey was going to be and why my father had avoided it. It was as though my mother was speaking directly to me for the first time and right there in her first words on the first page she made me a promise. A promise to look after me forever. I was two days old.

Why did she break her word? Hopefully, after so many years, these two slim volumes would finally give me some answers.

I needed less than two hours to read through the first diary which took me almost up to my second birthday. Mum kept her commitment to write something every day but often a single line or a couple of words were enough: 'great day!'; 'Sam's got a cold and is VERY grumpy'; 'Roop made homemade ravioli for my birthday. Actually quite good. I'm so lucky to have him.'. I could feel her love for me and Dad in every word.

I knew about the bad times, of course, but it was easy to forget that, even in the worst periods, most days were normal – daily life with its predictable ups and downs, laughter and happiness, tantrums and tears. It hadn't all been bad.

The things which happened to her in that first year – her 'incidents' – were recorded in detail, as were her counselling sessions. She was clear and precise in describing what had happened and in setting down her internal doubts and debates about what was happening to her. She seemed to be a logical thinker and, although she could never quite believe she was responsible for any of these incidents, she could also see that there was a weight of consistent evidence proving her wrong.

Overall, there hadn't been so many events – less than twenty – and none of them were particularly major, but her words shone on her increasing self-doubt; layer upon layer of uncertainty combining to form a cancerous black pearl, glowing and growing deep inside her.

After reading the pages about the missing car park ticket, I had to stop for a few minutes and went out to the balcony for an illicit smoke. Such a small event, but huge for her and it seemed as though something had snapped as she sat in the car screaming and pounding the steering wheel.

It was then that I had my first inkling of what might have happened to her more than a year later. She wrote at length about her fears and the animal terror which possessed her when she realised how little self-control she had at moments like this. She was becoming obsessed with the idea that she might do something in distraction, or by neglect, that could do me harm. I could taste the raw panic in each word.

When I came back inside and shut the door, the huge, empty flat echoed back at me and I felt an overwhelming urge to be around people, any people, it didn't matter who. Leaving the diary open and waiting in the middle of the table, I took the elevator down and pushed out into the chaos of early-evening Knightsbridge.

The noise and bustle was strangely calming; oversized, sharp-cornered shopping bags bashed and tangled, mothers struggled to keep hold of their children, young lovers strolled in double-width, self-absorbed bubbles and the river of humanity flowed along the pavement at its own pace. Any other day I would be dipping in and out of the traffic to try to move faster but just then I was perfectly happy to be a passive, canalboating passenger letting the stream guide me along.

As I walked I mulled over my mother's words, especially the parts which were completely new to me. The evening when the police had turned up and interviewed her about some anarchist called Jax Daniels was a surprise. The name Jax had also come up a number of times in earlier pages. Who was she? Why had I never heard of her? I would have to ask my dad. Or maybe Uncle Daz would be better as a first step?

Less surprising was a particular vein of frustration running through the entries from start to finish. Mum had struggled to find a good, balanced relationship with Granny and it was clearly an on-going sore that wouldn't heal. I wasn't even slightly shocked; I loved Granny dearly, but she was an incorrigible snob and the most manipulative, interfering person I'd ever met. Being her daughter-in-law was always going to be a challenge and, if you didn't come from the right sort of family ...

My body overruled the idea of stopping for a drink in Harvey Nichols, although a dry gin martini with a twist might have been the perfect cure. That was a worrying train of thought. Not the idea of a hair of the dog – that was still reasonable and logical. But when had I started seeing sixty-euro cocktails at exclusive bars as a 'normal' option?

With a drink off the menu, I switched flow and allowed myself to be drifted back to the flat. My mind was clear and I was ready for more. There would be time for regrets, sadness and questions later but first I needed to know everything.

The entries in the next half of the first diary – my second year – told the story of a normal, happy young family. Mum had finished her counselling, there were no more incidents and the pages were mostly filled with a comfortable optimism and peace. I learnt to walk and to talk, she wrote about going back to work and her need to find a different balance to her life once I was in nursery. She had even begun to think about the possibility of a little brother or sister for me and to ask herself when would be a good time to bring up the idea with Rupert.

Unfolding the memories of that simple, joyful year was more painful than reading the words of anguish and self-doubt which had gone before. As she wrote, she had no idea of what was to come. No suspicion of the tsunami that was building somewhere under a distant ocean. But I knew what was coming. I could see her optimism was misplaced and her future dreams were no more than that – dreams.

Empty knowledge. I was powerless. A passive observer wrapped in time's chains. Not able to do anything other than to watch the inevitable unfold.

It was almost midnight by the time I opened the second volume and, as I carefully unknotted the ribbon, a separate sheet of paper fell out onto the floor. It was folded neatly and, on the outside, 'My Darling Sam' was spelled out in her now-familiar flowing script.

I had to assume she'd written this after making her ultimate decision and my anger flashed. If my dad hadn't been too afraid to look at the diaries, he would have found this letter earlier and I wouldn't have needed to wait until now to hear what my mother had to say to me.

I didn't want to blame my dad though. He'd been through

enough. I was tired, it was late, and I still had the residue of half a bottle of grappa poisoning my blood. This had waited so many years. It would wait until the morning.

Two Halves Don't Make a Whole

July 20th 2013

The strangest thing happened to me last night. I got an email while I was up feeding Sam in the middle of the night. It didn't look like an ordinary email.

There was no address in the 'from' line. Only a row of stars. Nothing to say where it came from and all it said was 'you should have listened'. I must admit it freaked me out a bit. It felt like a warning.

I told Rupert about the mail as soon as his alarm went off and he took the phone to have a look. There was nothing there. The mail had simply vanished. Roops is good with technology and he dug around for about half an hour. There was absolutely no trace of the mail ever existing.

He said it must be some weird webmail glitch and that we should forget about it, but I'm not convinced. It was too personal, too full of menace.
I know I saw it. It's not the sort of thing you make up is it?

I slept better than I had in a long time. It was probably a combination of emotional and physical exhaustion, but I also felt a sense of calm and peace. I knew that I would never understand everything that happened to my mother, and that I would never really know her, but I did feel certain that she'd loved me and, whatever had happened, it wasn't my fault. That felt pretty good.

With Julie away and the book finished, I had a totally free day so went out for coffee and breakfast at Jak's Cafe on Walton Street. As always, it was full of chichi Kensington types and a great place to people watch. I was early enough to snaffle a corner table and settled in to enjoy a huge smoothie, great coffee and a couple of homemade croissants.

Looking at the name above the counter set me to thinking about the mysterious Jax and I messaged Daz to see if he could meet later. Uncle Daz always had time for me – whether or not I deserved it – and we agreed to meet at The Grenadier for an early pint. I had no messages from Julie which was ominous.

It was after eleven by the time I got back to the flat and I was ready to settle down for volume two. A part of me was relieved that I knew what was coming; if the renewed collapse of my mother's world had come as a surprise, it would have been devastating – as, of course, it had turned out to be for her.

It was still a harrowing read. There's something about an unexpected relapse that gives it extra power to cause pain and suffering; it comes suddenly, out of the blue, but you know what's happening instantly, and everything – all of those dark thoughts and emotions – flood in, rushing back in an uncontrollable wave.

After the fiasco on my first day at nursery, my mother was in hospital for a couple of days and the diary was silent but, on her return, she wrote down her thoughts and feelings without pulling any punches. Both the importance of the incident and the sudden unexpected reoccurrence were brutal blows and the tone of her writing changed from one entry to the next.

Her confidence and optimism were suddenly nowhere to be seen; every word on the page oozed paranoia and excuses, blame and shame. I was shocked at how quickly things changed and even more so at how negative she was about Granny. It was almost as though Mum was accusing her of having been responsible for what had happened.

Unsurprisingly, the following week's entries were messy and confused. There was a small hint of a return to her old self when she started work but it was only for a few weeks and was mixed up with frequent outpourings of her resentment of Granny. It seemed as though the more Granny helped out with me, the more angry and irrational Mum became.

Her daily entries stopped the day after the Facebook posting about Granny. Mum transcribed word-for-word the post which she had apparently made on her Facebook group and wrote underneath 'Does anyone who knows me believe I could write this? I am better than that! Someone is doing this to me.'

And, apart from a last, defiant curse on the day of her death, that was it. Whatever she thought or did during those final days was too personal and private even for her diary.

I closed the diary, tied the ribbon neatly and put it back in the box. Reading the second volume had done nothing to ease my sense that something was missing. The words on the page didn't quite fit with the facts they were describing nor with what I'd been told by my dad.

Until the end, there was nothing manic in her writing, no lack of coherence or logical thought, only a set of events that could only be explained by Mum having some sort of self-destructive second personality which was completely separate and independent of her normal self. If that was true, why didn't the other 'self' ever appear in the diaries?

I didn't know why, but reading everything laid out in detailed chronology, something seemed off. The timing was too perfect. Each step was so organised, structured and planned as though some sadistic deity was toying with her. She had talked about God and religion many times throughout the diaries and there was definitely some guilt there. Could her Catholic upbringing have played a role?

I was surprised at how calm I still felt after the initial shock of hearing her voice though her words. I also understood my suspicions might be driven by a desire to prove that my mother hadn't actually been mentally ill.

Whatever the reason, I needed to see this process through and the next step was to speak to Daz and my dad and to see if there were any clues on her phone. I would get it analysed as soon as I could and then, when I'd read through the diaries at least one more time, I would open her final letter to me.

There was a phone shop just around the corner in Sloane Street with a big 'We sell antique phones' sign in the window. It seemed like a good place to start.

'Good morning, I'm Serge,' said the young guy behind the counter. 'How can I help you?' He really was young. My mum's phone was probably at least ten years older than he was.

'Hi. I've got this old phone,' I said, handing it to him. 'I need to get the data off it, please. Something in a format I can read. Is it possible?'

'Yeah. Not a problem,' said Serge as he picked up the phone with two hands and twirled it confidently with the tips of his fingers. 'iPhone 5. It's a classic. Pretty good nick too. Let me know if you want to sell it. I'll give you a good price.'

'No ... Maybe ... Look, I don't want to think about that right now,' I said. 'I only want to know if you can get the data off it. Can you do that?'

'Of course,' he said. 'Easy. Do you want the full analysis? Emails, texts, apps, photos, system history, the whole shebang?'

'If it's not too expensive, that would be great.'

'I could do it for ninety euros including the memory tab, but I won't have it finished before the end of the week. OK?'

'That's fine,' I said. 'Take good care of it. It was my mother's.'

'Don't worry. It's in safe hands.'

And that was that. With Serge's help, I should have dug a couple more jigsaw pieces out from behind the sofa by the following week and might have a more complete picture. Meanwhile I was in waiting mode again and my old hamster friend was wearily climbing back onto his wheel.

I called Julie a couple of times during the afternoon but she didn't reply or ring back. Everything was happening all at once and my life had suddenly become untethered in a way which teleported me straight back into my fifteen-year-old self. I could almost feel the spots growing on my face.

I had no regrets about reading the diaries and it was wonderful to know Mum really had loved me, but that relief was only part of a truckload of more challenging thoughts and emotions – regrets, fears, confusion and, for the first time in years, biting loneliness.

And now it looked as though I might have blown everything with Julie. What an idiot I'd been. I was finding it difficult being the junior partner in the relationship, but I wasn't ready to break up with her yet, and not only because of the money and the crazy lifestyle. Being with her was amazing. I was probably more in awe of her than in love with her, but the two things were not so far apart. How often do you get to live with a goddess, after all?

In amongst everything else, I would need to find a way to mend things between us.

The Grenadier had been serving pints for over three hundred years and the walls oozed history and permanence. I remember Gramps talking about being a regular in the 1970s and I know my dad often used to go there after work when he lived in London.

They still had the same surprisingly-good sausages sitting on a heated dish at the bar and Daz had already lined up a couple by the time I arrived – along with pints, of course. Daz never seemed to change; it might have been the beard, his open smile or the fact that his clothes were always the same, but he definitely wasn't showing his years like my dad was.

In a way he'd filled a mother-shaped hole in my life growing up. He was always around and his burly, hairy bear-frame was wrapped around a sensitive – almost feminine – personality. There were definitely times when I felt more comfortable talking with Daz than with my dad.

The two of them couldn't have been more different. Dad was a product of his environment – one of the last vestiges of the near-extinct sub-species of stiff-upper-lip Englishmen who were bred to serve as army officers and civil servants in the days of empire. He tried hard, and we were very close, but it was always more natural for him to bottle up his thoughts and emotions rather than risk exposing them to the open air.

Two sausages each and a pint-and-a-half of familiar banter settled us deeper into the corner of the bar and it was time to get down to it.

'Who's Jax Daniels?' I said, watching Daz carefully.

He definitely twitched and his eyes widened for a brief moment. Jax wasn't just anybody.

'Now, I haven't heard that name for years,' he said. 'And I hoped I wouldn't. I knew she'd be back though. Her sort never actually get out of your life.'

'But who is she?'

'That's a long story and a half,' he said, sipping his pint. 'But before I tell you, you'd better let me know why you're asking.'

'OK. Fair enough. You remember a couple of weeks ago? When we were helping Dad to clear out of the house?'

'Yeah. So what?'

'Well, after you'd gone, Dad gave me Mum's diaries.'

'He did what?' Daz said, pint glass frozen in mid sip. 'I never knew about any diaries. Your dad's never said anything about them to me.'

'He never read them. He left them shut up in a shoebox at the back of a wardrobe.'

Daz was shaking his head slowly as he stared out of the window. 'All these years,' he said, a strange, sad smile poking its way out through the bush of his beard. 'All these years and she's not quite left us. Have you read them?'

'Yes,' I said. 'I finished them a few hours ago. I'll tell you more about them some time, but not today.'

'All right. You let me know. It would be magic to hear her voice one more time.' Daz was staring at the table with a glazed look. He was somewhere else. In a different time.

But I needed him here with me and waved my hand in front of his eyes. 'Hello. Earth to Planet Daz. Anyone in there?'

He looked at me, eyes soft with his memories. 'Sorry. Miles away.'

'Well I've told you why,' I said. 'Now it's your turn. Who's Jax? She was important to Mum, but I've never heard of her.'

'OK. I'll tell you. But it's complicated.'

I pointed to his empty pint glass and raised an eyebrow. 'I've got all night. What about you?'

And so we sat tucked in the corner as night fell and the pub filled with laughter and opinions. We were in our own bubble. Daz talking and me asking the odd question. I realised early on that I'd been right to ask Daz rather than my dad. He seemed to know more about this mysterious Jax than anybody.

I prided myself on being a modern, tolerant person without any of the built-in hangups which were still knocking around when my parents were young, but I was still shocked when I heard about my mother's relationship with Jax. My mother had been a lesbian before she met my father? I wasn't expecting that.

A bigger problem was trying to square their relationship with the way Daz described Jax. If he was telling it straight, the implication was that Mum had been blind, stupid and totally naive and that didn't fit with anything I'd been told about her before.

He really didn't hold back and I've never heard such a comprehensive character assassination. From the picture he painted of Jax, she was the embodiment of pure evil – Satan's favourite daughter. I'd always understood he must have been in love with Mum, but he wasn't the type to let jealousy get in the way of the truth. He was best friends with Dad after all.

I was probably being a bit harsh in any case. You don't need to be naive or stupid to fall in love and, although I'm not convinced love is blind, it's often quite shortsighted. Looking at my own romantic set-up, I wasn't in a great position to cast stones.

When he'd finished, I knew a lot more about Jax Daniels than I wanted to, but I had one more question.

'Do you think she could have had anything to do with Mum's death?' I asked him.

'Jax? I'd love to blame her, but don't see how. She'd been out of the picture for years. Your mum always made her own decisions, for better or for worse. She had her inner demons and they ended up taking over. Why are you asking, anyway?'

'It was only a couple of things I read in the diaries. It did sound as though she was becoming more and more paranoid though,' I said, managing to add a nervous laugh. 'She even thought Granny might've been behind things at one stage.'

Daz's laugh was more open than mine. 'Well, your mum certainly did pick 'em. I don't want to speak out of turn and you know I love Virginia to bits, but your gran is the second most manipulative bitch I've ever met, and I've met a few in my time.'

'Knock yourself out,' I said, with a smile. 'She's my grandmother and she's always been wonderful to me, but I totally see where you're coming from.' It was hard to find anything Daz said offensive, even when he was being exceptionally blunt.

'Anyway,' he said. 'I'm sure it was paranoia. Fabiola was in a bad way towards the end and I'd be surprised if she hadn't been looking for outside forces to blame.' He looked at me, holding my gaze without blinking. 'After it happened, we were all a bit crazy. It was such a shock and no-one could believe she was actually gone. I think all of us were looking to find someone or something to blame.'

'It must have been awful.'

'Yeah. Pretty grim,' he said. 'I'll never figure out how your dad managed. He somehow managed to hide his grief from you, even though he'd decided to blame himself for what had happened and it was eating him up. I think I tried to blame everybody – God, the universe, Jax, Virginia, myself – and I'm pretty sure your grandparents just blamed Fabiola.'

'Such a waste,' I said, lost for anything more substantial to say.

They called last orders and the noise of the crowded bar rose to a crescendo, melting our bubble and letting the real world back in.

We didn't need anything more to drink, but sat there for another five minutes, not speaking and letting the laughter and shouting ebb and flow over us. When we eventually stumbled out of the pub and said our goodbyes, I felt disengaged from reality, blinking and confused. It had been a crisp, sunny afternoon when I arrived and then, three hours later, I drifted out blank-eyed into the inky blackness of a London night and the world had changed.

I found my way home to bed on autopilot and slumped on top of the duvet like a sack of hops.

Toyboy

December 8th 2013

I've been a useless wife for too long; the whole passport mess was the last straw and we had a huge fight at the airport. I really lost it.

It was all my fault. I've started to see ghosts and villains everywhere. Rupert has actually been wonderful and, since we've been in Italy, I've been doing my best to let him know how grateful I am. I hope he can see that. I think he can.

I'm sitting alone on the terrace of Alberto's house as the morning mist floods a white lake into the valley below. It's beautiful.

Last night, me and Roop had our first romantic dinner out in ages. Sam stayed with Alberto and Maria and we walked down to a small trattoria in town. It was a perfect evening in every way and I can still feel the warm glow in my stomach.

I'm sure things are going to get better from now on. I can feel it.

The bees are all around me now – shimmering darts burning sunlight from their wings in golden vapour trails. I start to run in aimless panic. What Winnie-the-Pooh brainlessness convinced me to stick my hand into the hole anyway. I don't even like honey.

The first sting burns into my arm in a frenzy of boiling acid and I scream out loud like a four-year-old. Big mistake. My open mouth is a perfect round bulls eye and the stream of bees flows in before I have time to think.

The second explosion of pain is enough to make everything certain. I'm going to die this time. What a pointless, pathetic way to go ...

I snapped up in bed with my eyes wide open; my heart was hammering and, for a few seconds I couldn't breathe. My phone was still buzzing on vibrate but it must've fallen onto the floor and I couldn't find it in the dark. What time was it anyway?

By the time I'd found the light and the phone, it had stopped ringing and my heart rate was returning to normal. The sensation of small soft bodies in my throat was still real and, as I got up to go to the bathroom, I was gagging reflexively and waiting for the stings to come again.

My face in the mirror was reassuringly unswollen and a few seconds spent gargling tap water sent the bee memories back to honey land. Relieving myself of a bladderful of last night's beer took a bit longer, but I eventually staggered back to bed.

The message light was winking its devil's eye at me ominously. One-thirty in the morning. It had to have been Julie.

'Sam. Sam. Where the hell are you?' It didn't sound like I was forgiven. 'I'm about to get on the red-eye from JFK. I'll be landing at Heathrow at eight-thirty. Can you come and pick me up? I've only got hand baggage. See you there. Don't be late.'

That was a disaster. She wasn't supposed to be back for two more days. The flat was a mess. I was a mess. I'd planned to make everything perfect for her return – shiny clean flat, fresh flowers everywhere, well-stocked fridge, dinner on the table, champagne in an ice bucket and me, fragrant, groomed and grovelling.

I realised I had no time to panic. Military planning and precision were required. There were still risks but I might just get away with it. I texted Susie, our cleaner, and asked her to drop whatever else she was doing and get here first thing. I gave her detailed instructions for flowers and food and the promise of a hundred euro tip if she had everything in shape before nine o'clock. Hopefully she would be up early and pick up the text in time.

I took the box with the diaries and tucked it high up in the wardrobe behind the wedding hats. They should be safe there but I wanted them out of the flat as soon as possible.

The best thing I could do about myself was to get some more sleep, so I set my alarm for six-thirty and went back to bed.

Julie's flight landed early of course, but I was there in time, smartly dressed, showered, shaved and hopefully no longer oozing stale alcohol from every pore.

Her kiss was cold and close-lipped, but her eyes seemed pleased to see me and to be home.

'How was your trip?' I asked, as we walked out to the car park. 'Why are you back early? I thought you were going to be back on Thursday.'

'Crap, as you're asking,' she said. 'Our biggest investor has changed CEO and the new guy is a total arsehole who wants to make his mark. Nothing I can't deal with, but things would have been easier without the whole Imperial fiasco looming over me.'

'I'm so sorry about that,' I said, putting my hand on her shoulder and turning her to face me. 'I'll sort it out. Whatever you need.'

She pulled away roughly and carried on walking. 'Listen, Sam. I'm still pissed off with you and we need to have a proper talk, but I didn't get much sleep on the flight and I'm tired. This needs to wait until later.'

'Of course. I understand,' I said, opening the car door for her. 'Whatever you need.'

'I hope the flat isn't a tip. I can really do without coming home to a student house.'

'Of course not,' I said, giving her my best and most charming smile.

Meanwhile, my stomach was churning like an old-fashioned washing machine. Susie hadn't replied to my text and I had no idea what to expect when I walked through the door.

As we stepped into the flat, I was so relieved I almost tripped over my own feet.

Julie turned and stared at me. 'What's wrong with you today?

You're acting like more of a plonker than usual. The flat looks nice though. The flowers are lovely.'

I made a mental note to give Susie an extra fifty euros. She'd really delivered above and beyond.

'I'm sorry. I'm nervous because I know I screwed up. I knew the Imperial dinner was important to you, but I let myself get carried away.' I was working hard to deliver enough puppy dog contrition while keeping the attractive, manly boyfriend element. I was tempted to dust it with a bit of cheeky-chappy humour but that might have been a stretch too far.

'God, you're pathetic,' Julie said with a look of contempt. But was that a hint of a smile? 'I'll tell you what. I'm wiped out and I'm going to bed. If you can sort things out with Professor Bukowski and Imperial before I get up. I'll forgive you.'

'Done,' I said. 'I'll make it happen.'

'Oh.' Julie turned at the bedroom door. 'And I want supper on the table at seven o'clock. Deal?'

'Deal,' I said, my words falling on a closed door.

I was lucky and Dave was free for lunch. We met at Saki Saki, a new Japanese place on Sloane Street. The food was great; there was no menu and no choice which made it totally hassle-free. They brought out tiny tapas-like plates one after the other together with thimbles of saki or tiny shot glasses of craft beer.

'I'm still really pissed off with Julie,' he said, as we tucked into a single marinated and grilled octopus tentacle. 'The things she said the other night were completely out of order and frankly embarrassing. We were only having a laugh. Maybe we had a bit too much to drink, but so what?'

'I'm impressed you can remember what she said, to tell you the truth. My memories of the whole event are somewhat sketchy.'

'It was right after you dropped the carafe of port. The old profs were giving us both the evil eye and Julie came over and gave us a real earful. You must remember.'

'Mmmmh.' I was seeing flashes of a heavy cut-glass decanter falling silently in slow motion. As it hit the ground and shattered into ruby shards, my memory added the soundtrack and brought the playback up to normal speed. 'Ouch,' I said. 'I'd forgotten about the port.'

'Worth remembering. It was spectacular. Bit of a shame though, as we were having fun until then. It was excellent grappa, given to me by the Sapienza University. We probably shouldn't have followed it with port.'

'Maybe not.' I didn't want to think about grappa ever again. 'But going back to Julie, you can see her point, can't you? She's worked hard to build her relationships with Imperial and I'm sure she finds the academic bullshit as painful as you do.'

'That's probably true, but do I want to commit to working with someone like her for the next ten years? I've got plenty of other options.'

'Don't go there. You were happy enough before the dinner and you told me Pulsar is the most exciting partner by far. The thing is that it's all my fault ...'

'... That's not true. It was as much my fault as yours.'

'But it wouldn't have happened if I hadn't been there and I'm totally in the shit with Julie. I was hoping you could help me sort it out.'

'Of course I will,' he said. 'I'm only winding you up. You're a good bloke. What do you need?'

'Basically, I need everything to go back to how it was before, and we pretend Grappa-gate never happened. You tell the old profs to calm down and let Julie know everything is still on track. That's it.'

'I can do that,' he said. 'Pulsar actually is the best partner anyway. But, if you ask me, you should consider your own options going forward. It wasn't what she said to me that pissed me off. It was the way she was talking to you. That's not right.'

Dave wasn't telling me anything I didn't know, but I still wasn't quite ready. It was fine to think it through rationally, but I'd been surprised at the depth of my misery when I'd thought I was about to lose her. I told everyone - my dad, Daz, my mates, even myself - that I was only along for the ride and how I knew it wouldn't last. But was it true?

The idea of being apart from Julie was enough to leach all of the colour out of my life. Leaving her would be like leaving Oz and going back to a grey, dreary Kansas where Technicolor was either a dream or a distant memory. That was a real worry. I'd never planned to fall in love with her. It changed everything.

I spent the afternoon preparing supper. I'd done as much as I could to sort out the Imperial fiasco and I wanted to put together a special evening to complete my grovelling apology.

The star was going to be crab ravioli in a lobster bisque. Home-made pasta and some beautiful fresh crab which I'd found at my local corner shop. At five stories and taking up over a hundred metres of Knightsbridge pavement, Harrods was quite a big corner shop, but it was all relative.

When the table was laid and candles filled every corner of the room with warm, yellow flickering, I went to wake Julie. She was already up, sitting cross-legged on the bed, looking at her phone and smiling. She was so beautiful when she smiled. I needed to make her smile more. That would be a good plan.

As she saw me come in, she leapt up from the bed and hugged me. 'Who's a clever boy, then?' she said as she held my face in her hands. 'I just got a message from Professor Bukowski. Everything is going ahead and he's sent the contracts off to his lawyer for a final review. We should be able to sign next week.'

'Thank God for that,' I said, kissing her. I hadn't doubted Dave, but it was great that he'd come through so quickly.

'I don't know what you did to calm him down, but whatever it was, it worked. You're forgiven. And if supper's good, you're double forgiven.'

The half-wink she gave me as she said this made me very keen to find out what being double forgiven might entail and I ushered her through to the living room and the waiting champagne.

'You've made it so beautiful,' she said, spinning around. 'Not bad for a man. Not bad at all.'

That Doesn't Make Sense

January 15th 2014

I go back and forth and never know what to think. Deborah has convinced me that the mind is perfectly capable of playing these sorts of tricks, but I can't believe it. I know how idiotic it is to imagine someone is deliberately doing this to me. How could they be?

It's stupid, but I'm not crazy, so I can't stop thinking it. Who has it in for me? Virginia? Jax? It's all so ridiculous. As I write it down, I realise I really am sounding like a mad person.

Anyway, I persuaded Roop to buy me a new phone and I've changed all my passwords. If things still keep happening, I'll accept that everything is in my mind. I'll have to.

'Are you sure? Definitely not?'

Serge was nothing if not persistent. It must have been the tenth time he'd asked.

'Yes. Really sure. Thanks again for the offer. How much do I owe you?'

'It's ninety euros as agreed,' he said, handing over the phone and a tiny memory tab, stuck onto the corner of an A4 sheet of paper. 'I've listed the core contents by category and the chip is compatible with your vis screen ... And if you ever change your mind about selling the old phone ...'

'Don't worry, you'll be top of the list.' I handed over the money, picked up the paper and my mum's phone and turned to leave.

'Mr Blackwell?'

'Yes,' I said, standing in the doorway, halfway in and halfway out.

'Don't forget to check on those two forwarding numbers I've noted in the summary. It's unusual to have two bits of tracking software on the same phone. One is rare enough, but I've never seen two. I can do some tracing work if you want, but it's not cheap.'

I smiled. Serge was a young man who would go far. 'Thank you. I'll make sure to remember,' I said, closing the door behind me.

'Dad?'

'Yes.'

'Can you talk?'

'Yup. I've got ten minutes or so. What's up.'

'I've just picked Mum's phone up from the shop.'

'Oh.'

'Don't worry. I'm not going to share anything from the diaries or the phone unless you ask me to.'

'Thanks. Let's keep it that way.'

'But I do want to ask you about the tracking software.'

'Oh that. I told you about it years ago.'

'I know. And I can see the link to your phone number.'

'So, what's the problem?'

'Did you load up some other software before that?'

'No.'

'Well, someone did and it goes to different number. I've dialled it a few times but there's no reply.'

'That's strange. Nothing to do with me. Maybe your mum got someone to put it on for her.'

'Perhaps. But I'm not convinced.'

'You're not letting this get to you are you?'

'No, don't worry. I'm fine.'

'Good. I'm worried I might have made a mistake giving you the diaries.'

'You didn't. I needed this.'

'OK. But you take care not to get stuck in the past. Sorry, I have to go. See you soon. Love you.'

Julie was out at a conference until late, so I had the flat to myself. My plan was simple; I would go through the contents of Mum's phone looking for clues, and cross-reference everything I found. Then, and only then, I would read the letter. I couldn't put it off any longer.

There was a huge station clock hanging above the living room fireplace. It was over two feet in diameter and used to hang at Paddington Station. It was apparently chosen by Brunel and had hung over the main platform when the station first opened in the eighteen fifties. Julie was obsessed with the passage of time and would do anything she could to either slow it down or get more out of each wasting second. She'd bought the clock years before and it was one of her favourite possessions.

As I sat there with the diaries and my vis-screen in front of me, each swing of the gleaming brass pendulum ticked away the seconds until my moment of truth. I had no idea whether Mum's last words to me would make me feel better or worse and I would have loved an excuse to procrastinate a while longer.

The emails and texts were generally boring. Functional daily communications which didn't say much more about who she actually was and, unsurprisingly, didn't discuss any of the traumas and the emotional decline which defined her last months. Email wasn't the place.

There were some exchanges with my dad which were a bit more revealing, but mostly in a slightly uncomfortable, voyeuristic way. I actually didn't want to know anything about the pet names and euphemisms which made up their private world.

Probably the only thing that stood out was the way the number and tone of the emails declined over the period. Mum was definitely becoming worried about everything and everybody and I could see it in her words. More formal, cautious and evasive as the days and weeks moved on. I could almost see her open, trusting nature lashed down cord by cord like a captured lioness, muzzled and bound tight.

I knew from her diaries that she was starting to suspect that even those closest to her were potential traitors and threats. In her rational moments she realised she was imagining things, but in darker times, she saw betrayal after betrayal everywhere around.

There was no mention of the second set of spy software in the emails or the diaries and I couldn't believe she'd arranged for it to be installed to check up on herself. She would have referred to it somewhere. I would have to find a way to trace the number and also to get someone to double-check Serge's work. Maybe he'd made a mistake.

My Darling Sam,

I don't know when, or if, you'll ever read this, but I hope your dad finds the right time to give it to you.

Where do I begin?

I don't expect you to forgive me for my decision – how could you? I will try to explain why I don't think I have a choice anyway. Maybe it will help you to think of me a little more kindly.

I know Rupert will have told you what has been happening to me. He is too straight and honest to keep it from you. What he can't tell you is how I actually feel and how this is tearing me apart.

I have been to counsellors and psychiatrists and have tried my hardest to play along with their assumptions and conclusions. However hard I try, it doesn't change what I feel inside, and have always felt. I still can't lose this certainty that I'm completely sane and that everything that has happened to me is the work of some malicious and evil conspiracy.

I'm not unintelligent or ignorant and can see I am being ridiculous – I'm only an ordinary housewife and mother after all. But that's what terrifies me more than anything; the only other possibility is that I have another person living inside of me, but I can't feel their presence. Not at all. Can you imagine what that's like?

And, if I can't accept I have an illness, how can I hope to get better?

Which brings me to the reason why I've made this terrible choice. Why I've decided to abandon the two people I love most in the world. If I'm not even aware of my other self, how can I trust it with you? Can I be sure I won't have a car accident, or abandon you somewhere when I'm not in control?

Even if nothing dramatic happens, I can't stand the thought of forcing you both to worry about me year in and year out, or the way your friends will tease you about me, or of the ways I will let you down again and again. I have thought about this so much and I truly believe you'll be better off without me.

My greatest hope is that the man reading this is strong and happy, that he knows how to laugh and make others laugh. I look at you now, quietly sleeping in your cot, and have no doubt you'll grow into a beautiful man.

I will always love you and watch over you. Please try to forgive me.

All my love

Mum

I put the letter down on the table where it lay staring at me. Strange how a few dark squirls on cream paper could weigh so much and speak pain and loss across the years with such power.

It had been years since I'd last cried. Maybe it was about time.

I couldn't stay in one place and walked up and down through the flat. I moved from room to room to outpace my emotions but they were on my shoulder every step of the way. Eventually I ended up in the gym and switched on the treadmill.

No warm-up, no long distance rhythm, I ramped up the speed until I was at a full sprint and pushed forward like I never had before. My lungs were burning and I felt my legs turn to jelly as I quickly took myself past any sort of aerobic pace. I still kept on, pounding forwards and not willing to concede, until my legs suddenly gave out and I was thrown backwards to land in a tangled mess against the far wall.

The running machine continued to whine hysterically for a few seconds before the safety cut-outs kicked in and it gradually slowed to a safe speed before stopping completely and plunging the room into silence.

I lay in a sweaty heap for a long time, sucking deep, raw breaths in through my mouth and feeling my body and mind piece themselves back together bit by bit. Running had helped and I was scoured clean inside.

The outside needed some attention though and, as I stood under the shower feeling the heat of the jets pounding my back and neck, I felt relieved. That was it. The worst was over and I no longer had any new shocks in front of me. Having read the diaries, I wasn't surprised by what my mother had written in the letter. I was happy to have it and would read it again many times. There was no rush to decide how much I would be able to forgive her, if at all. That could wait.

The only remaining unknown was the mystery of the second phone number but I wasn't expecting any major new revelations. I would try it again a few times once I'd made myself a coffee and then go back and see Serge at the phone shop.

I dialled the number while the coffee was brewing. It rang and rang as before but still wasn't picked up. There was a slight buzzing echo which was unusual but no-one at the other end.

Coffee in hand, I hit redial and went back to the living room to read the letter one more time. No answer, but the echo was getting louder. Maybe it meant something?

I hit redial for the last time and, after a couple of rings, I put my phone down on the table and picked up the letter. The echo was just as loud as before, even though I didn't have the phone to my ear. It made no sense. Three more phantom buzzes and it stopped.

It took me a while to get my clumsy brain into gear. The echo wasn't an echo. It was a ringtone coming from inside the flat. My fingers were clumsier than my brain and I knocked my coffee flying as I grabbed for the phone to dial again. Hot acid coffee splattered the priceless, polished walnut and ebony gobbets of blackness sprayed out over the white carpets. I picked up the phone and left the coffee to do its worst.

Redial. I was certain now. It was in the flat. I started walking around, holding the phone in front of me like a water diviner's hazel wand and letting it lead me to the source. The sound was coming from Julie's private office; it wasn't locked, but was definitely a no-go area. I barged in without hesitation and the buzzing stopped.

Redial. It was definitely in the office. In Julie's desk. The drawers were also unlocked and I found the right one on my second try. There it was – an old-school glass and metal brick like Mum's, sitting at the back of the drawer, vibrating quietly against the polished walnut of the drawer and flashing its green and red phone symbols at me like a challenge.

I picked it up and carefully unplugged the charging lead, trying to remember to keep breathing. The on switch was fiddly and needed to be pushed in using a fingernail. A fingerprint lock symbol flashed up, but that wasn't why I dropped it clattering back into the drawer. Two smiling youthful faces filled the screen. One was my mother, and the other looked a lot like a younger version of Julie.

'Daz? Is that you?'

'Yeah it's me. What's wrong? You sound awful.'

'Can you come round?'

'What, now?'

'Yes, now now. Please. I need your help and I don't want to talk about it on the phone.'

'No problem, boy. I can skive off in a few minutes. I'll be about half an hour.'

'Thanks Daz. The door code is 1974. Come straight up.'

'OK. See you in a bit.'

The phone was fingerprint locked and I had nothing better to do while I waited so I reconnected the charging lead and went back to the living room. I cleared up as much of the coffee as I could and tried to polish out the white streaks and blobs in the walnut. I was beginning to realise that I was fighting a losing battle when I heard the doorbell.

I suspect Daz was anticipating a huge disaster when he came through the door. He was red-faced and breathing heavily and looked as though he'd been running.

'So where's the fire?' he said, looking around. 'I thought you'd murdered your girlfriend or something.'

'Don't be ridiculous. Although she might murder me when she sees what I've done to the table.'

He saw the cloths and polish spread out and walked over. 'No need to panic,' he said. 'It might need to be French polished again, but it'll be fine. Is that why you dragged me out of work and nearly gave me a heart attack?'

'No. Of course not,' I said. 'I'll show you.'

As we walked through the flat, I could hear Daz mumbling, more to himself than to me. 'Bloody ridiculous place. Twenty people could live here. What's the bloody point?'

'You know that I was going to get Mum's old phone analysed?'

'Yeah. I remember.'

'There were two bits of tracking software on the phone. One linked out to Dad's phone and the other went to another number.'

'I know. Your dad told me,' he said.

We'd arrived at Julie's office. I opened the drawer and took out the phone.

'This is the phone,' I said. 'I dialled the number and this phone rang.'

'What?'

'I dialled the phone number from the tracking software and this phone rang. That's how I found it.'

'Bloody hell. What's it doing here?'

'There's more,' I said, pressing the on button and handing it to him. 'Look.'

It took him a few breaths to get any words out and even then they were a mess. 'But ... Fabiola ... how? ... here ... Jax ...' He grabbed my arm – too hard. 'It's bloody Jax. Why has your girlfriend got a picture of Fabiola and Jax on her phone?'

'So it really is Jax?'

'Of course it bloody is. Not a face I'd ever forget.'

'I thought it must be,' I said. 'I've playing everything over in my mind while I waited for you, and it's the only explanation that works. It's Jax, but it's also Julie. They're the same person.'

'Oh fuck.' Daz slumped into the nearest chair. 'You can't be serious?'

'But I am.' I showed him a couple of pictures I'd managed to sneak of Julie without her full war paint and with her guard down. 'Recognise her now?'

'I think so. She must have had plastic surgery or something but, if you look carefully at the eyes, I'm ninety per cent sure.' His eyes flicked wildly around the room and he leapt up out of the chair.

'Jeezus H Christ. I don't know what's going on but I know we need to get out of here right now. We'll call the cops.'

'Me neither, Uncle Daz. I don't know what's going on either.' I took the phone gently from him, plugged it back in and closed the drawer. 'But I'll tell you one thing for nothing. I'm going to bloody well find out.'

A Monster Reborn

March 9th 2014

The police called around this evening, just as Daz said they would.

To begin with it was quite funny. There was a tall, lanky man and a short, dumpy, bubbly blonde. It was all a bit Carry On Policeman. I've never done anything wrong, so wasn't worried.

They were both quite senior and working for some sort of anti-terrorism team. The tall man did most of the talking and the woman jumped in from the sidelines from time to time. I could feel her watching me though.

The mood changed when they started talking about the ammonia-filled light bulbs. What sort of warped person would think up something like that? And then when she described what had happened to that poor policeman ...

That sort of thing was why I couldn't stay involved with the protest movements. Knowing there were monsters like that always waiting to hop on our coat tails and to twist all of our good intentions into violence and sadism. I couldn't stand it.

And then the two of them started implicating Jax in the attack and saying Jax had actually never existed and she had a false identity. It was way too much to deal with and I was grateful Sam woke up and distracted us. If it was true, how could I have loved her so much? What did that make me?

The only thing I remember after that was the way the blonde policewoman talked about the attack. There was something else there. Something personal. I could hear from the anger in her voice that the victim had been more than just a colleague.

It was a miserable morning and I got soaked in the hundred yards from Warwick Avenue tube to the little coffee shop on Formosa Street. I much preferred Little Venice to Knightsbridge. It had become almost as expensive and posh, but it hadn't always been and the area had managed to stay more bohemian than brash. I'd had my fill of money show-offs.

Daz was already there. I could see him through the windows, bent over a coffee cup and looking out of place in his own unique fashion. I'd managed to calm him down the previous evening and to persuade him to hold back on calling the police. He'd known Jax, but I knew Julie; the rules were different for people like her and, without a proper plan and solid evidence, she'd shrug off any accusations and probably sue us for slander. I also still didn't know what we were accusing her of anyway.

I sat down opposite him and ordered a short macchiato, putting the odds of getting something which wasn't a large cup of milk and foam at about one in ten.

'Did you speak to her?' I asked.

'Yeah. She remembered me from before. She retired last year, lives just down the road and is keen to meet. When I told her about Julie and the phone, she got very excited.'

'I think I know why,' I said. 'Mum wrote about her in the diaries. She thought DI Simpson and the dead policeman were an item.'

'That would explain a lot,' said Daz. 'She certainly remembered Jax Daniels. Even after thirty years.'

'Well, we'll find out soon enough. When can we see her?'

'Now,' said Daz. 'Finish your coffee and we'll go.'

I looked at the large cup of foamy milk which was nothing like a macchiato, took a sip and pushed it away. I would probably never learn.

The flat was on the fifth floor of a curving, white stucco terrace. No lift, and it was tiny, but still way outside the price range of a police officer – even a senior one.

'I inherited the flat from my father,' she said, pouring three strong teas. She must have been a mind reader. 'I love living here. Lots of trees and we've got a beautiful private garden at the back. Shame about the stairs, but it keeps me fit.'

'Thank you, detective,' I said, taking the offered tea.

'It was Detective Superintendent when I last looked,' she said. 'But I'm retired now, so please call me Liz.'

'Nice to meet you, Liz.' I lifted the mug of tea in a half toast.

'And nice to see you again,' she said.

'Have we met before?' I said, my confusion adding a squeaky inflexion to my voice.

Liz smiled. 'You were only ten months old at the time, so I'm not offended that you don't remember. I was so sorry to hear about your mother. We only met once, but she seemed to be a special person.'

'Thank you,' I said. 'I suppose Daz has told you what's been going on – the diaries, the phone, what we found in Julie's flat?'

She nodded and sat forward in her chair. 'And I think you were right to hold back before going to the police. By the time they blundered in, any evidence would be long gone. And with someone like Julie Martin, the investigating officers would probably have found a 'suggestion' on their desks. A suggestion to drop it and move onto something else.'

'That was what worried me,' I said. 'I've seen how she deals with people who cross her.'

'I've waited all of my life to get hold of this woman,' Liz said, almost spitting out the words. 'I'm not going to let her slip through my fingers again.'

Daz had been standing by the window and turned to face us. 'But what has she done?' he asked. 'I know you suspect she was involved in the attack on that copper years ago, but what's it got to do with Fabiola? And what's that phone doing in her flat?'

Liz turned to Daz. 'First of all, "that copper" was my fiancé, so that's why I care so much.'

'I'm sorry,' he said. 'I think Fabiola suspected something along those lines.'

She moved straight on. '... And secondly, I've been looking for this woman for my whole working life and, if she had tracking software on your mother's phone, it was there for a reason. My fiancé wasn't her first victim.'

'So you found out who she actually is?' I said.

'Yes. Or at least we're ninety-nine per cent sure. She was born Janice Cargill in Leicester in 1989. Not a great upbringing by all accounts. Her father beat her mother regularly and almost certainly abused Janice from an early age.'

'Are we supposed to feel sorry for her now?' Daz said. 'I wasn't expecting that from you.'

'I don't feel sorry for her,' said Liz. 'We all make our choices, however much shit is thrown at us on the way. It appears Janice chose violence and retribution. She knocked her father unconscious with a hammer, castrated him and left him to bleed to death on the kitchen floor. She was fifteen at the time.'

'Jeezus,' said Daz, hunching forward. 'I knew she wasn't right, but that's horrible.'

'It's best you know what you're dealing with,' said Liz.

'So, whose phone is it in Julie's flat?' I couldn't stop myself thinking about all of those times I'd been with her – everything exposed and vulnerable – and felt acid bile rise in my throat as I squeezed my knees together.

'The police may be able to run a trace on the number but I'm ready to bet it's Jax's old phone. We need to get hold of it and break the security.'

'Easier said than done,' said Daz.

'But worth it. The phone probably has evidence that Jax was tracking Fabiola and there might also be some record of her anarchist activities. I don't understand why she hasn't destroyed it. It seems unlike her.'

'I think she's never stopped loving my mother,' I said. 'I'm getting a nasty feeling that's why she's together with me. It can't be a coincidence. She must have engineered it.'

'That would fit with the Jax I knew,' said Daz. 'Obsessive, controlling bitch. Oh, and did I mention heartless?'

'You're probably both right,' said Liz. 'And that makes it even more complicated. And definitely dangerous. The safest thing would be to go to the police now. I'm still good friends with my old boss and I'm sure he'd listen. It would be great if we had the phone first though ...'

'But could it be used as evidence if we stole it?' Daz asked.

Liz was on her home turf now. 'Normally not,' she said. 'But if Sam takes the phone, it wouldn't be theft. He's got free run of the flat and the phone isn't locked away. It's treading a fine line legally, but it's the best I can think of. No-one would get a search warrant with what we have at the moment.'

'So you want me to go home, pretend everything's normal, take the phone and run?' I said.

'Not quite,' said Liz. 'I think it would be best if we swapped it for an identical one – with a dead battery maybe – and you played the boyfriend for a while longer. Until we've had time to see what's on it.'

'Easy for you to say. What if she catches me?' As I learnt more about Julie's past and thought about the tracking software and her relationship with me, I could feel the black dread growing inside me like a tumour. I had no proof, but I knew Jax/Julie had been behind my mother's misery and death. And then she'd seduced me? Why? What sort of sick person would do that? I shivered.

'That wouldn't be good.' Liz was the police detective again. 'Jax Daniels is a dangerous person. She's proven how resourceful she can be and you'd be at serious risk if she suspected anything.'

I was afraid, but my growing outrage and sense of betrayal outweighed the fear. I also felt foolish and dirty; I really had been only a toy for her – a puppet character in some sick Greek tragedy which she'd concocted in her twisted mind.

'I'll be fine,' I said, with more confidence than I felt. 'I have to do this.'

Daz and I didn't speak as we walked back down the five flights of stairs. I felt as though I'd agreed to jump off a cliff blindfolded with only vague assurances that the water below was deep enough and not dotted with jagged rocks.

235

As we stepped out onto Warrington Crescent, he broke the silence.

'Are you thinking what I'm thinking?' he said.

'I think so.'

'Your mother wasn't crazy, was she?'

'I don't think so.'

'But, at the time, none of us believed her. We let it happen.'

'How could you have known?'

'When your dad finds out, it's gonna kill him.'

We walked as far as the tube before he spoke again.

'This stays between us for now,' he said, squeezing my arm so hard it hurt. 'Just the three of us. We don't tell your dad. No-one.'

'Agreed,' I said. 'We'll figure out how to tell him when we've got that bitch cornered.'

My promise wasn't more than an hour old when I realised I needed to break it.

About ten minutes after I got back to the flat, my phone buzzed with a message from Dave Bukowski; 'Signing docs with your missus tomorrow. Fancy going out for a few after? No grappa.'

I'd forgotten all about the deal. That was a problem. Was I going to let Dave sign his life's work away to Julie and Pulsar without warning him? It was me who'd persuaded him to go ahead after all.

I messaged him back; 'Can you meet now? South Ken somewhere?'

His response was immediate; 'Sure. Zak's in ten.' Fortunately, world-famous professors didn't seem to have a lot of work to do.

We sat by the window and I allowed Dave five minutes to share his considered doctoral opinion about each and every 'bit of posh totty' and 'yummy mummy' in the cafe. This being South Kensington on a sunny day, the general rankings were high.

That done, I swore him to secrecy and gave him a short history lesson: my mother's life and death; her phone and diaries; the phone in the flat; Jax's involvement in the riots and, of course, the fact that Jax and Julie were the same person.

'... The thing is that I can't actually prove any of this. I'm certain it's true, but I don't have anything concrete yet. I just couldn't let you go ahead and sign without saying something.'

'Thanks,' he said. 'You've got no idea how much that means.'

For a moment, I thought he was about to cry. 'Are you OK?' I asked. 'You look terrible.'

'I'm sorry,' he said, shaking his head. 'You couldn't have known, but what you told me touched a bit of a nerve.' He ran his fingers through his hair a couple of times before looking up at me. 'Sorry. I'm OK now.'

'Do you want to tell me about it?'

'Not so much to tell. A tragic little story, really. It's just that ... when you told me about your mother ... it all came flooding back. My sister, Dana, killed herself when she was seventeen. She was two years older than me and I worshipped her.'

'Oh God. I'm sorry,' I said.

'Thanks. And I really do appreciate you telling me about Julie,' he said. 'There's more, you see. The reason why she did it was because of a stupid, vicious campaign of cyberbullying at school. No real reason why she was singled out, but it went on for almost three years and everything she tried to do to make it better only made it worse.'

'That's terrible. How awful.'

'And totally pointless. I went to the same school and knew a lot of the people responsible but nothing ever happened to them. Apart from anything else, they were all minors.'

'Yeah. I can just hear people saying how cruel children can be and how they didn't mean anything by it. Doesn't help your sister though, does it?'

'Too right. That's exactly how it was. I'll tell you one thing though - there's no way I'm working with Julie Martin now. I've got offers from two of her competitors and I'll do whatever I can to make things difficult for her.'

'Remember that I don't have proof.'

'I know, but you wouldn't have told me if you weren't sure and, for some unfathomable reason, I trust you. The deal's off.'

'Good,' I said. 'But you need to find a credible reason to delay signing for the time being. The last thing we need is for her to get suspicious.'

'Don't worry,' he said. 'She won't suspect a thing.'

The Beginning of the End

Something's not right.

I just picked up a message from Dave Bukowski. We were supposed to sign contracts this afternoon – the lawyers have agreed everything – but he called with some lame excuse about wanting to check on his tax status before signing. It's clearly bullshit as his lawyers did that months ago. He's a crappy liar; he's stalling and I don't know why.

Sam's being weird too. A couple of nights ago, he spilt coffee over my favourite table and all over the carpet. It's easily fixed and I don't actually care, but I expected him to be much more nervous and apologetic than he was. I've been noticing his change in attitude for weeks. If I didn't know better, I'd say he's thinking of breaking up with me, but doesn't quite know how to do it.

Who the fuck does he think he is? I'll decide when we break up and how. He's my last link to Fabiola – I can still almost see her in his eyes when the light is right – and I'm not quite ready to sever that cord.

It may be time soon though. The light isn't right so often these days. He's been fun and he's very pretty, but he's not his mother and he never will be.

I've always been good at knowing when to cut my losses and move on. It's something visceral. I start to pump adrenalin all of the time, I can't sleep and have no appetite. I can feel it now, but I don't want to listen to the warning. Not yet.

I love being Julie Martin. The Julie Martin. I love the power and the way people behave around me. It's as though I were a queen or an empress. Easy to sneer at, but you shouldn't knock it until you've tried it.

There's plenty of money stashed away, but it's too late to build something like Pulsar again. I'm tired. Much as I hate to even think it, I'm too old and I wouldn't want to try to change my appearance so much again. Cosmetic science has its limits.

If I leave now, I'll have to become a nobody, hiding away until the end. A lonely old woman, finding increasingly petty ways to vent her spinster bitterness on young, pretty shop girls and waitresses. I'm not ready for that.

Why can't things stay as they are? Maybe my pumping urge to flee is a false alarm. It could be something hormonal or I could simply be imagining things.

Who am I kidding? I've never been wrong before. I have to remember who I am. I can't trust anybody. I've known that all my life. If you trust people, they shit on your trust. Even Fabiola. I trusted her and she betrayed me. Look how far she was prepared to go to escape from me. That wasn't how it was supposed to end.

And now it's starting again. The cycle of betrayal. Well, I'm always prepared and there are more ways to reward treachery than bags of silver.

Thin Ice

March 15th 2014

I'm worried about Sam. Am I looking after him properly? It's not only the major disasters like the time I completely lost it in the car park. It's all the time. I'm distracted and nervous, waiting for something else to happen. I don't want that tension and edginess to affect him.

Rupert says I'm fine. That it's normal for young mothers to feel this way. He's a sweetie, but what does he know about young mothers?

I must try to get myself into a better place. I'm doing an exercise video every day while Sam has his nap and I'm taking much more care about my diet. That should help.

Surely Julie must have figured out something was wrong? I found myself staring at her – not in a good way – and she caught me a couple of times. If I'd been a good actor, I wouldn't have been laughed out of drama lessons at school.

To make it worse, my emotions were bouncing uncontrollably between terror and hatred and I felt like throwing up half the time. Under those circumstances, my loving toyboy role was an impossible part for anyone to play.

I'd forgotten we were going to be away for the weekend which made things even more difficult; there was not going to be any easy way for me to escape, even for an hour or two. We'd been invited to some ridiculous, snobby Polo event in Newquay sponsored by one of the big champagne brands. It would be Monday at the earliest before I could swap the phone and Monday was an eternity away.

The crazy thing was that Julie hated these events even more than I did, but still insisted that we went to them. Surely the point of having lots of power and money is to do what you want and never do what 'the man' tells you to do? I was obviously missing something.

On the way down to Cornwall, she was in a foul mood and sat simmering silently for the first half hour.

'I thought you said Professor Bukowski was happy to move ahead,' she snapped, as we turned onto the M4 at Chieveley.

'I did. He is. Isn't he?'

'He was yesterday but we were supposed to sign today and now he's delayed until next week.'

'Why?'

'Some bullshit excuse. Bloody academics – they always piss you around.'

'What d'you think happened? He was totally up for it when we had lunch.'

'How would I fucking know what happened? Look, I don't want to talk about it. Just get us there safely, will you. I'm going to catch up on some sleep.'

That suited me. The less time we spent talking together the better. Fewer opportunities for me to screw up. My biggest worry was sex. I wasn't sure I'd be able to perform and I definitely didn't want to. In normal circumstances, I didn't have hang-ups about sex and, for me, it definitely didn't need to be associated with love, but the image of a fifteen-year-old Julie standing over her father's body clutching a dripping kitchen knife was going to be tough to banish.

I always drove – using the autopilot was for wimps – and we had the new top-of-the-range Tesla which was a joy. My dad still rambled on about the old petrol classics, but he needed to try one of these. Gramps' old Aston Martin DB5 was still in the garage at Granny's. It was Dad's now, but since the ban on petrol cars came in, all he could do was polish it and run the engine every now and then.

The Aston was a pretty car, but so was the Tesla and, with twice the horsepower and half the weight, the Tesla was much more of a beast. A shame I never got to take my dad for a spin, but it was too late now – unless I stole the car when I made my escape, which would probably not be the smartest move.

Everyone still wanted electric cars to simulate the sound of classic petrol engines, and the roar we made as we flew westwards turned lots of heads. Seeing the beauty of the car turned them again in a classic double take and I smiled every time. I was going to miss this.

Daz and I had met in a cafe earlier and he'd handed me a bag with the dummy phone inside. It wasn't only the phone in the bag. Liz had also included a sticky plastic sheet to pick up some of Julie's fingerprints, a small plastic bottle for a lock of hair or a fingernail clipping and a tiny, tiny tracking device no bigger than a match-head. I felt like a spy.

Daz explained that the tracker was a back up in case Julie did a runner before we were ready to go to the police. I should try and attach it to something she wouldn't leave behind.

Really? And, without their advice, I would have stuck it to a table. Did he think I was totally thick?

I knew straight away where I'd put the tracker. Julie had a blue leather Mulberry purse which she'd had ever since I'd known her. It was old and shabby by her standards but she wouldn't consider replacing it. When I'd offered to buy her a new one soon after we met, she almost bit my head off. She then apologised – a rare occurrence in itself – saying, 'Sorry. It was a gift from an old friend and is special to me.'. I'll bet it was from Mum.

Julie had been either in her office or together with me the whole afternoon so swapping the phone would have to wait until we got back. I'd probably have a chance to do the other spy stuff over the weekend but would have to see what opportunities came up.

I only needed to hold it together for a few days. If Julie really had been responsible for Mum's death, I'd do whatever it took to make sure she didn't slip away again. As I looked at her sleeping next to me, I wondered if the best alternative would be to kill her myself. It wouldn't take much; I could just click off her seatbelt and drive us off the road.

Knowing my luck, the airbags would save her and, in any case, the inboard computer would record my actions and the police would find out what had happened. Strangling then? Accidental drowning?

But I wasn't a cold-hearted killer and Mum wouldn't have wanted me to throw my life away like that. No, the plan we had was a good one. I needed to man up and get on with it. It was only a couple of days.

We arrived in Newquay in the late afternoon with just enough time to change and go straight down to the beach for the welcome reception. All of the players and polo ponies were there to admire and it was a perfect midsummer's evening. The weather might have been expressly ordered for the throng of blazers, chinos and LBDs which littered the roped area.

The scene made me think of my Gramps. He'd generally kept a low profile at home – much easier not to get in Granny's way – but he'd always had a dry sense of humour. Granny had a bad cliché habit and, whenever the weather was kind to us, she'd inevitably declare that 'the sun shines on the righteous ...' normally raising a glass of champagne in toast to our righteous good fortune and the sun's dutiful cooperation.

Gramps would then lean over to me and Dad and, smiling all of the way, softly mutter '... and on the ungodly too.'. I don't think she ever heard.

Looking over at the polo players, I could see that this might be a suitable pond for Julie to hook a replacement Sam when the time came. Young, fit, handsome and Argentinian would fit the bill.

As always, Julie seemed to know everyone and we found ourselves chatting to Gonzalo Monteverde, the Captain of the Rest of the World team – Argentinian of course. Players from both teams were riding up and down the beach, showing off their horses and their trick shots.

'You ride, don't you Sam?' said Julie.

'I used to a bit as a kid,' I said. 'But nothing like these guys. And the ponies are amazing. It's as though they know exactly what the riders are thinking.'

'Actually Sam,' said Gonzalo, in perfect English. 'It's almost the other way around. When we train a pony, we say it's ready when it plays for you rather than the opposite. The horse knows what to do, so you don't need to tell it.'

'Incredible,' I said. 'I can totally believe that. I spent a couple of weeks on a hacienda just north of Buenos Aires when I was eighteen and we went out riding with the gauchos looking for new-born calves to check and brand. I loved it.'

'It's a beautiful country. What did you think of our gauchos?' he asked. 'And their horses?'

'I'd never seen anything like it. They were so skilful. And unbelievably fast. I think the bit that amazed me most was when they jumped off to check the calf. Their horses would stand there motionless, head down, waiting. Even if the calf's mother was upset and aggressive, the horses didn't spook or interfere. They waited patiently.'

'And this is why our players and ponies are the best in the world,' he said, smiling proudly. 'As you'll see tomorrow.'

'Could Sam have a try?' said Julie, with a mischievous grin.

'Julie, please. It's been years...'

'Of course he can,' said Gonzalo, ignoring my feeble protests. 'Just give me a moment.' He turned to one of the pony boys and gave him instructions in Spanish. 'Sam, if you could go with Juan please. He will sort some jodhpurs and a horse.'

Well, it clearly amused Julie, but I wasn't so convinced. It had been years since I'd been on a horse and these animals were a long way from ordinary weekend hackers.

My mother must have been looking out for me as the polo pony gave me a perfect excuse to avoid sex and generally behave awkwardly all weekend.

His name was Chico. He was ten years old, almost fifteen hands, and a beautiful horse. Ten minutes after leaving Julie and Gonzalo, I found myself sitting in Chico's saddle and setting out across the sand, mallet in my hand, wondering if he was as confused as I was about what was happening.

Apparently not. He spotted a group of players scrabbling over a ball about fifty yards away, and he was off. Chico obviously understood he was 'playing for me' but, if I wanted to stay connected to his back, I was also going to need to figure out what he was planning to do next.

As we approached the barging, biting, stick-swinging melee, I was sure Chico would swing left to follow the ball. It was only later that I learnt that the obvious tactic was to wheel right and arc around to the back of the group.

Unfortunately Chico was smart and well trained in polo tactics. I leant left and forward, Chico turned right and our short friendship was over.

Falling from a horse is never fun but when it's unexpected and you're carrying a long wooden mallet, it's even less so. I lay on my back, not moving as I struggled to get breath back into my lungs and to take stock of how much damage I'd done.

My head was all right, neck muscles a bit sore, but nothing seemed broken. I could move my fingers and toes which was good, but I wasn't sure about my back. It would probably be best to lie still for a bit longer in the damp sand.

The medics were quick to arrive and told me to stay still. I would have nodded my agreement but my neck was throbbing and, by then, I'd gathered enough breath to grunt my understanding.

While they were checking me over, Julie and Gonzalo rushed up panting.

'Is he OK? I'm sorry Sam. It was my stupid idea,' said Julie, her wide eyes and breathless voice betraying genuine concern.

'I'm sorry,' said Gonzalo. 'Chico is such a good horse. Predictable and smart. He always does the right thing. Why did you lean to the left, when it was obvious he would turn right?'

I was half in shock, starting to feel the pain and could barely speak, so my response to Gonzalo played only in my mind. My nostrils probably flared a little, but that was all.

Julie asked again, additional authority in her tone. 'Is he OK? Is he badly hurt?'

The doctor held up one hand to silence her as he finished checking me over. 'He hasn't broken anything as far as I can see,' he said. 'He's definitely got some whiplash and I can't be sure he doesn't have any back injuries. We need to get him onto a board and off this wet ground. We'll know more in an hour or two.'

The ambulance had arrived and they prepared to move me. The doctor told Julie to go back to the party and call in an hour and I disappeared in a flurry of blue lights and churning sand.

It was only after they'd completed the full checks that I understood what an amazing stroke of luck the fall had turned out to be. I had a big, obvious neck brace to ensure sympathy and a severely sprained back which didn't actually hurt too much. But no-one else knew that. The doctor said I'd be fine in a few days and fully recovered in two weeks.

I was able to go back to the party and play the wounded hero for half an hour or so before 'needing' to go back to our room for a rest. I found it easy to take on the martyr's role and spent most of the weekend on my own in the gorgeous hotel suite, abusing room service and watching Wimbledon.

Sex was out of the question and, whenever Julie offered to stay to keep me company, I gave her my best pathetic smile. 'Don't worry about me. I'll be fine. You just go and have a good time.'

A Simple Exchange

May 15th 2015

The first chance to write since I got back from hospital. I don't want to even think about the reasons why I was there, much less put them down on paper. It's too upsetting.

Even now I'm home, I can still feel the creeping suffocation, the iron hands around my throat, slowly choking off my breath.

They say it was only a panic attack and that I simply need to calm down. How can I do that? The walls are closing in on me again. Wherever I look, I see enemies.

I'm trapped and there's no way out.

I managed to drive us back on the Monday morning but wasn't exaggerating when I said I was exhausted afterwards. My back was seizing up, and the dull throbbing in my neck was ignoring the serious drugs that had been pumped into me.

Julie had meetings in the City all afternoon but promised to buy some fish and cook us supper when she got home. She was being unusually kind and thoughtful and, for a moment, I wondered whether she actually had a conscience hidden away somewhere.

Considering the frighteningly cold calculation behind her persecution of my mother and her seduction of me, if she did have a conscience, it must have been beaten into submission years ago and was only let off the lead on special occasions. Who could tell? She was probably just going through the motions of being kind to put me off my guard.

It didn't make a difference. Nothing she could do or say would stop me doing what I had to do. If it turned out I was wrong, and there was another explanation, I'd deal with the consequences. But I wasn't wrong. I knew it.

All I needed was to get that phone. It had been easy to put the bug in her wallet and take the DNA and fingerprint samples while I was the poor invalid. I now had plenty of time to grab the phone and give it to Daz. We'd arranged to meet in a pub down the road at four o'clock.

After Julie had been gone for half an hour, I got up and wandered around the flat, looking in every room to make sure she was definitely out. Following my lucky break at the weekend, I could feel the fear and tension tightening a spring between my shoulders, which did nothing to help my whiplash.

She wasn't there. I had my chance.

Her office was empty, but I still crept in on tiptoes, my heart in my mouth, waiting for an alarm to go off or someone to jump out. I opened the drawer inch-by-inch and there it was, just as before.

I picked it up and was unable to resist switching it on to look at the screensaver image. My mother was so young – probably about my age - and looked carefree and happy. How could she have known what was coming down the line? I stood there for a few minutes, talking to her in my mind, telling her how I was going to avenge her and to make her proud.

It was already after three and I needed to finish up and get out to meet Daz. I put the real phone in my pocket and took out the dummy – it was identical. As I reached forward to reconnect the charging lead, I heard a rustle of clothing behind me. I spun round and there she was, standing in the doorway, arms by her sides, no trace of emotion on her blank face.

I stopped breathing and sank back against the desk. 'Julie,' I croaked. 'Why are you here?'

'You little fool,' she said, taking a step towards me. 'I knew something wasn't right, but I wasn't expecting this.'

'Julie. I can explain ...' My mind was racing in panic-fuelled circles.

Why had she decided to sneak back? What did she know?

'Don't bother, sweet boy.' She looked at the phone in my hand. 'I think the situation speaks for itself. Don't you?'

I didn't know what to say and looked around for something to hit her with, or throw at her. I was bigger and stronger but she was dangerous.

There was a sharp crack and the open drawer slammed shut beside me, splinters flying. Julie was standing statue-still with a smoking black pistol in her hand.

'Fucking hell,' I screamed at her. 'Are you fucking crazy? That could've hit me.'

'Calm down,' she said. 'At this range, I'm pretty good. And if I want to hit you, I will. Just don't try and be clever.'

I stood shaking and looked at the cold, black eyes watching me from behind the gun. I couldn't see anger, sadness, or even disappointment in that gaze. I was now nothing more than an inconvenience. But she wasn't going to kill me. She had no reason to do that.

'Put the phone down on the desk,' she said. 'How did you find it anyway?'

I put the dummy phone down carefully. 'My father gave me my mother's old phone,' I told her. 'And I dialled the number on the tracking software. I heard it ringing in your office.'

'What are the chances of that happening?' she said, shaking her head slowly from side to side. 'I knew that keeping the phone was weak and sentimental, so I suppose I can't blame you entirely.'

'Blame me?' My voice was a falsetto squeak. 'Blame me. What the fuck else was I supposed to do?'

'Whatever,' she said. 'What's done is done. The problem we have now is that I need some time to get away safely.'

Was she going to kill me to keep me quiet? Surely not? 'Julie. Don't do anything crazy. I promise I'll keep quiet.'

She laughed. 'Don't be an idiot. I'm not going to shoot you. Whatever you might think of me, I'm not a murderer.'

I pictured my mother's desperate end, and Julie's father lying bleeding on the kitchen floor. 'I know that,' I said, trying to hide the doubt in my voice.

'But I do need to be sure you won't talk to anybody until I'm long gone.'

'I promise I won't say anything ...'

'Of course you will. You'll tell them everything you know. But not until you get out of the safe room.'

After buying the flat, Julie had installed a fully armoured panic room, well stocked with food and water as well as independent ventilation and communications systems. If a burglar or kidnapper was in the flat, you could hide there until the police came.

'I'll tell the police where to find you in a couple of days. It'll give you a chance to catch up on some sleep.'

I felt the fight wash out of me like the last gurgling gasps of an emptying bath. I wasn't going to die today.

I let myself be guided through to the panic room which was hidden behind a mirrored panel in the main bedroom's ensuite bathroom. Julie opened the door and motioned me in. I turned in the doorway and looked at her.

'Was there really nothing between us?' I said. 'Nothing at all.'

'Of course there was. We had lots of fun and you reminded me a little of your mother. But now it's over. We both know that.'

'... And my mother? Were you responsible for what happened to her?'

'Come along. Enough is enough. This isn't a James Bond film. There's no time for more chit chat. In you go.'

I heard the door close behind me with the hiss of pneumatic seals.

I'd been in the room a couple of times before when Julie was explaining the emergency drill. The remarkable thing was the silence. Her flat alway felt quiet and tranquil – it was on the fifth floor with triple-glazing everywhere – but, when the safe room door closed behind you, the silence was something different. Solid, tangible, something you could scoop up with a spoon.

There was a big, high-tech control panel on the wall which

managed all of the systems including the door release, the radio beacon and the panic alarm. It was too much to hope that I would get to any of these before Julie, and I watched as each of them flashed up 'Manual Override - System Inactive'. I would be stuck here for a few days; I might as well get comfortable.

There was a small bed in one corner, a chemical toilet and a tall, metal cupboard filled with water, food and medical supplies. No entertainment. It was going to be a long wait. I imagined how worried Daz would be when I didn't turn up for our meeting, but there was absolutely nothing I could do about it. I was trapped and Julie was escaping again.

I felt the shape of the real phone in my pocket and smiled to myself. At least I had that. And the tracker. Maybe things weren't so bad after all.

A steady beeping was coming from the control panel and when I went over to look, a bright red triangle was flashing insistently in the centre of the screen. 'Warning. Ventilation systems disabled. Enter password to reset.' I looked at it blankly. Was the display broken?

It took a while for the horrible truth to sink in.

If she'd deliberately disabled the air supply, then she had no intention of telling anyone where I was. Julie knew I didn't have the password. She was leaving me here to die.

I didn't know how long the oxygen in the room would last, but it was a small room, so my guess was not more than a day. I could already taste the air becoming stale and the walls closing in on me.

I sat down on the small bed and started to cry.

Not This Time

I've now been waiting for twenty minutes and no sign of Sam. I've called his phone ten times and there's no answer. Something must have gone wrong and, if that bitch Jax is involved ... if she caught him poking around ... I wouldn't put anything past her.

I told Liz we shouldn't let him do it. I'm the only one who knows what Jax is actually like. She's got this kind of sixth sense – almost like magic – and she's always one step ahead. Back in the day, there were times when I thought that Fabiola must see through her, but Jax always came up with something to twist things in her favour. Often making me look bad in the process.

If she knows she's been rumbled, she'll be looking to disappear again and it won't take her long. She always had a back-up plan, even when we were only innocent young idealists, playing at changing the world. She had at least two grab bags, with clothes, money and fake IDs, stashed with friends or in left luggage somewhere. She told the rest of us we were fools if we didn't have our own escape plans. 'You never know,' she'd say. 'Better safe than sorry. Don't trust anyone.'

That was the thing I remember most about Jax. She didn't trust anyone. She always covered her options and assumed people would let her down. The only exception was Fabiola. I think Jax trusted her and that probably explains everything.

In my job, I'm trained to behave with empathy and understanding to the patients – even those who've done terrible things and, given a chance, would do them again. We learn how it isn't their fault; either their biology or their experiences have driven them to this point.

Jax is different. Maybe it's because of Fabiola and the way I felt about her? Maybe it's because I knew her from outside work? Whatever it is, I can't give her the benefit of the doubt. I've always believed she was simply evil; a black soul set on Earth to cause mischief, misery and pain.

Jax had a favourite escape plan. She always talked about it as Plan G. 'G' as in 'Get the fuck out of here'. She'd done an analysis of surveillance camera angles and transport links and was convinced that Kings Cross station was the best starting point. Left luggage right next to the loos, a quick change of appearance and you could stay in camera black spots until you were well gone.

It was over a quarter of a century ago and everything's completely different now. My only hope is that she hasn't changed. If she's on the run, my gut says that'll be where she goes first. Sam's now forty minutes late. Something is definitely wrong.

I hope I'm not too late or in the wrong place. The Ladies is still right next to the left luggage and I've found a good spot behind a pillar where I can see everyone who goes in or out. I think I'll recognise her from the photos Sam showed me but I'm not a hundred per cent sure.

I've been here for twenty minutes, which makes almost two hours since Sam was supposed to meet me; I'm afraid I've missed her. God, I hope not. I know in my gut that this is my one chance.

When I told DS Liz what was going on, she called in a favour with some of her old colleagues and they went to Julie's flat. A flash of ID and the concierge let them in.

There was no-one there and they didn't have a search warrant, but it was difficult for them to miss the bullet hole in Julie's desk. Something bad has happened. Sam is in big trouble.

Wait! Is that her? Different hair and high street, off-the-rack clothes, but there's something about her movement. It has to be Jax. She's taking care to keep close to the wall and it looks like she's heading down Caledonia Street towards Caledonia Road. It's not dark yet, so I need to find a good place to tackle her. Somewhere less public.

I'm not cut out for sneaking around tailing people, but luckily Jax isn't expecting anyone to be following her. She's focused on keeping in camera blind spots as much as she can. Her head is bowed and the long, black hair of her wig is falling in front of her face.

Apart from the usual bumper-to-bumper traffic, there are very few people about. If I can find the right place, I should be able to grab her without being seen.

There's an underground car park up ahead. It might be a possibility, but I'll need to be quick. I run towards her as quietly as I can, but she's already turning and the whites of her eyes show her shock when she realises that it's me. The confusion gives me a vital fraction of a second head start and I manage to grab her and bundle her down the concrete ramp and into the darkness.

Tackling and restraining strong, struggling patients is something I've been doing all of my life, but I can't remember any of them fighting like Jax. She's swearing, spitting and scratching like a wildcat and, for a second or two, she comes close to breaking free. I have one knee on her back and lean closer.

'Jax. If you don't stop struggling, I swear I'll break your fucking arm.'

I tighten my grip and increase the leverage on her elbow, one degree at a time.

'OK. You've made your point,' she spits the words out through the agony, but stops struggling. 'What the fuck are you doing here?'

'Where's Sam?'

'How would I know where Sam is?'

'You always treated me like a stupid piece of shit,' I say, applying more pressure to her elbow. 'But I'm not that thick. The police found the bullet hole in your desk. Where's Sam?'

'I don't know. We had a fight. He left. That's all I know. Let me go. I never did anything to you.'

I can feel the rage flood my skull. I need to keep myself under control. I need to find Sam. But all I want to do is to break her arm like a stick and then pound her head into the hard concrete. Again and again. Again and again. Until it's over.

'Never did anything to me?' She must surely hear from my voice that she's gone too far. 'You took the only person I ever loved away from me, you fucking witch. And you did it out of spite. Out of fucking spite, for Christ's sake.'

'I loved her too,' she says. 'It wasn't supposed to end like that. I didn't mean ...'

'I don't give a fuck what you meant. If you're not going to tell me where Sam is, let's see what the police have to say.' I use my free hand to take out my phone and start dialling.

'Wait,' she says. 'If you call the police, you won't find Sam in time.'

'What are you talking about?'

'You heard me. He'll be out of air in a couple of hours. Let me go and I'll tell you where he is. Don't and I won't.'

'You want me to trust you?'

'Do you have a choice?'

The war going on in my head is physical. A battle between rational thought and primeval apocalypse. Seconds quickly become hours of raging conflict and I start to shake with the effort.

'How do I know you're not lying?'

'Give me my phone. It's in my jacket.'

I reach into her pocket and pass her the phone, still keeping her right arm twisted almost to breaking point. As she shifts her body round to see the screen I can hear her breath coming in sharp bursts. She must be in agony – most people would probably have passed out by now.

After a few seconds, she hands me the phone.

'Look,' she says. 'Still think I'm lying?'

It's my turn to gasp. The image on the screen is grainy and black and white, but there's no doubt it's Sam, lying on the floor of a dimly-lit room, pale face covered in beads of sweat.

'When was this taken?'

'Look more carefully,' she says. 'Zoom in.'

I look again and this time I see the movement. Sam's chest is rising and falling – almost imperceptibly – and his eyelids are half-closed and flickering.

'What the fuck is this?'

'You know exactly what it is,' she says. 'It's a live feed of the room where I left Sam.'

I can feel the cold of the concrete floor seeping into me. It's real. Sam's dying.

'What would Fabiola want you to do?' says Jax, knowing her trump card and, as always, playing it at the perfect moment.

'Fuck you,' I say, tightening the armlock until she cries out. 'What would she want *you* to do? Let her son die?'

'Don't treat me like an idiot,' she snarls. 'Remember who locked him in the room in the first place.'

'Jax, please. He's just a kid.'

'... And he doesn't have to die. You can still save him,' she says. 'It's not too late.'

'Give me your word,' I say, realising how weak that sounds.

'I swear. Let me go and I'll tell you where to find him.'

I stare at the white face on the phone screen; it's as though I can see the life seeping out of him and I can feel tears warm on my cheeks. If I let Jax go, she'll be gone for ever, but Sam is dying. If there's even the slightest chance of saving him ...

I let go of her arm and slump forwards onto my knees. Jax is a psychopathic bitch but she's always had her own warped ideas of right and wrong. I can only pray that, in her world, keeping her promise is 'the right thing to do'. I've got no other choice.

Jax stands up, holding her elbow and clearly in a lot of pain. She picks up her bag and backs away towards the car park entrance.

'Stay here,' she says. 'I'll message you in five minutes.'

'If you fucking let me down, I'll ...'

She lifts her good hand to stop me. 'Don't worry. A deal's a deal. A life for a life. I'll see you Daz.'

And then she's gone, leaving me kneeling on the cold, hard floor, emotionally-drained, exhausted and praying I've made the right decision.

It was only five minutes, but five minutes is an eternity when you're watching the seconds ticking away and wondering if you've made the biggest mistake of your life.

The phone screen is blurring as tears of rage and frustration start to fill my eyes. She's not going to text me. I shouldn't have trusted her.

When the message flashes up, I'm almost surprised.

'There's a secure panic room in my flat. Behind the mirror in the main bathroom. I've disabled the ventilation system and the door lock. Tell them to bring drills. He can't have long.'

The Walls Close In

May 21st 2015

I lost Sam today.

It was only for quarter of an hour but I don't know how it happened. I turned around for a second and he was gone.

I keep seeing flashes of the empty pavement where Sam was supposed to be sitting in his pushchair, right where I left him. It's as though my mind sliced out a short wedge of time, threw it aside and seamlessly joined up the edges.

What will I say to Rupert when he comes home? I have to tell him, but I don't know how.

I eventually stopped crying. What was the point? A small voice was still coming from the Pandora's box deep inside of me promising that all was not lost. Julie would tell someone after all. Daz and Liz would definitely call the police if I didn't turn up. There was always hope.

But would anyone arrive in time? I suspected my initial estimates of a day's worth of air were optimistic; I needed to do whatever I could to conserve what was left.

Lying still was probably the best option, but it didn't work. After a few seconds, I started to feel the panic well up inside me and my breaths became short, desperate rasps, hungry to grab as much air as possible before it was all gone.

I stood and paced slowly around the ever-shrinking box, concentrating on my surroundings and working to bring my hyperventilation under control. There wasn't much to see; I'd already made a full inventory of the cupboard, my phone wouldn't work inside here. There was nothing to help me and the room had heavy steel reinforcing on all sides.

The small spyhole in the wall gave me a fisheye view of the huge, marble bathroom but Julie wasn't sitting on the edge of the bath waiting to let me out and tell me that she hoped I'd learnt a lesson. Of course she wasn't.

The only option I had was to wait. Either that tiny voice of hope was toying with me or it wasn't. There was nothing I could do about it. I needed to keep calm and to stop time coming to a complete stop but, as each minute passed, I could feel the walls closing in and the air becoming musty and stale.

And the nagging harridan of the ventilation warning alarm wouldn't stop prodding a bony finger between my eyes reminding me over and over again. 'You ... are ... running ... out ... of ... time.'

I did my best to ignore it and found a simple routine which worked for a while. Timing it carefully and not allowing myself to cheat, I would first sit for five minutes looking at the image of my mother on the phone, willing my thoughts to reach her. The messages I tried to send were a confused mix of begging her to help me, apologising for letting her down and raw feelings of loss and missed opportunities.

After sitting with her for five minutes, I would get up and walk – slowly – around the room, looking through the cupboards again and peering out at the empty bathroom before returning to the bed and starting again.

It wasn't much, but it gave me something to help fight the fear and the desperate sense of foolishness which were telling me to give in to my emotions, to scream and to shout and to smash my head against the wall.

I'd been locked in for less than two hours when I saw them.

Completing my routine for the tenth time with a cursory look at the empty bathroom, I saw that it wasn't empty any more. Two men were inside, looking around. They weren't wearing uniform but, even blown up and distorted by my fishy eyes, they looked a lot like policemen.

My heart leapt. They'd sent people to rescue me. Julie must have had second thoughts and told them. I shouted as loudly as I could and banged my fist against the door. Surely they could hear me?

One of them walked towards me. He can't have been more than three or four feet away. I shouted and banged again, but all he did was to turn sideways, suck in his doughnut-filled belly and throw back his shoulders in a classic male self-deceiving mirror pose.

'Help. In here.' I was screaming now, smashing both hands against the steel of the door.

He turned and walked over to his friend who was poking through Julie's things with the absent-minded nonchalance of the professional voyeur.

'Oi! Help. I'm in here.' I kicked at the door as hard as I could and felt a sharp stab of pain as something broke in my foot.

Neither of them even flinched and I watched them saunter out of the room. It wasn't their first wild goose chase and they hadn't expected to find anything anyway.

This couldn't be happening. I screamed and shouted, smashed my bruised and bleeding hands against the door again and again, but no-one came.

That was it. I was going to die. No-one would get here in time. I sank to the floor in a heap, breathing hard, legs like jelly and tiredness wrapping me in its soft blanket.

Was it really going to end like this? Was Julie going to kill me as well? I wasn't even as old as my mother had been.

And that bitch was going to mosey off into the sunset again.

I don't know how long I lay there. It must have been for hours. My phone was on the bed and it was too much effort to drag myself over and check the time.

I was breathing fast now, panting like a dog on a hot summer's day. The carbon dioxide levels must be getting high. The pain in my foot and hands had been replaced by a ripping headache which was threatening to make me vomit and the room had begun to shimmer and dissolve in flashes of light. I was sure that none of these things were good signs.

The flashes were accompanied by a dull rumbling sound which became louder as the seconds passed. I remember thinking that it might be important but I couldn't imagine what it was or where it came from. It was so hard to concentrate. My thoughts were dancing mayflies; no sooner had they dipped into my consciousness than they swooped up and away again.

The rumbling was deep and soporific and I thought I could hear my mother's voice calling to me as I sank slowly into the blue blackness of the floor. At least I would be able to meet her at last.

Roll Away the Stone

May 28th 2015

I had a dream last night. I dreamt I was Jesus rising from the dead. There was silent darkness.

A bass rumbling filled the silence and cracks of light appeared, splintering the darkness shard by shard.

A hand reached through the circle of light and helped me to stand and make my way out into the brightness of day.

The hooded figure then bent and heaved the stone back into place before walking away and leaving me standing alone, blinking in the sunlight.

I needed more air. I needed more air.

There was something blocking my mouth and throat. I tried to reach up to pull it out, but couldn't move my hands. I shook my head from side to side trying to free it, but it wouldn't budge.

I needed more air.

'Mr Blackwell?'

I could see a woman's face leaning over me. It wasn't my mother. Brown hair, brown eyes, blue paper hat – I was in a hospital. It appeared that I wasn't dead.

'Mr Blackwell. Nod gently if you can hear me,' said the voice.

I nodded.

'Good. Now I want you to stay calm and listen carefully. OK?'

Another nod.

'My name is Susan Miller. I'm your nurse. Everything's fine, but we needed to put a tube in your throat to help you breathe. Do you understand?'

My mind was beginning to function again and I'd seen enough hospital dramas to know what intubation was. I nodded.

'You tried to pull it out a couple of times while you were unconscious, so we had to restrain you. I'm going to take it out now. It will be a little uncomfortable, but only for a few seconds. Is that all right?'

I nodded several times.

'I'll count to three and, on the count of three, I want you to breathe out as hard as you can. One, two, three ...'

It wasn't pleasant, but the sensation of being back in control of my breathing was fabulous. I lay there for a long time taking in long, deep breaths of clean air and didn't even notice her removing my wrist restraints.

'Do you want to try speaking?' she said, eventually. 'Your throat will feel a little sore, but you should be able to talk.'

'Where am I?' I croaked.

'You're in the Chelsea and Westminster hospital,' she replied. 'You've been here since Tuesday morning. You came in with severe hypercapnia, which is carbon dioxide poisoning. You were unconscious so we elected to put you into a chemically-induced coma while we ran tests and allowed your body to recover. But don't worry, you're going to be fine.'

'Thank you,' I said. 'I don't feel fine. Every part of me aches in some way. Could I have some water please.'

'Of course,' she said, handing me a paper cup of water. 'Now, there are some people outside who've been waiting to see you for two days. I'll go and get them.'

The water trickling down my throat was wonderful.

First in was Dad, pushing ahead and reaching to take my face in his hands.

'Thank God,' he said. 'You're OK. We were so worried.'

'Yeah. I seem to be fine. It's good to see you old man.' My throat was hurting and I was the one with the nursing home voice.

'You wouldn't have been fine if the police had arrived any later. What were you bloody thinking, you idiot?'

'I clearly wasn't. Things didn't exactly go as planned. I'm sorry, Dad.'

'You were lucky to have a friend in Uncle Daz. He was the hero of the day. Without him, you'd be dead.'

Daz was lurking in the background, trying – and failing – to look small. He stepped forward and stood by the bed, hands clasped, shoulders hunched and head bowed.

'Not sure about the hero bit,' he said, mumbling through his beard. 'It was all my fault in the first place. I shouldn't have let you do it. If we hadn't got you out in time ...'

'But we did. Apparently you did, and thank you. Anyway, I made my own decisions. I'm not fourteen any more.'

'But I was the one who understood Jax,' he said. 'I should've known better.'

'Whatever,' I said. 'Don't beat yourself up about it. We were all trying to do what we thought was the right thing. You saved my life, for Christ's sake.'

'So, tell us what happened,' asked my dad.

I could feel the terror rising in my throat and it was only the sight of those familiar, kind faces that stopped me from screaming out loud. 'Can we leave that until later?' I said. 'I don't want to talk about it yet ... Tell me how you found me.'

'Of course,' said my dad. 'We can talk about it whenever you're ready.'

'I'll keep it brief,' said Daz. 'You look like you're wiped out anyway.' He took a deep breath. 'When you didn't show up at the cafe, I knew something was wrong and guessed Jax would be making a move. I took a punt she'd be keeping her escape bag at Kings Cross like in the old days and went there to wait for her. I rang Liz on the way and she arranged for a couple of plods to go to the flat and look for you. Fat lot of good they were!'

I shivered as I thought about the moment when the two policemen had walked nonchalantly out of the bathroom.

'Anyway,' Daz continued. 'I was lucky and leopards don't change their spots. Jax still used the same place and I spotted her coming out of the Ladies – new face, new hair, new crappy clothes. It was lucky you showed me those recent photos of Julie.'

'So, what did you do?'

'I followed her and dragged her into an underground car park. She said she didn't know where you were, but I knew she was lying. I swear I nearly bashed her brains out there and then.'

I almost laughed out loud. My ordeal hadn't been wasted. Julie hadn't got away.

'That's amazing,' I said. 'Do the police have her under arrest.'

'I'm afraid not,' he said. 'I let her go.'

'You did what,' I squeaked. 'Why?'

'She gave me a choice,' Daz shrugged. 'Your life or her freedom.' Were those tears in his eyes? 'I chose you.'

I smiled as I imagined how much it must have cost him to let her walk away.

'Thanks Daz. Good choice.' I said, reaching out my bandaged hand to squeeze his arm.

The three of us were silent for a while as we took stock. Daz was the first one to speak.

'I went with your dad to meet up with DS Liz,' he said. 'She said they might get something on the tracker at some point, depending on where Jax turns up and whether she's still got it, but it's extremely unlikely unless there's an active arrest warrant in force. The DNA may or may not be useful but, without the phone, she doubts that they'll get an international arrest warrant anyway, let alone a conviction.'

'So she wins again?' I said.

'Looks like it,' Daz said. 'It seems like she always will.'

I looked at the two of them standing there and thought about everything Julie had done to our family. It wasn't right that she should get away with it. As I shovelled coal into the furnace of righteous indignation, my fuddled brain exploded into life.

'Wait a minute,' I said. 'Could one of you call the nurse?'

Dad went out and came back a few seconds later with Nurse Miller.

'Do you need something?' she asked me.

'Yes. Have you got the leather jacket I was wearing when you brought me in?'

'Of course. It's right here.' She opened the cupboard door, took out my jacket and handed it to me. 'Here you are.'

I reached into the pocket and there it was. Right where I'd put it.

'Sorry,' I said, pulling out the phone. 'My brain wasn't working. I'd already swapped the phones by the time Julie came back. She's got the dummy.'

The sight of the phone stripped ten years off both Daz and my dad.

'You beauty,' said Daz in his best Aussie accent. 'That changes things completely. Let me get this to the police straight away. I'll see you guys later.'

He took the phone and left, shooing the nurse ahead of him.

Which left me and my dad. His eyes were sad as he looked down on me and the enormity of recent events loomed over us like a pregnant storm cloud.

'Why didn't you come to me?' he asked, finally breaking the silence.

I'd been dreading that question. I had my reasons, but hadn't wanted to spell them out.

'You know why,' I replied. 'First of all, I thought Daz would know more about Jax than you and then, when I found the phone, I was sure there was more to Mum's death than everyone thought.'

'... That doesn't really explain why you didn't speak to me.'

'Yes it does,' I said. 'You told me why you'd never read the diaries and I knew this would tear open that wound. I wanted to be sure of my facts first.'

'But I'm your dad. I'm supposed to be here to look after you,' he said. 'You shouldn't have to worry about me ... Not for a few years yet I'm hoping.'

'Well, you're no spring chicken,' I said, managing half a smile. 'It won't be long.'

The brief moment of levity didn't last and Dad's lips were pressed tightly together as he pulled up a chair and sat next to the bed. 'Do you seriously believe Jax was involved in what was happening to your mum?'

'I'm certain of it,' I said. 'I don't know how exactly, but I can't see any other reason why she installed the software on Mum's phone. God knows how she got hold of the phone in the first place.'

'But she didn't admit anything to you?'

'What, before she locked me in a box and switched off the air? No. I asked her, but she ignored me. She did admit that keeping the phone was a mistake though.'

'I guess we'll know more when they've finished analysing it?'

'I hope so.' I said.

My dad stood up. 'Look, I need to go home for a bit. I've not had a shower for two days and I could use a change of clothes. I'll be back soon.'

'No problem. I'm pretty knackered to be honest.'

'It's wonderful to see you back in the world of the living. I couldn't stand watching you lying there with all those tubes and thinking about what might have happened.'

'Trust me. It's good to be back.' I looked up at him. 'Dad ...?'

'Don't worry boy. I know you think I'm going to beat myself up about my failure to trust your mother. Well, I'm not going to. Maybe I will at some point but, for now, I'm going to wait until we know more. OK?'

'OK. Good. See you in a bit.'

Redemption

June 1st 2015

The days seem to be blurring together now. Accelerating towards something unknown. Every moment is touched with inevitability and my life is no longer my own.

But I haven't forgotten my promise to Sam.

Whatever happens to me, I'll watch over him. I made him a promise on the day he was born and I'll keep it.

I was out of hospital two days later and went to stay with Dad and Granny. Where else could I go? I had nowhere to live and no job. I was going to have to start my life over at some point but, right then, I didn't have the energy to think about it.

The headaches were slowly getting better, although my recovery was taking too long and I was worried about the amount of painkillers I was taking. When I wasn't doubled up in pain, I felt like I was walking on a trampoline.

The nightmares weren't getting better at all. Every night, often two or three times, I would wake up to soaking sheets, forehead clammy and cold, pulse racing and breath coming in short, panicky bursts.

It was the same dream every time. I was back in the safe room, peering out of the spyhole, knowing I was out of air but transfixed by the sight of the two men who'd come to save me. A surge of relief would lift me up like a surfer's wave, high and strong until I suddenly realised they couldn't hear me and didn't know I was there.

The wave of elation would disappear from under me but, for an instant, I knew how to fly. It was a dream within a dream and reality quickly dropped me hard onto the scouring sand to be pounded down by the heavy, roiling waters, spinning over and over until I would snap awake, screaming out loud, dripping wet and with my eyes stretched wide and staring into nothing.

I was up early and went down to the kitchen. No-one else was awake, but it didn't matter; the room was a sanctuary filled with a lifetime of happy memories. I put the kettle on and sat down to read yesterday's paper, my heart still pounding in my chest and the metallic taste of fear lingering on in my spearmint mouth.

It was only a few minutes before Granny appeared, standing beside my chair. She didn't make noise any more – she simply appeared.

'D'you want a cup of tea, Granny.'

'Yes, that would be lovely. An Earl Grey please.'

We sat sipping our teas in the morning quiet, the silence occasionally punctuated by squabbling jackdaws.

'Difficult night?' said Granny eventually.

I nodded in reply.

'We were all so worried,' she continued. 'When you were missing, and then afterwards in the hospital. It was as though it was all happening over again. I thought we were going to lose you.'

'Well, to be fair, Gran, I thought you were too. They only just got to me in time.'

'It doesn't bear thinking about,' she said, gazing out through the French windows and into the garden. When she turned back to face me, the look on her face had changed – she looked sad, but serious and determined as well.

'What is it?' I said. 'What's wrong?'

'We've never talked properly about your mother, have we?'

'No, I suppose not.' I said, thinking about all of the terrible things which my mum had said about my grandmother in her diaries. 'Dad and I talked about her a lot, though.'

'I would like to now if you don't mind. Bear with me if I ramble on.'

'Of course.'

'It was a long time ago and it's not easy,' she said, pursing her lips and sitting straight up in her chair. 'Fabiola was a wonderful girl. Beautiful, clever and totally charming when she wanted to be. She loved your father very much. And you, of course.

'She and I never really hit it off, unfortunately. I tried hard, and I think she tried too, but there was something about me that always threw her on the defensive. Part of it was related to class – she thought I was an awful snob, and I probably was – but that wasn't everything. I think she felt a need to compete with me for Rupert's affections. It probably would have been much easier if we'd lived further away.'

'Surely that's not so unusual, is it?' I said. 'It's the classic evil mother-in-law syndrome. There's a reason why so many stand-up comedians love it.'

'Maybe,' she said. 'But anyway, for us, it had become difficult even before she started having her problems. Everything I did was wrong. If I offered to help, I knew Fabiola thought I was interfering and being critical, but I didn't mean to be.'

I had already decided I wasn't going to mention the diaries and kept my lips firmly pressed together.

'When she started to have difficulties, it became much worse. We were all worried about you, but she hated the idea that she might not be capable of looking after you properly on her own. That was, of course, understandable, but you were so little and vulnerable and I felt you had to come first, no matter what.

'That night, that terrible night, I think she overheard me talking about my concerns with your father and I think it may have been that which pushed her over the edge.'

'I don't think you ...'

'... Let me finish, please,' she said. 'It was bad enough when I was certain she was mentally unstable. But now. Now we've learned that she probably wasn't ill at all, I'm struggling. I can't help thinking, "what if she hadn't heard us talking that night?", "what if I'd minded my own business in the first place?".

'Oh Granny. Poor you,' I said, knowing she was telling me the truth – at least the truth from her perspective. 'You can't blame yourself. You didn't know what was going on and you were trying to make the best of a bad situation.' I could hear the sound of Dad clumping down the stairs. 'Let's not allow Jax to do any more harm than she already has. We have to remember who's really to blame for what happened to Mum.'

'Thank you darling,' she said, sagging down into her chair. 'I'm sorry to burden you with this, especially now, but I do feel better for telling you.'

'What happens now?' said Dad.

'Now we wait for the system,' said Liz. 'It'll take its own time and you can't do anything to make it move any faster.'

'But you must have an idea?' I said. 'You've seen this sort of thing before?'

'Nothing quite like this,' she said. 'But I can take a guess. I wouldn't expect anything much to happen for at least three or four months.'

'Three or four months!' said my dad. 'That's ridiculous.'

'Not really. They'll be working on an international arrest warrant now which will kick things off, but some countries will process it faster than others and, if she's left the UK, we have no idea where she is.'

'She'll have left all right.' I said. 'Somewhere sunny.'

We were sitting on the terrace in Granny's garden. For some inexplicable reason, Daz and Granny had become good friends over the years and they'd been in the kitchen chatting. He strolled out carrying a bamboo tray laden with a teapot, cups and what looked to be a lemon cake, glistening with stickiness.

'Got it all sorted, have you?' he said, putting the tray on the table.

'Apparently, nothing's going to happen for months,' said Dad, still oozing disappointment. 'We need to wait for the system.'

'Might as well have a cup of tea while we wait,' said Daz. 'Cake looks good too.' He busied himself pouring tea and slicing cake, pretending he wasn't interested in the conversation.

'What about the tracker?' I said to Liz. 'I'm sure she'll have kept the purse. Can't someone trace her with that?'

Liz smiled. 'If only it were so simple. Something that small can't exactly broadcast a signal around the world. It needs to be within a few miles of a tracking station and the tracking station needs to be specifically looking for it.'

'I get that,' I said. 'But there must be some sort of process to make it happen.'

'There is. First you need the warrant. Then Interpol needs to notify all of its members. They then need to prepare proper paperwork to comply with local laws as well as circulating the identification codes for the tracker. Then she needs to come within range of one of the monitoring stations. All of that takes time and remember the evidence they have that she was actually the one who threw the ammonia is not the best. If the victim hadn't been a policeman, I don't think they'd be bothering at all.'

Daz and Liz took their tea and wandered off to admire Granny's roses, leaving me and Dad on our own at the table.

'What's up with Uncle Daz?' I said. 'It's like he's not interested in what happens now.'

'He's having a hard time,' said my dad. 'He hates that he allowed you to get into such a dangerous situation, and he can't forgive himself for letting Julie trap him into letting her go. I think he believes he's let your mum down all over again.'

'But that's rubbish,' I said. 'He saved my life.'

'I know that, but it's going to take him a while to get there.'

'How can that vile woman go on fucking up people's lives and get away with it untouched?'

'It's not over yet,' he said. 'But I still can't understand why she's not going to be prosecuted for Fabiola's murder as well.'

'Yeah. I've been trying to get my head around that too,' I said. 'It seems as though the phone proves Jax was tracking Mum and that she was responsible for at least some of the emails but not much more.'

'But surely that would be enough to convict her? The phone was registered in her name.'

'It might be,' I said. 'But convict her of what? Sending a few malicious emails? Using Mum's Facebook account to create a fake group? You'd struggle to get a court interested if it happened last month.'

'But Fabiola died,' he said, tears in his eyes. 'This is different.'

'Yes, Mum died,' I said. 'But Jax didn't kill her. It was her fault, but she didn't actually do it.'

'I know that, but it's still wrong. Don't you want to get back at her for what she did to your mother?'

'Of course I bloody do, Dad. Why do you think I've been doing this? Taking her company away from her will have hurt her badly. It's something, but not enough.'

'Then everything you went through to get that phone was a waste of time?'

'No. That's not true. Liz told me the phone has traces of deleted emails and texts which might be enough to prove that she planned the ammonia bulb attack. Without them, there wouldn't be enough evidence for an arrest warrant.'

'But even if they find her and prosecute her for that attack, you won't actually be getting revenge for your mother.'

'I think I will. If we can take her down, destroy her life completely, I don't really care how.'

'I don't know,' he said, shaking his head. 'It might have been better if I'd burned the diaries and thrown the phone away. We could have got on with our lives. You'd have split up with her sooner or later.'

'Maybe you're right, but we can't turn back the clock. I actually wonder if she'd have ever let me go – thinking about how she must've deliberately targeted me in the first place terrifies me.' I twisted round and stared out into the garden, the dream taste of sand and salt suddenly overwhelming.

I could see Daz and Liz strolling back across the lawn, arm-in-arm like an old married couple.

I turned back to my dad and smiled. 'Look at that,' I said. 'What do you reckon?'

All Roads Lead to Rome

The woman in the blue dress sat at the metal table, sipping her coffee. It was still early and the air was cool under the canvas awning. Her broad, white hat and oversized Chanel sunglasses whispered 'film star' in the ears of passers by and most of the men couldn't resist a second, sly stare.

It was her favourite time of day. The May nights were still cool enough to chill down the stones and a gentle breeze picked up a fine mist from the fountain and carried it over to the restaurant.

All too soon the oppressive heat would reach out into every corner of the square, through each window and spread its invisible fingers into every room of every house. By midday, it would already be unbearable.

The only solution was air conditioning, which she hated, or to leave for the coast, which she was about to do. She'd bought a cliff top villa in Peschici and the renovations were now finished. A month overdue, but still in time to escape the unbearable heat of a Rome summer.

The sun blazed even more strongly in Puglia but the forests and the sea breeze would make a huge difference. Her new villa was three hundred years old and had belonged to twelve generations of the same wealthy merchant family. They'd known exactly where and how to build. Old stone, thick clay tiles and the whole thing planted into the hillside by local knowledge. She knew it would be perfect all year round.

The previous year hadn't been her best year. It wasn't because of worries about being found; her new identity was bulletproof and there were no links at all to her former selves. She also had more money than she could ever need, stashed in numerous, untraceable accounts and safety deposit boxes.

Nor was it because Sam had survived. If he'd died, she would probably have regretted her petulant malice in any case. He was all that was left of Fabiola and she knew she would see him again one day.

Fear and regrets weren't what had almost destroyed her – it was the feeling of having been defeated and outsmarted. She hadn't felt like that since she was a child – not even close. She knew she'd made some small errors of judgement but that didn't explain everything.

She'd made her escape – again. She'd proven who was smartest – again. She'd won – again. So why did the victory taste so sour and bitter?

Her problem was that she knew the real root cause of her pain and could do nothing about it. It was already too late. Powerlessly observing what had happened to Pulsar after she'd left had driven her almost insane with rage and frustration and she would never be able to fix it.

Pulsar had been hugely successful. She'd built the business from nothing to become one of the world's top ten companies and had taken great care to put in place structures – legal, financial and managerial – which would make it impregnable even if she wasn't around.

Pulsar was her legacy, her Taj Mahal built from the grief, despair and fury which had engulfed her after Fabiola died. Pulsar was supposed to stand for ever as a monument to their perfect love. How could it have crumbled into ruins in six short months?

Dave Bukowski had driven the wrecking ball but she didn't understand why. For whatever reason, he'd turned overnight from being the saviour of her legacy to its nemesis. It wasn't only business. He was on some sort of evangelistic crusade.

She'd made the mistake of sharing too much of her vision with him and given him the tools to use against her. Why had she done that?

Within days of her sudden departure, Pulsar's largest competitor,

MySafe, had announced their partnership with Bukowski and outlined radical, visionary plans for the future of digital security. Based on the professor's unique nano-genetics research and approved patents, they would be the only company able to provide the radical solutions which were urgently needed.

It was time for a new kid on the block and they would now save the world from technological Armageddon as Pulsar had done twenty years earlier. The chief executive of MySafe even had the patronising audacity to thank Julie Martin and Pulsar for their contribution to the industry. 'On the shoulders of giants ...' or some such drivel.

The story made extremely convincing reading – it was her strategy after all – and Pulsar's share price dropped by forty per cent almost overnight.

The treacherous professor wasn't finished and his next step was to approach the Pulsar board with a hostile takeover bid. They'd laughed him out of the building the first time, but he was well funded and his PR machine was working overtime. Pulsar *was* Julie Martin and she'd disappeared. There were tabloids full of scandalous rumours, and the global media smelled blood.

It only took three more takeover offers and four months before those lily-livered puppets crumbled and accepted the bid. Six months later, Pulsar was no more.

That was in January and she'd barely stepped out of her flat for six weeks afterwards.

She'd always had a cause, a project, a focus to keep her tied down. All at once, she found herself floating, untethered and at the mercy of every capricious puff of air. She had no idea how to stop it, how to take back control and, perversely, she began to unravel.

A few threads at first, then more and more until she could see her fraying outline blurring in the mirror and she understood that she would soon be completely lost. Everything which she'd once been would be pulled apart and wafted away. Meaningless strands scattered and lost forever.

She was over that now, but it had been a close call.

In her more coherent moments, she would buy every newspaper she could find and read them all, back-to-back, word-by-word, looking for answers. Looking for salvation.

It was in one of the Italian papers that she found it. In a glossy Sunday supplement. There was an article called 'Una tragedia pugliese' and it was Fabiola's family story. Some enterprising journalist had linked Fabiola's suicide to the post-war workers' exodus and told the tale of three generations of Puglians, their ups and downs, the death of Fabiola's parents, and the ultimate tragic ending.

She'd stared at the picture of Fabiola for hours. It must have been taken when they were together. She looked young, strong and immortal. That was how she remembered her. On the facing page was a beautiful photo of Peschici showing the Carlantino's hometown nestling into the cliffs and there, overlooking the harbour and the beach, was the villa.

It was as though she had an old-fashioned circuit breaker in her head and someone had suddenly pulled down the lever with a clunk of springs and violet-blue sparks. The faint and bitter smell of ozone was left hanging in the air, but she was back. She'd known exactly what to do next.

'Il conto per favore.' Her Italian was flawless. If there was any accent, it might have been German, or maybe something Eastern European.

'Sì signora, subito.' The waiter made a short half-bow and disappeared inside.

As she waited for the bill, she smiled at the hundreds of pigeons mobbing a little old grandmother dressed head-to-toe in black. La Signora dei Piccioni came here at the same time every day with a big bag of breadcrumbs. Her friends were always waiting, dirty town-grey plumage blending into the stone flags and sharp beaks eager for their breakfast. Rome had its own charm and she would make sure to spend a few weeks here every winter.

'Ecco qui, signora.' The small plastic tray with her bill materialised in front of her and she turned to the waiter.

'Grazie mille,' she said, with a gleaming smile.

The waiter walked away feeling a little taller, a little stronger, a little more 'male'. She hadn't lost her touch.

The lady in blue took a twenty-euro note out of her worn leather purse, tucked it under her coffee cup and stood up, carefully smoothing her dress. It was time to move on. She'd never allowed regrets to rule her and the disappointments of the past year were already fading.

Her ability to airbrush history to match her preferred version was a wonderful talent. She could never make a mistake that endured because she would simply change the narrative; everything that happened, happened because *she* wanted it to happen. She was always in control.

Except for Fabiola. Try as she might, she couldn't make that right.

When he saw the lady in the white hat ask for the bill, the tall man standing in the corner of the square held his right hand to his cheek and spoke quietly to himself. One of the two young men standing by a scooter next to the fountain nodded almost imperceptibly and looked up stretching his shoulders and neck.

She walked across the square towards the tall man and the narrow street which led to her apartment. She shivered despite the strong sun. Something was out of place. Why was the man walking towards her? Who was he?

'Buongiorno, signora,' said the tall man. 'My name is Capitano Roberto de Alfaro of the Guardia di Finanza. I have a warrant for your arrest. Would you come with me please.' He reached into his suit pocket and took out a plastic wallet which appeared to be some sort of ID.

'There must be some mistake,' she said, turning and looking behind her, eyes flicking from side to side, trying to understand what was happening. The two men from the scooter were closer now, spaced apart and watching her. She turned back to the tall man.

'Signora Martin. I must insist that you come with me.' He waved some folded sheets of paper in front of her. 'I can assure you that the paperwork is all in order. It would be best not to create a scene.'

He knew who she was? How was it possible? How had they found her? No point in asking any of these men and there was no hope of immediate escape. She would have to wait until she had spoken to her lawyer.

'As I said, Capitano, there must be some mistake but, if you insist, please lead the way.'

She sat in the cold, square interview room wrapped in a borrowed blanket and stared at the pale green paint peeling away from the walls. She was on her own. They had tried asking her questions but she'd insisted on waiting for her lawyer. He was the top defence lawyer in Rome and would clear up this mess soon enough.

She still didn't understand why she'd been arrested or how they'd found her. The Italian police had an English detective with them, so it must relate to something that had happened in the UK. They couldn't have any real evidence. She was certain of that.

The only thing which could have caused a few problems was her old phone, but she'd thrown it in the canal straight after she'd left Sam. It had been weak and sentimental to keep the phone in the first place, but it was gone now.

The English detective had brought an older woman with him as an observer; she was apparently a former colleague, recently retired. That was strange in itself, but there was something more, something about the way that the woman had looked at her. Intense anger, hatred, bitterness – who was she?

She leant back in her chair and tried to quieten her thoughts. Nothing to do but wait.

A cold, damp room, a blanket and a paper cup of water. That wasn't how she'd pictured the day unfolding.

Is That All?

June 10th 2015

It's time to close this diary. I can't believe I'm actually going to do what I'm going to do, but there's no better way. I'm certain now.

A part of me still wants to believe that I'm not losing my mind and that someone has been deliberately tormenting me. It can only be God and, although I know I'm not perfect, I don't understand what I have done to deserve this.

Whatever, or whoever, is responsible, I curse you. I curse you with my innocent death. I pray that my death will be a crushing yoke around your shoulders to remind you of what you have done to me, my husband and my innocent child.

To remind you for every day of your life and then into the hereafter forevermore.

I curse you.

'It's not looking good, is it?' I said.

'I'm sorry, Sam.' Liz was on her third double G&T and showed no signs of slowing down. 'As far as I've been told, things could be better. The police still need something to link Jax with the ammonia attack itself. The video footage is reasonably damning, but it's grainy and from an angle.'

'... and the phone evidence doesn't do enough?'

'Not really. At the moment the prosecution doesn't think a jury will convict on what we have.'

'And if they don't, she'll walk away?'

'Free as a bird. And she won't be the only thing to sprout wings. My friends in the force tell me that legal actions will start flying around within days.'

'I can't believe she's going to get away again. It's too depressing.'

'No point in assuming the worst at this stage,' Liz said, forcing a smile. 'We've still got a week before the trial and there's one more bit of DNA forensics which might give us what we need. Funnily enough, it's based on the nano-genetic technology developed by Professor Bukowski and he's agreed to work on it personally. We'll know more in a few days.'

'We'll just have to keep hoping I suppose.' I said, even though it sounded like a desperate long shot. 'If she's acquitted, she'll be coming after us as well.'

It was the first time I'd been 'inside' and, even though it was a women's prison, my overwhelming impression was one of too much testosterone. Doors clanged, locks clicked and clunked, and all around there were eyes staring.

For them, I was the equivalent of a woman walking past a building site. A piece of meat on display. Presented for assessment and comment – lewd, complimentary or dismissive – and then forgotten.

I hoped my dad hadn't been right when he'd warned me not to come. I think he was worried Julie would work her witchcraft on me one more time and make me suffer. He might also have been afraid that she would manage to convince me of her innocence and bring me over to her side.

I understood his fear, but he was wrong.

I could see her through the reinforced glass. She was sitting at the table, as beautiful as ever, calm and relaxed. It was easy to imagine how she was manipulating everyone around her – guards and prisoners alike – to get whatever she wanted.

As I walked in, she looked up at me and smiled. It was as though nothing out-of-the-ordinary had happened and we were meeting in a cocktail bar before dinner.

'Sam. How lovely to see you.' Julie's inner fire was undimmed. 'I hear you managed to lock yourself in the safe room and nearly died.'

I'd promised myself I wouldn't let her make me angry but she really was a twisted bitch. She was able to rebuild history brick-by-brick and make it true.'

'The fact that you forced me in at gunpoint might've had something to do with it, don't you think?' I said, sitting on the metal chair opposite her.

'Don't be such an idiot,' she said, laughing. 'Why would I do something like that? I told you the life support systems were faulty.'

'What? The systems you disabled?'

'You do have such an active imagination.' She leant towards me over the table. 'Was it a cry for help?'

'Like mother, like son. Is that it?'

She arched her eyebrows. 'Your words, dear boy. Your words.'

I found myself strangely immune to her digs and barbs. As I'd discovered more about her past – and especially the details of what she had done to my mother – it made it easier to see past her actress mask, to see through to the writhing snake pit of malice that lay within.

Contrary to my dad's fears, I was fine. If anything, I might have felt pity for her, but that was too much to ask and I was stuck with a cold contempt. Seeing her locked in here with the guards looming by the door was very satisfying.

'So, the trial starts tomorrow? You'll be old and wrinkled by the time you get out of here,' I said. Age scared Julie more than anything.

'Do you seriously believe they'll convict me?' She filled the words with condescension and contempt. 'I've got too much money, I've got the best lawyers and there are far too many people who'd rather not be my enemy.'

She looked at me with sad eyes. 'A little late for you, I'm afraid. When I get out ...' Her voice was hard and sharp, digging into me and I could feel my hands and knees shaking under the steel table.

Julie hadn't finished. 'You should have just stayed pretty and not tried to be clever. It was the same with your mother. Why couldn't you both have simply stayed happy and pretty rather than ruining everything?' Her melodramatic sigh was straight out of drama school. 'Never mind. I thought I'd taught you how the world works, but apparently not. People like me don't get convicted. There's no evidence. I've done nothing wrong.'

'You actually believe your own bullshit, don't you?' I said, pressing my quivering hands hard against my thighs. 'It's not working out so well for you so far though, is it? Six months in jail with no bail. And what about Pulsar? That must've stung a bit.'

If I hadn't known her so well, I might not have noticed the twitch at the corner of her mouth and the way she dropped her head. She wouldn't want me to see what was going on behind her eyes.

'A shame really. After all of that work.' I continued to work the knife in deeper. 'Still, Dave Bukowski's a great guy and it's all based on his research after all.'

'Great guy,' she spat and spluttered out the words, unable to stop herself. 'He's a lying Judas. His 'discoveries' weren't worth a thing on their own. It was my work. My strategy ...'

'Shame you didn't have a contract, then.' I was enjoying the unique experience of seeing Julie losing control. 'You know he would have signed with you, don't you?'

'What do you mean 'would have'?'

'I mean that he would have signed the contract with you as planned if only I hadn't told him what you did to my mother.'

Julie's eyes stretched wide open. 'But you had no proof I did anything. He wouldn't break our partnership just on hearsay. There was far too much at stake for him and for Imperial.'

'You really, really don't get it do you?' I said. 'You've actually not got a clue how normal people think. He believed me because he trusts me.'

That was Julie's Achilles' heel. She couldn't grasp the concept of trust.

I twisted the blade deeper still. 'Did you know that Dave's older sister killed herself on her seventeenth birthday? She was being cyberbullied and jumped in front of a train? When I told him about you and my mother, he was disgusted.'

Julie was snarling now, her lips pulled back from those delicate pointy incisors which I'd found so pretty once upon a time. 'You don't seriously think any of you will get away this, do you? I've got friends everywhere. When I get out, I'll break you both, just like I broke your mother.'

I had already stood up and was half way out of the door. If it hadn't been for the two prison officers, I think she might have physically attacked me.

Julie was still certain she would win and, as I looked at her, I could feel my mother standing beside me, holding my hand and giving me strength.

Julie was unbroken, but I wasn't finished.

'One more thing,' I said. 'I probably shouldn't tell you this, but you'll find out soon enough. They've got a positive DNA match on the glass from the ammonia-filled light bulb.'

She sneered and spat out her reply. 'I knew that already, but it proves nothing. I was young and ignorant and shouldn't have had them in my backpack, but that doesn't mean that I did anything with them. It doesn't link me with the attack on that policeman.'

'Sorry, I wasn't being clear,' I said. 'I'm not talking about the intact light bulbs that were in the backpack.' I could feel the weight of the heavy door pushing against me. 'As you say, that's old news. Now they've found your DNA on the shards of glass which they pulled out of the policeman's face and eyes. Nano-genetic analysis apparently.'

The door swung shut behind me and I saw a different person through the glass pane – shoulders slumped, eyes darting from side to side and deep furrows appearing in her brow as if from nowhere.

The magic was gone and she looked old and tired.

The Old Orchard by Tony Salter

The family thriller that will grip you until the last page.

Finance Director, Alastair Johnson, is in trouble. He needs a lot of money, and he needs it very soon.

Alastair's solution is unorthodox and completely out of character – the fallout leaves his family torn apart.

But everything is not what it seems ...

———————————————————

"What a cracking story! Loved the way it all unfolded at the end. Really clever and credible and I didn't see the twists coming."

"FLIPPIN' BRILLIANT!"

"The Old Orchard is a pacy, tense, domestic thriller which builds an original and satisfying plot around real characters we can believe in. The prose is light and evocative with vivid descriptions and many moments of real insight and human wisdom."

———————————————————

The Old Orchard is AVAILABLE NOW in paperback or eBook format from Amazon and most booksellers.

Printed in Great Britain
by Amazon

28445923R00169